RED FLOOD

RED FLOOD

WILLIAM C. DIETZ

This book is for my grandson, Wyatt George Franta

CONTENTS

ACKNOWLEDGEMENTS

Many thanks to my editor, Marjorie Dietz.

You are wonderful!

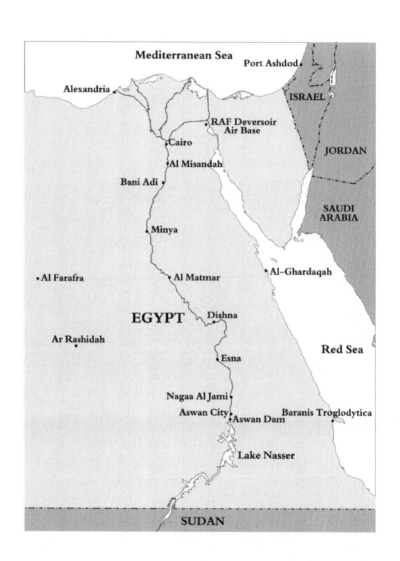

CHAPTER ONE

Khmeimim Air Base, Latakia, Syria

Dawn was still hours away as the hangar doors parted to reveal a Boeing 727. The plane was 36-years old, and had seen service in the United States and Brazil, before being sold to Syrian Air. Now, thanks to a fresh paint job the aircraft appeared to be the property of Israel's El Al airline. The main difference being the Star of David emblazoned on the jetliner's vertical stabilizer.

A tug towed the 727 out onto a taxiway on the civilian side of the Khmeimim Air Base, previously known as Bassel Al-Assad International Airport, and still referred to as such by the local population. Once the plane was in position, the pilots asked for and received permission to take off.

After taxiing onto the main runway the pilots paused to run the engines up prior to releasing the brakes. Mustafa Kantar felt gravity push him back against leather upholstery as the plane gathered speed. This was only his third trip in an airplane and he feared it would be his last. It wouldn't do to let that show however. Not with subordinates seated around him, most of whom were listening to music, or settling in for a nap.

The 727 could theoretically carry 189 passengers. But only 150 men were aboard, all of whom had a need to store weapons, ammo, and other supplies inside the cabin.

Kantar was in command of the 96 fighters seated in the forward section of the jet. The *albarabira* (barbarians) were in back, where they were conversing in Russian, and passing a bottle of vodka back and forth. They called themselves Spetsnaz, or special forces troops, and were said to be part of the Russian military intelligence service called the GRU.

But the only thing "special" about the *kafirs* (unbelievers) was how loud and obnoxious they were. Kantar felt the wheels leave the runway and waited to die. He didn't.

The fear had always been there, starting as a little boy slinging rocks at Israeli soldiers, continuing as a member of Hamas, and later Hezbollah—which sent him to Iran for more training. Then there were missions. A dozen or so ... All of which terrified him.

Hiding the fear, that was the key, and Kantar had. And that made him the right man to lead a mission which, if Allah willed it, would force Egypt to join the Russian-Syrian-Iranian-Pakistani-Chinese Axis. Thereby denying Egypt to the so-called "Allies."

Kantar would be a hero then, and a man with a future. Would he become a *wahda*? (Head of a Hezbollah division.) Anything was possible.

Kantar managed to take a nap after that. He was dreaming about his brother's wife when his second in command, Amir Alawi, touched his arm. "Mustafa! Look! A plane!"

Kantar leaned forward to look past Alawi, and sure enough lights were visible off the 727's starboard wing. A voice came over the intercom. "Don't be alarmed. Keep the window shades down. A pair of Israeli F-15s were sent to intercept us. We're talking to them. Everything is under control."

Kantar knew the pilots were supposed tell the Israelis that the 727 was on a charter flight, taking a professional soccer team from Lebanon to Cairo, having been cleared by the understaffed Beirut Area Control Center. Would they buy it? Kantar felt the fear return. What if the Jews saw through the story? What if the

F-15s shot them down? *Then Jannah* (paradise) *awaits*, Kantar reminded himself.

"We're good to go," one of the pilots said. "And cleared into Egypt."

Kantar felt a profound sense of relief. "See?" he said. "Our plan is working."

Alawi nodded. "The Jews are stupid. We will kill all of them."

Kantar knew that neither one of those assertions were true, and he was about to warn Alawi about the dangers inherent in underestimating an enemy, when he thought better of it. Why bother? Alawi might be dead soon.

After freeing himself from the seatbelt Kantar made his way forward to the cockpit. The door was unlocked. The pilots turned to look. Both men had parachutes stored behind their seats. "What's our ETA?" Kantar inquired.

"We will enter controlled airspace in thirty-six minutes," the copilot replied.

"Good," Kantar replied. "We'll get ready."

Kantar returned to the main cabin where he saw that the Russians were putting their parachutes on. The narrow aisle made the process difficult, so it was necessary to take turns.

Each man would get up, move to the aisle, and strap his chute on while Colonel Arseny Gortov watched. He had the unwieldy title of, "Chief of the Directorate of Operations at Military Unit 64722." An organization which was described online as "mysterious," and of "unknown purpose." Although Kantar felt pretty sure that he was *looking* at Unit 64722, and knew exactly what its purpose was.

Much to Kantar's embarrassment *his* troops were chatting, sleeping, and eating snacks. Kantar grabbed the mike normally reserved for flight attendants and thumbed it on. His voice boomed throughout the cabin. "Put everything away. Those occupying aisle seats will retrieve the parachutes from the overhead bins and hand them out. After putting their gear on they will rotate to a window seat. *Mulazim* (lieutenant) Alawi will check each fastener, on each man."

That was news to Alawi, who hurried to comply. And a good thing too, because the process took every bit of 30 hectic minutes.

At one point Kantar's eyes came into contact with Gortov's. The Russian smiled. There was no humor in it. Just contempt. That made Kantar angry. But anger, like fear, could be concealed. And Kantar did so.

"Take your positions," the pilot ordered brusquely. "We're about to enter restricted airspace. The back ramp is going down."

Kantar knew the pilot was referring to the so-called "airstair," that opened from the airliner's rear underbelly, and allowed passengers to deplane quickly. The original airstairs could be lowered in flight. That came to an end after hijacker D.B. Cooper bailed out in 1971. But, thanks to the Syrian makeover, the 727's airstair was fully operational again.

As Kantar eyed the aisle he realized how smart Gortov was. Rather than claim the first class seats for himself, the Russian allowed Kantar to take them, knowing that the troops seated in the back of the plane would jump first. A definite advantage if the jetliner was damaged.

Kantar felt resentment mixed with fear. There was nothing he could do other than stand there and fume. Maybe it wouldn't make any difference. Maybe things would go smoothly. The Muslim Brotherhood controlled the dam, and the airspace around it, but surely they would …

"Jump!" the pilot shouted over the intercom. "The Brotherhood thinks we're Jews *pretending* to be Arabs. They're about to fire on us."

Kantar swore. That was the trouble with the Middle East. The lie that saved your life in one place, could get you killed somewhere else.

The "Brotherhood" the pilot referred to was the transnational Sunni Society of Muslim Brothers, commonly referred to as the Muslim Brotherhood, which assumed power in 2011, only to lose it less than a year later. Hundreds of Brotherhood members had been imprisoned or murdered by the military-backed interim government. And the organization was banned in 2013.

But when WWIII began, and the military government had to institute rationing, surviving elements of the Brotherhood took advantage of the resulting discontent to lead a counterrevolution. By systematically assassinating military leaders, the brothers tried to ensure that their organization couldn't be suppressed again. What remained of the military struck back, and would have been victorious, if they hadn't split into rival factions.

Air swirled and candy wrappers flew around the cabin, as the airstairs deployed, and the Russians began to jump. Kantar was impressed by how quickly the heavily loaded Spetsnaz troopers could shuffle forward and disappear.

The lightly armed Hezbollah fighters were right behind the Russians. But there were more of them. And Kantar knew that three or four-minutes would pass before he could make his own escape. Fear battled fear. Which was worse? Flying on a doomed plane? Or plunging to his death from 500 feet in the sky?

Yes, he and his men had some training, which was to say a single jump. What Kantar's troops didn't realize was that their commanding officer screamed all the way down. And, because he landed in a pond, they couldn't tell that his pants were already wet.

There was a loud bang as something hit the plane. The 727 jerked wildly, and started to shake. "We're on fire!" the pilot shouted. "Jump! Jump! Jump!"

Kantar was six-feet away from the airstairs at that point. Panic threatened to overwhelm him. Something was wrong! A fighter named Omaya had balked. Two men were trying to force him onto the ramp.

Kantar felt as if his heart was going to beat its way out of his chest, as he ordered the men to release Omaya, which they did. Kantar drew his pistol and shot Omaya in the head. Blood splattered onto the lavatory door. The body blocked the aisle. "Drag the *nadhil* (bastard) out of the way!" Kantar shouted. "Then jump!"

The men obeyed. A missile struck the front end of the 727, killed the crew, and threw the plane's nose up. Kantar fell onto the airstair and bounced. Cold air swallowed him up. Kantar caught a momentary glimpse of the flaming jetliner as he tumbled head over heels. Then the jetliner was gone. Kantar was wearing an American-made BA-22 aircrew bailout kit. One of hundreds the Kurds had captured and sold shortly after the beginning of the war.

The BA-22s had a number of virtues including the fact that they were compact. But, at altitudes below fourteen-thousand feet, it was necessary for the parachutist to pull a manual ripcord. Kantar hurried to do so. He felt a reassuring jerk as the canopy opened and slowed his fall.

Street lights were visible in the city of Aswan. It was home to more than a quarter-million people. Hundreds of them began to die as Russian submarines launched cruise missiles from the Mediterranean Sea. The lights went out as explosions rippled across the city.

The plan was to help the paratroopers take the dam by inflicting so much damage on Aswan that none of the locals could rush south to oppose the invaders. That's why the missiles targeted power stations, military detachments, and police stations.

Kantar could steer, *should* steer, into the wind to reduce the possibility of injury, but to *where?* A fire was burning to the south. The plane? Everything else was blacked out. All Kantar could do was pray as he fell from the sky.

The ground came up hard. His boots hit, but Kantar fell, and was being dragged along the ground when a Russian stepped in to grab hold of his risers. The skid came to a halt. English was the lingua franca that bound the two teams together. "Whoa! You're supposed to spill the air out of the chute after you land. Remember that next time."

There wouldn't be a "next time," if Kantar could help it. "Thanks," Kantar said, as he gathered the chute into his arms.

"You can put it with mine," the Russian said. "Then we'll go after the bastards who shot us down."

Kantar dropped the pack and chute next to the Russian's. "That sounds good. But how will we find them?"

"They're civilians," the soldier said contemptuously. "They will flock to the burning plane. That's when we'll shoot them. But we must move quickly. The sun is rising."

The Russian's plan made sense. And Kantar knew it was important to kill as many members of the Brotherhood as possible, both because they were Sunni, and because they controlled the dam. "Lead the way," Kantar said. "I'll follow."

The heavily encumbered Russian began to run, and Kantar was able to keep up, but just barely. They were crossing the uninhabited plateau that lay just north of the dam. The ground was flat, bare of vegetation, and cut by gullies. And each time the men had to traverse one of the ravines it slowed them down.

Kantar was wearing a headset and a radio. Alawi answered right away. "Twenty-one fighters were with the *mulazim*. The rest were scattered far and wide."

"Lead the men to the plane," Kantar ordered. "But be careful. The brothers may be there. Kill them if you can."

The two men continued to run, and were nearing their goal, when a brisk firefight broke out up ahead. The Russian had a radio too. "The brothers walked into the colonel's trap," the soldier reported. "We must slow down. Some of the bastards are running our way."

Kantar had been in combat before. But the fear was there, waiting for him. Not as an enemy, but as a friend, who would help keep him alive.

Kantar was alert to the smallest sound, and the slightest sign of movement, as they crossed a stretch of hard-packed sand. The sun had broken company with the horizon by then. And Kantar could see a gully up ahead. The fire continued to burn in the distance, and that's what he was looking at, when three silhouettes lurched up out of the ravine. Two charged Kantar. He shot one in the chest, and was about to fire again, when the second man bowled him over.

The handgun went flying. And, as the brother started to choke him, Kantar realized that his assailant was far too heavy for him to dislodge.

Fortunately the *janbiya* (dagger) was there at his side. The one left to him by his father. The blade was curved, and according to a family legend, home to a blood thirsty *jinn* (spirit). Kantar's lungs were close to bursting, and his vision was blurry, as the blade came free. There was nothing scientific about what occurred next. The knife went in between two ribs.

The brother uttered a grunt, and rolled away. He was busy pulling the blade free when the Russian shot him. And shot him again. "If he's worth one, then he's worth two. That's what they taught us at Hatsavita. (The GRU Mountain Training Center in Labinsk.) Good job, comrade. The others are dead too."

Kantar bent to retrieve his knife. He wiped the blade on the dead man's sleeve, thanked the *jinn*, and returned the weapon to its sheath. His pistol was five-feet away.

Next came the grisly process of gathering weapons, ammo, money, food, and ID from the dead. All of which was second nature for any guerilla fighter. So Kantar was carrying a heavy burden, as he followed the Russian across some hardpan, to the pile of smoldering wreckage.

Colonel Gortov and most of his men were present. A row of bodies were laid out on the blood stained sand, and judging from their clothing, all were members of the Brotherhood.

Alawi was there too, and hurried over to greet Kantar. "Men continue to trickle in, sir ... But we haven't been able to contact two of them."

Omaya was dead. So, if two of Kantar's fighters had been killed during the jump, then 93 men remained. Not bad really, given the need to bail out of a burning plane.

"There you are," Colonel Gortov said crossly, as he arrived. "As you can see, the scum sent to secure the crash site are dead."

Kantar eyed the bodies. "Yes, sir. No prisoners?"

"No," Gortov replied. "They fought to the death. Their families would be proud."

Kantar knew Gortov was lying. The prisoners had been executed. But, since they were Sunnis, that was reasonable. "We have work to do," Gortov said. "To capture the dam we'll have to fight the rest of the Brotherhood's security people. And they know we're coming."

"How many are there?" Kantar inquired. Prior to the mission he'd been told to expect roughly 100 defenders at the dam, not counting the troops assigned to outlying missile batteries, like the one that blew the 727 out of the air. But what would Gortov say? The Russian's answer came as an unpleasant surprise.

"Our drones have overflown the dam for weeks," Gortov said. "We believe that about 250 men are defending the dam."

Kantar felt a sinking sensation. The number was *twice* what he'd been told to expect! Why? *They thought you might balk*, Kantar reasoned. *So they lied.* He felt the first stirrings of fear. Gortov smiled thinly. "We're outnumbered, but we aren't outclassed. We are Spetsnaz. You are Hezbollah. They are dogs. We will crush them."

Kantar forced a smile. "Yes, sir. We'll do our part."

The plan was for the combined force to reach the vicinity of the dam as quickly as possible. Then it would split into two groups, one large, and one small.

Most of the troops would be under Gortov's command, with Alawi in charge of the Hezbollah contingent. Their objective was to secure the dam itself.

Kantar was to lead the smaller team against the administration complex located adjacent to the dam. "That's where the bureaucrats and engineers have their offices," Gortov said. "And we need them. Some of them anyway. So don't harm a single hair on their mostly bald heads. Do I make myself clear?"

"Yes, sir," Kantar replied. It was a formidable task, or would be assuming that he and his men faced armed opposition. How could he eliminate the guards while protecting the civilians? A partial answer occurred to him. "I want snipers, sir. Two of them."

Gortov frowned. "That's a big ask, Captain. But I like the way you're thinking. Your request is approved."

The sun was up. Columns of smoke rose from the north, where some of the buildings in Aswan continued to burn. The raiders split into columns and jogged south.

Kantar had a map. So he knew that a long, narrow, tree-lined inlet lay ahead, with an industrial area beyond. That was where the invaders were likely to encounter initial resistance. And, if things went well, they would capture some vehicles.

But if things went poorly the larger team could find itself locked into a prolonged firefight. That would give the Brotherhood time to summon reinforcements.

A dirt track appeared from the east and turned south towards the trees. A sure sign that the inlet and a bridge lay up ahead.

Gortov's scouts were in among the palms by then, glassing the enemy. Kantar could hear them speaking to Gortov in Russian. The translation came shortly thereafter. "The enemy is waiting for us," Gortov announced. "They're on the south side of a wooden bridge. Deploy your troops along the east side of the tree line, but don't advance until I give the order. We'll tease them onto the bridge, pull back, and open fire."

Kantar gave the necessary orders. There were 28 Hezbollah and 2 Russians under his command. They took up defensive positions as the larger group opened fire on the Brotherhood. The defenders had heavy weapons and put them to use. There was no mistaking the thump, thump, thump of a fifty-caliber machine gun, interspersed with the occasional crack of an RPG.

That wasn't good. Or so it seemed to Kantar, until two large drones bored in from the east. One of them was intercepted by a surface-to-air missile and blew up. But the other made it through ... And was flying so low it was lost in the ground clutter.

It was carrying bombs under its wings. And as it swooped over the enemy the weapons tumbled free. The defenders had revealed where they were. And, when the brothers surged onto the bridge, they were concentrated in one place.

Explosions threw human bodies high into the air, where they seemed to pause, before raining down. Columns of water rose and collapsed. The center section of the bridge was gone.

The Brotherhood fighters fired as they withdrew, but the skirmish was over, and Gortov issued new orders. "The water is shallow," the Russian said. "My column will cross while you, and your men, provide security."

Kantar moved his unit westward in accordance with Gortov's orders, and told them to deploy facing north, ready to protect the larger force should reinforcements appear. After fifteen minutes had passed Kantar received orders to turn south, and cross the inlet.

The well-worn track led to the shattered remains of a wooden bridge. Bodies, and parts of bodies, lay on the wreckage or floated in the languid waters below. Tracks left by the first column led into the inlet. Kantar and his troops soon found themselves knee-deep in blood warm liquid. A man wearing a dirty turban and a gray *gallabiya* (gown) floated face down. The body rocked slightly as Kantar pushed past it.

The south bank was steep, and difficult to climb, after the passage of so many feet. And by the time Kantar made it to the top his boots were heavy with black mud.

Low-lying buildings were visible ahead. Kantar kept an eye out for vehicles as he jogged south. But those that were available had been hotwired and were pulling away. Troops clung to them like fleas to a pack of dogs.

That meant Kantar and his men would have to hoof it. The dam rose in the distance with white water spewing out into the Nile. But Kantar's objective was closer. In fact the road they were on led to it.

Some of the locals were on the street by then. Egyptians mostly, but dark-skinned Nubians too, decedents of people who'd been displaced by the dam. They stood and stared as the column of heavily armed men double-timed past them. Who were the strangers? Members of a private militia? Anything was possible after the recent revolution—and the onlookers knew better than to try and interfere.

Gunfire could be heard in the distance. A sure sign that Gortov's men were in contact with the Brotherhood. But Kantar had his own challenge to face. The three-story building was off to the right with the dam behind it. "On the roof!" a man shouted, as an RPG sped their way.

It landed short of the column, exploded, and hurled shrapnel in every direction. "Disperse!" Kantar order. "Find cover. Snipers to me."

Kantar was crouched behind a wall where the Russians joined him. One was named Yezhov, the other Anishin. Both men were carrying VKS 12.7X55mm suppressed sniper rifles. And, since Kantar was well aware of the prominent role Russian snipers had played in WWII, he expected great things from them. "Kill the men on the roof. If others engage us, kill them too. But no noncombatants. The colonel wants to capture them alive. Do you understand?"

"Da," Yezhov said stolidly. "We kill." It was a sweeping response. Kantar hoped that the sniper understood the need to protect civilians.

Kantar's team had its own frequency to avoid the possibility of confusion. He spoke to them. "The snipers will neutralize the men on the roof. Squad one will circle around to the west side of the building and stand ready to enter through the back door. Squad two will remain with me. Execute."

Shots rang out as the brothers on the roof saw movement and stood up to fire at it. But that made them visible. A sniper fired and one of the brothers toppled forward. His body fell three stories and smacked onto the ground. A cloud of dust billowed into the air.

The defenders became more hesitant. But as the attackers came closer, they were forced to respond, thereby exposing themselves to sniper fire. The casualties continued to mount. Eventually, after suppressing fire from the roof, Kantar prepared to make entry. "Remember," he told the men. "Take prisoners. If you kill a noncombatant, I will kill *you*."

All the Hezbollah fighters had heard about Omaya by then. So they were inclined to take the threat seriously. And Kantar was counting on that. When both squads were ready, he gave the order, "Go!"

Kantar was running. But it felt as if he were standing still. *Shoot me in the head*, he prayed. *I won't feel it that way.* Men carrying AK-47s spilled out through the front door and raised their weapons. One fell to a bullet from Yezhov's rifle. And another toppled over backwards as Kantar fired. But, when he tried to fire a second shot, his pistol jammed.

A third fighter remained upright and Kantar watched with a sense of dread as the defender's Kalashnikov began to swing his way. Then a man named Hassan yelled, "*Allah Akbar!*" and shot the defender in the head.

Kantar and Hassan entered the lobby together. The other squad was inside by then, and chaos raged, as men shouted orders. "Get down! *Face* down. Hands behind your heads!"

It took about five minutes to subdue thirty-plus men and a handful of women. "Search the building," Kantar ordered. "Find the ones who are hiding."

Two men were. And they received rough treatment as fighters herded them into the now crowded lobby. "Tie their hands behind them," Kantar ordered. "And lead them out front.

"Yezhov and Anishin will take positions on the roof. Abbar, Erakat, and Fadel will patrol the perimeter. Take nothing... And no one is to enter. Do you understand?"

All of the men nodded. "Good," Kantar said. "Call for help if you come under attack."

The prisoners were marched heads hung, away from the building, and onto the road that ran east and west across the top of the dam. Kantar had done his homework. He knew that the new Aswan Dam was equipped with 12 Francis turbines, capable of producing 2,100 megawatts of electricity. But the structure wasn't, in all truth, that impressive to look at.

The belly of the concrete beast pushed south, from whence the 4,258 mile long river flowed, as if to keep Lake Nasser at bay. And there, running parallel to the road, was a well irrigated strip of carefully manicured trees. The planting curved in concert with the dam, thereby providing a welcome touch of green to what would have otherwise been an entirely drab structure.

Signs of fighting were visible ahead. Bodies lay sprawled on the pavement, the pools of blood already drying, as flies ate their fill. Most of the dead wore Egyptian garb. But there were Russian and Hezbollah casualties too. Both readily identifiable by their uniforms.

A Russian lieutenant and his men were guarding a metal door which had clearly been blown open. "Take the prisoners below," the officer ordered curtly. That, in spite of the fact that Kantar outranked him.

Kantar was careful to keep a check on his emotions as he gave the necessary orders. A Hezbollah noncom led the prisoners inside. Kantar and a contingent of his soldiers followed. Two flights of stairs led down to a large room with high ceilings. The air was artificially cool, and machinery hummed nearby.

Flat screen monitors covered most of the left wall. Some displayed schematics with colored indicator lights. Others featured lines of scrolling code. The rest were devoted to shots from external security cameras. Including one that displayed the bodies lying out front.

Two rows of consoles, all equipped with computer screens, filled the center of the room. A dead man sat slumped in a chair, blood pooling at his feet. The rest of the seats were empty. And that made sense because the control room's staff were standing against the right hand wall with hands clasped behind their heads. "Put your prisoners over there," Colonel Gortov said, as he pointed to the wall partially obscured by stairs.

"Good," Gortov said, as the Egyptians were chivvied into place. "Now, you will act as interpreter. Tell these people that they have a choice to make. They can run the dam for us, and live, or be martyred. Go ahead. Tell them."

The prisoners included the 22 people that Kantar's men had captured, plus the eight individuals who'd been on duty in the control room when Gortov's troops entered. They were understandably terrified. A man had peed himself, and a woman was sobbing. A strong indication that both understood English.

"You have a choice," Kantar told the prisoners in Arabic. "Work for us or die. Please raise your hand if you want us to shoot you."

All of the administrators, engineers, and technicians had been employed by the government before the country split into factions, and been forced to work for the Brotherhood after it took control. Now another group had taken over. The decision was easy. Not a single hand went up. Kantar turned to Gortov. "All of them want to work for you, Colonel."

Gortov nodded. "Excellent. I believe you have some administrative experts among your men. Am I correct?"

That was true. The need to supervise the dam's staff had been apparent from the beginning, and due to the potential language barrier involved, Hezbollah had been chosen to handle the task. Kantar nodded. "Yes, sir."

"Put your men to work," Gortov ordered. "Capture each prisoner's name, title and function. Collect the names of off duty personnel and send members of your team to find and bring them in. And last, but not least, pay each prisoner a 1,000 E£ bonus. Tell them they will receive a raise as well."

That, in Kantar's estimation, was pure genius. The Russians had a metal suitcase full of money, and what better way to spend some of it? Especially if the Brotherhood had been forcing the staff to work for free. "Sergeant Burhan, you heard the colonel," Kantar said. "Execute."

The next four hours were spent treating wounds, scouting the area, and feeding the troops. The American MREs were labeled "*Dhabihah Halal*," indicating that the meat in the meal came from animals which had been properly slaughtered. The Russians ate the *Halal* rations too, and none of them complained. How the MREs had been obtained was a mystery.

Kantar was sitting on a chair in the control room when a Russian came looking for him. "The colonel wants you to join him. He says that 'it's time to put the baby to sleep.' Whatever that means."

Kantar knew exactly what it meant. The "baby," or *"Rebenok"* in Russian, was a sixty-pound tactical nuke with a yield of 1K, or 1,000 tons of TNT. Though similar to the backpack devices that the United States, Russia, and possibly other countries had developed over the years, the "baby" had been purpose-built at the Budker Institute of Nuclear Physics in the Siberian town of Akademgorodok. And it had been in the possession of a huge noncom ever since the 727 left the ground in Syria. Putting the "baby" to sleep, and doing so quickly was an important part of the plan.

Kantar set the remains of his meal aside, wiped his mouth with a paper napkin, and took a final swig from his water bottle. After a quick radio conversation with Alawi he stood. "I'm ready. Lead the way."

A door opened onto stairs that led down to the third sub-level, where huge turbines labored around the clock. The ceiling was at least fifty-feet high, rail mounted hoists were mounted on the ceiling, and the smell of lubricants hung in the air.

The Russian led Kantar past the brightly painted machinery to a numbered door and into the tunnel beyond. It stretched for what seemed like a city block before terminating at a second numbered door. This door opened into a chamber large enough for ten men. A circular plate had been removed from the floor, and eight bolts were resting next to it. The "baby" was dangling above an open pipe. It was supported by a wire cable and a folding tripod.

Five men were present including the colonel, two Spetsnaz, and two Hezbollah fighters. "Finally," Gortov said. "Dorkov will take a picture of the moment, which will be uploaded to the internet. Then we'll finish the job."

Dorkov took half a dozen photos. Gortov gave an order in Russian once the soldier was done.

Kantar watched the "baby" descend into the vertical pipe. He was impressed by how perfect the fit was. The winch produced a ratcheting sound as the bomb sank out of sight.

"*This*," Gortov told them, "is an excellent example of Russian superiority. Back in the fifties, when western nations refused to help Egypt construct the dam, Russia stepped forward with a $1.12 billion dollar loan at 2% interest. Work began in 1958. The Soviet Union sent engineers and heavy equipment to do the job.

"One of those engineers was a KGB officer named Ivan Dragovich. It was his idea to install this pipe, the compression chamber below, and the blast ducts designed to channel the full force of the explosion into the dam's core. Tactical nukes hadn't been invented yet ... So Dragovich's plan called for the use of TNT.

"*Why* you ask?" Gortov asked rhetorically. "Did Dragovich intend to destroy the very thing that he and his team were striving to build? No. But he knew that relationships change. He knew that today's friends can become tomorrow's enemies.

"So Dragovich installed the *means* to destroy the dam. And, if we pull the trigger, the force of the resulting blast won't destroy the dam directly. But the structure will be weakened. And Lake Nasser's weight will do the rest. A wall of water will wipe the Nile River valley clean of life."

Most of the dead would be Sunnis, Kantar thought. *Millions of them. Inshallah.* (If Allah wills it.)

The ratcheting noise stopped and some slack appeared. "It's on the bottom," a Russian said.

"Test the relay box," Gortov ordered.

An insulted wire was wound around the cable by which the "baby" had been lowered. It was connected to a black box, or "sender," affixed to the bottom of the metal plate. Assuming everything worked properly, Colonel Gortov would be able to trigger "baby" using the remote clutched in his beefy hand. The technician flipped a switch and a green light appeared on the sender. Gortov eyed his device and nodded. "Replace the hatch and bolt it down."

Gortov turned to a knapsack at that point, withdrew a bottle of vodka, and removed the cap. Then he raised the bottle to his lips and took a drink before offering it to Kantar. "I know alcohol is forbidden … But a lot of your people drink anyway."

"Some do," Kantar admitted, as he drew his pistol. "But I'm not one of them."

The gunshot was very loud in the enclosed space, and echoed by more, as the Hezbollah fighters shot the rest of the Russians.

A blue-edged hole appeared between Gortov's eyes and brain tissue splashed the wall behind him. The bottle shattered on the floor as Gortov's body collapsed. Gun smoke eddied in the air. Kantar opened his mike. "Alawi."

"Sir."

"Kill them. Snipers first."

"*Yajib alqiam bih.*" (It shall be done.)

Kantar bent over Colonel Gortov's body, felt for the remote, and found it. He turned to face his men. Dead bodies lay sprawled all around. Kantar held the trophy high. "Egypt is ours!"

"Egypt is *ours!*" the Hezbollah fighters shouted. "*Allah Akbar!*"

CHAPTER TWO

Port Ashdod, Israel

The port of Ashdod was protected from the Mediterranean Sea by a long curving breakwater. And there, within its rocky embrace were freighters, transports, and naval vessels of every description—all waiting to discharge troops, effect repairs, or receive orders.

The 70-foot fishing boat *Galene* (named for the Greek goddess of calm seas), was shoehorned in between a German destroyer and an Italian tug. The *Galene* was what had been referred to as a "Q-ship" back during WWII, when armed merchantmen were used to lure enemy submarines in close, in an effort to sink them. The strategy met with only limited success.

But with the advent of WWIII Q-ships were back in fashion. Not to combat submarines, but to combat pirates, who were preying on small boats. A crime made considerably easier by the chaos of war.

Civilian workers were onboard the *Galene*, working under the watchful gaze of Ralph Hanson, the boat's XO. The wheelhouse had been blown to splinters during the boat's most recent engagement—and tools clattered as a replacement was bolted into place.

After being removed from an ancient trawler, the wheelhouse looked right at home on *Galene's* 63 year-old metal hull. Fishermen don't salute each other, so Hanson nodded, as

Lieutenant Commander Harley Kydd appeared from below deck. "Good morning, sir."

"*Really?*" Kydd inquired. "What's so good about it?"

Hanson grinned. Kydd was generally even tempered. But he'd been summoned to what promised to be a tongue lashing from flotilla commander Rear Admiral Hal Ducey. "We're alive, sir."

Kydd nodded. "Barely. Keep them on it Ralph … And count the tools before they leave."

"We will, sir," Hanson assured him. "And our wallets too."

Kydd was careful to step over the cables that crisscrossed the deck, as he made his way to the head of the gangplank. That's where gunner's mate Mary Kay Wilson was stationed. She was small, leathery, and busy splicing an eye into a length of rope. A Heckler & Koch MP5 was within easy reach. Some of the workers were Muslims. And even though they'd been screened, terrorist attacks weren't unknown. "Morning, sir."

Kydd forced himself to be civil. "Good morning, Wilson. Who knew that a gunner's mate could splice?"

"A gunner's mate can do *anything*," Wilson replied. "But don't tell the chief … I have enough work already."

"My lips are sealed," Kydd assured her, as he stepped onto the ramp. It led to the top of the breakwater. It was a steep climb but the cross cleats helped. A two-lane road occupied the top of the seawall. Trucks both large and small growled in both directions. There wasn't any sidewalk. That meant Kydd had to share the street with the trucks, and be ready to jump when they approached.

The prefab that served as Flotilla Six's headquarters was a mile away; the sky was mostly clear, and the sun was halfway up. So it wasn't long before Kydd's ball cap, tee shirt, and trousers were damp with sweat.

When the breakwater came to an end, Kydd took a right, and made his way between the low-lying buildings to a prefab.

It had been red once. But years of harsh sunlight had turned it pink. According to the sign the nondescript "fab" was the home of "Kinzo Marine."

An old pickup was up on blocks next to the building, and two men were working on it. Or *pretending* to work on it because, despite the civvies, both of them were marines.

One came forward to intercept Kydd, while the other watched, prepared to draw a concealed weapon. "Lieutenant Commander Kydd. Here to see Admiral Ducey." His ID was ready in the palm of a hand.

"Thank you, sir," the marine said. "Today's door code is 4112."

Kydd made his way to the entrance and entered the code. A green LED appeared, followed by a click. An artificially chilly room waited beyond. A yeoman was stationed at the front desk. The 9mm went back into the in-box. "Good morning, Commander. The admiral is on the horn. Please take a seat."

The waiting room was equipped with four chairs and one magazine. The much-thumbed issue of *Vanity Fair* was a month old. An actress in a fanciful uniform graced the front cover.

Kydd was two pages into an article about the many ways in which New York's elite were suffering from the war, when a door opened and Admiral Ducey appeared.

He was sixty-something and handsome in a Ralph Lauren sort of way. After investing over 30 years in the navy Ducey had retired, only to be called up weeks after the war started, and shipped to the Med. Something he welcomed. Kydd rose. "Good morning, sir."

Ducey frowned. "You look like hell."

"That's the plan, sir."

"Maybe so," Ducey responded. "But there's no need to look *that* authentic. You are a navy officer after all. Come in."

Kydd followed Ducey into a small, sparsely furnished office. Blackout curtains hung over the windows to keep light in during the night, and foil snipers during the day. Ducey gestured to a chair. "Have a seat. How are the repairs going?"

"We're working around the clock, sir," Kydd replied. "We hope to make the *Galene* seaworthy by the day after tomorrow."

"Good," Ducey responded. "Pirates boarded a ferry. Two women were abducted and the rest of the passengers were robbed."

Kydd winced. "I'm sorry to hear that, sir."

"We're doing what we can," Ducey said. "And that brings me to the situation at hand. Saudi Royal navy Captain Abdul Aziz bin Al Saud, better known to his people as *Prince* Abdul, since he's one-thousand five-hundred and fifty-sixth in line for the throne, filed official complaints with the Navy and the Department of Agriculture—charging you with numerous offenses, including insubordinate behavior, and the use of foul language during the *Princess Charlotte* incident."

"The Department of Agriculture, sir?"

"Yes. I don't know why. And don't try to change the subject."

"Sir, yes sir. The *Charlotte* was under attack. So we intervened and requested support from the so-called 'quick response' vessel captained by Prince Abdul. It arrived forty-five minutes *after* the engagement was over. I lost two men, and my boat was severely damaged."

"True," Ducey admitted. "Then you called the prince, and I quote, an 'incompetent asshole.' I'm sorry about your men," Ducey added. "But the reality of the situation is that our European Allies no longer receive oil from Russia. That makes Saudi Arabia more important than it was. So, when they whistle, the people in D.C. hear it."

"And?" Kydd inquired.

"And you were up for full commander," Ducey replied. "But not anymore. The secretary of the navy told the Saudis that we are going to bust you from 05 to 04. So you get to keep lieutenant commander."

"Oh, good," Kydd said. "I feel better now."

"It's going to be a long war," Ducey responded. "Don't worry, you'll make captain before it's over. If you live that long."

The meeting came to a close when a general called. The yeoman was waiting for Kydd in the front office. "I have mail for the *Galene*," she said. "Please take it with you. Yours is on top."

Like Q-ships, letters were back in fashion. The internet, and the traffic that rode on it, was subject to censorship. Emails rarely got through. That meant everyone looked forward to mail from home. "Will do," Kydd said, as he accepted the canvas satchel with "*Galene*" stenciled on it. "Thank you."

It was like stepping into a furnace as Kydd left the air conditioned building. He'd been planning to return to the boat. But now, in the wake of the conversation with Ducey, and mail to read, Kydd took a detour.

The Mariners Club had been founded by the Brits who, as they had for hundreds of years, knew how to make themselves comfortable during a war. Officers from all the Allied powers were welcome to enter the cool interior, and order some refreshment.

A five minute walk took Kydd to a low, unassuming building. A pair of Royal marines were stationed out front. One, a corporal, was clearly suspicious of Kydd's appearance. He barred the way. "Can I help you?"

Kydd presented his ID. "Sorry, it's my day off."

The corporal ignored the attempt at humor. "Welcome, sir. Sorry for the inconvenience."

The air inside the club was *too* cold, if such a thing was possible, and Kydd shivered. It was barely lunchtime. So very few people were present. Kydd chose a table in a corner where he hoped to escape being noticed. The last thing he wanted to do was shoot the shit about the war.

A waiter arrived to take his order, which consisted of a sabich sandwich, a gin and tonic, and a slice of lime. Kydd's mail was secured with a blue rubber band. An invitation to purchase life insurance was on top of the pile. That made him laugh. *What would they charge,* he wondered. *A hundred dollars a day?*

There was a birthday card from his mother too. It had been mailed a month earlier. Kydd felt guilty. He should write but hadn't.

And there, third from the top, was the most precious item of all. An envelope with Jamie Everson's military style block printing on it. He held it up to his nose. Nothing. No perfume.

Well, Jamie was stationed aboard the carrier *Carl Vinson*, and smelly stuff could be in short supply. Kydd tore the letter open and started to scan. "Dear Harley... Sorry to tell you... I met a pilot... Lots in common... I will always be your friend... Watch your six. Jamie."

"Here you are," the waitress said, as she placed the sandwich and drink on the table. "Will there be anything else?"

"Yes," Kydd replied. "Another gin and tonic."

$$* * *$$

The next 24 hours were extremely hectic. Once the "new" wheelhouse was secured to the deck, the cables that controlled the boat's steering had to be repaired, and new electronics installed, including radios, radar, a depth finder and more.

Ideally that sort of work would have been carried out by civilian contractors. But repairing an ancient Q-ship was at the very bottom of the military harbormaster's list of things to do.

So, it was up to the *Galene's* crew to do most of the work themselves, while unskilled civilians were left to plug holes and paint. Lieutenant Hanson was in charge of the overall effort. But Chief Boatswain's Mate Sergio Lazio was the *real* taskmaster. And "Boats" was everywhere.

He was a small man, with a big attitude, and a pencil thin mustache. The slightest mistake could set him off. But Lazio was fair ... And an important bridge between the boat's officers and crew.

While the repairs were being made Kydd sat in his tiny cabin, filling out forms on his laptop, and printing them down. An old fan stirred the air as it swung back and forth but did little to cool him. At 1800 hours the civilians went ashore and Hanson stuck his head in through the open hatch. "Dinner is served, sir ... Dress whites are mandatory."

Kydd chuckled. "Of course, nothing less would do. Give me a sitrep."

"We're ready for sea trials," Hanson replied.

"Excellent," Kydd said as he stood. "We'll cast off after chow. Speaking of which please send a sailor up to the road. I'm expecting an important delivery."

Kydd was on deck, decorating a cheeseburger with condiments, when three Styrofoam chests arrived. Each was filled with ice cold beer. And not just *any* beer, but Goldstar, a very popular lager. A cheer went up, moral soared, and Kydd grinned. His crew consisted of 26 people, and there were 52 bottles of beer, which meant the crew would still be sober as the *Galene* slipped into the night.

The port was very busy. That meant all arrivals and departures had to be scheduled in advance. So when the harbormaster's office gave the *Galene* permission to leave at 2000 hours, they meant 8:00 pm, not 8:15. Once chow was over Kydd ordered the crew to secure all gear, clear the decks for sea, and run the standard systems checks. Amber lights appeared, but were quickly cleared.

Because the *Galene* was sandwiched in between a destroyer and tug, and equipped with a single screw, the process of warping out might have been difficult. However, one of the reasons the *Galene* had been "bought into the service" was her recently installed engine, plus the external bow, side, and stern thrusters added by previous owners.

All the quartermaster had to do was press a rocker switch to activate the port side thruster and push the Q-ship out of its berth. Skillful use of the bow-stern thrusters was required to prevent yawing. Applause was heard from the destroyer's aft deck—indicating that the Germans had been expecting the worst.

Once clear of obstacles Kydd instructed his radio operator to notify the harbormaster that the *Galene* was underway, ordered "slow ahead," and felt the deck vibrate in sympathy with the powerful 803hp Mitsubishi diesel engine.

The oily black waters of Ashdod harbor parted in front of the *Galene's* sheer bow and slid back along her hull to produce a V-shaped wake. A buoy swayed in response. Kydd felt a surge of happiness. In command and underway. There was nothing better.

An inbound frigate passed to port, running lights on, as it returned from a mission. To battle Russian Shmel Class gunboats off Cyprus? To escort a freighter into Athens? Anything was possible. The *Galene* wallowed as the warship's wake hit her.

Kydd had served on large ships, half a dozen of them, since his graduation from Annapolis. But he felt no sense of envy for the officers on the frigate's bridge. He had chosen the brown water navy, and the boats appropriate for that kind of work.

Once the *Galene* was well off shore, and well clear of other vessels, it was time to kill her running lights, don tactical gear, and exercise the boat's systems. The steering came first. And, thanks to the new cabling, it was more responsive than it had been before.

Then came the rest of it. The radios, the nav gear, and the boat's weaponry. The most important part of which was the GAU-17/A minigun concealed below flip-off hatch covers in the bow. The 7.62X5mm NATO six-barrel rotary machine gun could fire up to 6,000 rounds per minute. It was mounted on a hydraulic lift, and could be deployed in less than two minutes, thereby transforming the *Galene* from a fishing boat to a bullet-spewing sea monster.

In addition to the minigun there were pintle mounts for two Browning heavy machine guns in the stern, and two medium machine guns mounted just aft of the wheelhouse. Those weapons plus the crew-carried grenade launchers, assault rifles, and shotguns added up to what Chief Lazio called "A bad-assed boat."

After an hour of drills, Kydd declared the shakedown cruise a success, and told Hanson to "Take her in." And that too was part of the training cycle. If Kydd were killed Hanson would assume command.

Rather than stay, and look over Hanson's shoulder, Kydd went below. A sign of his faith in the XO, which would be noticed by the crew, and help to build his credibility.

The bunk was narrow, and too short for Kydd. But it felt good to get off his feet. A breeze had come up by then and the *Galene* rolled gently as she plowed forward.

It was a sensation that would have been familiar to a sea captain 2,000 years earlier. Some things never changed while others had. Take Jamie for example. Maybe he had misjudged her. Or maybe the relationship had been more about sex than love. Kydd smiled. Go navy.

***

With the exception of the *Galene's* watch keepers, the crew was allowed to sleep in the next morning. And all of them knew why. Once darkness fell, the boat would leave port, and head north.

Kydd rose early, had two cups of coffee, and left for the local operations center. The one story building was located near Flotilla Six's headquarters. That made for a long walk. But, thanks to a high overcast, the temperature was in the low 80's.

After wading through two levels of security Kydd entered a large dimly lit room. Flat screens covered one wall, Intel techs sat in worshipful rows, and the low murmur of their radio conversations was reminiscent of monks praying.

A female petty officer was in charge of the "take out" counter at the back of the room, where a uniformed 06 was busy reviewing the latest "buzz." Something the captain could do aboard her ship if she chose to.

But lesser beings, Kydd among them, had to visit the OC to obtain the latest weather forecast, eyeball aerial surveillance imagery, and review all of the after-action reports filed during the last 12 hours. Of the thirteen contacts that had taken place during that time Kydd was most interested in two of them.

The first had to do with an Israeli tug which had been attacked by three armed RIBs (Rigid Inflatable Boats), but been able to fend them off with machine gun fire.

The second had all of the hallmarks of an attack by the so-called "Lucky Strike" gang. Lucky Strike cigarettes had been discontinued in the U.S. many years before, but were still popular in Europe, and pirates were said to have taken their name from the brand.

Maybe that had something to do with the "cigarette boats" they used to launch lightning fast strikes against ferries, coastal freighters, and larger fishing vessels. The pirate boats were typically about 30-feet long, powered by a couple of 400hp engines, and capable of speeds up to 60mph in choppy waters.

And because the low-lying cigarette boats were difficult to detect by radar, except in flat seas or at close range, they were hard to intercept. That's where the *Galene* came in. Her job was to look helpless, wait for the Lucky Strikes to attack, and blow them out of the water.

In this case a pair of high-speed boats had overtaken a 75-foot motor yacht which, ironically enough, was being moved from Benghazi to Israel, where it would theoretically be safer. Unfortunately the boat had been boarded, the crew had been forced into a dinghy, and the owners had been abducted. Making the situation worse, from an Allied point of view, was the fact that the owner, Mr. Abdel Kubar, was an important official in Libya's Sunni led government.

Kydd slid the printouts into his envelope-style briefcase, thanked the PO behind the counter, and took a doughnut with him. The air was warmer on the way back—and the doughnut made him thirsty.

The rest of the day passed slowly. And Kydd felt grateful as the sun began to set. The trip out to sea passed without incident. Then it was time to flip the floodlights on and pretend to fish. A *real* trawler would drop a net over the stern and pull it along at a specified depth.

But since Kydd didn't want to catch fish, only a short length of carefully weighted net was deployed. Not much, just enough to look realistic, thereby inviting pirates to attack.

The sun rose above a calm sea. A tanker followed a warship across the horizon while contrails clawed the sky. A seagull perched on the radio mast. A pair of bottlenose dolphins came by for a look as a shot-up life raft floated by. And, as the sun sank lower, the light gradually faded. Once darkness fell the cycle started over.

The following day was no different. Nor the one after that, except for the increasingly choppy seas. When night fell Kydd decided to call it quits.

The *Galene* was running low on fuel, all of the fresh food was gone, and one of the seaman had a terrible toothache. A problem hospital corpsman "Doc" Parley couldn't do much about.

After setting the course, and passing the con to Hanson, Kydd stepped outside. His favorite resting spot was on the steel deck, with his back to the wheelhouse. Other people liked it too. So a beat-up cushion was available to sit on.

The bow rose and fell as the *Galene* broke through the low-lying waves. And there, high above, thousands of the galaxy's 100-billion stars glittered. It was a sight never seen by people who spent their entire lives in cities. "Excuse me, sir," Wilson said. "The XO wants to see you. He's down below."

That's where the radar was. Kydd felt his pulse quicken as he stood. "Thanks, Wilson. Who knows? Maybe our luck is about to change."

After entering the wheelhouse, he placed his feet on the side rails, and slid down. The *Galene's* Operations Room was so small it barely qualified as such. The radar and radio operators sat back-to-back separated by a narrow passageway.

The boat's "blip chaser" was a young man named Peterson. Hanson was looking over the operator's shoulder, and turned when Kydd arrived. "Two targets, sir. They're southwest of us, and headed west."

Kydd stepped in to look. And sure enough, there they were, two blips headed west. "How fast are they going?"

"No more than 10 knots," Peterson replied. "If that."

Kydd considered what he'd heard. He was expecting to encounter cigarette boats. But cigarette boats were unlikely to travel so slowly. He turned to the radio operator. "Hey, Lee ... Did you try the IFF?" (The Identification, Friend or Foe system.)

"Yes, sir," Lee answered. "There was no response."

Kydd took a moment to consider that. The failure to respond could indicate that they were tracking enemy vessels. Or, it could mean that the radar targets were friendlies, who couldn't receive or transmit for some reason.

This wasn't anything like the kind of situation Kydd expected to find himself in. It took effort to put his brain in gear. He turned to Hanson. "Change course to put us behind the targets and add power. Oh, and pass the word... The crew will report to battle stations. This is not a drill."

It was a pro forma order for the most part because, with the exception of those who were asleep, the rest of the crewmembers were at battle stations. Hanson said, "Yes sir," and turned to climb the ladder.

Kydd remained where he was, watching, and waiting to see what, if anything, the other vessels would do. If the unknowns had radar, they would see the *Galene* change course, and turn to meet the threat. Or run like hell.

The deck shifted under Kydd's feet as the Q-ship turned. The engine noise grew louder and there was no reaction from the blips. Kydd turned to Lee. "Try the IFF again."

Lee tapped some keys, waited, and shook his head. "Nada."

Kydd thanked Lee before climbing the ladder to the wheelhouse. Hanson lowered a pair of night vision binoculars. "No visual as yet, sir. What's the plan?"

"The first priority is to see what we have," Kydd replied. "I think one boat is towing the other. Maybe they don't have any electronics due to a power failure."

"So *both* of them had power failures?" Hanson inquired skeptically.

Kydd grinned. "You've got me there, Ralph... How long before we catch up?"

"No more than fifteen minutes, sir."

"Good." Kydd turned to the intercom. "Lee... Get operations on the horn. Give them our position, course, and speed. Tell them we're about to make contact with two unidentified vessels, one of which might be under tow."

"Roger that," Lee replied.

Time slowed. The bow rose and fell. The helm made soft clacking sounds as the helmsman turned it right and left. A fan blew warm air at the back of Kydd's head. Then the call came in. "Bow here, I see a vessel dead ahead. I don't see any weapons."

"Prepare to light it up," Kydd said. "And prepare to engage."

Kydd wasn't wearing night vision gear, and didn't want to take the time to put it on. All he could see was the black-on-black bulk of something to starboard. If the other vessel's crew was aware of the Q-ship there was no sign of it. "Hit 'em with the spots," Kydd ordered, and watched as the mystery ship popped into stark relief.

Kydd wasn't looking at a fishing boat, but a yacht. And there was something familiar about it. *Why?*

Then it came to him. He was looking at the *Sea Star*! The boat that had, along with its owners, been captured by pirates! And judging from appearances the yacht was definitely under tow.

Suddenly everything changed. Who was towing the *Sea Star*? The pirates most likely. Something had gone wrong. An engine failure perhaps, forcing them to tow the unwieldy yacht to their home port, wherever that was. And what about Mr. and Mrs. Abdel Kubar? Were they on board? "Don't fire on the yacht," Kydd ordered. "Even if it fires on us. Hostages may be aboard."

"The lead boat dropped the tow!" a lookout announced.

"It's a cigarette boat!" a second voice added.

"There are *two* cigarette boats," the bow lookout warned.

Kydd's brain was churning. *Two* cigarette boats? How could that be? He'd seen two blips on the radar. *They were side-by-side*, Kydd told himself. *And both had towlines out. But, being so close together, they looked like a single image.*

That was when the first speedboat opened fire with a deck mounted LMG. Bullets clanged as they struck the Q-ship's metal hull. "Smoke 'em," Kydd ordered, as the minigun rose from its hiding place in the forward hold.

Wilson was sitting on a plastic chair, protected by a ballistic shield. The minigun produced a sustained roar as he pulled the trigger. A steady stream of 7.62X5mm slugs, mixed with tracer, drew a straight line between the *Galene* and the oncoming boat.

There was no contest. The incoming fire shattered the cigarette boat's composite hull. And, when a tracer found a fuel tank, the vessel exploded.

Burning chunks of debris continued to fall as the second speedboat attacked from astern. It had turned, and circled around the far side of the yacht, in order to get in position. And Wilson couldn't fire on it without hitting the wheelhouse. That left the stern gunners to handle the job.

The machine guns began to thump as a spotlight found the incoming target. The heavy weapons hit, and hit hard, but it was a grenade from Chief Lazio's launcher that finished the job.

The explosion blew a hole in the bottom of the boat and it went under in a matter of seconds. "Cease firing, but standby your weapons," Kydd ordered. "Drop fenders. We'll go alongside. Lieutenant Hanson will lead the boarding party."

"Three people on the bow with hands in the air," a gunner announced.

"Two on the stern!" another added. "A man and a woman."

The Kubars? Quite possibly.

Kydd was forced to put a hand on the wheelhouse, as the *Galene* bumped into the yacht, and the chief's deck crew took lines across. "Don't fire unless fired upon," Kydd ordered. "Search the prisoners, and watch for IEDs. Chief Lazio, have the crew rig a cable. We'll take the yacht in tow. Lee, get operations on the horn, and explain the situation. We need air cover."

Two extremely frightened civilians were brought aboard minutes later. They were disheveled, and Kydd could see that the man had been beaten. "Do you speak English?"

"Yes," the man replied. "Who are you?"

"Lieutenant Commander Kydd, United States Navy," Kydd replied. "And you're Minister Kubar, if I'm not mistaken."

A look of relief appeared on the woman's face. "The pirates took us to Cyprus," she said. "Then, after two days, we left. But there was a fire in the engine room."

"All of the electronic controls were destroyed," Kubar explained. "And the pirates couldn't figure out how to operate them manually."

"They hit him," Mrs. Kubar added. "But Abdel said he didn't know. So they tried to tow us."

"I'm glad you survived," Kydd said. "Simms will take you below. I will notify the Naval Operations Center—and they will contact your government."

The planes arrived five minutes later. A tugboat announced itself an hour after that, and with a fine display of seamanship, took the tow.

Then, when the Q-ship was still three hours from port, a sleek Super Dvora Mk III patrol boat arrived to take the Kubars off. Once they were gone the *Galene* was all alone.

Kydd took stock. Two sailors had been wounded, but not badly. And the Q-ship would need more repairs. But, all-in-all, Kydd was satisfied.

And so, it seemed, was Admiral Ducey. The message read, "Not bad for a fishing boat. Come see me after you get in."

* * *

After returning the *Galene* to the harbor, and getting his wounded sailors ashore, Kydd granted himself six hours of sleep. His alarm went off at 0900. That was when he discovered the sheet of paper someone had slipped under the door. The handwritten note was on Admiral Ducey's stationary. "Please join us in the Operations Center at 1000. Ducey."

Kydd swore. That didn't leave much time to shower, get dressed, and complete the requisite hike. So he sent for petty officer Simms, better known to his shipmates as "the fixer." He had close cropped hair and dark skin. A pair of board shorts completed the look. "No problem, sir," Simms said. "I'll take care of it."

Kydd showered in the same grungy cubicle that everyone else used, donned fresh civvies sans socks, and went up on deck. Simms was polishing brass. "Your car is waiting up on the street, sir."

Kydd thanked the sailor and climbed the gangway to find that a shiny Hyundai was there, with flashers on, blocking a lane of traffic. Truckers were honking their horns at the driver, but he seemed to be blissfully unaware of it, as he got out to open the rear door. "Commander Kydd? Good morning, sir."

Cool air flowed around Kydd as he got inside and the car pulled away. "You know where we're going?"

"Naval Operations," the man said.

Kydd allowed himself to relax. It took less than five minutes to reach his destination. "What do I owe you?"

The man eyed Kydd in the mirror. "Nothing, sir. Lieutenant Simms took care of it."

Lieutenant? The fixer indeed. Kydd grinned. "Thank you."

Kydd got out, worked his way through security, and entered the building. A civilian was stationed behind the reception desk. "How can I help you?"

"My name is Kydd. I'm here to meet with Admiral Ducey."

The man consulted a screen. "Your meeting is in room C, sir. It's down the hall."

Kydd followed the pointing finger, saw C, and went inside. A dozen people were in the conference room, drinking coffee, and shooting the shit. Ducey came over to greet him. "Good morning."

"Good morning, sir," Kydd said, as he looked around. "What's going on?"

"Nothing good," Ducey replied. "A team comprised of Hezbollah fighters, and Russian commandos, took control of the Aswan Dam in Egypt. They have a tactical nuke, and are threatening to blow the dam, unless Egypt surrenders to the Axis."

Kydd stared at him. "You're kidding."

"Nope," Ducey replied. "I wish I was."

"That's terrible," Kydd said. "But, if you don't mind my asking, what am I doing here?"

"That will become clear during the presentation," Ducey said. "Grab a cup of joe and strap in."

After collecting a cup of coffee Kydd sat down. Ducey took the dais moments later. "I believe all of you know me, and vice versa, so let's dispense with the introductions. As you know we've got a major problem to deal with. Cassandra Cole just arrived from D.C., and she's going to read us in. Cassandra?"

The woman who replaced Ducey on the stage had short blond hair. She was wearing sunglasses and a set of well-pressed khakis. *Uh-oh, CIA,* Kydd thought. *Never a good sign.*

Cole removed the sunglasses. She had even features and full lips. A remote was waiting for her. "Some of what I'm going to tell you is classified, and some of it isn't," she began. "I think the difference will be obvious.

"About 48-hours ago Russian attack submarines fired two flights of cruise missiles at the city of Aswan in Egypt. Aswan is located just north of the dam bearing the same name, and has a population of a quarter-million people.

"The purpose of the attack was to destroy key infrastructure, and kill the city's first responders, in an effort to ensure that a joint Hezbollah-Russian special ops team would face minimal resistance when they fell out of the sky.

"The secondary objective was to scare the crap out of the civilian, mostly Sunni, population and cause them to evacuate. Both goals were achieved. As I speak tens of thousands of civilians are fleeing north."

Drone footage appeared at that point. Entire sections of Aswan had been destroyed. Columns of black smoke rose to stain the otherwise blue sky. A major highway was clogged with people. "Meanwhile," Cole continued, "the commandos defeated the Muslim Brotherhood's militia, and took command of the facility. Then they placed a nuclear device deep inside the dam." That statement produced expressions of surprise and concern.

Cole nodded. "Within hours a Hezbollah produced video appeared on internet sites in Lebanon, Iraq, and Iran. But *not* in Russia," Cole added. "And there's a reason for that. Watch this."

The video showed a mixed group of Russians and what Kydd assumed to be Hezbollah fighters lowering a cylindrical object into a pipe. "My name is Captain Mustafa Kantar," a voice said, as the footage rolled. "Many years ago, when the Aswan Dam was under construction, Russian engineers had the foresight to create a repository deep inside the dam's containment wall. The purpose of that chamber was to receive conventional explosives which, if the need arose, could be used to destroy the dam. And that day has arrived.

"However, thanks to advances in technology made during the intervening 60 years, we are lowering a tactical nuke into the repository instead of TNT. That means we can destroy the dam with the press of a button. All prayers to Allah, such a moment will never arrive.

"But *if* it does," Kantar continued, "It is my duty to remind you that approximately 6-trillion cubic feet of water will be released into an area where 10-million Egyptians live."

A tight shot appeared. Kantar had dark hair, a widow's peak, and heavy eyebrows. *"Please,"* Kantar said. "There is no need to die! Accede to our demands and live. The moment that Egypt creates a single government, and that government welcomes Axis forces into the land of the Pharaohs, we will remove the device from its tomb—and embrace our fellow Muslims as comrades in arms."

A picture of a soaring monument appeared on the screen. "Sadly our Russian comrades were killed in a firefight after the nuclear device was lowered into place." Kantar said. "They were buried next to our Hezbollah fighters adjacent to the monument of Arab-Soviet friendship that stands on top of the dam."

Cole thumbed a button. The image disappeared. "And *that*," she said, "is Grade-A bullshit. Based on satellite imagery we know that Hezbollah troops launched a surprise attack on the Russians, gunned them down, and dumped the bodies into a common grave.

"And our vodka swilling friends know that. According to signals intelligence the Russians, the Lebanese, and Iran are engaged in a three-way pissing match. But the Russians *need* the Shia countries. Especially their airbases. So they're going to back down, and Hezbollah, which is to say Iran—knows that."

Cole's eyes roamed the room. They were bright blue. "So," she said. "By now you're asking yourselves what the Allies plan to do. I'll begin with the things we *can't* do.

"We can't drop troops in because the Brotherhood placed rings of surface to air missiles around the dam.

"The second thing we *can't* do is destroy those missiles with other missiles. Because if we try to do so Kantar will blow the dam."

"The third thing we *can't* do is attack from the west, because a 263,000 square mile desert is in the way. That gives us a choice. We can attack from the Red Sea, or straight up the Nile valley. Both strategies have advocates. But the pro-Nile crowd came out on top, and that's how it's going to be.

"That leaves us with a surface attack," Cole said. "And there are two ways to accomplish it. We can send vehicles up one of the highways that run parallel to the Nile, or we can make use of the river itself. Each option has advantages and disadvantages. Suffice it to say that the brass settled on the river."

"So here's the skinny," Cole continued. "Operation Pharaoh will be led by Marine Colonel Martin Goolsby, with support from a naval task force consisting of American and British forces. The colonel has orders to take a battalion of marines south, assault the dam, and neutralize the nuke. Do you have any questions?"

Kydd raised a hand.

Cole frowned. "And you are?"

"Commander Kydd."

"Okay, shoot."

"No offense ma'am, but that plan won't work. Barring a political miracle—the tangos (terrorists) will blow the dam once we get close to it. They won't wait for an assault."

Cole nodded. "There's an additional element to the overall plan. One which I'm not authorized to share at this time. But I can assure you that your concern will be addressed. Are there other questions? No? Thank you for your time."

And with that Cole put her sunglasses on and left the room. Kydd turned to Ducey. "Don't tell me, let me guess. I've been assigned to the naval support group."

"Nope," Ducey replied. "You're in *command* of the support group. Reporting to Goolsby. Who, by the way, is said to be a by-the-book asshole."

"Gee, thanks," Kydd said. "*Why?*"

Ducey grinned. "Because you did a good job yesterday. Operation Pharaoh is your reward."

CHAPTER THREE

Aswan Dam airport, Egypt

The sun was up, but just barely, as Mustafa Kantar stood on the tarmac—and scanned the cloudless sky. Two Kenya Airways planes carrying much needed troops were due to arrive. But what if they'd been shot down? What if he and his tiny command would be forced to defend the dam alone? Fear of death, fear of failure, and fear of fear caused his palms to sweat. Why *him*? Why was he so weak?

"There!" a man shouted. "Coming in from the south!"

Kantar squinted. And sure enough, two specks could be seen. Kantar spoke into the boom mike attached to his headset. "Attention all missile batteries. Two friendly aircraft are inbound from the south. *Do not*, I repeat, *do not* fire on them."

The same message had been sent earlier. But Kantar knew that endless repetition was required to keep some people from making mistakes.

And the fact that members of the Muslim Brotherhood were manning most of the batteries, and doing so under duress, made the situation even riskier. But the incoming planes were carrying Iranian missile technicians who would replace the brothers. So that problem would be solved.

The first plane circled the airport so as to land from the north. The words "Kenya Airlines" were clear to see on the plane's white fuselage.

The country of Kenya was theoretically neutral. But everyone knew that Kenya's new railroad system had been financed by China, constructed by Chinese engineers, and was under their control. So, when an Axis country called, Kenya answered.

Engines roared forcing Kantar to pull the earmuff style hearing protectors down over his ears. It took the better part of fifteen minutes for the plane to land, taxi in, and park.

The airport personnel were Sunni. And it seemed safe to assume that many, if not all of them, were sympathetic to the recently defeated Muslim Brotherhood.

But they hurried to do their jobs, and for good reason. Each had been required to surrender a family member, all of whom were housed in the terminal building, where they were being cared for.

That arrangement would end soon however, when 95-percent of the employees were dismissed, leaving a handful of technical experts behind. Just enough to handle occasional Hezbollah flights.

Kantar watched with pride as a company of fighters, all heavily laden with gear, made their way down a set of rollup stairs to assemble on the tarmac. The second plane had arrived meanwhile, and was unloading its passengers.

And that was to say nothing of the machine guns, RPG launchers, and mortars being removed from baggage compartments. The newly arrived weapons, plus those captured from the Russians and the Brotherhood, would ensure Hezbollah's ability to defend what had been taken.

Allawi appeared at Kantar's side. The lieutenant's lips were moving but Kantar couldn't hear. He pushed the safety muffs up and out of the way. "Yes? What is it?"

"The secretary general!" Alawi said. "He's here! To see *you*."

"No."

"Yes! I saw him with my own eyes."

Kantar could hardly believe it. Hassan Haddad! The head of Hezbollah ... In Egypt to see *him*. The visit was unexpected, exhilarating, and terrifying all at the same time. Kantar's thoughts were racing. "Find a guide ... Show the secretary general to a nice room. Summon food and drink. Send the guide back to me. Tell Haddad that I must greet the incoming troops ... But I will meet with him immediately thereafter." Alawi took off at a run.

Kantar forced himself to stroll over, greet the fighters from plane one, and welcome them to Egypt. "Most of you are veterans," he said. "And that's why I sent for you. We took Aswan Dam by force of arms. Others will attempt to capture it. But you, the *Almuqatlin Alumuqdasin* (holy fighters), will send them to *aljahim* (hell)."

A cheer went up, and Kantar smiled. "We'll get acquainted after you settle in. *Ila-liqaa* (until we meet again)."

After receiving a positive response from the first group, Kantar saw no reason to invent new remarks for the second. And they were equally enthusiastic.

A second cheer was dying away when an obsequious middle-aged man in a shabby business suit appeared. "This way sir, if it please you, to the executive dining room."

Kantar followed the functionary through a door, up two flights of stairs, and across an empty room to a waiting elevator. It carried them to the 2nd floor where Alawi was waiting. "Please follow me."

A carpeted corridor led to a door guarded by two men. Both carried AK-47s. They had sour expressions and matching beards. "This is Captain Kantar," Alawi told them. "The secretary general wants to meet with him."

The security measures weren't surprising since there had been two highly publicized attempts on Haddad's life during the last 12 months. "Surrender your pistol," one of bodyguards demanded, and Kantar complied.

"Face the wall," the second man ordered. "Put your weight on it and spread your legs."

The ensuing pat-down was very thorough, *too* thorough for Kantar's comfort, but necessary in the age of suicide bombers. "All right," the second bodyguard said. "You may enter. The pistol will be waiting when you depart. The lieutenant will remain here."

Kantar opened the door and went inside. A huge window looked out onto the sunbaked runway. Heat waves shimmered around the planes. A table large enough to seat 12-people occupied the center of the room. Two additional guards stood with their backs to an inside wall.

Secretary General Haddad rose from a chair. He was wearing a black turban, glasses, and a gray-streaked beard. He was fat in a way that even his voluminous robe couldn't conceal.

Both men stepped forward. "*Marhaban,*" Haddad said. (Hello, greetings.)

"*Ahlan wa Sahlan,*" Kantar replied. (Welcome.)

Kantar was ready for the handshake. But not the kiss on both cheeks, normally reserved for close friends and family. "My apologies for the wait," Kantar said, as they parted.

"Those who fight must come first," Haddad replied. "Please join me lest I consume everything. I am on a diet."

They sat across from each other, and as they ate, Haddad launched into a stream-of-consciousness rant. Kantar welcomed the narrative because it allowed him to remain silent and absorb any useful information that could be gleaned from it.

"The entire world was astonished by what a handful of Hezbollah fighters could accomplish," Haddad told him. "Meanwhile the Russians are unhappy, *very* unhappy. They came close to accusing Hezbollah of murder. But without support from the Iranians, or the Iraqis, the *kafir* must allow the matter to rest. But I wouldn't vacation in Moscow if I were you."

It was a joke, and Kantar laughed, but felt slightly nauseous too. The possibility that his name had been added to a Russian hit list hadn't occurred to him.

Kantar put his fork down. Haddad continued to talk between bites of *fuul* (cooked mashed fava beans) on pita bread. "Our spies claim that the Allies will attack up the Nile valley," Haddad said. "But that's a waste of time. You can kill the *kafirs* whenever you choose. But that isn't our goal ... Our goal, no *your* goal, is to reconstitute Egypt's government—and bring the country into the Axis. Then we will attack Saudi Arabia from the west. Oil is critical ... Without it Europe will fall to the Russians."

"And remember," Haddad added. "Don't kill millions of Sunnis unless you must. Such an act would strengthen Sunni resolve, and turn the world against us."

The overall plan was brilliant, or so it seemed to Kantar. And the extent of his enthusiasm must have been clear to see. "You're a good boy," Haddad said, as he wiped a gob of *fuul* off his lips. "I have a present for you."

Haddad snapped his fingers. A guard came forward with a case—and the secretary general stood to open it. And there, sleeping on a bed of satin, was a beautifully crafted scimitar. It had a gently curved blade and an oval shaped pommel. Such weapons were perfect for mounted warfare because of their lightweight and saber-like design. That's why generations of Arab horsemen favored them.

"Come," Haddad insisted. "Come and receive your gift. The blade is made of stainless steel. The hornbeam handle is wrapped with the finest leather and hand-stitched in place. "

The secretary general turned as Kantar rounded the end of the table. "Take it Wahda (colonel or general) Kantar," Haddad said, as he offered the weapon with both hands. "For this is the *Sayif al-Dawla* (sword of state). Use it to conquer Egypt."

Kantar felt tears roll down his cheeks as he accepted the gift. "*Inshallah.*" (If Allah wills it.)

* * *

Three days had passed since the Kenyan planes had departed, taking Secretary General Haddad and his bodyguards with them. And that was a good thing because Kantar had a lot of work to do. The first task was to establish checkpoints on the roads that led south from Aswan City, and close that section of the Nile as well, in order to keep former residents and looters from flowing back in. The last thing Kantar needed was to have more than a quarter-million Egyptians living 10-miles from the dam. Should a Sunni activist manage to mobilize the locals things could get dicey.

Kantar's second priority was to make sure that the missile systems were operating properly and training was underway. Kantar planned to install at least one member of Hezbollah on each missile crew to ensure that the Iranians couldn't trick him. Did he expect trouble from that quarter? No. But Colonel Gortov didn't expect to get shot in the face either.

In addition to the external threats Kantar had to face, there was a religious challenge as well. It was Thursday. And while it was permissible to pray at home, or at work if necessary, Muslims were expected to gather for the Jummah prayer time on Friday.

That's why Kantar felt he had no choice but to arrange for a trip to Aswan City. Half of his men would go, and half would stay, knowing their turn would come the following week.

So when Friday came a wild menagerie of vehicles was waiting to transport half the battalion into town. All of them had been "borrowed" from the locals.

Because the Hezbollah fighters hadn't been required to organize a convoy before, mistakes were made, and time was wasted.

But Kantar welcomed the process knowing that his men would learn from it.

With the exception of a single heavily laden donkey, the dusty road was empty at first, and for good reason. Kantar's men had a checkpoint at the outskirts of Aswan city. And motorized traffic was forbidden south of that point. The fighters manning the checkpoint waved the 15-vehicle convoy through.

Kantar was seated with a squad of heavily armed fighters on the back of a flatbed truck. He knew, as all leaders did, that riding in a car could be suicidal. Especially a fancy car like a Toyota SUV. The Americans were so rich they thought nothing of firing a $115,000 Hellfire missile at suspicious looking targets. Just in case. So it paid to blend in rather than stand out.

A great deal of Aswan had been destroyed by the Russian missiles and the fires that jumped building-to-building afterwards. But hints of the old city remained. Clusters of palm trees stood untouched and a scattering of one, two, and three story buildings endured.

And signs of life could be seen even in the ruins. Kantar spotted a line hung with brightly colored clothes, a tendril of gray smoke curling up from a hidden cooking fire, and a mangy dog foraging in the rubble.

The first vehicle in the convoy was a dump truck with a dozer blade mounted up front. Metal screeched, and sparks flew, as the blade hit a wreck and pushed it out of the way. Then Kantar heard a cry of pain as rocks fell on the convoy.

"Don't fire!" Kantar ordered, as the people around him ducked. "They hate us enough. Don't make it worse."

Had the rock throwers known the convoy was coming? That seemed likely given the security preparations Alawi had made. If the rocks had been bullets the column would've been destroyed. A lesson learned.

The ambush fell away as the truck picked up speed and started uphill. Kantar had thrown rocks as a boy. One of many provocateurs sent forward to harass the Israeli soldiers in the hope that one of them would shoot a child. Not *him* the young Kantar assumed, but someone else, so the Jews would look bad on the news. "Look!" a fighter said, as he pointed. "A minaret!"

Kantar stood to peer over the top of the cab. The El-Tabia mosque was famous for its central dome, as well as the minarets that flanked it, except that one lay broken on the ground. Mosques were neither Shia nor Sunni. They were Muslim. And Kantar felt a pang of guilt. Could Allah forgive him? *Maybe,* Kantar thought. *If what I accomplish is sufficient.*

Alawi and a platoon of fighters were waiting when the convoy arrived. They'd been sent to secure the mosque, set up the tent where female worshipers would be searched, and to provide force protection during the service. By the time the convoy arrived the local muezzin was up in the remaining minaret, calling the faithful to prayer. Kantar never tired of hearing the melodic rise and fall of the eternal words:

Allah is most great.
I testify that there is no God but Allah.
I testify that Muhammad is the prophet of Allah.
Come to prayer.
Come to salvation.
Allah is most great.

Kantar's boots produced puffs of dust as he jumped down off the truck. A black tent stood well clear of the mosque and the Hezbollah vehicles. Did Kantar expect suicide bombers? No. But such things weren't unheard of in Egypt. In November of 2017 a bomb had gone off inside a Sufi Mosque on the Sinai Peninsula.

The explosion, combined with the subsequent machine gun fire, killed 305 people–and wounded 128 others. And it was logical to suppose that any number of Egyptian militias would be eager to slaughter the Shia invaders if they could.

But Shia, or no Shia, at least a hundred locals had lined up by then. The women filed into the tent one at a time. The men were searched out in the open.

Once cleared the worshipers were free to approach the mosque and perform the Wudu. The ritual cleansing included prayers and physical ablutions as well.

After completing the Wudu, Kantar entered the mosque, where he paused to examine the interior surface of the dome. It was decorated with alternating stripes of green and red. Beautifully executed geometric designs covered the walls around the dome and an exquisite chandelier dangled from the center of it.

There was nothing in the Qur'an that required men and women to worship separately. But every Mosque Kantar had worshipped in was set up that way. El-Tabia was no different. The sexes were separated by no more than woven mats on wooden frames so that sound could travel freely.

A green and red carpet covered the floor. Kantar led his men forward to kneel, with weapons resting beside them. Would the Sunni congregation disapprove? Probably. But Kantar didn't care. He and his men were vastly outnumbered, and only a fool would go unarmed.

The imam was a kindly looking man, who began by welcoming "visitors" to the mosque, and emphasizing the many beliefs that Muslims had in common. That was when Kantar heard a male voice shout, "*Allahu Akbar!*" (God is great.)

The center of the explosion was on the female side of the mat partitions. But the barriers did nothing to protect the neighboring men. The explosive vest was loaded with nails. The pressure wave propelled the shrapnel outwards. Sunni and Shia alike were swept away by the force of the blast. Kantar felt a sharp pain as something struck the surface of his left shoulder. The impact was enough to throw him forward as more metal passed over his head.

A brief moment of negative pressure followed. It sucked hats, scarves, and bits of paper back to the point where the blast originated.

Kantar lay there for a moment staring at the carpet as he struggled to gather his thoughts. His ears were ringing and blood was dribbling from his nose. Kantar's inner voice spoke to him as he pushed the floor away. *You are alive. You are in command. Take action.*

Kantar struggled to his feet. Bodies lay all about. A woman was screaming. A man's *galabeya* (robe) was soaked with blood. "First aid!" Kantar shouted. "Stop the bleeding! Do we have a doctor?"

They had a doctor. Two of them. And a nurse who, amazingly enough, had been kneeling only yards away from the suicide bomber. But explosions can be fickle. And by the will of Allah she was alive. Kantar left the woman to help the wounded, but made a mental note to keep track of her, as he ordered his men to pitch in.

The hospital had been destroyed by a Russian missile, and most of Aswan's first responders had been killed, so there was only so much the doctors could do for those who had serious wounds. "This is your fault," one of them said, as he made use a ballpoint pen to pry a nail out of Kantar's shoulder. "You are cursed in the eyes of Allah." Kantar knew the doctor was wrong, but understood his anger, and thanked him anyway.

The final death toll was 58, including 37 Sunnis, and 21 Shia fighters. And as the effort to save lives began to taper off, Kantar told Alawi to detain the nurse, along with five people who'd been close enough to see the bomber.

Some basic facts were apparent by then, including the way the bomber had been dressed. "Who was chosen to search the women?" Kantar demanded. "How could she miss the fact that the bomber was a man wearing a *niqab*?" (A burqa-like garment designed to hide a woman's face as well as her body.)

Alawi hung his head in shame. "I thought it would be dangerous to entrust the task to a Sunni, so I chose a Christian," the junior officer confessed.

That made sense. But Kantar wasn't ready to let Alawi off the hook. "Did you approach her? Or did she approach you?"

Alawi's eyes were focused on the bloody floor. "She approached me."

The other officer's voice was so low that Kantar could barely hear it. Everything was clear. The advance preparations had been enough to trigger an attack by Sunnis who were willing to kill Sunnis in order to slaughter Shias. And, because they knew female worshippers would be searched, the plotters sent a Christian woman to perform the task. And Alawi fell for it.

I could have fallen for it, Kantar thought. He couldn't let his sympathy show though. Maybe their superiors would write the loss of 21 men off to the hazards of war. If so, Alawi would go unpunished. *But, if someone has to suffer it will be Alawi*, Kantar decided.

"You made a mistake," Kantar said coldly. "A serious mistake. I assume that the Christian woman fled."

"Yes, sir."

"We need to find her. Who would you recommend to lead the effort?"

"Sergeant Boustani, sir."

"Bring him here."

Alawi returned a few moments later with a noncom in tow. Kantar recognized him as being one of the men who had arrived with Secretary General Haddad. Boustani was an ex-ISIS fighter, if Kantar remembered correctly, and a devout one judging from the darkened callus located at the center of his forehead.

The *zabib*, or "raisin," was the result of frequent prostration in prayer. The callus was a sign of piety and devotion. The more a man prayed, the larger the callus, or "raisin." And Boustani's was the size of a pebble.

But there was something more about the man as well … A fervor that was visible in his eyes—and seemed to surround him like a cloak. If anyone could find the fugitive Boustani would. He came to attention. "Sir."

"A Christian woman let the bomber through. Find her, but under no circumstances will you harm her, do you understand?"

Boustani's eyes were alight. "Sir, yes sir."

"Take your men and go." Boustani did an excellent imitation of a British soldier doing an about face, and departed.

Kantar turned to Alawi. "Interrogate the nurse and the others seated close enough to observe the bomber. Be sure to take notes."

Alawi nodded. "Yes, sir. I'll take care of it."

Kantar gave orders. Alawi and his platoon would remain behind to conduct the investigation. The unit's dead were loaded onto trucks, and would be buried near the dam. The wounded were placed in cars. The rest sat or stood wherever they could, clinging to vehicles, weapons ready. And for good reason. Kantar put the odds of being ambushed during the return journey at 80-percent.

But despite Kantar's fears the attack never came. And for that he was grateful. After seeing to the wounded, and giving instructions regarding the dead, Kantar retired to the gallery adjacent to his bedroom—which was to say the room directly above the sleeping bomb.

It hurt when a medic cleaned his wound, but Kantar made no complaint, knowing the entire unit would hear about it if he did. Then it was time to take a sponge bath next to a utility sink, put on a clean set of clothes, and eat a surprisingly good kebab sandwich prepared by the group's newly hired Nubian cook.

Kantar was still seated at a table when Alawi and Boustani escorted a female prisoner into the gallery. "Sergeant Boustani found her, sir," Alawi said. "This is Marta Abdelmesseh (servant of Christ.) She was hiding in a Coptic church."

Abdelmesseh appeared to be middle-aged, had a white scarf over her head, and was dressed in baggy clothes. Her eyes darted all around. "Please show mercy, sir ... I have children."

"And dogs produce puppies," Kantar replied coldly. "You killed 21 of my men. Who paid you to let the bomber through?"

The woman looked at Alawi. "I told him."

"Then tell me."

"His name is Rafa Jabr."

"And?"

"He's a Sunni. From Baranis Troglodytica."

The name meant nothing to Kantar. He looked to Alawi. "It's a city, sir," Alawi put in. "Directly east of here on the Red Sea."

Kantar frowned. "Why would someone from Baranis Troglodytica attack us? Because we're Shia?"

"A man named Maaz Nadwi was in charge of the dam when we arrived," Alawi replied. "He died in the fighting. And a man named Kamran Nadwi rules Baranis Troglodytica now."

Kantar stared at him. "Brothers?"

"Yes, sir."

So that's it, Kantar thought. *It's more than a religious thing. It's a family grudge.* "You did well," Kantar told them.

"What shall we do with *this*?" Boustani inquired, as he pointed to the woman.

Kantar gave the matter some thought. Had Aswan's Sunnis been aware of the impending attack? Sunnis so loyal to Nadwi that they'd been willing to let him slaughter their own? That seemed unlikely. So he had no reason to punish the Sunnis.

But *Christians?* Everyone hated them…And Marta Abdelmesseh had admitted her guilt. "Go to Aswan," Kantar said. "Find a Christian carpenter, and order him to construct 13 crosses. One for him, one for the bitch in front of us, and 11 more. You can choose the other apostles at random. Then, once everything is ready, crucify them. Our Sunni brothers and sisters will thank you for it."

Boustani nodded eagerly. "Yes, sir…And where should the crucifixions take place?"

"In front of the Coptic church," Kantar answered. "Where else?"

The woman was sobbing as they led her away. Kantar barely noticed. His thoughts were on the city of Baranis Troglodytica, and a man named Kamran Nadwi.

***

Two days had passed since the crucifixions in Aswan. Kantar told Alawi that he was too busy to attend. That was a lie. Two years earlier he and a company of his peers had been forced to watch a noncom execute a western journalist. The executioner performed the task with a knife, sawing back and forth until the German's head came free, and Kantar threw up. And a Wahda couldn't afford to show that kind of weakness.

But according to what Alawi told him, the executions had drawn a large and mostly enthusiastic crowd. The exceptions being the people nailed to the crosses.

As for Kantar's dead, they had been laid to rest in graves adjacent to those of men killed during the initial assault, each with a carefully inscribed metal marker.

Now Kantar was free to kill Kamran Nadwi, and secure his eastern flank. The intelligence reports suggested that the Allies would attack from the north. But who knew? What if that was a feint? So, it made sense to establish an outpost, and rely on it to provide him with an early warning should the *kafirs* land in force.

Kantar felt a jolt of fear as he felt the Russian-made Mi-17 helicopter lift off the ground. The aircraft had been Muslim Brotherhood's property prior to the moment when the liberators took control of the dam. But this was Kantar's first ride in a helo. And, when it wobbled, he felt the desire to grab something. But that wouldn't do. Not with Sergeant Boustani sitting across from him, eyes watching.

At some point along the way Kantar's feelings regarding the Ex-ISIS fighter had shifted from admiration to wariness. What was the brute thinking about anyway? Could he detect the fear in Kantar's belly? *No*, Kantar decided. *He's thinking about women. Or lunch.*

But the feeling persisted as the chopper began to follow the two-lane road east. Kantar had done his homework. Baranis Troglodytica had been founded in 275 BC by Ptolemy II Philadelphus (285–246 BC), who named it after his mother— Berenice I of Egypt.

Troglodytica referred to the aboriginal people of the region, known as the "Troglodytai" or "cave dwellers." The settlement subsequently became a trans-shipping point for trade between India, Arabia, and upper Egypt.

The town had an indifferent harbor, but improvements had been made over time, and the bay was sheltered from the northeast wind by the island Ophiodes—which was known for its topazes. But that was then. Now, according to what Kantar had been able to learn, the port was nearly filled in—and a sandbar kept large ships from entering. A fact that might explain why the Allies were going to attack up the Nile river valley.

The "city" consisted of 20–30 wood houses, and a store that catered to fishermen, smugglers, and slavers. And that's where

Nadwi came in. He owned the store which, thanks to the complete absence of competition, did very well. So well, that Nadwi could give money to a Sunni group which did his bidding.

Kantar couldn't see the road that led east. Only some of the limitless desert was visible through the open hatch. But he knew that their destination was an hour away.

Kantar closed his eyes. Engines droned. Hot air buffeted his face. He fell into a reverie. Death. Was it waiting for him at Baranis Troglodytica? Not if Allah wanted him to control Egypt. Kantar felt for the remote. It was there, safe in a pocket under his chest protector.

But was that wise? What if he was killed, or captured? Someone else would have the remote... And what then?

Kantar opened his eyes to find that Boustani was staring at him. *Why?* Then it came to him. Boustani was thinking about the remote too! Would the noncom kill in order to control the bomb? No, yes, Kantar wasn't sure. But the possibility still lingered in the back of his mind when the pilot spoke into his ear. "We're there, sir."

Kantar wanted to see. He released his seatbelt, made his way over to the hatch, and felt the slipstream tug at his clothes. As the helo banked Kantar saw acres of tan-colored sand and a scattering of buildings. Some were larger than he'd been told to expect.

And there, moored to a substantial pier, was a small ship. So that aspect of the intelligence he'd been given was wrong as well. Larger vessels *could* access the harbor.

But right in the middle of things, was a big one-story building. The roof was home to solar panels and a small antenna farm. Nadwi's store? Yes, Kantar thought so, and it soon became apparent that the helicopter hadn't gone unnoticed.

Tiny figures spilled out onto the flat roof. Some were armed with RPGs. Kantar was wearing a headset and trailing a wire behind him. "Kill the men on the roof."

"We'll use rockets first," the Iranian pilot replied. "Followed by gun runs. Hang onto something."

The Russians sold Mi-17s in a variety of flavors, and that particular model was half-transport, and half-gunship. The pilot entered a tight left-hand turn and fired. Rockets flashed off the ship's pylons and explosions rippled across the roof. Satellite dishes fell, solar panels shattered, and bodies were tossed into the air.

"Good work," Kantar said. "Finish them off, and land on the roof."

The pylon-mounted, four-barreled rotary machine guns roared as the helo made a second pass. Gunmen fell as twin streams of 7.62mm rounds chewed them up. Kantar turned to his men. There were five of them. Six including Boustani.

But they were, according to the noncom, the most lethal fighters in Kantar's command. And they certainly looked the part. Each and every man was gunned to the max. "We're going to land on the roof," Kantar told them. "We'll fight our way down through the building, and out onto the street, where the chopper will pick us up. Kill everyone you see. Do you have any questions?" None of them did.

Kantar returned to his seat. As the helicopter started to lose altitude small arms fire pinged the fuselage. It seemed some of the defenders were still alive. Boustani grinned happily. *Keep him in front of you*, Kantar thought, as the pilot spoke. "Everyone out, and make it quick ... We're taking fire."

Rather than put his aircraft down on the now uncertain roof, the pilot hovered above it so the team had to jump. Boustani went first, followed by Kantar, Tharwat, Salah, Rasi and Fahri.

Kantar let his knees absorb the shock. Because of the need to handle radios and maps Kantar preferred to enter close quarters combat armed with a pistol. Or, in this case, *two* pistols—both acquired from dead Russians. They could hold 18 rounds each—and Kantar had 4 spare magazines.

A man with an AK-47 emerged from the drifting smoke. Kantar fired twice. One bullet missed. The other destroyed a knee and dumped the defender onto the roof. Boustani shot him in the face.

Every team member had a radio and headset. "Stay together!" Kantar told them. "Head for the stairs at the northeast corner of the roof."

Two men appeared from that direction firing as they came. Massed fire from everyone other than Kantar cut them down. He arrived at the stairway first. That left him with no choice but to precede Boustani and risk being shot in the back. Kantar braced himself for an impact that never came.

The door at the bottom of the stairway was unlocked, and Kantar held it open, as the team poured through. The warehouse had high ceilings and was spotlessly clean. Yellow storage racks were filled with shrink-wrapped barcoded boxes. The air was relatively cool.

Kantar was taking all of that in when a shot rang out and Tharwat collapsed. Boustani yelled, "Sniper!" and fired his rotary grenade launcher. A flash of light marked the top of a stack. The sound of the explosion was still echoing between the walls as the body fell to the floor.

Kantar knelt to check Tharwat's pulse. But when he saw the finger-sized hole in the fighter's forehead he knew there wouldn't be one.

Kantar stood. That was when he noticed the neatly painted yellow line and turned to see where it led. "Follow me!" Kantar said, as he took off at a run.

But he hadn't gone far when a motorized forklift rounded the stacks ahead. The operator was invisible behind the steel bin that he held high. Two men were riding inside of it. They fired AK-47s without showing themselves. Bullets flew every which way. The Hezbollah fighters were forced to take cover. "RPG!" Kantar said. "Hit the bastards."

Corporal Rasi was carrying an RPG-7. He took a knee. The rocket propelled grenade flew straight and true. Kantar saw the flash and heard a resounding BOOM! The forklift slewed sideways and came to a stop.

Kantar stood and began to run. Salah tossed a grenade into the bin as they passed. Kantar heard a bang but didn't turn to look back. The office was up ahead. Was Nadwi holed up inside? They were about to find out. "Open the door!" Kantar ordered. There was a loud boom as Salah fired his shotgun and half-a-dozen holes appeared around the lock. Kantar rushed forward to finish the job with a kick.

The door slammed open to reveal a startling tableau. Kantar saw a desk, the body sprawled next to it, and two men beyond. Their backs were to an old fashioned safe. They raised their hands.

Kantar fired, saw his target slump sideways, and knew he couldn't nail the second man in time. But Salah could. The blast from his shotgun struck *both* targets and splattered blood all over the safe. Kantar put his pistol away and drew the other one. Gun smoke drifted on the air as he spoke. "Boustani, Rasi, Fahri ... Stand guard."

Kantar knelt next to the body by the desk. He felt for a wallet and found it. An Egyptian driver's license was inside. Sure enough, the man lying in front of him was Kamran Nadwi.

Kantar tucked the ID away as he looked up at Salah. "Take his picture, grab the laptop that's sitting on the desk, and go through the drawers."

"Yes, sir."

Salah went to work as Kantar approached the safe. It was necessary to drag a dead body out of the way. The safe's door was open. Kantar could imagine the scene. Nadwi had been there, intent on salvaging what wealth he could, when two of his own gunmen entered the office. They saw the opportunity, and killed him. They were loading gold into Nadwi's briefcase when Salah blew the door open.

Kantar chose a coin at random, felt how heavy it was, and took a closer look. It was a Saudi Arabian one guinea piece. The gold, combined with the money Colonel Gortov had brought with him, would keep the battalion going for quite a while.

Kantar hurried to sweep the rest of the coinage into the case and zip it closed. Then, after a quick 360, he left the office. A yellow line led the team to an open door and the blistering heat beyond. There weren't any gunshots. And no wonder. The chopper was aloft, and circling overhead. Kantar turned to Boustani. "Pop smoke."

Then he spoke to the pilot. "Kantar here…Land by the smoke."

"Will do," the pilot replied. "How did it go?"

Kantar's thoughts turned to Tharwat. "As well as it could. *Alhamdulillah*." (All praise is due to God alone.)

CHAPTER FOUR

Cairo, Egypt

The navy patrol boats had been underway for more than six hours, and the sun was starting to set, by the time they reached Cairo. The red-orange disk was barely visible through the perpetual haze that hung over what travel brochures called "the city of a thousand minarets."

Their journey had begun near the city of Izbat Al Burj, which was situated at the mouth of the Damietta River, a major tributary of the Nile. From there the Riverines had to follow the river's twisting-turning flow past hundreds of villages, towns and cities before arriving in Egypt's capital.

Lieutenant Commander Harley Kydd was aboard a rakish looking 53-foot Riverine Command Boat or RCB. Its appearance was similar to the patrol boats (PBRs) that followed. But the RCB was equipped with a broad array of command and control gear the other boats lacked.

Kydd was standing just aft of the wheelhouse, sipping a Coke, when Master Chief Lester Jones approached him. "Jones" was a big man with a shaved head, ebony skin, and a square jaw. "The crew wants to play their theme song, skipper ... What do you think?"

Kydd frowned. "Theme song? What would that be? *Anchors Aweigh*?"

Jones grinned. "No, sir. *Fortunate Son*, by Credence Clearwater."

Credence was a very retro group … But Kydd was aware of it, and knew that *Fortunate Son* was a Vietnam War era protest song that was critical of the draft. The draft was back now, and so was the song.

A lot of COs would have dismissed the request out-of-hand. And Kydd understood why. Protest songs were assumed to be bad for morale.

But, as the senior noncom in Kydd's command, Jones was the critical link between the enlisted personnel and the officers. And the fact that the chief had asked permission implied that he was comfortable with the request. "Sure," Kydd responded. "Let the bastards know we're here."

The boat's external speakers were good, *too* good to be navy issue, but Kydd wasn't about to go there. The music was so loud he could understand the lyrics in spite of the noise generated by the RCB's twin diesels. The combination of the music, along with the sensation of speed and the cityscape, reminded Kydd of the famous helicopter scene from *Apocalypse Now*.

"Incoming!" a sailor yelled, as bullets clanged against the armor plated hull.

"Got 'em," a gunner named Ellis responded. "They're on the port side at seven o'clock. Requesting permission to fire."

"Take evasive action," Kydd said, as he looked through his glasses. Kydd had to steady himself as the helmsman turned the wheel. The red tracers looked like beads on a string as they floated his way. "The port fifty only," Kydd said. "Fire!"

The .50 caliber machine gun began to chug. Brass casings flew through the air, landed on the deck, and rattled as they rolled back and forth.

"Two-boat," Kydd said over the ship-to-ship frequency, "Fire. Three-boat, fire."

Now *three* fifties were pounding the shore target. One of them found a stash of ammo. A sudden flash of light rippled across the river, flames shot high, and a loud boom echoed between the shoulder-to-shoulder skyscrapers that lined the waterfront. "Cease fire," Kydd said. "Secure weapons."

It was amazing how well the Riverines were able to respond given how quickly the unit had been thrown together. One week earlier Kydd had been in Port Ashdod getting new orders. That was followed by the handoff to Lieutenant Hanson, a helo flight to the ship on which the patrol boats were traveling, and the subsequent hurried preparations.

Now the RCB was headed upriver on its way to rendezvous with Colonel Goolsby near Bani Adi. The command boat passed under a bridge. Someone fired down at it but missed. There was no time or need to respond.

Kydd entered the wheelhouse to eyeball the sat map. The flotilla could travel at night if forced to do so, but Kydd hoped to avoid it. According to what he'd read the Nile was littered with shifting sandbars, old wrecks, and underwater cables. Some of which would be more visible during daylight hours.

That meant it would be best to drop anchor. But *where?* An island caught Kydd's eye. It was located 25 miles upriver, just short of a town called, Al Ikhas Al Qibliyyah. A diminutive ET (Electronics Tech) was standing next to him. Her name was Chu, better known to the rest of the crew as Chu-Chu, and "a good sailor" according to Jones. That was a considerable compliment coming from the chief. "We'll anchor *there*," Kydd said, as his finger stabbed the screen. "Pass the word."

There was barely enough light to see by as the flotilla neared the island half-an-hour later. The water was deep enough for the shallow draft boats to pull in close. The quartermasters kept their engines running just fast enough to counter the current as Kydd gave his orders. "The three-boat will circle the island and report back. The one and two-boats will put armed personnel ashore and secure the area. Over."

It took the three-boat, under the command of Ensign Miller, about ten minutes to complete the circuit. "This is Three-Six. The island is being farmed. But there are no signs of habitation. Over."

"So they commute to work," Kydd observed. "All boats will put lines ashore and stop engines. We'll set three four-hour watches with the command boat going first.

"I want two people on each boat at all times, the duty crew will post lookouts to the north, east, and south and monitor radio traffic. Sweet dreams. Over."

There was a lot more to do, such as distributing meals, performing routine maintenance on the boats, and digging privies. But the individual boat commanders, and their noncoms, could not only handle such matters—they'd be resentful if Kydd tried to micromanage their activities.

Once the boats were properly moored, Kydd went ashore. The temperature was likely to drop to about 60 degrees during the night, so the crews were busy deploying their army issue patrol bags, and a dozen headlamps could be seen moving around. Once settled they would heat their MREs using the flameless ration-heaters.

When Kydd came across a sailor digging a latrine by himself, Kydd offered to lend a hand. That wasn't required of course, but it was good for morale, and gave him a chance to shoot the shit with one of his sailors. The dirt was soft and black. But, according to what Kydd had read, the soil wasn't as nutrient-rich as it had been in the early 1950s. The Nile flooded every year back then, and the process swept fertile soil downriver.

But, once the high dam was built the natural cycle came to and end. Now it was necessary for farmers to buy expensive fertilizers in order to maintain yields.

Still, the more the river narrowed, the more land was exposed. And the entire population had access to electricity. Even if it was increasingly expensive.

"Bug juice," a voice said loudly. "You need it, and I have it." As Kydd turned the blob of light from his headlamp came to rest on the face of the always affable "Doc" Niles. Each boat had its own medic, and Niles was the senior hospital corpsman.

"*Bugs?*" Kydd demanded. "What kind?"

"Mosquitoes, sir. But this stuff should keep 'em at bay."

Kydd accepted a pump bottle, as did his ditch digging companion, a fuzz-faced storekeeper named Bartley. They finished the job five minutes later. As Kydd left Bartley was preparing to "test" the latrine.

The night passed peacefully for the most part. The single exception was the moment when an empty felucca (small fishing boat) struck the two-boat's starboard side, causing a resonant boom, and scaring the crap out of the watch keepers. Then the Nile carried the felucca toward Cairo, and a rendezvous with its new owner.

Kydd called a command meeting for 0830. His officers and their senior noncoms were present, all clutching coffee mugs. Kydd sat on a log. "So, Jim," he began. "Did you change your shorts?"

Lieutenant JG Jim Altman was the twenty-something heir to a tech fortune, and known for his easy going personality. As the flotilla's XO he would take command if Kydd fell. "Yes, sir. So much for my constipation." The rest of them chuckled.

"The drifter was a wakeup call in more ways than one," Kydd told them. "What if the felucca was carrying an IED? A whole lot of people would be dead, and the two-boat would be history. So pass the word … We won't anchor in the current unless we're absolutely forced to do so. And if we do we'll rig booms to deflect anything that drifts downstream which, come to think of it, could include naval mines. Although it's hard to imagine where the bad guys would get their hands on them. Agreed?"

Kydd heard a chorus of, "Yes, sirs."

"Good. Let's go over the plan for today. Our destination is Bani Adi which, judging from satellite photos, is a good sized town. That's where we'll join Colonel Goolsby and his marines.

"Bani Adi is about 170 miles from here. So, assuming that we can make a steady 30 miles-per-hour, we'll arrive in six hours. Here are some factors to keep in mind: First, due to the fact that the river twists and turns, our forward visibility will be limited.

"And remember... This is a heavily populated area. So we can expect to see a lot of boat traffic. That means hostile forces could blend in. Tell your lookouts to stay sharp, and report anything that looks suspicious.

"Second, there are sections of the river where thick foliage grows to the water's edge. Enemy forces could use it for cover.

"To the extent possible stay in the middle of the river and out of RPG range. And be ready for anything if the river narrows. All right... Do you have any questions? No? Okay... Recall all personnel. Take a headcount, single your lines, and prepare to pull out."

Crews were at battle stations, guns ready, as the patrol boats pushed their way upstream. But as the west bank slid past there was nothing other than peaceful countryside for Kydd to look at. A heron took to the air with a great flapping of wings. Two women, water jugs balanced on their heads, stared. Armed vessels were a rarity. Especially those with American flags snapping in the morning breeze.

Further back from the Nile green fields could be seen. All dependent on water from the Nile. Columns of smoke were visible too, along with spindly minarets, and cell phone towers.

The scene changed as the boat passed under a steel bridge. Had hostile forces wanted to attack the flotilla the bridge would have been the perfect platform to do it from. But as Kydd looked up he saw three children. They waved, and he waved back.

The patrol boats passed the town of Nazlat Ilyan soon thereafter. It was on the left bank. Buildings crowded the river as if daring it to rise.

Kydd thought about that as he sipped his coffee. If the Allied mission failed, and Hezbollah destroyed the dam, *all* the residents of Nazlat Ilyan would die. Along with his sailors and millions more. It was a sobering thought.

River traffic had picked up by then. Most of it consisted of 12-foot metal feluccas. Some were rowed with clumsy two-by-fours functioning as oars.

Others bore triangular sails, and tacked to and fro, constantly getting in the way. Tanaka was at the wheel, and he swore a steady stream of oaths, as the river traffic forced him to steer the RCB through a veritable maze of unpredictable small craft.

When Kydd looked astern he saw that the RCB's wake was a very unprofessional twisting-turning thing. Boats two and three could plow through the waves. But the feluccas weren't so lucky. They pitched and rolled. Kydd knew very little about local customs, but assumed the palm-out gestures were the Egyptian equivalents of "fuck yous."

The next town was Al Misandah on the right. And, like Nazlat Ilyan, structures extended down to the water's edge. But in this case Kydd saw that a rectangular harbor had been excavated from the river bank. And there, moored side-by-side, were half-a-dozen colorfully painted tour boats. All sidelined by the war—and left to bake in the sun.

The flotilla passed a burned-out oil storage facility minutes later, a sure sign that Egypt's civil war had been visited upon Al Misandah, and a reminder of how deceptive the pastoral countryside could be. That was when the shit hit the fan.

The attack helicopters were on the ground, hidden behind the fire-blackened oil tanks. The pilots knew the *kafir* boats were coming upstream because *everyone* south of Cairo knew. No more than 30-seconds passed between the time the Russian-made "Black Shark" attack helicopters took off, and the moment when they appeared.

Ellis had already opened up with the minigun when Kydd gave the order to fire. But Egyptian rockets were on the way by then. Twin explosions bracketed the RCB and sent columns of water high into the air.

That was when the second Shark scored a hit on the two-boat's bow. Armor plating prevented the weapon from penetrating the hull. But the splash effect destroyed the boat's minigun, killed a kid named Bowers, and smashed the windscreen. Lieutenant Altman stepped up to take the wheel as the helmsman went down.

The fifties in the command boat's stern swung around to follow the enemy aircraft as they attacked the three-boat. Armor piecing shells stitched lines through the water, cut a felucca in half, and scored hits on the PBR as the helos passed over.

It was impossible to say whether the three-boat's mini found the first attack ship, or the two-boat's fifties deserved the credit, but the result was spectacular. The orange-red fireball was so bright Kydd had to avert his eyes. Chunks of flaming wreckage tumbled out of the sky and produced clouds of steam as they hit the water.

But the battle wasn't over. The second helo was circling the boats preparing to make another gun run. A fully prepped FIM-92 Stinger was racked against the starboard bulkhead. Kydd took the weapon, brought it up onto his right shoulder, and took aim.

A steady tone signaled that the seeker head had achieved lock-on. Kydd pulled the trigger. He felt the weapon jerk as the launch rocket fired, quickly followed by the solid rocket that propelled the Stinger toward its target. The missile was traveling at 1,500 miles-per-hour when it sensed the heat produced by a whirling rotor and homed on it.

The explosion destroyed two rotors. That caused the Ka-50 to whirl like a top. Kydd watched what remained of the helo lose altitude and disappear behind a clutch of palm trees. A dust cloud marked the spot where it crashed. Kydd expected an explosion. There was none. He turned to the right. "Chief! If that pilot is alive I want him. Take the doc and two gunners. Oh, and grab some photos. The Intel people will want to know who attacked us."

"Aye, aye sir," Jones replied. "Doc! Ellis! Collins! Gun up and launch the RIB boat. We're going ashore."

Kydd turned his attention back to the flotilla. "One-Six to two and three … Remain at battle stations. Hold your positions relative to shore. What's your status, two? Over."

"This is Two-Six actual," Altman replied. "We can fight if we need to. Bowers was KIA. Sanchez has a chest wound. The doc says he's stable. Over."

Kydd took a moment to consider his options. Should he send two upriver by itself? Send two *and* three? Or call for a med evac? The latter being the fastest. He turned to Chu. "Get battalion on the horn. Tell them we need to air evac a casualty."

Chu nodded. "On it skipper."

The reply came quickly. "They can't respond at this time, sir. Their helos aren't available."

Kydd swore. "Okay … Raise the chief."

There was a burp of static, followed by the sound of Jones' voice. "This is One-Seven. We're on the scene. The pilot is alive. He's got some minor cuts and a broken leg. Doc Niles is splinting it. Over."

"What about security?"

"We're drawing a crowd, sir. No firearms that I can see, but a lot of shovels."

Kydd felt a rising sense of concern. "Fire over their heads, and pull out *now!* Over."

"Roger that," came the reply. "Over."

Kydd heard the distant rattle of automatic fire moments later. Fifteen long, tension-filled minutes passed before a lookout spotted them. "Shore party at three o'clock!"

Kydd turned to the helmsman. "Take her in as close you can."

Water churned at the stern as the helmsman went slow ahead. When the bottom came up he shifted to reverse. After that it was a matter of turning the bow into the current, and holding the boat in place as the prisoner was hoisted aboard. The shore party followed.

Once the RIB boat was recovered Kydd ordered the flotilla out to the center of the river and called for more speed. The sooner they could get Sanchez to the battalion surgeon the better. But due to all of the river traffic, 35mph was the best they could do.

Once underway Kydd took the opportunity to make his way aft. The pilot was seated on an ammo locker with a leg stretched out in front of him. He had a black eye and an assortment of lacerations. Doc Niles was taping a dressing into place as Kydd arrived. "How's he doing?"

"I survive," the pilot answered. "You kill please."

Kydd looked at Niles. The corpsman shrugged. "He failed," Niles explained. "So he wants to die."

Kydd sat on a folding chair. "You attacked us. *Why?*"

"You destroy dam ... Flood valley. Kill me."

"Who told you that?"

"General Ahmar," the pilot replied. "Republican Guard protect president. We fail. Now our modo: *Win or die.*"

"I think you meant, 'motto,'" Kydd said. If he understood the pilot correctly, the Republican Guard was supposed to protect Egypt's president, and having failed to do so, they were determined to die. Or was this Ahmar person using them?

"What's your name?" Kydd demanded.

"Hasan Farook."

"Listen, Hasan … What the general told you isn't true. We're here to *fight* the people who took control of the dam. Maybe there's been a misunderstanding. Or maybe General Ahmar has been lying to you. Understand?"

"*No,*" Farook said emphatically. "He not lie. Kill me."

Kydd stood and turned to Jones. "Chain Hasan to the boat, and put him on suicide watch. We'll let battalion S2 sort this guy out. Oh, and tell the crew to watch what they say around him."

"No worries, skipper," Jones said. "We'll take good care of Mr. *Farook.*" Jones pronounced the name as "far-rook."

Kydd was hyper alert as the flotilla made the long run past Al Jazirah Ash Shaqra on the left, Al Widi on the right, and Al Khurman before closing in on an island east of Bani Adi where Colonel Goolsby's battalion was based.

Alhadiqi (Garden) was actually *two* islands divided by a passageway so shallow even feluccas couldn't navigate it. So, in the functional sense, Alhadiqi was a single land mass. It was shaped like an inverted V, with the point aimed upriver, and a harbor within.

But, before the flotilla could enter the harbor, a 38-foot SURC (Small Unit Riverine Craft) had to tow a log boom out of the way. Though not very big in diameter the logs would be more than enough to prevent a hostile boat from invading the harbor. Lengths of chain linked them together.

Kydd approved. The chains could be cut. But enemy forces would have to do so while taking fire from the bunkers located on both sides of the passageway.

As for the island itself, other than clusters of palms and some scattered banana trees, neatly aligned tents, rows of steel cargo containers, and a tidy antenna farm had replaced the Egyptian "Garden." And since all those goodies were well within range from both banks of the Nile, two barge-mounted C-RAM (Counter Rocket, Artillery, and Mortar) systems sat ready to defend the base from incoming fire.

A couple of self-propelled Avenger Air Defense systems were stationed on barges too. And should General Ahmar send helicopters in to attack the forward operating base he'd be sorry. One thing bothered Kydd however ... Why did FOB Pharaoh look so fucking permanent? Wasn't it supposed to be a jumping off place?

Kydd put the thought aside, as the boom opened to let the flotilla through. The PO in charge of the SURC threw a salute and Kydd returned it.

Now that the RCB was in the harbor, Kydd took a moment to assess the boats anchored there, starting with the most eye-catching of all—a three-decked side-wheeler that looked like something left over from the colonial era. Judging from the beautifully varnished wheelhouse up forward, and the rows of red doors that lined each deck, it had been a cruise ship before the war.

The paddlewheels were concealed by white wooden boxes. A long sway-backed gangplank connected the paddle boat to the shore. And based on the number of people coming and going Kydd felt certain that the riverboat was Operation Pharaoh's headquarters.

Equally striking, but in a different way, were two pristine patrol boats that floated above shivering reflections of themselves. They were roughly the same size as the flotilla's command boat, and so glaringly white, that they were difficult to look at.

Had it not been for the shark's teeth painted on each bow, Kydd might have mistaken the boats for yachts. *The British are not only coming*, Kydd thought, *they're here.*

Consistent with orders from the harbormaster the two-boat went alongside the refueling barge first. A medical team, plus a handful of marines, were waiting to receive Sanchez, the prisoner, and Bower's body. Kydd had met Bower, and exchanged a few words with the sailor, but never gotten to know him.

Once the stretchers were gone the rest of the flotilla was permitted to pull in for fuel. A smart looking corporal was waiting to greet Kydd. "Commander Kydd? I have a message for you, sir... Colonel Goolsby wants you to report to the *Nile Queen* right away."

"Thank you, corporal. I assume you're referring to the floating palace behind me."

The marine grinned, said "Yes, sir," and popped a salute. That was the *second* salute Kydd had received since arriving. Salutes were normally frowned on in combat zones.

Snipers loved nothing more than to have the enemy identify targets for them. So were the salutes a matter of coincidence? Or an indication of how Goolsby ran things? What had Admiral Ducey called the marine? A "by-the-book asshole?" Something of that sort. A sense of impending doom descended on Kydd.

It seemed safe to assume that "right away" meant right away. So Kydd ordered Altman to complete fueling, make contact with the harbormaster regarding anchorages, and find somebody to carry out a damage assessment on the two-boat. Could repairs be made on the spot? Or would it be necessary to send the patrol boat downriver?

There was no need to seek directions once Kydd was ashore. The *Nile Queen* was visible from everywhere on the island. To reach the cruise ship he had to pass a row of cargo containers, a sandbagged LAV-25 (light armored vehicle), and "tent city," before crossing over to the other leg of the inverted V. A well-trod path led to the foot of the gangplank, where a pair of marines were checking IDs.

One of them eyed Kydd's ID card with great care, while the other looked him up and down. "Are you armed, sir?"

"No, should I be?"

"Yes," the private replied, as if speaking to a child. "Officers are required to wear side arms."

"You can go aboard," the first leatherneck said, as she returned his card. The sentence was punctuated with a salute.

Kydd replied in kind, felt the gangplank bounce under his boots, and crossed the gap. A first class petty officer was waiting to greet him. "Commander Kydd? Welcome aboard, sir. My name is Evans. I'm your yeoman. I saw you arrive."

Kydd offered his hand. "It's a pleasure to meet you Evans. I was told to report to Colonel Goolsby. Can you show me the way?"

"Yes, sir. Please follow me."

Kydd followed Evans out of the heat, up a flight of metal stairs, and down a gleaming corridor. A lance corporal stood guard next to a door. A sign read, "First Class Lounge."

"This is it," Evans told him. "A meeting is underway. I will make arrangements for a cabin. It will have to serve as your office too I'm afraid."

Kydd was about to say, "I don't need a cabin," but the yeoman was walking away by then. Kydd flashed his ID at the marine and entered the room beyond. The air was cool. Fans turned lazy circles above. Beautifully executed murals covered the bulkheads. All of it was there. The pyramids, the Sphynx, and a portrait of Cleopatra.

A table split the room in half. About two-dozen people were present, leaving two chairs unoccupied. Kydd was about to sit on the nearest chair when the man at the head of the table spoke his name. "Lieutenant Commander Kydd, I presume?"

Goolsby had a high forehead, beady eyes, and a long lugubrious face. And there, seated next to a major, was CIA agent Cassandra Cole! Her face remained empty of expression as Kydd rose to stand at something just short of attention. Every eye was on him. "Yes, sir."

"You are out of uniform Commander."

At that point Kydd was painfully aware of the fact that he was the only person in the room, other than civilians, who was wearing a ball cap, blue tee, and cargo pants.

"Sir, yes sir. This was the approved uniform for my last command. My gear is in transit somewhere."

"Please request a full set of uniforms," Goolsby said. "I expect my officers to look the part."

Cole's head was turned toward Kydd. And, much to Kydd's surprise, he saw a wink... As if to say, "Goolsby is full of shit. Don't worry about it."

That changed the way he felt about being dressed down in front of his peers *and* how he felt about her. Maybe, just maybe, a human being lurked behind the blond good looks. "Aye, aye, sir. I'll take care of it."

"Good," Goolsby said. "How is Sanchez doing?"

"The doctors are working on him, sir... I plan to check on him once the meeting is over."

Goolsby nodded. "Keep me informed. I'm sorry about Bowers. I'll write to his family."

In a single stroke Goolsby was transformed from a complete asshole, to a partial asshole, and Kydd filed him accordingly. Cole smiled as if she knew what Kydd was thinking. "Thank you, sir," Kydd said. "I'm sure the family will appreciate that."

"Grab a chair," Goolsby said. "Major Waller is our S-2, and he's most interested in the helicopter attack. You took a prisoner I believe?"

Kydd was seated by then. "Yes, sir... He suffered a broken leg, so the medical folks are working on him."

Goolsby nodded. "Andrew will drain him dry. In the meantime please share you impressions with us."

Kydd gave a brief report, and concluded by saying that General Ahmar could be a threat in the future. Waller had dark hair, wore wire-rimmed glasses, and was toying with a pen.

"He's a problem," the S-2 admitted. "The general was a captain with the Republican Guard, and better known for his delusions of grandeur, than for his leadership abilities. We will, as the colonel put it, 'drain your prisoner dry.'"

The meeting moved on to other matters after that, including threats to the supply chain. "Because we have to bring our fuel all the way up from the Med," the battalion supply officer began, "the chain is very vulnerable. A tug towing two or three barges would be easy pickings for a well-armed militia. We've been lucky so far ... But it's only a matter of time before our luck runs out."

"And that," Goolsby put in, "is one of the areas I expect Commander Kydd to address. We have five patrol boats at our disposal now ... And I'm of the opinion that each supply convoy should be accompanied by at least one of them."

All Kydd could do was agree even though he understood the toll such an assignment would take on his people and their boats. "Yes, sir ... We'll make it happen."

And so it went until the meeting came to a close half an hour later. Some of the participants took the opportunity to introduce themselves. Then, as the room cleared, Cole approached him. "So," she said. "We meet again."

"Yes," Kydd agreed. "I suppose it would be a waste of time to ask what you've been up to."

"I help where I can," Cole replied evasively. "And that brings me to a request. My team and I will need a boat at 1900 hours tomorrow night."

"To do *what?*"

"To go upriver, find a retired engineer, and bring him back."

"Because?"

"Because he knows Aswan Dam like the back of his hand. He spent 27 years working on it prior to the Brotherhood's takeover."

"So he's friendly."

"Maybe, and maybe not. We'll find out. But he's Sunni, and the Hezbollah fighters are Shia, so that will cut our way."

"It's as simple as that."

"I hope so, yes."

"Should I check in with the colonel?"

"No."

"I see," Kydd said. Maybe Cole was on a solid footing—and maybe she wasn't. He would check. "How large is your team?"

"Four marines. A fireteam."

Kydd nodded. "Tell your team to be on the fuel barge. I'll meet you there."

Cole raised a carefully plucked eyebrow. "So, you're coming?"

"Of course. There's nothing like a moonlight cruise on the Nile. Or so I've heard."

Cole put her sunglasses on. "It may have been that way once … But not anymore." She turned her back on Kydd and left. He watched her go.

CHAPTER FIVE

Khartoum, Sudan

Darkness was falling on the city of Khartoum. The man in the ankle-length *jellabiya* was no different from other pedestrians, except that he was Chinese, and carrying a stick. Yet, minimal though those distinctions were, they marked the man as a *kafir* and a target.

Lights from adjacent buildings were reflected in the gently roiling waters before him. Al-Khartum was the capital of Sudan, and located at the confluence of the White Nile and the Blue Nile, which combined to become the Nile.

As a student of military history, Colonel Shing Bo was fascinated by the battle that raged in and around Khartoum during the summer of 1884, and the winter of 1885. "Study the past," Confucius said, "if you would divine the future."

The lead-up to the battle began when a self-anointed Mahdi (religious leader) led a successful revolt against the government of Egypt, which was a British protectorate at the time.

After a muddled response a general named Charles George Gordon was sent to evacuate the British garrisons in the Sudan. This, despite Gordon's personal belief that, should he succeed— the Mahdi might gain dominion over the entire Muslim world.

Bo paused to look out over the churning waters. They were black, like congealed blood. Shadows shifted nearby. Scuffling sounds were heard. Bats swooped. A siren bleated in the distance.

Gordon arrived in Khartoum on February 18, 1884. But instead of preparing the garrisons for withdrawal, as he'd been ordered to do, Gordon went about the business of administering the city in hopes of gaining support from its citizens. Gordon made improvements to the judicial system, lowered taxes, and ironically enough—legalized slavery. A horror which *he*, as Governor-General, had abolished years earlier.

In the meantime Gordon sent a series of proposals to the British government all of which favored staying rather than leaving. The entreaties were refused.

Bo *felt* rather than saw movement behind him. He moved his feet. Right foot forward. Left leg bent.

Knowing that the Mahdists were closing in on Khartoum, Gordon finally got around to strengthening the city's fortifications. But his efforts came too late. The city was surrounded. Citizens and soldiers alike began to starve. Gordon organized a force to break through enemy lines.

But when Mahdi forces heard about that, they decided to attack, rather than continue to wait. On the night of January 25th a force of approximately 50,000 Mahdists approached Khartoum. And, because the Nile was low at that time of year, the attackers were able to wade across it. After circling around *behind* the city's wall, they launched an attack on the governor's palace.

The British garrison was slaughtered. Four-thousand civilians were taken into slavery. And Gordon died fighting. The lesson? *The soldier who fights for himself, fights for a fool*, Bo concluded. The *correct* path was spelled out in the PLA (People's Liberation Army) oath.

"I am a member of the People's Liberation Army. I promise that I will follow the leadership of the Communist Party of China, serve the people wholeheartedly, obey orders, strictly observe discipline, fight heroically, fear no sacrifice, loyally discharge my duties, work hard, practice hard to master combat skills, and resolutely fulfill my missions. Under no circumstances will I betray the Motherland or desert the army."

"*Khadhah*," (take him) a male voice said, and three men rushed Bo. The telescoping staff was made of metal. And, as Bo gave the weapon a twist, it was transformed from a 22-inch baton, to a 60-inch long fighting stick. Bo held the weapon in both hands as he turned to face his attackers. The right tip came up to whack an assailant across the bridge of the nose. The man stumbled backwards clutching his face, trying to stem the flow of blood with his hands.

In the meantime the left end of the staff stabbed sideways, penetrating deep into the second attacker's left ear. He screamed and reeled away. The third man was close by then, *very* close, and might have been able to make contact had it not been for Shao wei (2nd lieutenant) Wang, who shot the would-be thief in the back. The Norinco Type 92 pistol was equipped with a suppressor—and produced little more than a gentle cough.

The 9mm bullet threw the man forward to land at Bo's feet. He frowned. "Lieutenant Wang … What are you doing here?"

The rebuke was obvious. Though dressed in a Sudanese business suit, Wang snapped to attention, weapon straight down along his right leg. "Many apologies, sir. I have orders to follow and protect you."

"Orders from whom?"

"Orders from Major Zhou, sir."

Zhou was Bo's executive officer who had been obliquely critical of Bo's "wanderings." It was a compliment in a way, since Bo was the only thing that stood between Zhou and a command, which his second-in-command sorely wanted. Still, a private word with Zhou was in order.

Bo took a quick look around. The surviving attackers had fled. The body lay in a shadow. Another casualty in Khartoum's long list of casualties. "At ease, Wang … I understand. Orders must be followed. Come, we'll buy food from a vendor on the way back."

That was a rare honor. And as close as Bo would ever come to thanking Wang, because to do so, might involve a loss of *mianzi* (face). And that would compromise both of them though in different ways.

To reset the staff it was necessary to push each end of the pole against the pavement. Once that evolution was complete they left. The Nile whispered softly as it departed for Egypt.

***

The new day dawned the way most did, which was to say clear and already warm. That made it the best time for calisthenics since later, around noon, the temp would hover in the upper nineties.

Bo's battalion was quartered in the old Cosmopolitan Hotel which, with its fortress-like exterior and spacious inner courtyard, was an excellent example of the colonialism imposed on China in the past. Yet the hotel offered numerous. Among them was the fact that the battalion had control of the entire structure. And the surrounding gardens could be mined, and converted into a free-fire zone, if the complex come under attack.

Additionally the "Cosmo" was only blocks from Sudan's most important government buildings. That was important because Bo's men were in the city to protect the China-friendly Sudanese government—and China's considerable investments in oil production.

Though not a military power, Sudan had the kind of oil reserves that China lacked, and would need in the future. A *Chinese* future which would rule Africa and India.

The calisthenics were well underway by then, and the troops were performing jumping jacks, when Zhou appeared at Bo's elbow. "Excuse me, sir."

"Good morning, Major."

"Good morning, sir. A visitor is here to see you. An old friend."

"I doubt that," Bo replied.

"His name is Fan Leong."

Bo frowned. "Describe him."

"He's shorter than you are," Zhou said, "and stocky. A scar cuts diagonally across his face."

Bo felt a sense of shock. It *was* Leong. Which was to say *Major General Leong,* who, for reasons unknown, was in Khartoum rather than Beijing. "Where is he?"

"In your office."

"Thank you."

Zhou watched Bo leave. Mysterious were the ways of commanding officers.

***

The Cosmo had elevators, but they had broken down decades earlier, and never been repaired. So Bo followed a flight of sweeping stairs down into a cavernous lobby. The paint, the furnishings, and the carpets were long overdue for renewal. But in spite of that the high-ceilinged room still managed to convey a sense of bourgeoisie elegance.

The entrance to the manager's office, currently Bo's office, was located near the massive front desk. Both the duty sergeant and a private 1st class snapped to attention as Bo passed them.

The door was ajar. And as Bo entered, he saw that General Leong was on his feet, inspecting the oil painting that hung over the fireplace. It was a portrait of Queen Elizabeth as she appeared in 1956. The general was dressed in a retro Mao suit which, in his younger days, had been standard formal wear for men.

Bo came to attention as Leong turned. "Colonel Shing Bo, reporting as ordered, *sir!*"

When Leong smiled it did nothing to lessen the scar's visual impact. Most people assumed that the scar marked a battle wound. That despite the fact that up until the moment WWIII started hardly anyone within the PLA had fired a shot in anger. Bo included.

No, the scar was the result of an auto accident on the Jingping Expressway, more than 20 years earlier. "At ease, Colonel ... You look surprised."

"I am, sir," Bo confessed, as they shook hands. "Please have a seat. Would you care for some tea?"

"That would be welcome," Leong replied.

Bo went over to his desk and used the house phone to call the kitchen. Then he went back to sit across from Leong in front of the seldom used fireplace. The men knew each other well. Leong was a friend of Bo's father and had been Bo's mentor.

Such a relationship could be very advantageous if all went well for the mentor. But, should Leong fall into disfavor, Bo would go down with him.

Fortunately Leong had proven himself to be an adept politician. And that, in all truth, was something *every* general had to be. "So," Leong began. "The people in our embassy tell me that you are doing a good job. Your parents will be pleased."

"I'm glad to hear that," Bo replied patiently. He knew Leong was on his way somewhere, and would arrive in his own good time.

"For the most part the war is going well," Leong added. "Especially in situations where our forces can engage the enemy alone."

Bo was quick to pick up on the cue. "And when they don't?"

"Then problems arise," Leong said.

The tea arrived. Once it was served the civilian employee left. Leong slurped some of the liquid and smacked his lips. "Lu'an Melon Seed, if I'm not mistaken."

"You are correct," Bo assured him. "It's from my private supply."

"You chose well," Leong said. "As I was saying, much as we appreciate our allies, they are prone to errors. Take the Russian plan to invade Alaska for example ... That was motivated more by national pride than strategic necessity. Now, to the north of you, there's another example of how rash they can be. And Iran as well."

Bo knew little more than what was available in the Intel briefings that came his way. A team of Russian and Hezbollah fighters had parachuted into Egypt, captured the Aswan Dam, and planted a nuke deep inside of it.

Then, in a surprising turn of events, the Hezbollah fighters killed the Russians. Now *they* were the ones who controlled the bomb. And if the Egyptians failed to form a Shia friendly government, and join the Axis, the fanatics were going to destroy the dam. "Capturing the dam was 'rash' sir? In what way?"

"Our government fears that the Egyptians won't be able to establish a central government," Leong replied. "And, without the Russians to keep the Shias under control, the Central Committee fears that they will blow the dam.

"Should that occur," Leong continued, "Something on the order of 10-million Sunnis will die. That would not only constitute an atrocity, it would stir unrest among the Muslims who reside in *our* country, all 21-million of them. Most of whom are Sunnis.

"That's to say nothing of the damage done to the relationships we built throughout the continent of Africa. We warned our allies about the potential consequences of their plan—but they went ahead."

Bo felt a sense of shame. None of those possibilities had occurred to him. Fortunately the men and women of the Communist Party's Central Committee were more insightful than he was. But, according to Confucius, "Humility is the solid foundation of all virtues." And Bo felt very humble indeed. "So what are we to do?" he inquired.

Leong slurped some tea. "*We*, which means *you*, are going to take two companies of infantry north—and neutralize that bomb. I brought two scientists in for that very purpose. A primary and a spare." It was Leong's idea of a joke. He smiled. "Please return them if you can."

***

The next few days were very busy. The most pressing matter was the need to acquire transportation for the 865-mile journey from Khartoum to the Aswan Dam. Bo's first inclination was to hire boats and float down the Nile to Lake Nasser. But because of the cataracts north of Khartoum, Bo's newly hired guide argued against it.

The local's name was John Jal. He had intelligent eyes, brown skin, and prominent teeth. Though born in Sudan, Jal had lived in the U.S. And Jal could speak Dinka, Nuer, Bari, and Zande as well as English. And since Bo spoke English that was the language they used to communicate. "We will use the highway," Jal announced. "But you must be ready for bandits."

"We will be," Bo assured him. And that was true since his soldiers were trained and ready to fight. But, like many Chinese officers, Bo had never seen combat. So was *he* ready? *I must be,* Bo thought. *I will be.*

Bo went to work securing the vehicles and supplies required for the trip. He couldn't take more than two companies of men without weakening the larger force to the point where it would be vulnerable to attack if a Sudanese military officer launched a coup.

So the expeditionary force would be limited to 160 soldiers give or take. However, based on intelligence estimates, that should be enough to overwhelm the Hezbollah fighters and neutralize the bomb.

After that the Shia fighters could pretend to have a bomb or leave Egypt if they chose to. The Central Committee didn't care.

Would other Axis countries be furious? Yes. But the committee wasn't worried about that either. "They can't win without us," Leong had said. "And they know it."

According to Bo's calculations he would need 12 trucks to carry personnel, plus supplies, along with two gun platforms and a couple of motorcycles for scouting. Thanks to the additional authority granted to Bo by General Leong he was able to commandeer 8, but only 8, trucks from China's National Petroleum Corporation's (CNPC) extensive operations in south Sudan.

All of the vehicles had been manufactured by a state-owned company called JAC motors. And they were, according to CNPC's regional operations manager, "…in excellent condition."

Bo didn't believe that… But he hoped the trucks would be serviceable.

That left Bo 4 trucks short of the number he needed. He was about to go shopping when Jal intervened. "I know people, who know people," Jal said mysteriously. "I will find what you need."

That freed Bo to buy two used Toyota pickup trucks and put mechanics to work converting them to Middle East style gun trucks. The greatest challenge involved through-bolting the KPV-14.X114mm weapons to the trucks' frames so that the recoil wouldn't break them loose. Then came the need for rotating pintle style mounts, seats for the gunners, and bullet proofed ammo bins.

Once that work was underway Bo and Jal went shopping for motorcycles. After looking at nearly two-dozen dirt bikes, they settled on two Suzuki RM2450s, both of which were about four-years old. Bo rode each machine before putting his country's money down.

When he arrived at work the following morning Jal was waiting in his office. "Good news, boss. I have them. They're parked outside."

"You have *what?*"

"Two buses," Jal replied. "They can carry 60 passengers each, more like 40 given how much gear your soldiers have, and they're air conditioned! All you need to do is pay for them."

Bo made some calculations, and decided that Jal was correct, two buses *would* fill the gap. But what kind of condition were they in?

A mechanic was summoned and the three of them went out to the driveway that fronted the hotel. The Mercedes-Benz buses hadn't been washed in quite a while. Their owner was a voluble man in a white turban and a blue *jellabiya*. He aimed a torrent of Sudanese at Bo, waved his arms wildly, and continued to babble as Jal led him away.

Bo ordered the mechanic to check both maintenance logs, and spot check some of the work recorded in them, prior to driving each. Then he left for breakfast.

He was at his desk when the mechanic entered his office three hours later. The man popped to attention. "Corporal Lau Chang, sir."

Bo looked up from the pre-operation report he'd been working on. "Yes, corporal … What did you conclude?"

"Both vehicles are fully operable, sir, and appear likely to function without breaking down."

"*How* likely?"

Chang's eyes were fixed on a point over the officer's head. "About 90 percent, sir."

"Good," Bo said. "Dismissed."

Chang performed a smart about-face and marched out of the room.

The trucks had arrived from the south by then, been inspected, and pronounced serviceable. Bo sent for Jal. Time was of the essence. They would leave in the morning.

After working far into the night, and grabbing what sleep they could, Bo's soldiers rose to confront something rare: A rainstorm.

The balcony outside Bo's two-room suite faced the inner courtyard. Clothed in nothing more than a pair of white boxers, he went out to stand in the downpour.

The raindrops hit hard. But they were blood warm, and Bo delighted in the rare feel of the rain, as water trickled down the length of his body. He closed his eyes. Should he take his soldiers north? In spite of the flash floods that they might encounter? Or should he give the thirsty desert time to swallow?

The rain will slow us down, Bo decided. *But every mile matters. And the men expect to go. They want to go. And, come to think of it, so do I.*

Bo went back inside, took a *second* shower, and got dressed. His pack and personal weapons were waiting. The expeditionary force was ready an hour later.

After shaking hands with Major Zhou, and assuring him that all would be well, Bo climbed into the first truck's front passenger seat. Jal was in the back, legs up, reading a magazine.

Bo felt sorry for the gunner, and assistant gunner, both of whom were exposed to the rain. But nothing could be done about it. An attack could come at any time.

The gun truck was followed by 2 tarp-covered troop trucks, 2 supply trucks and a bus. His executive officer was riding in gun truck two—followed by the same combination of vehicles. Should the convoy be cut in two, both halves would have leadership, troops and supplies.

The highway took them through light traffic, over the Blue Nile, and north through Alkadroo, El-Kabashi, Al-Sagi, and Wad Ramli before delivering the column into the Sudanese version of a traffic jam. The back-up consisted of a heavily loaded flatbed truck, a donkey cart, an ancient tractor and about twenty rain-drenched pedestrians.

The rain continued to fall as Bo got out and made his way forward. A wooden bridge had been washed out. And because of the rushing water no one could cross. Bo turned to find Jal at his side. "Ask them how long it will be before someone comes to repair it."

Jal spoke to an old man in a rain slicker. Then he turned back. "He says it will be a day or two, boss."

"So why are they waiting?"

"We have a saying," Jal replied. "Patience is beautiful."

Bo understood the sentiment, but was in no mood to practice patience. He brought the handheld radio up to his lips. "Xu… Send supply truck 4 forward—along with two squads of men. They'll need shovels, axes, rope and a chainsaw. We're going to build a bridge."

Bo's XO was a young officer named Captain Xu. And, if the mission went well, it would be the making of him.

The first step was to clear away some of the debris, being careful to preserve key cross beams, so that the perforated steel planks (PSPs) would have something to rest on. Next a squad had to battle its way through the raging torrent of water to the north bank. And repeat the process until all of the necessary gear was in place.

Then, and only then, could they manhandle the 12-foot long sections of PSP over the eight-foot-wide channel and drop them into place. Given how wide the truck/bus tires were Bo thought it best to lay down 2 sections of PSP on the left and the right so that there would be very little chance of straying off the temporary span.

And it was then, just as they finished, that the rain stopped. Not gradually, but all of a sudden. As if a giant faucet had been turned off. It was only a matter of minutes before the clouds dissipated and the sun appeared. Ground fog rose to shroud truck 4 in mist as a noncom drove it out onto the PSP bridge. Civilians watched in wonder as the steel planks gave, wood creaked, and the truck's diesel engine spewed black smoke into the air. Then with a final bump and rattle the truck was across. A cheer went up.

One-by-one the rest of the vehicles followed. "Allow the civilians to cross," Bo ordered. "And retrieve the planks. We could need them later."

While the civilians crossed Bo consulted his map. The original plan was to reach Al Dabbah before darkness. But it was a good 300 miles away, and Bo didn't think it made sense to travel at night. So he settled on a goal of driving 150 miles prior to making camp. That would leave the battalion with enough daylight to erect tents, establish a perimeter, and eat before darkness fell.

Even though the two-lane highway ran parallel to the Nile, which was five-miles to the west, all signs of agriculture vanished as the convoy continued north. There was nothing to see but brown desert to the left, right, and straight ahead.

Drifts of windblown sand covered the pavement in places. Wrecked vehicles, some of which were half-covered by dunes, marked the locations where accidents had occurred.

The convoy had to stop after two hours so the troops could relieve themselves and stretch their legs. Bo took advantage of the opportunity to have both motorcycles unloaded. Then with a sergeant acting as his bodyguard, he took off. It felt good to escape the close confines of the gun truck, and feel the hot air buffet his face.

With very little to break the monotony, Bo was looking forward to reaching the town of Wahat Saghira (Little Oasis) which, according to Jal, was little more than a truck stop. Still, something was better than nothing. So when Bo saw the water tower up ahead, and the tops of some palm trees, he felt his spirits rise. Maybe the store would have something cold to drink. Some iced tea would be nice, and … Then Bo noticed the vultures circling above the town. He spoke into the boom mike. "Slow down. Something's wrong."

The sergeant downshifted. Bo saw the bodies as they approached the edge of town. They were badly bloated. Some lay in the streets. Others were sprawled by vehicles. Men, women, and children. All had been shot. A halo of dried blood surrounded each corpse.

Bo stopped to scan the scene for any signs of danger. A dog nosed its dead master. A red toy lay next to a child. Flies buzzed. Other than that the town was still.

The sergeant's name was Wong. The machine gun that had been slung across Wong's back was in his hands. Bo got off the motorcycle and drew his pistol. "We'll stay together. Check the store first."

The screen door squealed as Bo pulled it open. The proprietor, or the man Bo assumed to be the proprietor, lay face down on the floor. He'd been shot in the back. His shelves were nearly bare.

A dead woman was slumped over the counter with an open cash box sitting next to her arm. The smell was horrible. Bo gagged. He led Wong outside. "Bandits," Bo said thickly.

The sergeant nodded. "Yes, sir." If Wong felt sick, Bo could see no sign of it on the noncom's moon-shaped face. He spoke into the mike. "Captain Xu."

"Sir."

"The town of Wahat Saghira was attacked by bandits. It appears that all of the inhabitants and some travelers are dead. Place the convoy on high alert. Sergeant Wong and I will be waiting for you on the south side of town. Over."

Bo turned to Wong. "Take the west side of the street. I'll take the east. Alert me if you see something suspicious."

Bo eyed the street ahead. Except for the bird-pecked bodies it appeared to be normal. The pavement was intact—and there were no piles of trash. The kind that might conceal explosives.

He stuck his head into a trinket shop. A radio was playing the drum heavy music many Sudanese enjoyed. A blood stained turban rested next to its owner's head.

And so it went until Bo arrived at the south end of town and saw gun truck 1. It was getting larger with each passing second and shimmering like a mirage.

The heat combined with the smell caused Bo to feel nauseous. Did that make him weak? He was trying to decide when he heard a high-pitched whine. It was similar to the noise a mosquito makes only louder. He looked up. And there, hovering above, was a consumer-grade drone!

Thoughts flashed through Bo's mind. The bandits were nearby ... They were watching ... And they were waiting. But for *what?* Then it came to him. They knew about the convoy, and planned to steal whatever they could.

Bo turned to the south. The convoy was close, *too* close to stop short of the town. "Hit the gas!" he ordered. "Go as fast as you can!"

The gun truck seemed to leap forward. But the larger vehicles couldn't accelerate so quickly. The drivers were still shifting gears when the gun truck bounced over a woman's body. The corpse exploded ... And that caused the Toyota to flip and skid.

The first explosion was followed by another, and *another*, as a dozen command-detonated mines went off in quick succession. That was the moment when Bo realized that the explosives had been hidden *inside* the bodies. And, had he taken the time required to roll them over, that would have been obvious.

A machine gun rattled as Wong blew the drone out of the sky. That was followed by a resounding BOOM, as one of the supply trucks exploded. Pieces of smoking wreckage fell as a bus bounced through a crater, swerved to avoid the burning supply truck, and came back on course. "They're close by!" Bo shouted into the radio. "Find them!"

The bandits *were* nearby. But there was no need to find them—as well concealed bandits came boiling up out of holes, stood on flat roofs, and rolled out from under the town's elevated walkways. Bo heard gunfire as a wild-eyed man with a scarf wrapped around the lower part of his face dropped from above and landed off balance.

Bo reached out to grab the bandit's AK-47 with his left hand andfired the pistol with his right. The man let go of the rifle as he fell backwards. Sergeant Wong fired short bursts, and laughed every time a bandit went down.

A body, or what *looked* like a body, came to its feet. The AK seemed to fire itself. "And stay down," Bo said, as he put a slug into the man's head.

Wong yelled, "On the roof!" as bullets kicked up geysers of dust around Bo's boots. Both men fired at a black silhouette. It jerked spastically, and fell head first into the street, where it produced a puff of dust.

Another bandit left a blood trail behind as he tried to crawl under a car. Bo shot him in the ass with the AK, ran out of ammo, and fired his pistol. He was fumbling for a fresh magazine when someone spoke. "Colonel, it's me … Xu."

The magazine clicked into place, the slide snapped forward, and Bo turned. The gun was pointed at Xu. His hands were up and his eyes were huge. "Sorry," Bo said lamely, as he lowered the weapon. "There were lots of them."

The next four hours were spent dealing with a long list of problems, the most urgent of which consisted of two wounded soldiers, both in critical condition. The battalion surgeon was doing what he could—but feared it wouldn't be enough.

Bo made contact with Major Zhou by radio, told him about the firefight, and the need for an air evac. "Make sure they have a doctor on board," Bo said. "And notify the embassy. Ask them to contact the Sudanese government. There are a lot of people to bury here."

There were minor wounds to cope with too … But nothing the surgeon and his medics couldn't handle themselves.

Three soldiers had been killed in action. Bo decided to bury them outside the town. Zhou would send a platoon north to disinter the bodies and take them to Khartoum for cremation.

Bo led a platoon of troops west toward the Nile and two palm trees. "There," he said, pointing to the ground. "Side-by-side. Make sure they have their tags on. Take a picture of the palms— and get a GPS fix on this location."

The shifting sand made it difficult to dig the common grave. As quickly as the men shoveled sand *more* poured in. And it was hot. *Very* hot … That meant the grave diggers had to take turns and drink lots of water. Eventually the job was finished.

The dead soldiers lay on their backs, blind eyes staring up at the sun, as their comrades formed two ranks before them. *How many?* Bo wondered. *How many of Genghis Khan's warriors were laid to rest thousands of miles from home? Now we're going to found a new empire, a Chinese empire, and a price must be paid.*

There was no Buddhist funeral prayer as such, and with no monks to assist him, Bo had to improvise. "After fighting bravely, our brothers fell in battle, freeing their spirits to enter samsara or nirvana–the end of suffering. They live on in our memories."

Then, as soldiers shoveled sand into the grave, Bo allowed himself to reflect. His battalion had been blooded. *He'd* been blooded. And emerged free of shame. His parents would be proud. Bo opened his eyes to discover that the grave had been filled in, and a platoon of soldiers was staring at him. "Don't just stand there," Bo said. "Get to work. We have things to do."

And that was true. The loss of a gun truck, and a supply truck, were very much on Bo's mind. Especially the supply truck which had been loaded with 25% of the battalion's ammo supply. The rest was divided equally between the other trucks.

Jal was waiting at the edge of town. Bo felt a sense of shame. The possibility that Jal had been wounded or hurt hadn't occurred to him. "Jal!" Bo said. "What happened?"

"The truck did a somersault," Jal replied. "The driver and I were strapped in, but our gunner was killed."

Bo hadn't made the connection until then. Private Chen had been riding in the back of the truck, and now he was lying under a foot of sand. It was hard to keep up. "I'm glad you're okay," Bo said. "Did any of the townspeople survive? And if so, were you able to speak with them?"

"Yes," Jal replied. "I found an old man. He hid in a shed along with his goats. And that's where he was, when a Land Rover pulled up, and a warlord named Hussain Urabi got out."

"He *knew* the warlord?" Bo inquired skeptically. "That seems unlikely."

"That's what I thought," Jal agreed. "But the old man says that Urabi and his men passed through Wahat Saghira a month ago. And he saw Urabi quite clearly."

"And that isn't all," Jal added. "A woman identified Urabi as well. She says he's Egyptian."

"Perhaps we killed him," Bo said hopefully.

Jal shook his head. "No such luck, Boss... I made the old man look at everybody."

It was unfortunate that Urabi had escaped, but it wasn't critical to the mission, and that was Bo's focus. "You did well," Bo said. "I won't forget."

There was a roar as a helicopter passed overhead, banked, and came in for a landing next to a column of red smoke. Bo went over to watch as the wounded men were loaded onboard.

The helo took off five minutes later and turned south. "They have a pretty good chance of making it," the battalion surgeon said.

"Thanks to you," Bo replied.

The sun was hanging low in the western sky by that time, and any hope of logging 150 miles was lost. But Bo wasn't about to spend the night near Wahat Saghira. That would be hard on morale—never mind his nose.

So with Xu's help Bo put the convoy back together minus two trucks. Then they headed north. The plan was to camp in the desert. But not just anywhere. What the battalion needed was a position that it could defend should it be necessary. Would Urabi attack during the night? Bo didn't think so. But assumptions could get people killed. As was the case in Wahat Saghira. Explosives hidden *inside* people. A lesson learned.

Gun truck 2 was in the one-slot. Rather than ride in the cab, Bo stood in the back, and peered over the cab. That gave him added height and a 360-degree view. It was an exhilarating experience. The dry wind in his face, the desert all around, and the speed with which the landscape flew by.

But there was nothing at first. No sign of the refuge Bo had been hoping for. He was ready to give up after fifteen minutes, and settle on a spot in the desert, when a rocky outcropping appeared in the distance. It was the sort of elevation that would give the battalion an advantage if attacked.

Bo opened his mike. "This is the colonel. I see a hill up ahead. It's on the west side of the highway. I want all vehicles to slow down and pull over while I take a look. Over."

Bo heard a chorus of "Yes sirs," as he spoke to the driver. "You heard me Hu… Turn off the highway—and circle the hill."

Bo's primary concern was the depth and consistency of the sand. The trucks had six-by-four drives, but the buses didn't, and if one of them was to bog down, the wrecker would have a hard time pulling it free. Bo had to grab the gun mount as the Toyota bounced off-road.

The first thing Bo noticed was the fact that they weren't the only people to turn off there. Tire tracks led to the hill. And that wasn't surprising, since others would want to climb the hill, and take advantage of the view.

"Pull up," Bo ordered, as the gun truck rounded the north side of the hill. As Bo jumped down he noticed that the ground was solid. And once the vehicles were parked on the west side of the elevation they would be screened from the highway.

"Follow our tracks," Bo said over the radio. "Buses first, followed by the trucks, and the wrecker. Captain Xu… Once all the vehicles are off the highway, send a squad out to sweep the first fifty-feet of our tracks away. Over."

"Yes, sir."

The moon was up by the time all of the vehicles were parked, tents were erected, and guards posted. That was when Bo gave himself permission to climb the hill. Two lookouts were there to greet him. Both had night vision gear.

Bo made his way along the ridge to a ledge where he could sit and look out over the moonlit desert. It was breathtakingly beautiful. *Quiet Night Thought*, was a famous poem written by the Tang Dynasty poet Li Bai. It spoke to the moment.

> *"Moonlight before my bed*
> *Perhaps frost on the ground.*
> *Lift my head and see the moon*
> *Lower my head and I miss my home."*

CHAPTER SIX

Bani Adi, Egypt

Though doubtful at first—Kydd was thankful for his combination cabin-office aboard the *Nile Queen*. It was air conditioned for one thing… And he had to have a place where he could fill out the endless reports that Colonel Goolsby not only insisted on, but clearly delighted in, never missing a chance to dot an "i" or cross a "t."

Fortunately Kydd's yeoman, a first class petty officer named Marty Evans, was able to handle most of the work on his own. He was working in a corner when Cassandra Cole entered. Evans turned to look. "Agent Cole is here to see you, sir? Are you in?"

Kydd, who was only six feet away from Cole, frowned. "I am, but I'm busy. Ask her to take a seat in the waiting room." Both men laughed.

Cole made a face. "That's the best you can do?"

"Yup," Kydd replied. "Please have a seat on the guest stool that Evans liberated from the ship's bar."

Cole perched on the stool, and Kydd moved his laptop around, so the agent could see the screen. The satellite photo showed Bani Adi, a large island immediately to the south, and a small island just beyond that.

The town of Ezbet Sherif was west of the smaller island. That's where an Egyptian engineer named Asem El-Baz had chosen to retire after working on the Aswan Dam for 27 years. The

Allies would need a guide after they took control of the sprawling structure. Would El-Baz be willing to serve in that capacity? That was Cole's problem.

"This is where we're going," Kydd said, as he pointed to Ezbet Sherif.

"I know that," Cole said. "It's my mission. Remember?"

"I do," Kydd replied. "But what you don't know is that some yahoo moored a barge *here*, between the small island, and the west bank." His pen tapped the spot. "And he has a Russian Kord-12.7mm heavy machine gun mounted on it. And that's all he needs to make commercial vessels pay his tolls. The fishermen can avoid the barge. But, if we were to motor past, the odds are pretty good that he would open fire on us."

Cole stared at him. "The National Reconnaissance Office didn't mention any of that."

Kydd shrugged. "It's a barge ... And a single gun would be easy to miss."

"Then how come you know about it?"

"I bought a *jellabiya* and hired a fisherman to take me up-river at 0500 this morning."

Cole's expression changed. "That was smart."

"Thanks," Kydd replied. *What does Evans think of this conversation?* he wondered. *And why am I attracted to Cole in spite of her snotty attitude?*

"So, how do we handle it?" Cole inquired.

"The water between the large island and the east bank is shallow. But our jet boats are equipped for that. We'll pass under a bridge *here*," Kydd said, as he tapped the screen with his pen. "Once we reach the end of the big island we'll pass between it and the small island. Then we'll go alongside the barge and board it.

"Meanwhile you, and your marines, will be on Lieutenant Altman's two-boat. He will put you ashore just east of town. You'll have to hoof it from there. What kind of condition is El-Baz in? Will he be able to reach the two-boat under his own power?"

"Yes," Cole replied. "We think so. He ran marathons prior to the war."

"Good. I'll see you on the fuel dock at 1900 hours tonight."

***

Kydd gave Evans a two hour lunch break after that, took a nap, and awoke feeling refreshed. Then he went down to visit the American boats. Chief Jones was waiting to greet him. "Good afternoon, Skipper... How's life on the floating pleasure palace?"

"Terrible," Kydd deadpanned. "My eggs benedict was cold this morning."

"Tell them to turn the AC down," Jones replied. Both men laughed.

"So how's our readiness?" Kydd wanted to know. "According to the scuttlebutt we're going up-river soon."

"The wrench turners can't replace the minigun on two," Jones replied. "But they patched the hole—and repaired the wiring. Lieutenant Altman talked the marines out of an LMG. We're fabricating a mount."

"That's better than nothing," Kydd replied. "How's morale?"

"We rigged awnings over the decks," Jones said. "But the heat wears people down. Especially since we have to wear full uniforms."

"I don't like what I'm seeing Chief," Kydd said. "Those boats are filthy. Hose 'em down once a day. That's an order."

Jones grinned. "Our personnel would have to dress accordingly."

"Let it be so," Kydd replied. "But only one boat at a time. In case the shit hits the fan."

Jones nodded. "Aye, aye, sir."

***

After going boat-to-boat, and shooting the shit with the sailors, Kydd went to visit the Brits. Their Scimitar class boats were 52-feet long. They were powered by twin diesel engines, and armed with two machine guns each, both mounted aft.

Each vessel carried an officer and a six person crew. Senior Lieutenant Fox-Smith was there to greet Kydd as he came over the side. "Welcome aboard, sir."

"Good afternoon, Lieutenant. Are you ready for our outing?"

"Very much so, sir." Fox-Smith had an Oxford accent, which meant that he could have passed for an American, had it not been for some of the idioms he used.

"Excellent."

After going over the mission Kydd gestured to the machine guns mounted in the stern. "No offense Lieutenant, but what if the enemy is up ahead? Will you turn? And go full astern?"

Fox-Smith laughed. "We were on coastal patrol before they sent us to the Med," he explained. "And one weapon per side was considered to be sufficient."

"So you wouldn't object if we were to up-arm your boats?"

"No, sir. Please do."

"Good. Please inform Sub-lieutenant Hawkins that I'll be on the fuel barge by 1830."

***

Kydd ordered the sailor running the RIB boat to take him to the *Nile,* where a raft, and a set of steeply slanting stairs led to the main deck. It was dinnertime and the dining room was nearly full. Kydd sought permission to join some marine officers at their table, and received a hearty "Welcome aboard," from a major.

The leathernecks were discussing the complexities involved in pushing upriver, as well as what would happen when they reached the dam. "Once we're ten miles away the tangos will blow it," a captain predicted.

"Even captains are correct sometimes," the major said. "So, if you don't know how to swim, now's the time to take lessons."

Kydd remembered what Cole had told the assembled officers back in Port Ashdod. "There's an additional element to the overall plan. One which I'm not authorized to share at this time." Kydd hoped there was.

He finished his meal, excused himself, and went to his cabin. Evans was gone for the day. Kydd's tactical vest was stored in the closet. It was set up the way he liked it, and since it served well aboard the *Galene*, why change?

All Kydd had to do was remove the shoulder rig that carried his M17 pistol, move the semiauto to the vest, and secure it in place. Extra magazines for the 9mm and the suppressed H&K MP7 were already in their slots.

As Kydd put the vest on he felt the familiar weight, plus the rising sense of fear, and a sense of anticipation. The latter being something he was hesitant to admit to, since no one in their right mind *wanted* to see action. But action would be required in order to move upriver and seize the dam.

It was almost dark by the time Kydd left the *Nile Queen*. A different Cole was waiting on the fuel barge. She was wearing a heavily loaded tac vest and carrying an MP7. "Good evening, Agent Cole .... I see you dressed for the occasion."

"This ain't my first rodeo," Cole replied. "I was a platoon leader in a previous life."

Kydd realized how little he knew about her. A platoon leader ... Then it occurred to him. Cole was a member of the CIA's Special Operations Group (SOG)! That made her the perfect candidate for the job at hand. "I should have known," Kydd replied. "Even so, I hope you'll be careful tonight."

Cole looked at him. "*Why?*" It was both a question and a challenge.

Kydd shrugged. "In spite of your obnoxious personality, you have some latent charm."

Cole's eyes searched his face. "I can see where this is headed sailor boy… And, if things were different, I might go along for the ride. But I lost someone recently… And I don't have anything to give right now. I hope you understand."

Suddenly Cole looked like a little girl playing soldier. Kydd had a strong desire to wrap his arms around the agent, and tell her that everything was going to be okay, even if that was by no means certain. He forced a smile. "Message received. But, like I said before, be careful out there."

The conversation was interrupted by the rumble of powerful engines as a British patrol boat pulled alongside. A sailor jumped off to hold the vessel in place. Once Kydd was aboard the sailor followed. As the first boat pulled away the second arrived.

"Welcome aboard, Commander," a voice said.

Kydd turned to find a British officer standing two feet away. "Sub-lieutenant Hawkins?"

"At your service, sir," the young man replied cheerfully as they shook hands. He had a round face, an infectious grin, and the manner of a schoolboy on vacation.

"Good," Kydd said. "You were briefed?"

"Yes, sir. Up the east channel, between the islands, and alongside the barge."

Hawkins made the whole thing sound so simple. "That's correct," Kydd said. "But here's something new. Assuming all goes well, you will see three blips from a flashlight as you enter the channel. They will appear on the port side.

"As you get closer you'll see a felucca anchored in the stream. I want you to pull in and take the occupant aboard. His name is Jamil. He's been fishing this stretch of the Nile since he was ten. Jamil will act as our pilot."

Hawkins nodded. "Yes, sir. And if things *don't* go well?"

Kydd chuckled. "You were paying attention. I like that. If things *don't* go well, we'll see three blips of light, pull in and come under fire from the east bank."

"Because Jamil sold us out."

"Precisely," Kydd said. "But here's why I'm willing to take the chance... Jamil is a Sunni. And he knows we're going south to take the dam away from the Shias.

"Add the fact that he can't fish the west channel so long as bandits occupy the barge, plus the money I promised to pay him, and Jamil has three reasons to help us."

"So there's nothing to worry about," Hawkins said.

Kydd laughed. "I like your style Sub... Please pass the word."

The log boom had been towed to one side so the boats could pass through. Kydd was in the stern looking back at the ghostly two-boat. Cole was on it. *Ah well,* Kydd concluded. *Some things aren't meant to be.*

Strangely, given the fact that World War III was raging all around the globe, lights were visible port and starboard. There were two reasons for that. The first was the lack of a central government which, had it existed, would have almost certainly imposed a blackout.

The second was that in spite of their threat to kill 10-million Egyptians, the terrorists had been able to keep power flowing from the dam. That was intended to prove how reasonable they were—and smother the resentment outages would cause. Someone knew what he was doing.

"There it is," a sailor said. And Kydd turned just in time to see blip two and three. The H&K was ready to fire as he stepped over to the rail. It was a scary moment. If things went wrong British sailors might die. Hell, *he* might die.

But if Jamil kept his word the fisherman could help them avoid most of the shoals in the east channel. It would take hours to find their way through the maze otherwise.

Kydd heard something bump the side of the boat. A light flashed on and off. And in that brief moment Jamil looked up at him. The fisherman spoke English surprisingly well. "I see you Effendi."

"And I you, Jamil. Please come aboard."

A sailor reached down to take Jamil's hand and pull him up. Kydd had been holding his breath. He let it go. Hawkins was at his side. "Take Jamil forward. Order the helmsman to follow his instructions. And tell the two-boat to close it up."

Even with a pilot, the trip south was still a long, torturous process. Jamil tried using night vision gear, but ultimately rejected it, choosing to rely on his memory instead. And for the most part the Egyptian was successful. The boat was halfway up the length of the island before it ran aground. "I sorry, Effendi," Jamil said. "River play tricks."

Thanks to the fact that the boat was moving slowly, Hawkins was able to back off the shoal without difficulty. The turning-twisting journey continued. But the next time the boat ran aground, it was on some thick, glutinous mud. Hawkins ordered the helmsman to go full astern, but to no avail.

That forced the crew to pass a line over to the second boat, which succeeded in pulling the first Scimitar off. In the meantime Kydd struggled to control his impatience and let Hawkins do his job.

Finally, after what seemed like an eternity, the one-boat rounded the south end of the large island, putting the small islet to port. A lantern had been hung on the south end of the barge making it easy to spot. The diesels were throttled down in hopes of catching the bandits by surprise. Then, as they drew close, Hawkins called for more power.

A bandit shouted something in Arabic and fired his AK-47 at the oncoming boat. The patrol boat's machine gun responded in kind. The heavy slugs tore the watchman apart.

The Scimitar hit the barge hard as it came alongside. Kydd yelled, "Now!" and made the leap. A dozen men had been sleeping on deck. Half were on their feet and were trying to bring the Russian Kord machine gun to bear on the British boat.

The plan to keep things quiet was out the window. Kydd fired. The gunner slumped sideways and fell to the deck. "Cease fire!" Hawkins shouted. "Check each man, collect weapons, and search the barge."

Kydd eyed his watch. The battle had lasted no more than 20 seconds if that. The two-boat was nowhere to be seen, and that was good, because the mission was on track.

A man moaned, a dog barked somewhere, and the Nile gurgled happily. Cole was gone. The waiting had begun.

***

Ezbet Sherif, Egypt

Floating docks were moored to pilings along the riverbank east of Ezbet Sherif, and connected to the shore via wooden planks, one of which gave under Cole's boots.

The team consisted of Staff Sergeant Owens, Corporal Ortiz, Lance Corporal Kelly, and Lance Corporal Landro. All of whom belonged to the corps' Force Recon—a legendary unit which was trained to carry out amphibious reconnaissance, intelligence collection, and raids. They wore headsets, night vision goggles, and heavily loaded tac vests.

Two of the men carried suppressed MP7s, and two had what Owens referred to as the "boom-booms," meaning a 12-gauge shotgun for opening doors, and a 40mm rotary grenade launcher for "crowd control." All were armed with suppressed pistols in custom thigh holsters.

But, if push came to shove, a CIA controlled Predator drone was circling over Ezbet Sherif, and could provide valuable Intel, plus Hellfire missiles if it came to that. Cole figured the odds of getting in and out without difficulty were good.

But a smalltime bandit named Abdel Tuma was not only in charge of the barge hustle, he had a tollbooth on the nearest highway, and ran the village. So his heavies could be out and about. The team began to jog. Ortiz was on point, his MP7 ready for a quick takedown, followed by Cole, Kelly, Landro and Owens who, if the agent was killed, would assume command.

The house that Asem El-Baz and his wife lived in was located a mile-and-a-half from the river. The first half-mile or so consisted of a dirt path that ran through a moonlit banana tree plantation.

Then came the smell of animal pens, followed by small houses with TV antennas, and darkened stores. Everything had a green hue thanks to Cole's night vision goggles. The definition was excellent however—and a source of comfort.

The town was a maze of winding streets. Fortunately Ortiz had a GPS device that could guide him to the target. And they were making good time when Ortiz raised a hand with palm back (stop). The rest of them obeyed. When Ortiz spoke his voice was little more than a whisper. "Two men. Stationary. AKs."

Cole considered that. Tuma's thugs? Probably, but not necessarily. Lots of people went armed in wartime Egypt. She eyed her GPS. "Go left. Loop right."

Ortiz made the OK sign with his fingers, turned into a narrow passageway, and disappeared. Cole followed. The path led past a store and a communal water fountain. Water gurgled down the drain and flowed back to the Nile.

A right-hand turn put them on the street where El-Baz lived. As seen through their goggles everything was glazed with moonlight like frosting on a cake. "On the right," Ortiz said.

"Roger," Cole replied. The El-Baz residence was two-stories tall. That made it a mansion by local standards. The upstairs lights were on.

"Kelly," Cole said. "Try the door."

The rest of the team scanned for threats as Kelly went forward. Three minutes passed before Kelly spoke. "I'm in. Dog down. Noise upstairs."

Cole winced. Killing the dog made sense because if they didn't, it might bark, or attack. But how would El-Baz feel about the loss of his dog? Would that prevent him from cooperating? "Hide the body," Cole said, as she hurried forward. "Ortiz has the overlook. The rest of the team on me."

Judging from the splinters the door had been jimmied. Kelly was inside. There was no sign of the dog. Once all of them were in the house Cole touched Kelly's arm and pointed at the door. He nodded.

A narrow stairway led upstairs. Cole pointed to Landro, then Owens, and signaled "Go."

Boots thundered on wood as the marines hurried upstairs. Cole followed. A woman screamed. Cole heard a man say, "Please! Don't hurt us," in Arabic.

Cole paused to look around. She saw a bed with a brass frame, an ornate wardrobe, and a TV which was tuned to a black and white American sitcom. Lucy with subtitles.

Cole had been raised in the Middle Eastern countries where her peripatetic parents taught school, and spoke fluent Arabic. "We're Americans," she told them. "We won't hurt you."

Mr. and Mrs. El-Baz stared at her in disbelief. Because she was female? Because she was blond? Because she spoke Arabic?

There was no way to know. "You know about the Shia?" Cole inquired. "And the plan to blow the dam?"

Mr. El-Baz nodded.

"Good. We're going to stop them. But, once we reach the dam, we will need some expert advice from a person like *you*. Will you help us?"

The team was going to take El-Baz with them no matter how the engineer answered. But, if he would go willingly, then so much the better. El-Baz turned to his wife. She nodded. He looked back. "Yes, I'll go."

"Thank you," Cole said. "Please change into your running gear. You can bring your ID, but nothing more. If all goes well, you'll be sitting in that chair three weeks from now. Please hurry."

She was on the stairs when Ortiz spoke. "Tangos at nine, twelve, and three. Danger close."

Cole was on the ground floor by then. The night had a thousand eyes, at least two of which, had seen the team enter Ezbet Sherif—and move through the streets. Kelly was waiting. "Push them back," Cole ordered. "Don't let them form up."

Kelly was carrying the grenade launcher cradled in his arms. "No problem, ma'am ... Betsy and I will mess 'em up." Then he was gone.

Cole switched frequencies. "Six-Six to One-Six. We have him. Exfil route-two. Tangos closing. Engaging. Over." The transmission was punctuated by a loud boom, as Kelly dropped a grenade on someone.

The reply came quickly. "One-Six actual. Exfil two. Engaging. Roger that. Over."

Kydd came across as cool, composed, and competent. The three C's. Cole liked that. She heard a second boom as El-Baz came down the stairs. He was wearing a ballistic vest over an Addias running outfit plus shoes. The marines were right behind him.

Cole switched to the team freq. "We will exfil via route-two. Ortiz first, followed by me, the target, Landro, Owens and Kelly in the six slot. Move."

Kelly was still laying down fire as Cole led the others outside. Once Betsy ran dry Ortiz fired short bursts from his SMG. AK-47s answered in kind. But the bandits were disorganized and their shots went wide.

Cole said, "Go," and Ortiz went. Route-two took them to the right, and north along a narrow street. Some lights came on as others were extinguished. If an ambush was waiting on route-one the bandits would be disappointed.

That was the good news. The bad news was that route-two was half-a-mile longer than route-one. But that couldn't be helped. Once the team broke out, the tangos had to give up or follow. They followed.

Kelly paused to reload the grenade launcher and fired. Clack-pause-boom! Clack-pause-boom! Clack-pause-boom!

Then, eager to catch up with the others, Kelly turned and ran. He was a few yards behind Owens when a bullet hit the back of his right leg, broke his femur, and plowed through. He uttered a yelp and fell. "Man down," Owens said. "Turning back."

"Covering fire," Cole ordered. "Ortiz, you know what to do."

Ortiz *did* know what to do. He didn't speak Arabic, but the shove said it all: "Get going." El-Baz began to run.

Owens had pressure dressings on both wounds and was binding them in place. A splint would have to wait.

Landro was kneeling. He had Kelly's 40mm launcher. Grenades arched away, fell, and exploded. Cole switched to command frequency. "Six-Six to Blue-Bird. Over."

"This is the Bird," the drone operator replied from a base in Libya. "You have one-five tangos on your six. Over."

"Smoke 'em," Cole replied. "Over."

Thirty long seconds passed, followed by a bright flash, and the sound of thunder. Cole heard a burp of static followed by Blue-Bird's voice. "Screens clear. Three on the racks. Over."

"You rock," Cole said. "Over."

Owens and Landro had Kelly in a four-hand seat-carry. It was effective, but slow. So the team was vulnerable to attack as the street turned into a path.

Erie moonlit gardens lay to both sides—with darkness gathered beyond. Cole was about to call Kydd when his voice boomed through her headset. "One-Six actual to Six-Six. On your twelve and closing."

Kydd could have remained on the one-boat. Could have sent sailors to meet the team. But he hadn't. *Duty*, Cole thought. *No more than that. But still…*

The train of thought was interrupted as Kydd arrived with three British sailors in tow. Kydd smiled. "El-Baz is aboard the one-boat by now… Not bad for a civilian. Welcome back."

***

Bani Adi, Egypt

After returning to Bani Adi, and delivering Kelly to the battalion surgeon, Kydd went to bed. Evans rapped on the door five hours later.

And, when Kydd went to pull it open, the yeoman made a face. "You're due at a staff meeting in an hour, sir. I figured you'd want to shower and shave first."

Kydd yawned. "Thanks, Evans. What's going on?"

"We're going to pull out at 0600 tomorrow morning," Evans replied as he entered the cabin. "So the marines are taking the camp down and loading the barges."

Kydd considered that. The jarheads would have to move the antenna farm, the generator, and tons of supplies. It was a big job, and likely to last into the night. "What's the scuttlebutt on our destination?"

"People are guessing," Evans said, as he began to make coffee. "But if anyone knows for sure they aren't talking."

"Roger that," Kydd replied. "Does the XO know that we're pulling out?"

"Yes, sir."

"Good."

A mug of piping hot coffee was waiting for Kydd when he emerged from the bathroom. Kydd thanked Evans, got dressed, and had just enough time to grab an egg sandwich from the dining room before heading for the First Class Lounge. As Kydd entered he saw that Cole was seated near Goolsby. He sat next to the surgeon. "How's Kelly?"

"He's in Israel by now," the doctor replied. "We flew him out."

Kydd was about to ask a follow-up question, when Goolsby cleared his throat. "Good morning. As most, if not all of you know, we're pulling out of Bani Adi at 0600 tomorrow. That means there's a lot of work to do.

"With that in mind I'll keep the meeting short. I'd like to get things going by highlighting last night's raid. Agent Cole led a team comprised of Force Recon marines, with significant support from our British Allies, operating as part of Commander Kydd's flotilla."

The announcement produced a smattering of applause, along with some enthusiastic "Oorahs" from the marine contingent.

Goolsby nodded. "You'll be glad to know that Lance Corporal, soon to be *Corporal* Kelly is doing well, and is going to keep his leg."

The news produced sustained applause.

Goolsby turned to his right. "Agent Cole? I believe you have some news for us."

Cole nodded. "Based on Intel from numerous sources we know that a battalion strength contingent of PLA soldiers are traveling north from Sudan. We don't have any signals intelligence to rely on. But, since Iran and China are part of the Axis, and Iran maintains an important relationship with Hezbollah, it's logical to believe that the PLA troops have orders to support the terrorists. That means we might face *two* battalions when we attack the dam."

That provoked a buzz of conversation, as well as a rebuke from Goolsby. "Belay the bullshit, people … Please remember that effective though they may be in certain circumstances, Hezbollah fighters don't have much training, and aren't well led.

"As for the Chinese, the battalion Agent Cole referred to has never seen combat, and compared to our forces has a top-heavy command structure. So there's no need to soil your pants yet."

Kydd heard some chuckles, as Goolsby turned to his left. "The S-2 is going to brief you on the trip from Bani Adi to Minya, which is roughly 100-miles upstream. That information is classified for obvious reasons. Major Waller? Over to you."

Waller began by clicking through sat photos of the river. They went by rather quickly, and Kydd made a note to study them later. "Units from Commander Kydd's flotilla will lead the way," Waller informed them, "and suppress shore based attacks if any. They will also be on the lookout for feluccas, rafts, or other flotation devices that could carry IEDs."

Kydd made another note. The river was lousy with small craft—and interdicting them would be a fulltime job.

At that point Waller turned the session over to the S-3, and S-4, who had shared responsibility for loading the barges and riverboats with supplies and troops. It was important stuff, but Kydd's thoughts were focused on the responsibilities that he'd been given, and how to best carry them out.

After the meeting ended Kydd went to visit the flotilla where he met with his direct reports, including Chief Jones, and began to assign specific responsibilities.

"Let's start with the need to scout ahead and protect the convoy from IEDs. We have two SURC (Small Unit Riverine Craft), and I'm putting the chief in command of both."

Jones smiled. "Yes, sir."

"I suggest that you operate at least two miles ahead of the convoy," Kydd said. "There's no way that two boats can stop and search all the feluccas on the river so don't try.

"Tell your civilian translators to order the fishermen over to the west bank where they are to wait until the convoy is well upstream of them. Fire warning shots if you need to, and if a felucca tries to intercept the convoy, destroy it.

"Make sure both boats have plenty of water rations, fuel and ammo. Do you have any questions? No? Okay … That brings me to the second line of defense.

"Two patrol boats, one American and one British, will operate downriver from the SURCs, and ahead of the *Nile Queen*, which will be the lead vessel." Kydd would have preferred to put *two* of the more heavily armed American boats in the two-slot, but knew the Brits would feel slighted, and he wanted to keep the Allies happy if he could.

"When we come up on islands the lead patrol boats will have responsibility for checking *both* channels," Kydd added. "Plus they will respond to shore based attacks if any, watch for drifting mines, *and* provide support to the SURCs should they come under attack.

"The American two-boat will operate halfway down the length of the column, where it can respond to delayed attacks, and rescue any personnel who fall off the troopships. The last thing we want is for the convoy to stop, or for boats to turn back in an attempt to rescue people," Kydd added.

"The American three-boat, and British two-boat, will operate downriver from the convoy. Their job will be to protect the boats and barges from attack—and lend assistance should a vessel run aground. I will rely on Lieutenants Altman and Fox-Smith to make specific assignments."

The rest of the day, and half the night, was spent preparing for departure. Kydd hit the sack at 2300, got up at 0430, and was aboard the *Nile* when she got underway an hour-and-a-half later. It would have been nice to start the day on any one of his boats, but Kydd figured it was best to stay with Goolsby in the morning. Later, when the convoy was five or ten-miles upstream, he would go boat-to-boat and visit with the crews.

So Kydd was standing in the *Nile's* bow as the riverboat's port paddle stopped turning, and the starboard wheel churned the water, causing the boat to turn upstream.

As Kydd looked south he could see the lead patrol boats cruising along both banks in an attempt to keep the feluccas from relaunching, and to respond to an attack, should one come. But there was no attack. And, thanks to the soft morning light, the scene took on a magical feel.

Kydd was amazed by the way the eastern desert dunes crowded the Nile. Dark shadows marked each dune just as they had when explorers like Richard Burton, John Hanning Speke, and David Livingstone passed by.

As for the right bank, it was as different from the left as night is from day. It was lined with palm trees, greened by well-irrigated crops, and postcard perfect. Women carried jugs of water on their heads, a distant call to prayer could be heard over the rhythmic thump-thump-thump of the *Nile's* engine, and a stork took to the cool morning air. "It's beautiful, isn't it?"

Kydd turned to find that Cole was standing next to him. "Yes, it is," he agreed. "How is Mr. El-Baz doing?"

"Pretty well," Cole said, "although he's worried about his wife."

"That's understandable," Kydd said. "And *you?* How are you doing?"

Cole looked away. "A little better with each passing day. John was killed in Europe. His tank took a direct hit from a Russian missile."

"I'm sorry."

"Yeah," Cole said, as she put her sunglasses on. "So am I." Then she was gone.

CHAPTER SEVEN

The Aswan Dam, Egypt

Kantar awoke in what felt like a cold, clammy tomb. He didn't *want* to sleep in the chamber located over the nuclear bomb. But the door could be locked from the inside. And, while he was in the room, no one else could gain access to the nuke.

That seemed even more important after his conversation with Alawi two days earlier. Most of the noncoms liked Alawi and were willing to share information with him. "There are rumblings, sir," Alawi said. "Expressions of discontent among the troops."

When asked to be more specific Alawi shrugged. "*All* of our troops were chosen for their dedication to the Shia cause, but some are more fervent than others, and they grow impatient. The overall strategy means nothing to them. They want to blow the dam, kill millions of Sunnis, and claim their places in Jannah (paradise)."

Kantar asked if Sergeant Boustani was one of the fanatics, and Alawi answered by saying, "Boustani is their leader."

Kantar was reminded of what Secretary General Haddad had said. "Don't kill millions of Sunnis unless you must. Such an act would strengthen Sunni resolve, and turn the world against us."

But Boustani and his kind lacked the capacity to appreciate the big picture. It had been Kantar's hope that the fanatical noncom would get killed during the mission to Baranis Troglodytica. But the bastard emerged from the battle unscathed. *Maybe I can come up with another way to get him killed*, Kantar mused, as he rolled off the cot. *It's something to consider.*

Kantar checked to ensure that the bomb's trigger was securely zipped into a pocket, before leaving the chamber, and making his way down the hall to a restroom.

Following a sponge bath, and a shave, Kantar donned a fresh uniform. Then after taking his shaving kit and dirty clothes to the chamber, and locking the door, he made his way to the control room. The engineers were at their consoles and running the dam with the same efficiency they had prior to the takeover. But they were Sunnis... And it was safe to assume that they would vehemently oppose the sort of mass slaughter that Boustani and his fanatics had in mind. Still another variable to track.

Kantar walked past them to the office once occupied by the dam's chief engineer. A ragged Egyptian was seated outside with a guard stationed beside him. The man's eyes were focused on his sandal clad feet.

Alawi stood when Kantar entered. "Good morning, sir. Your breakfast will arrive soon."

Kantar smiled. "Thank you. Why is a beggar sitting outside my office?"

"His name, or one of his names, is Burhan Al-Bishi," Alawi said. "And in spite of appearances Al-Bishi isn't a beggar. He's a thief, a bandit, and an informer."

"Oh," Kantar responded as he sat behind the desk. "My mistake... I hope Mr. Al-Bishi will forgive me. Like I said, why is he here?"

"Al-Bishi works for a warlord named Hussain Urabi," Alawi explained. "He was with Urabi's men when they attacked a Chinese army unit in Sudan. A unit which is coming our way."

Kantar stared. "*Chinese?* You're joking."

"No sir," Alawi replied.

"Why did Al-Bishi come to us?"

"For money," Alawi answered. "The gold you brought back from Baranis Troglodytica has been very useful."

"What about proof?"

"Al-Bishi took some photos prior to the attack," Alawi answered. "Here's his phone."

Kantar accepted the device, and swiped from photo-to-photo. All were wide shots taken from a hilltop. So he couldn't see faces. But there was no mistaking the flag that flew from a long whip-style radio antenna. Kantar saw five gold stars on a field of red. He handed the phone to Alawi. "You did well, Amir ... Bring him in."

Al-Bishi was ushered into the office and ordered to sit on a chair. The informer's eyes darted from face-to-face as he dry washed his hands. The story was revealed in fits and starts. Urabi wanted to kill the Chinese and take their weapons.

But the Chinese were more capable than expected, and Urabi's men were forced to leave Sudan empty-handed. That meant no pay for fighters like Al-Bishi, who made their money looting dead bodies.

No, Al-Bishi didn't know why the Chinese were headed north. He assumed they'd been sent to help Hezbollah. China was aligned with Russia, Iran, and Pakistan after all.

But, Kantar mused, if there was an agreement to send Chinese troops his way—why hadn't he been notified?

Kantar thanked Al-Bishi, warned him to keep the conversation to himself, and urged the informer to keep Alawi up to date regarding Urabi's activities. Al-Bishi promised that he would, stuffed some gold coins into a pocket, and left in a hurry.

The more Kantar thought about the Chinese, the less he liked the prospect of their arrival. Yes, more troops would be helpful, but at what cost? Kantar had Shia fanatics to cope with, a contingent of Sunni engineers he couldn't entirely trust, and was about to enter negotiations with a warlord named Umar al-Hudaybi. And a battalion of Chinese would sap some of his attention.

Even worse the officer in command of the Chinese troops might try to take over. And Kantar would have more mouths to feed. "Call the airport," Kantar said. "Tell them to prepare the helicopter. I want you to fly south, locate the Chinese, and find out what their orders are."

Alawi was visibly surprised, and pleased, to be trusted with such an important mission. "Yes, sir!" he said enthusiastically, and rushed out of the office.

Kantar smiled. In spite of all the difficulties that faced him, there was one person he could count on, and that was Amir Alawi.

***

Dongola, Sudan

Rather than a single day as Bo first imagined, the journey from the village of Wahat Saghira to the ancient city of Dongola consumed four days. Two of which had been spent in the city of Al Dabbah waiting for engine parts to be flown in. Now, rather than travel at night, the battalion was hunkered down in the town of Dongola.

After establishing a defensive perimeter within a U-shaped wall built by the British, and setting a schedule for patrols, Bo gave two-thirds of his troops permission to do as they pleased. Some wandered about buying trinkets and snapping selfies.

Others, far too many in Bo's opinion, sat in scraps of shade playing a card game called Dou Dizhu, or Fighting the Landlord. As for Bo—he'd done his homework, and knew Dongola had been a center for Nubian civilization. Traces of which were still visible.

Bullet shaped tombs dotted the surrounding desert, crumbling walls suggested structures long gone, and a row of free-standing columns marked the remains of an ancient temple.

There was military history to contemplate as well. Dongola was the location of British Field Marshal Herbert Kitchener's victory over Mahdist tribes in 1896.

Of course Kitchener was equally well known for his scorched earth tactics against the Boers in South Africa, and the creation of civilian concentration camps, where thousands died of starvation and disease. Not the kind of career Bo wanted to emulate, no matter how celebrated it was at the time.

Bo was touring the open ruins of a 900-year-old tomb when a helicopter roared overhead. That wasn't especially remarkable since Dongola had a small airport. It wasn't until 20 minutes later that Xu's voice came over the radio. "Sorry to bother you, sir … But we have a visitor. Over."

"What does he want? Over."

"He claims to a member of Hezbollah, sir … And part of the unit that controls the dam. Over."

That was a surprise. Bo felt his pulse quicken. "Thank you. Offer him refreshments. I'll be there shortly."

A brisk walk took Bo back to the compound. A tan tarp was stretched over crisscrossing ropes. It threw shade onto some folding chairs. A tea set sat atop an ammo crate.

Xu, and a young man in desert camos, were waiting for him. They stood. "Colonel Bo," Xu said, "This is Lieutenant Alawi, 2nd in command of the Hezbollah commando detachment that controls the dam."

Alawi snapped to attention and offered a salute which Bo returned. Then they shook hands. "Welcome to Dongola," Bo said. "Please, have a seat. We have tea … Would you care for some?"

"Yes, please," Alawi said, as he sat down.

Once they were settled, Bo poured, and each man took a sip. "That's delicious," Alawi said. "What kind is it?"

"Lu'an Melon Seed," Bo replied. "I'm glad you like it. So, Lieutenant, what brings you our way?"

The answer to that was obvious, but Alawi recognized the question for what it was, an opening gambit. And chess was a game he knew well. "Our intelligence agents keep a close eye on the North Sudan," Alawi lied. "One of them told us that you were attacked by a warlord named Urabi. Wahda Kantar sent me to see if you need assistance."

Bo couldn't help but be impressed by the fact that Hezbollah not only knew that the battalion had been attacked, but knew who was responsible. As for the offer of help, that was clearly spurious, because if Hezbollah knew about the attack—they knew about the battalion's state of readiness as well. "We don't need any help," Bo replied. "But thank you."

"Good," Alawi replied. "May I inquire as to your plans?"

Bo took a sip of tea. Alawi's commanding officer was clearly concerned about the fact that a battalion of PLA soldiers was traveling north. And that was understandable. But how should he play it? Should he claim to be on a mission unrelated to the dam? Such as securing a site for a drone base? Or, should he claim to be Hezbollah's best friend?

Bo decided that the answer, like so many answers, could be found in The Art of War. A book written more 2,500 years earlier by a Chinese general named Sun Tzu.

"True excellence is to plan secretly, to move surreptitiously, to foil the enemy's intentions and balk his schemes, so that at last the day may be won without shedding a drop of blood."

"Our plans are simple," Bo lied. "My orders are to travel north, place my battalion under Wahda Kantar's orders, and to defend the dam. Of course your commanding officer may decide to flood the valley. Or is that a bluff?"

The Chinese were going to help. That's what Alawi wanted to hear. But he didn't believe it. First, Kantar was suspicious of the Chinese, which meant Alawi should be suspicious as well.

Second, the reference to a "bluff" was jarring, because anyone who was familiar with Hezbollah's history, would know that the threat was very real.

Third, if Colonel Bo's battalion was going to help, why hadn't the Wahda been notified of that in advance? "That's good news," Alawi said. "The sooner you arrive the better. The Allied expeditionary force is moving up the Nile as we speak."

"We're agreed then," Bo said with a smile. "Please join us for lunch... And invite your pilot. It won't be fancy, but we're soldiers, and used to hardship."

Alawi thought it was best to accept the invitation, and agreed to inspect the battalion with Xu, while arrangements were made. And it would have been fun to talk to Xu if he hadn't had so many things on his mind.

Lunch consisted of Haricot beans in a spicy tomato sauce with chunks of lamb. It was served in a local restaurant under a slow-motion fan. A boy wearing a red fez and matching vest stood by to swat the flies.

Much to Alawi's surprise the food was good. So good that his pilot requested more. The fact that the principals didn't know or trust each other meant that conversation was stilted.

Pleasantries were exchanged once the meal was over. Alawi and his pilot left for the airport shortly thereafter. Bo and Xu were back at the battalion's compound, hands shading their eyes, as the helicopter took off.

Bo held out his hand so that Xu could place the remote on it. *I'm sorry Lieutenant Alawi,"* Bo thought. *But, based on your organization's track record, I know your Wahda will press the button when the time comes. As would you.*

Bo pressed the button. There was a bright flash of light as the explosive charge went off. That was followed by a resounding BOOM, and a cloud of black smoke. What remained of the helo spiraled into the ground. A cloud of dust rose. "Take some men," Bo ordered. "If you find survivors kill them. Bury the bodies."

***

Aswan Dam, Egypt

Could Allied drones penetrate the dam's air defenses? The officer in charge of the Iranian missile techs said, "No." But Kantar wasn't so sure. *Three* Hezbollah leaders had been assassinated by Allied drones since the start of the war. And he had no desire to be the fourth. Besides, even if drones couldn't attack, satellites could photograph him from space. Or so Kantar had been told.

All of which meant Kantar couldn't go out for the walks that had long been part of his daily exercise regimen. But what he *could* do was hike through miles of corridors, tunnels and passageways inside of the dam complex.

Some sections of the walk were more enjoyable than others. The enormous power house was his favorite. It had the high ceilings of a world class mosque, sliding gantries, and evenly spaced yellow turbines. And as he entered the west side of the cavernous space Kantar's thoughts were on Alawi.

The helicopter was overdue, and repeated efforts to reach it by radio had failed. Maybe it had developed mechanical trouble and been forced down. Did the helo carry emergency supplies? Kantar hoped so, because it was impossible to survive in the desert without water.

A shot rang out and Kantar's lead bodyguard fell dead. Kantar had no idea where the shot came from nor did he take the time to look around. There was a yellow railing on his left. He threw himself over the top and fell twelve feet to the ramp below. Bursts of AK-47 fire raked the area above as the surviving bodyguard was fired on. Then the noise stopped. Kantar drew his pistol. Damn it! Boustani … It had to be.

Kantar's hand went to the remote. It was buttoned into a cargo pocket. He hurried down the ramp into the depths of the dam.

Bullets spanged off metal as a rifle was fired from above. He recognized the voice as Boustani's. "Don't bother to run *alkalb* (dog)… We'll find you."

Kantar fired two shots. Then he followed the ramp down and out onto the face of the dam. He could hear a steady roar and see water shooting out of the pipe located twenty-feet below. There was nowhere to go. A bullet snapped past his head. Kantar jammed the pistol into its holster and jumped. The jet of water from the outfall hit his body two-seconds later and propelled him out and away from the dam. Gravity pulled him down. *I've never been with a woman*, Kantar thought. *And now I'm going to die.*

Kantar's feet broke through the surface of the roiling water and he plunged down into the depths of the Nile. *Swim*, Kantar told himself, *even though you don't know how.*

Kantar's arms flailed, his feet kicked, and his lungs started to burn. Then his head broke the surface providing him with a brief opportunity to gulp air.

But not for long. The weight of his combat boots and uniform were pulling him down. Kantar tried to reach his boots in hopes of untying them. But the effort was futile.

So Kantar kicked as hard as he could. He broke the surface again, arms splashing in a desperate attempt to remain afloat. Someone grabbed his belt. "Get a grip boy," a voice said. "Help pull him in."

Kantar felt hands grab his armpits and heard the voice say, "Together now."

Metal scraped the surface of Kantar's back as the fishermen hauled him out of the water. Kantar fell onto the bottom of the boat where he stared up into the achingly blue sky. *Thanks be to Allah. I'm alive.*

Kantar managed to sit. Half a dozen perch were sliding around the bottom of the felucca. Two men, one younger than the other, stared at him. "Look at the uniform," the younger fisherman said. "He's a Shia. From the dam."

The older man nodded. "Kill him."

Kantar fumbled for the pistol, managed to draw it, and fired. The first bullet struck the younger man's left arm. The second entered his left ear and blew the right side of his skull out.

The surviving Sunni attacked with a spear. Kantar felt a searing pain as it passed between his left arm and chest. He fired again. The slug struck the man's bare chest. He fell back into the bottom of the boat. Had the shots been heard? Kantar took a desperate look around. No, there were some fishing boats to the north, but none of them were coming his way.

Kantar's breath came in short gasps. He started to shake as the adrenaline drained from his system. He needed to rest, to think, but the boat was drifting downstream toward Hiesa Island, and the people who lived there. *The bodies*, Kantar thought. *And my uniform. I need to get rid of them.*

An eddy caused the boat to turn as Kantar removed his shirt, pants and boots. He was about to drop the bundle overboard when he remembered the remote. Was it still there? What if it wasn't? Kantar felt a sense of desperation as he felt for the lump and found it.

After removing the remote, Kantar threw the rest into the river, confident that his boots would weight everything down. Next came the difficult task of dumping the old man into the Nile. Would someone notice the body? Probably … But he hoped to be on land by the time that occurred.

Then came the unpleasant task of pulling the other Egyptian's filthy shorts off, and removing his cheap sandals, before rolling the body up and over the side. The current carried the corpse away. The shorts were a little baggy—but Kantar managed to cinch them in.

Hiesa Island was closer by then and Kantar had no intention of landing on it. The oars were secured to vertical posts with cord, and unexpectedly crude, being little more than lengths of lumber. Still, something was better than nothing.

Kantar settled himself onto the middle seat and began to pull. His goal was to land on the east bank of the river near the area where the Russian-Hezbollah fighters originally came down. From that point a two-mile hike would get him to Launcher # 4, which was part of the dam's missile defense system. The noncom in charge of the facility was an Iranian named Babak Marwan. A man who wasn't likely to be part of Boustani's plot.

One of Kantar's Hezbollah loyalists was stationed at the facility both to learn about the launcher, and keep an eye on the Iranians. With assistance from the two men Kantar planned to recruit more personnel from other missile sites.

Kantar looked over his shoulder occasionally, in hopes that the trip would soon end. But due to the clumsy oars, and his lack of skill, the endeavor took twenty minutes.

As the felucca neared the shoreline it was time to look for a landing spot. A small cove offered Kantar the opportunity he was looking for. Another felucca was pulled up on the beach, but the owner was nowhere to be seen.

Once the hull scraped the bottom Kantar got out and checked to ensure that the remote was in his pocket. It was. But a horrible thought occurred to Kantar. What, if anything, had the water done to the device?

After removing the remote Kantar flipped the protective cover out of the way. It wasn't watertight, and the inner surface was wet.

There were three buttons, each labeled with Cyrillic script, and three matching indicator lights. What Kantar assumed to be the firing switch was located at the bottom of the remote and protected with a sliding cover. A green light was on. Did that mean what he hoped it meant? That the device was on, and functional? It seemed logical, but there was no way to be sure.

Kantar removed a bottle of water from the boat and gave it a push. It took a moment for the current to find the felucca and drag it away. Then Kantar put the remote down long enough to wade out into the river, before returning to shore, and retrieving the device.

Kantar's wet skin and clothes helped to keep him cool as he followed a trail east. But not for long. The merciless sun bit into the skin on Kantar's back, and sucked the moisture out of his shorts within fifteen minutes, leaving him hot and dry. And the fisherman's flip flops were far from ideal for the rocky ground.

It wasn't long before the trail turned into a dry creek bed through which water flowed two or three times a year. Kantar knew he was headed in the right direction...But was the missile base directly ahead of him? Or off to one side? Maybe, if he was lucky, he would catch a glimpse of the facility's communications tower.

Kantar scanned the horizon as he walked, paused to take an occasional sip of water, and wondered what was happening at the dam. Alawi was missing. That left Sergeant Major Damji in command. Kantar's bodyguards were dead, and he was missing. What would Damji make of that? Or had he been killed as well?

Doubt and fear continued to plague Kantar as he climbed up out of a ravine and spotted a palm tree! No, *two* palm trees, both standing next to a deserted building.

Suddenly Kantar knew where he was. The highway that led from the dam to Aswan city was up ahead. And, after turning south, he would come upon the dirt road that led east to the missile battery. Kantar felt a sense of renewed energy as he walked past the ruins and out to the highway. There wasn't any traffic and for good reason. His men had established a checkpoint just south of Aswan City and the locals weren't allowed to proceed beyond it.

The pavement was hot, but easier to walk on, and Kantar was eager to reach the base. After fifteen minutes he came to the unmarked turnoff, took a left, and followed the dirt road east. It wasn't long before Kantar came to a cyclone fence, a gate, and a post with a phone mounted on it.

Beyond the barrier Kantar could see the triangular signs that marked the facility's protective minefield. The mines had been laid by the Muslim Brotherhood to protect the missile battery and left in place by Kantar. Attackers could destroy the gate, and proceed on the road, but even a small force of men would be able to stop them.

Kantar hurried over to the phone. He lifted the protective cover and pushed a button. Nothing happened. He tried again and again. The man who answered was clearly annoyed. "This is a military facility, in a restricted area, and you must leave immediately."

"This is Wahda Kantar … Send someone to open the gate. That's an order."

There was a pause as the technician thought that over. "Yes, sir," he said finally. "But if I arrive at the gate, and someone other than Wahda Kantar is waiting there, I will shoot that person in the face."

Kantar grinned as he replaced the phone. He saw a dust cloud before he heard the engine, and an American made jeep with Egyptian markings skidded to a halt. A noncom hopped out and drew his pistol. "I told you I would …" Then he saw Kantar's face. "Wahda, is that *you?*"

"It is," Kantar answered. "Open the gate. We have a lot of things to do."

Tech Sergeant Babak Marwan was shocked to see a half-naked Kantar appear inside the air conditioned prefab. The unit was located adjacent to the transporter-mounted S-300VM surface-to-air (SAM) missile system, which consisted of a launcher, a command post, four radars—and a supply of SAMs that could destroy incoming targets up to 200-miles away.

Marwan was clearly shocked as Kantar described the attack, and the ordeal that followed. "That's terrible, sir ... I had no idea."

"So you haven't been in touch with the dam? What about the 0900 status report?"

Marwan's eyes widened. "I spoke with Sergeant Boustani."

Kantar nodded. "That would seem to indicate that he's in charge. Can we communicate with the other missile batteries without Boustani knowing?"

Marwan frowned. "Not if he's monitoring radio transmissions."

Kantar made a face. "I think it's safe to assume that he is. Put Basri in charge of communications. No radio messages will be sent without my approval."

Corporal Basri was the man Kantar had sent to keep an eye on Marwan. If the Iranian resented that he managed to conceal it. "Boustani doesn't know I survived," Kantar added. "Let's keep it that way."

"Yes, sir."

"I need a shower, a uniform, boots, a holster, ammunition, something to eat and a driver. I will visit each missile battery, brief the man in charge, and provide them a frequency that Boustani won't know to monitor. Then we will assemble a force consisting of men from each location and retake the dam. Do you have any questions?"

Marwan shook his head. "No, sir."

"Good. I am promoting you to acting lieutenant, subject to approval by your superiors, and to the position of executive officer in Alawi's absence."

Marwan looked pleased. "Thank you, sir. I will obtain everything you requested."

There were six missile batteries in all, established to defend against multiple threats and provide redundancy. Three were located on each side of the dam.

Sites five and six were closest so Kantar went to visit them first. Once each noncom had been briefed, and the new frequency tested, Kantar left.

Kantar was hidden in the back of the jeep as his driver took him across the top of the dam to the west side. Such battery-to-battery visits weren't uncommon, and no effort was made to stop the vehicle as it passed the control building.

As Kantar peeked through the gap between the fabric top and its frame he took note of the fact that a single sentry was posted out front. Normally there would be two. Was Boustani short-handed? Or had the second sentry gone inside to take a pee? There was no way to know.

After visiting the batteries on the west side of the Nile, Kantar chose to remain at site two, rather than cross the dam again. Now that all of the missile sites were under his control Kantar could send Marwan to Aswan city with orders to take command of the fighters stationed there. That left 46 men who were allied with Boustani, being held prisoner, or dead.

Kantar felt tired, but wasn't about to let the mutineers settle in. Maybe Boustani knew his commanding officer was alive and maybe he didn't. It made no difference.

Rather than attack from the top of the dam, which Boustani would expect, Kantar was going to approach from the peninsula of land that jutted out in front of the dam.

Kantar gave orders for the men on both sides of the dam to secure feluccas, prepare for battle, and perform the Isha (night) prayer. After praying Kantar took a nap.

A private woke him at 2400. Fear was waiting for him. But so was Kantar's pride. *Boustani took the dam from you,* Kantar thought. *Like candy from a child. Will you allow him to win?*

No, Kantar decided. *I won't.* The anger was sufficient to overwhelm the fear. Kantar got up, put his uniform on, and checked both pistols. The one he'd arrived with, plus a Russian PB with suppressor. The other fighters had Russian weapons too.

Each missile site had been ordered to contribute three men to the larger team, which meant that Kantar had a combined force of 18 men, 19 counting himself. A truck carried the western contingent down to the Nile where two large feluccas were waiting. Street lights marked the top of the dam.

Other lights were visible too, on the island of Hiesa, and beyond. That seemed to indicate that the Egyptian engineers were still alive and on the job. But for how long? Even if Boustani couldn't detonate the bomb, and didn't know how to operate the dam, he *could* execute the staff. And with no one to run the dam's equipment millions of Sunnis would lose power.

Kantar sat in the stern where he could control the rudder, as the first boat departed the bank. There were two oarsmen, but they weren't used to pulling in unison, and the one on the right swore as he missed a stroke. "Silence!" a noncom said harshly. "Or you will regret it."

Cordage creaked as the oars splashed into the Nile, and men heaved. The current from the outflow was strong, and it grew even stronger, as they neared the dam.

Kantar was wearing a headset. He whispered into the boom mike knowing that all the team members could hear him. "Careful now, we're getting close. Snipers, find your targets."

The sharpshooters had Chukavin sniper rifles with night scopes and suppressors. They were prone, weapons on sand bags, at the bow of each boat.

There was no wind to speak of. So once past the turbulence the nearly black water was flat. "This is Farhad. I have a target, *one* target, at six o'clock."

"Confirmed," a second voice said. "One target, at six o'clock."

"Kill him," Kantar said coldly. As he said it Kantar knew there was a chance, a *slim* chance, that he was putting an innocent man to death. But only if loyal soldiers had been able to overpower the mutineers, and post sentries, and did so without notifying the rest of Kantar's command. He heard a series of soft pops. "Target down," the second soldier said. "Scanning."

That was wise. Perhaps a second man was present, but wasn't visible for some reason. Or another soldier could suddenly arrive. "Assume nothing and survive." That was a lesson every Hezbollah fighter had been taught. But as the feluccas converged on the peninsula no additional targets were observed.

Kantar was holding the Russian pistol in his right hand as he stepped into a foot of water. He was barely aware of the discomfort as he made his way up the beach to the spot where the dead sentry lay. His name was Kazem. A boy really, no more than 18, and impressionable. "Search him."

A minute passed while a fighter searched the body. "Here's his radio, sir ... And a key."

The radio would allow Kantar to monitor Boustani's radio traffic. As for the key, that would open the access door at the foot of the dam, and allow them to enter.

"Remember," Kantar told the men, as they prepared to enter the dam. "Boustani may have prisoners. So be careful who you shoot. Oh, and one more thing ... Take Boustani alive if you can. Let's go."

The key turned in the lock, the door opened, and an Iranian started up the stairs. A Hezbollah fighter carrying a shotgun was right behind him. Kantar was third. The dead man's radio burped static. Kantar recognized Boustani's voice. "Sentries will report." Such checks were part of the standard operating procedure Kantar had put in place. They were made at random times and intended to keep sentries on their toes. The metal stairs shook slightly as the assault team hurried up them. "Addi." "Gamil." "Ismat."

Three, Kantar thought, *plus an equal number who are sleeping. And some more in the control area. Something like 16 men.*

"Kazem!" Boustani said. "Wake up."

Ten seconds passed without a reply. Then Boustani spoke again. "Chances are that the idiot fell asleep. I'll check. But keep a sharp lookout just in case."

As the team arrived on level three of six, Kantar herded them into the shadows. "Boustani's coming! Remember, I want him alive."

It wasn't long before metal rattled and heavy footsteps were heard as a person descended the stairs. Kantar wasn't about to deliver a warning. The Russian pistol made a clacking sound as Kantar fired two bullets. One hit the mutineer in his right leg. He uttered a cry of pain and fell sideways. Two Iranians jumped him.

Boustani tried to struggle but it was useless. It took less than a minute to strip the noncom of weapons and bind his extremities. "Put a pressure dressing on that wound," Kantar ordered. "Keep him alive so I can kill him." A guard was left to make sure that Boustani couldn't escape.

The mutineers were leaderless now. But Kantar was under no illusions. Boustani's followers would fight to the death. They had no choice.

The assault team continued up the switch backing stairs and soon arrived on the main level. "Be careful," Kantar cautioned.

"There's likely to be one or two guards in the control room, and one or two out front."

But when the challenge came it was from *behind* the group. "Stop right there!" a voice ordered. "Who are you?"

That was when Kantar realized that Boustani had been smart enough to have guards roaming the facility—as well as standing guard at specific points. And, as his men turned to face the threat, a grenade clattered across the floor. The device exploded with a loud bang and sent knee-high shrapnel flying in every direction. Two of his men fell, their legs cut out from under them, as others fired into the darkness.

Kantar knew that would bring other fighters on the run. He turned just in time to see two men round a corner, their AK-47s at the ready. Kantar fired the Russian pistol, saw a fighter fall, and was about to shoot at the second attacker, when someone else cut him down.

A burst of gunfire was heard, followed by a terse, "Traitor down."

"Medics!" Kantar shouted. "See to the wounded. The rest of you on me."

Kantar led the team down the corridor and paused just shy of the control room. Then, careful to expose as little of his body as possible, he took a peek around the corner.

Terrified engineers were huddled against a wall with their hands raised. No mutineers were visible. That seemed to suggest that the men killed moments earlier had been on duty in the control area prior to being pulled away. "Check out front," Kantar ordered. "There should be at least one man out there."

Two fighters went to check. One of them responded by radio. "There's no one here. I think the sentries ran."

"All right," Kantar said. "Remain there until you are relieved."

Kantar turned to an Iranian corporal. "Take some men. Search for prisoners."

Then it was time for Kantar to speak with the engineers. It turned out that they knew about the mutiny, believed Kantar to be dead, and had been on the receiving end of Boustani's rage. "He threatened to kill us many times," one man said. "And forced us to remove the bomb from the hole."

That was a surprise. *"Why?"*

"Boustani wanted to take the bomb away, and find experts who could make a trigger for it," a second man said. "But, when he wasn't around, his men talked about selling it."

Kantar considered that. What would a baby nuke bring on the black market? A lot. That was for sure. "Where is it?" he demanded.

"In the chamber where you sleep," the first man answered.

"Well, it's going back in the hole," Kantar told them. "Nothing has changed. Return to work."

Kantar went to his chamber, and sure enough, the bomb had been reeled up out of the pipe and was dangling from a tripod. His bed lay on its side. His personal effects were scattered about. *The sword*, Kantar thought, as he scanned the chamber. *Where is it?*

Kantar left the room and made his way to the broom closet which, as a noncom, Boustani had been entitled to. The ceremonial scimitar was hanging from a hook. Kantar took it down. Carefully. Reverently. His radio was on. "Corporal Zaki."

"Sir!"

"Summon help. Bring Boustani up to the main entrance."

"Yes, sir."

That was when the Iranian corporal arrived. "Boustani had 12 prisoners, sir ... All locked in the same room."

Kantar felt a surge of relief. "Thanks to Allah. "Take me to them."

The prisoners were in the employee break room, eating and drinking when Kantar entered. A cheer went up. That was followed by a gabble of conversation, man hugs, and joyful backslapping. Once the celebrations were over a fighter looked Kantar in the eye. A bloody bandage was wrapped around his head. "Did Boustani survive?"

"Yes."

"We want him."

Kantar nodded. "Follow me."

Boustani had been delivered to the control room by the time the men arrived. He was lying on the floor, clutching his leg. "It hurts! I need a doctor!"

"Drag the traitor outside," Kantar ordered.

Two ex-prisoners took the instruction literally, grabbing the noncom's arms and dragging him out through the main door. The civilian engineers sat silent—eyes glued to their screens.

The cool night air felt good. Kantar took a deep draught of it. Then he pointed to the circle of light thrown off by the nearest streetlight. "There … Put him there, on his knees. Bind his hands behind him."

That was when Boustani saw the sword. "No! I am a soldier for Allah!"

"You're a piece of dog shit," Kantar replied. "You can recite the Shahada if you wish."

Boustani mumbled the words as he was positioned on his knees. "I testify that there is no god but Allah, and I testify that Muhammad is the messenger of Allah…"

Kantar planted his feet, and raised the sword high. Light glinted from the blade.

Kantar had read stories about how Saudi executioners could sever a head with a single blow. He had no such ambitions. The Sayif al-Dawla (sword-of-state) rose, fell, and rose again. Finally, when Kantar felt the last bit of gristle part, Boustani's head rolled free. Dead eyes stared up into the light. The newly freed prisoners shouted, "*Allahu akbar!*" Justice had been done.

CHAPTER EIGHT

Esna, Egypt

The first sign of trouble was just that, a large freshly painted sign which was mounted on a raft, and anchored in the middle of the river. "LOCK FEE $1M U.S." That was followed by a phone number. "They saw us coming," a petty officer named Murphy said.

"Yeah," Kydd replied. "They sure as hell did."

The two men were standing in the bow of a 38-foot SURC just aft of the gun position. The boat rocked gently as Kydd opened his mike. "One-Six actual to Two-Six. Over."

"This is Two-Six actual," Altman replied. "Over."

"Someone posted a sign in the middle of the river," Kydd said. "They want a million dollars if we use the locks. We're going upstream to take a look around. Over."

"Roger that ... I'll pass the word. Over."

"Okay, Murph," Kydd said. "Let's knock on the door. Action stations."

Action stations in the SURC's case consisted of three .50 caliber machine guns. Two in the bow and one in the stern. Murphy had three gunners plus the engineman at the wheel. "Here," the petty officer said, as he handed Kydd a Heckler & Koch HK416 rifle. "Just in case."

Kydd's eyes were on the river ahead as the boat accelerated, came on step, and threw waves port and starboard. A dozen feluccas, some with sails raised, were tacking back and forth. They rocked wildly as the SURC roared past. None of the Egyptians waved.

The town of Nuju an Nawasir was visible off the starboard side. Kydd saw a mix of two- and three-story tan colored buildings backed by a minaret and a cell tower further inland.

***

The countryside east of the river was more agricultural. Sun baked dunes could be seen out beyond the verdant farms.

Kydd turned his binoculars upstream. Esna's locks, the *only* locks on the Nile, were up ahead. In order to proceed upriver, which was Goolsby's plan for the convoy, the Allied vessels would have to transit the locks one-at-a-time.

Once a boat entered, the gate was closed behind it. Then as water was pumped from the high Nile to the low Nile the boat would rise. Then the upper gate would cycle open, allowing the vessel to proceed. "Gun emplacement," Murphy said. "Starboard side, one o'clock."

Kydd swung his glasses to the right. There was a puff of smoke followed by a bang as a shell rumbled through the air. It landed half-a-mile ahead of the SURC and tossed a waterspout into the air. That was followed by a *second* column of water as a battery on the east bank fired. The boat performed a nosedive as the helmsman cut power. "Warning shots," Kydd observed.

"Yup," Murphy agreed. "The cannons look like Russian-made 122mm D-30s. They're old, but effective."

Kydd frowned. "How do you know *that?*"

Murphy looked offended. "I'm a gunner's mate, sir. It's my business to know."

Kydd laughed. "So it is ... My bad. So, if those tubes have a weakness, what is it?"

"A slow rate of fire," Murphy replied. "We're talking 5 to 6 rounds per minute. And, in order to track a moving target, the cannon-cockers will have to spin them around by hand."

Kydd took that in. He didn't have any big guns, but maybe he didn't need any. A couple of Hellfire missiles could do the job. Then Kydd saw why he was wrong. The guns had been incorporated into the lock's structure.

That meant it would be nearly impossible to use a Hellfire without inflicting damage on the lock itself. And that was why the artillery pieces were positioned where they were. Someone had a brain. "The lock is opening," Murphy observed. "And there's something inside."

Kydd jerked his glasses to the left, and sure enough, a vessel had started to emerge. Not just any vessel … A gunboat. Kydd could see the turret on the bow. "Grab some photos," he ordered.

Both SURCs carried digital cameras for reconnaissance purposes. Murphy's was close at hand. He was snapping away when the vessel fired. There was a loud bang followed by the rumble of a shell passing through the air. Smoke drifted away from the gunboat's turret. "What do you think, Skipper?" Murphy inquired, as a gout of water shot up into the air. "Should we back off?"

"This is show and tell," Kydd replied. "They're showing us what they have so we can run and tell. Let's wait to see if that boat will turn broadside to us. I'll bet the S2 would love some pictures of that."

The enemy vessel obliged. It had a mottled desert-sand and black-striped paint job. Kydd could see the bow gun, the rocket launcher aft of the boat's superstructure, and the turret in the stern. And that was to say nothing of secondary weapons like machine guns and grenade launchers. "Holy shit," Murphy said. "That sucker must be 90-feet long."

"Yeah," Kydd agreed. "It looks mean as hell. All right, let's go home. Slowly though—no wake."

Murphy grinned. "Right . . . Fuck them."

Kydd got on the horn. "One-Six actual to Two-Six. Over."

"This is Two-Six actual . . . Go. Over."

"There are two shore batteries, plus what looks like a 90-foot gunboat waiting for us. Please inform battalion command that I think the convoy should drop anchor.

"I will report aboard the *Nile* in an hour or so. In the meantime Bat-Six might want to have someone call that phone number. This is Egypt. Who knows? A million might translate to 50K once the haggling is over. The fee might be worth it. Over."

Kydd knew Goolsby would be pissed off about a delay, *any* delay, for any reason. So it made sense to take the SURC downriver and confront the lion in his den.

When Kydd arrived he was pleased to see that the convoy was anchored about 100-yards off the west bank. Marines were being ferried ashore to secure the area beyond.

The helmsman brought the boat in with a flourish and came to a sudden stop. One of the *Nile's* civilian crew stood ready with a boathook. Kydd took the HK416 with him. He liked the feel of it. Steep stairs took him up to the main deck where Evans was waiting. "The colonel will see you in his cabin sir."

"And?"

"And he has a full head of steam."

"Oh goody," Kydd replied. "Please lead the way."

Kydd hadn't been invited to Goolsby's private quarters before. It was located on the main deck in the stern. Two marines stood guard outside. Kydd was required to produce ID and leave his weapons with them. As Kydd entered he saw that Goolsby was seated behind an ornate desk framed by a view of the Nile. No one else was present. Goolsby nodded. "Have a seat."

There was something foreboding about the moment. Or was that his imagination? But the feeling persisted as Kydd took one of two guest chairs. Goolsby formed a steeple with his fingers. "I understand there are some obstacles up ahead."

"Yes, sir."

"Please share the details."

Kydd told Goolsby about the sign, the shore batteries, and the gunboat. Once the report was complete the marine nodded. "Thank you… The S-2 sent a drone up to look around. Your assessment is consistent with his."

"However," Goolsby added, as he put some weight on his forearms. "Lieutenant Altman says you want to pay our enemies rather than fight them. *If* that counsel had originated from an officer with a combat record less sterling than your own I would question his or her courage.

"But, since that isn't the case, I'll say this… We aren't here to pay people off. We're here to fight. I will instruct the S-4 to call the number, pretend to enter negotiations, and drag the process out. If he's able to discern who we're dealing with, then so much the better.

"In the meantime you will use the forces under your command to go up river, clear the way, and take control of the dam by noon tomorrow. Need I remind you that 10-million lives are at stake?"

Kydd's heart was pounding in his chest, he knew his face was bright red. Admiral Ducey had it right. Goolsby *was* an asshole. "Sir, yes, sir."

The chair creaked as Goolsby leaned back. His eyes resembled black stones. "Dismissed." Kydd got up, performed an about face, and left.

Face burning, Kydd retrieved his weapons, and made his way to the deck below. The S-2 and his staff occupied adjoining cabins. Both were packed with marines and their electronics. Waller was peering at a screen as Kydd entered. A smile appeared on his face as he turned. "Commander Kydd … Welcome to my den. What can we do for you?"

"Can I speak to you for a moment?"

"Oh," Waller said. "It's like that, is it? Please join me on my private verandah. It's in the shade."

All of the more expensive cabins had balcony-like verandahs where, prior to the war, guests could sit and watch Egypt glide by. Kydd followed the S-2 out. "Don't tell me," Waller said after closing the door. "Let me guess. The colonel chewed your ass. Some nonsense about fighting instead of paying."

Kydd's surprise must have been visible on his face. Waller chuckled. "Welcome to the party, Commander. Very few of us escape unscathed. That said, Goolsby is quite competent, and that's the thing isn't it? Personally, I'd pay, if the price was right. But I'm a major."

Kydd smiled. "Thanks… That helps. I have orders to go south, and capture the locks. What, if anything, have you got for me?"

"Follow me," Waller said, as he opened the door. "I'll share what I have."

"Meet Corporal Tanaka," Waller said, as they stopped behind a chair. "He's one of our drone operators."

"The *best* operator," Tanaka said, as he turned to Waller.

"But not the most modest," Waller added. "This is Commander Kydd. He'd like to see the parade footage."

Tanaka touched a series of keys and video began to roll. Kydd watched from above as a drone swept over the SURC he'd been riding on and went straight for the lock complex.

A group of armed men were gathered on the bridge that crossed the top of the locks. The gunboat was below and nosing its way out. "Now watch *that* guy," Waller said, using his pen as a pointer. "The one with the red checkered *keffiah* (scarf). We think he's the man."

The gunboat fired, and as gray smoke drifted away from the gun turret, the men raised their rifles. "The show's over," Waller said. "So Red Scarf leaves. Fortunately Tanaka had the good sense to follow the parade rather than bring his drone back."

"I'm a genius," Tanaka added, as the drone followed the pedestrians over to a street where four vehicles were parked. Two motorcycles were positioned in front of them. Each with an armed rider.

A classic gun truck, complete with a .50 caliber machine gun was next in line, followed by a white Land Rover. A subordinate held the door open as Red Scarf got in. A military transport loaded with bodyguards brought up the rear.

The motorcycles took off and the drone followed as the "parade" turned onto a main thoroughfare. People scattered as the procession made a series of turns and stopped in front of a three-story building. Kydd saw that sentries were posted on the roof.

"Esna was called Latopolis in ancient times," Waller said. "And it was a bishopric. Meaning an area overseen by a bishop. He lived in that building. A long succession of Egyptian officials have used it since."

"So, who's living there *now?*" Kydd inquired.

"According to one of our civilian interpreters the man in the red scarf is named Hussain Urabi. He's an Egyptian colonel turned warlord who's known to raid cities as far south as Sudan."

"I'd like to have a copy of that footage," Kydd said.

"Done," Tanaka replied, as he passed a USB stick back over his shoulder.

Waller smiled. "Tanaka is a full-time pain in the ass. Okay, let's discuss the gunboat."

A new video locked up. "That," Waller said, as the drone hovered above the vessel, "is a Russian Shmel Class, Project 1204 river patrol boat which, along with a sister ship, was sold to Egypt back in 1986. It has a crew of 14, it's nearly 90-feet long, and draws about three feet of water."

Kydd produced a low whistle. "The same as my command boat. That's amazing."

"The fun doesn't stop there," Waller added. "That sucker mounts a deck gun, plus rocket launchers, and lots of secondary weapons. So when that dog barks, you'd best pay attention."

"Why not tease the gunboat out of the lock and drop a missile on it?" Kydd inquired.

"That would be ideal," Waller conceded. "Unfortunately the lock is located inside the area protected by terrorist controlled Russian S-300VM surface-to-air missiles that encircle the dam. If we fly a Pred or a plane into the area they'll shoot it down."

Kydd thanked Waller and went to his quarters. Evans was there, and eager to get approvals on numerous requests and reports. "That stuff will have to wait," Kydd told him.

"Contact Altman and Fox-Smith. Tell them to report aboard an hour from now. Oh, and contact the S-1. Tell her I'm going to need a platoon of marines. After we capture the lock we've got to hold it."

Evans looked at him. "I want to go."

"No, you don't," Kydd said. "I need you here."

Evans was clearly disappointed. But he went back to work.

The balance of the day was spent planning and organizing. The British boats had been sent down river to escort a tug and three barges up from Cairo. That meant the American contingent would have to get the job done on their own.

Each boat commander had at least one job. As did the lieutenant in charge of the marines. And all of them would have to work as a team.

The operation began shortly after darkness fell. Chief Jones, and an engineman named Hawley, drove a dilapidated cruise ship south—and ran it aground half-a-mile short of the locks. The next task was to set the cargo of cotton bales on fire.

It was a tricky business. Too little air, and the blaze could go out. Too much air, and the ship might burn far too quickly. But, if everything worked as it was supposed to, the fire would act as a diversion.

Gunmen fired on the ship from the community of Bani Himayd on the west bank even as the sailors ran from compartment-to-compartment lighting fires. Finally, with bullets snapping all about them, it was time for Jones and Hawley to jump into a RIB boat and flee. "One-Seven to One-Six," Jones said, "We're clear. Over."

"This is Six-actual," Kydd replied. "Roger that... We're underway. Over."

There were numerous reasons to attack at night. Kydd wanted to take advantage of the navy's night vision technology, cloak the flotilla's movements, and minimize civilian casualties.

He was aboard the command boat which, along with three-boat, was going after the shore batteries. The strategy was simple. Zigzag in to take advantage of how unwieldy the D-30 cannons were, get so close that the gun crews couldn't depress their weapons any further, and open up on the bastards.

The key was speed. And, thanks to its twin engines the command boat could hit 40+ knots wide-open. As Kydd stood next to the helmsman he couldn't help but glory in the rush of wind that blew back around the windscreen, the rhythmic thump-thump-thump as the hull slapped the Nile, and the adrenaline surge associated with a small boat action.

Kydd laughed as *Fortunate Son*, by Credence Clearwater, blared out of the loudspeakers, and a shore battery fired on them. Kydd's goggles were on. He saw a column of green water leap into the air off the starboard bow—and heard the minigun roar. Tracers drew a straight line to the shore battery, and remained on-target, as the boat swerved.

That revealed the D-30 to the marines located just aft of Kydd's position. Custom-made straps held their bodies steady as they fired their rocket launchers. The resulting explosions produced overlapping claps of thunder and flashes of light.

But the guns were well protected, and as the command boat turned to the east, the Russian-made cannon was still operational.

Meanwhile the three-boat, with Ensign Miller in command, swept in for *its* run. Another minigun roared, more rockets flashed away, and Kydd saw a hit.

That was followed by a rising ball of fire, and a resounding BOOM, as the second rocket found the D-30's ammo supply. A warm wind blew across the river, and Kydd felt it wash past his face, as a rebel yell came over the radio.

The celebratory moment was short-lived however, because the Shmel Class patrol boat had come out to play, and its commanding officer knew what to do. The gunboat's bow gun could pump out 200 rounds per minute, and put the shells where they counted—which was out front of the three-boat.

Miller and her crew were still celebrating their victory as they ran into the stream of high-explosive rounds. The patrol boat seemed to expand before it exploded and ceased to exist.

Kydd closed his eyes and opened them again. All that remained of the three-boat was some debris and patches of burning fuel. A lump filled his throat and his voice was a croak. "One-Six to SURCs one and two. Search for survivors. Over." But Kydd knew there wouldn't be any survivors. Just bodies.

Only seconds had passed and the RCB was closing with battery number two. The enemy shell made a shrieking sound as it passed over the one-boat to explode a hundred-yards astern. "Go in all the way!" Kydd shouted. "Get *under* the gun and stop."

The helmsman put the wheel over, the boat entered a tight turn, and the mini began to fire. If the RCB could get in close, *so* close the D-30 couldn't fire down on it, the sailors could pound the gun position into submission. Meanwhile the Russian-made gunboat couldn't fire on them without hitting the cannon too.

The one-boat skidded sideways, threw spray into the air, and began to wallow as the helmsman cut power. When the D-30 fired Kydd saw a flash above him. The RCB was in the pocket!

The shore gun continued to fire impotently as the minigun and the starboard machine guns sought to find a weakness. Then the marines fired. Both rockets were dead on.

An enormous explosion threw pieces of concrete high into the air. A blast wave passed over the boat while chunks of cement fell out of the sky. Kydd feared that a 100-pound piece of debris would land in the cockpit and plunge straight through. Fortunately none did.

But what about the locks? Had they been damaged? Goolsby would go batshit crazy if he couldn't go up-river. There was no time to worry about that so long as a Russian gunboat was on the loose. "Hit it!" Kydd yelled. "Before they can nail us!"

The one-boat seemed to leap forward just as tracers slashed through the space where it had been. "Four-Six," Kydd said. "This is One-Six actual. What's your status?"

***

Lieutenant Altman was standing on the bridge of a tugboat with the wheel in his hands. He was wearing night vision goggles—and the scene was clear to see. A riverboat continued to burn on the west bank. Flames shot up out of the shore battery on the east side of the lock. And there, in front of the tug, was a barge. It was positioned crosswise to current. That made it hard to push—but there wasn't any choice. Not if Kydd's plan was to work.

Two Marine Corps eight-wheeled LAV-25 reconnaissance vehicles were chained to the barge. Their engines were running and their 25mm M242 Bushmaster autocannons were ready. Each weapon could fire 200 rounds a minute in the

High-Rate-Fully-Automatic mode, and they were full-up with M791 armor-piercing tracer rounds.

Taken together the LAVs were Kydd's answer to the Russian gunboat and its deck turret. But someone had to put the barge in the right place at the right time. And that job fell to Altman. He could see the enemy vessel, which meant the people on the gunboat could see *him*, and would respond soon. "This is Two-Six," Altman replied. "We're almost in position. Give us thirty seconds."

***

"Go for the gunboat," Kydd ordered. "Run along the starboard side. Then haul ass."

"Aye, aye sir," the helmsman said stoically. "Starboard side, then haul ass."

Both boats were headed straight for each other at a combined speed of 60 mph. And both were firing. The mini roared and brass rattled around the cockpit.

Red tracer whipped past on the starboard side as the enemy gunners tried to acquire and hold the speeding target. Then, for one brief moment, the opponents were side-by-side.

Hundreds of machine gun rounds sleeted back and forth. A marine fell dead as the other one fired. The rocket struck the side of the enemy vessel's superstructure and exploded.

But as the helmsman put the RCB into a tight turn there was no indication that the enemy gunboat had been seriously damaged. Spray flew from its bows as the American boat fled and the barge-mounted LAVs opened fire.

***

Flames stabbed the night as the M242 Bushmaster autocannons opened up. Taken together they were pumping more than

400-rounds per minute down-range. And, thanks to the high-tech targeting systems the LAVs had, almost every round struck the enemy gunboat.

The Russian-made vessel was bow-on to the barge, which meant the incoming fire converged on its front turret, and burrowed through steel. A shell found ammo. There was a flash of light and a dull thud as flames shot up through a blackened hole.

But, thanks to the gunboat's automatic fire suppression system, the flames vanished as quickly as they appeared. Altman watched in horror as the enemy commander put his vessel about. The gunboat had two racks of rocket launchers plus a stern turret which housed a heavy machine gun. And all of those weapons were pointed at *him!* Rockets sleeted into the air as the machine gun fired.

A rocket hit the tugboat's stern, another exploded next to a LAV, and a third crashed through the front of the elevated wheelhouse. Altman stared at it. Nothing happened. A dud.

It was enough to make a guy pee his pants. And maybe Altman would've except that Kydd was making another pass. After a rocket struck the gunboat's bridge it continued to turn circles and was no longer under control.

Altman was about to order a ceasefire, when the enemy vessel belched flames, and began to sink. The Egyptian tug captain entered the wheelhouse. He'd been battling the flames on the stern. "That enough. Fire out. You go."

***

The naval battle was over … But the operation wasn't. Marine Lieutenant Jonathan Sommers and his platoon were waiting to come upstream and secure the dam.

Sommers and his leathernecks arrived on a 75-foot tour boat, pulled up next to the floating dock, and hurried up a flight of metal stairs to the bridge above. Kydd had been expecting a fight but, much to his relief, there was none. It seemed that the naval engagement had been enough to scare Urabi's guards away. And there were no police or firemen on the scene either.

Sommers kept most of his men at street level, but a team of snipers was sent up to secure the elevated control room, and function as an overlook. "Good job, Lieutenant," Kydd told him. "Now, since our mission goals have been met, I have something more in mind. But it's outside the scope of our original orders. So there's no need to sign aboard if you feel that you shouldn't."

Second Lieutenant Jim Sommers was clearly intrigued. "Yes, sir. What do you have in mind?"

"As you know a warlord named Hussain Urabi has been in control of the locks. I think I know where the bastard is. And, if you're willing to loan me some marines, I'd like to go get him. I want volunteers though … This outing would definitely fall under the heading of 'above and beyond.'"

Sommers was hooked. "I'd like to volunteer, sir … And I have some men in mind. How many do you need?"

Kydd shook his head. "No way, Lieutenant … Your place is here in case the bandits try to retake the locks. But thank you. Three volunteers should be enough. If one of them happened to be a sniper that would be perfect."

Sommers was clearly disappointed. "Aye, aye sir. I'll ask around."

Kydd was wearing his tac vest, night vision gear, and carrying the HK416 in addition to his pistol. During Sommers's absence Kydd took the opportunity to pick up some additional magazines for his assault rifle, two grenades, and an individual first aid kit. He was stowing the items away when Sommers reappeared. Three marines were with him. "This is Private Givens," Sommers said. "And this is Private Lopez. Lance Corporal Stiles is a sniper."

Kydd looked them over. "What's the first thing you learned in the Marine Corps?"

"Never volunteer for anything," Lopez responded.

"Exactly," Kydd replied. "Yet here you are." The marines laughed.

"Okay," Kydd said, "We're going after the asshole whose been running this facility. His name is Urabi. We'll capture him if we can, kill him if we have to, and get the hell out.

"Thanks to a download from the battalion S-2, I know where Mr. Urabi lives. And it's only a mile and a half away. That's the good news. The bad news is that he has something like 20 AK-toting yahoos guarding the area. But, since there are only two or three men on the roof, we'll use that as our point of entry."

Stiles had wideset eyes, a pug nose, and a firm mouth. "No offense, sir," she said. "But how are we going to get up there?"

"None taken," Kydd replied. "A minaret is located next to Urabi's building. And it's higher than the roof we want to access."

"That's where I come in," Stiles said. "I nail the guards from above, we jump, and enter."

"Exactly," Kydd agreed. "Do you have any questions?"

"Yeah," Lopez said. "I have one … Let's say everything goes to hell in a handcart. What then?"

"Exfil to the river," Kydd replied. "Two SURCs will be patrolling just offshore. Anything else? No? Then we're almost ready to go. We're going to need some climbing rope, and pair of bolt cutters might come in handy. "

"One of my squads will be on standby," Sommers put in. "My call sign is Mambo-Four. Call if you need back-up."

"Thank you," Kydd said. "Okay, let's go."

It was 2235 by then, and the road was empty as Kydd jogged west. He was careful to stay in the shadows to the extent that was possible. The route was burned into his brain. First right, second left, next right. The lights were on in the buildings along both sides of the road.

Kydd was afraid that someone would look outside and report the suspicious activity to one of Urabi's men. On the other hand, the locals might decide it was better to ignore people with guns, rather than piss them off.

Kydd paused in a shadow. The marines took up positions covering their left, center, and right. The faint strains of a rising-falling Arabic pop song could be heard. A horn honked somewhere … A donkey brayed in the pen behind him. That was all.

Kydd led the team around a corner and up a street lined with shops. They were dark or dimly lit. He felt his heart jump as a cat dashed across the sidewalk in front of him. Stiles was in the two slot, with Lopez behind her, and Givens was walking drag. His job was to watch their six. The roar of a motorcycle engine drove the team into a darkly shadowed passageway, where they hid while the bike rattled by. Kydd led the team out and up to the second left.

They hadn't gone far when a man with an AK-47 slung over his shoulder backed out of a door half a block ahead of them, locked it, and turned away. Stiles lowered her rifle.

When the man was gone Kydd waved the marines forward. The right hand turn came up quickly. The front of Urabi's residence was washed with light. Guards loitered out front.

Thanks to the drone footage Kydd knew that a narrow passageway led back to the alley behind both the mansion and the minaret next to it.

It wasn't unusual for Egyptians to pee in public, and the corridor reeked of urine. An ancient bicycle was leaning against the wall to the right, a window box hung off the building to his left, and a maze of clotheslines ran back and forth above.

When Kydd came to the alley he paused to look both ways. Nothing. A left turn led him to the mosque. He turned to hold a finger to his lips. Urabi's complex was only a 100 feet away. And if they...

A dog growled and charged out of the darkness. The unexpected attack bowled Kydd over. He fell and the animal landed on top of him. Stiles fired. The dog jerked and went limp. Kydd pushed the body off and rolled to his feet. His heart was pounding and his hands were shaking. Could the marines see that? Kydd hoped not. Of more importance was the fact that the incident seemed to have gone unnoticed.

Kydd turned and led the team back along the north side of the mosque to the Ottoman style minaret. What made Ottoman minarets unique were the walkways that circled around them every 50 feet or so. Not only were they pleasing to the eye, the local muezzin could choose how many stairs he wanted to climb, which in the case of the older men was fewer.

A high wall separated the minaret from Urabi's residence, but the structures were only 15-feet apart, and Kydd was counting on that to make his plan work. A curved door provided access to the minaret. It was secured by a hasp and padlock. Givens stepped forward. The bolt cutters made short work of the lock. Then they were inside.

It would have been nice to leave someone at the entrance. But that was a luxury the tiny team couldn't afford. The blob of light from Kydd's headlamp led him up the winding stairs. The risers were high—and Kydd figured that the Mosque's muezzin had thighs like tree trunks. Up, up and up Kydd went, until he was short of breath, and a doorway appeared.

The first, or lowest walkway, was the one they were seeking. Kydd paused to turn his headlamp off before stepping onto the stone surface. It was about 3-feet wide.

The wall was chest high. Kydd looked over the side. Thanks to the overhang, Urabi's roof was about 10-feet away, and perhaps 15-feet lower than the walk around. Kydd turned to Lopez. "I need the rope."

"No offense, sir," the marine replied. "How old are you? Thirty-five?"

"Thirty-six."

"I rest my case," Lopez said. "I'll drop down, swing back and forth, and drop onto the roof. The rest of the team can slide down."

"He can do it, sir," Stiles assured him. "Right after I kill the sentries."

Kydd grinned. "So this is a unanimous decision?"

Givens nodded. "Yes, sir."

"Okay," Kydd said. "Rope up."

Lopez cut a section of rope off the coil, fashioned a Swiss Seat out of it, and prepared to rappel. Kydd looked down before turning to Stiles. Her rifle was resting on a pair of gloves.

Kydd was about to tell the marine that there were three sentries, that speed was of the essence, and that she needed to make kill shots. Then he realized how stupid that was. "Okay, Corporal, drop 'em."

***

Names had been bestowed on the sentries by that time: One, two, and three. Stiles planned to smoke them in numerical order. The key to success was her M110 Semi-Automatic Sniper System (SASS) with Sniper Night Sight. Had it been necessary to work a bolt, precious seconds would've been lost, and the movement could pull the barrel off-target.

Stiles took a deep breath, let go, and squeezed. A gentle cough was heard as a 7.62X51mm NATO round hit the Egyptian's head and blew his brains out.

Stiles was already swinging left by then and lining up on number two. She touched the trigger. It gave.

Three had good peripheral vision. He saw movement out of the corner of his eye, opened his mouth to shout a warning, and jerked spastically as a bullet passed right through his teeth. The sentry's body appeared to wilt. Then, like the professional she was, Stiles put an extra slug into each body.

***

Givens said, "Go!" and Lopez dropped out of sight. Kydd leaned out to watch, but couldn't see much, until the marine swung out and into sight. Then it was time for Lopez to repeat the performance. Once, twice, and the third time was the charm.

The marine's boots made a barely audible thump as they hit the roof. Lopez spent the next three minutes freeing himself from the rope, and securing it to a vertical plumbing vent, before signaling the people above.

"You first, Stiles," Kydd said. "Check the perimeter around the house. But don't drop anyone."

After slinging her rifle, and pulling her gloves on, Stiles went over the side. The first bit was the most awkward. Then it was boot camp stuff. Stiles wrapped her legs around the rope and slid down, using her hands to brake. Kydd took note. "Your turn," Givens said, and Kydd agreed.

After slinging his rifle, Kydd worked his way out onto the rope, and was surprised by the amount of effort required to lift his legs up and onto the line. Gravity took over from there. And, having neglected to bring gloves, he was forced to hug the rope with his arms. Once Kydd felt his butt touch the roof he let go and rolled to the right.

Givens was on the way by then, and managed to land with more grace than Kydd had. Then he cut the rope.

Stiles appeared out of the gloom. "There are three guards in front," Stiles said, "and two out back."

Kydd nodded. "Nothing on the sides?"

Stiles shook her head. "Not that I could see."

"Okay, let's do this. Odds are that Urabi's bedroom is located on the top floor…But that's far from certain. If we fail to find him there we'll keep looking.

"Stiles, you're the only person with a suppressed weapon, so you'll be on point. If the rest of us have to fire then so be it. But here's hoping we don't.

"Once we have the bastard, gag his mouth, and secure his wrists. We'll fall back on the river. Okay, Stiles, hit it."

A large cupola marked the spot where the stairs emerged onto the roof. It was intended to provide access and allow warm air to escape from below. Cables squirmed up out of the doorway and wandered over to a small antenna farm.

The door hung open, and lights led the way, as the Americans followed a circular stairway down. Shadows played on ancient walls, and a depression marked the center of each stone step, testifying to many years of continual use.

The stair came to an end on a circular landing. A conventional staircase was waiting ahead. Catholic murals decorated the walls. And, judging from the multiplicity of doors, the 3rd floor rooms were accessed from the central core. "We'll take them one at a time," Kydd told them. "Stay on me."

Kydd had assumed that Urabi's quarters would be located on the top floor. He was wrong. One door provided access to a storeroom. Two doors opened into vacant guest suites. A forth provided access to a filthy bathroom. The one the sentries used? Probably.

The cables led down the stairs, across the 2nd floor landing, and into a room. The door stood open. And, as a man carrying a teapot stepped out onto the parquet floor, Stiles shot him. Twice. The teapot shattered when it hit the floor. The sniper stepped over the body.

Another man appeared, took two bullets, and collapsed. Stiles entered the room and took a look around. "Room clear, sir … It's their com center."

Kydd nodded. "Okay, let's find Urabi."

That, as it turned out, was easy to do. A red runner ran under a pair of brass inlay doors and into the room beyond. "Let's take him alive if we can," Kydd whispered. "Okay Givens, open sesame."

Givens took hold of a massive handle and pulled. As the right hand opened Stiles entered. Kydd followed. It was a big room. And seemingly larger because of the mirrors fastened to the walls and ceiling. And there, sitting on a riser, was a king-sized bed.

A man was on top of a woman, his hairy back exposed, when he heard the sounds of movement. He rolled sideways in a clumsy attempt to reach the pistol that was resting on a side table, but Lopez got to the weapon first. "Oh, no you don't," the marine said. "No bang-bangs for *you*!"

The man fell back against some pillows. Kydd aimed the HK at him. A red dot drew circles on the man's furry chest. "Colonel Urabi?"

The Egyptian shrugged. He had a British accent. "Of course. And you are?"

Kydd was about to answer when the woman slapped a hidden button. A klaxon began to bleat. Urabi laughed. "So you managed to get in … But, now my American friend, how will you get out?"

CHAPTER NINE

Esna, Egypt

"The answer to your question is obvious," Kydd replied. "I have a hostage. Which is to say *you*. And, if we're about to be overrun, you'll die before I do."

Kydd turned. "Stiles, Givens, block the stairway up from the first floor … I saw weapons in the com room. Use those first. Go.

"Lopez, hogtie the colonel first, and the woman second."

Urabi was about to say something when Kydd jammed a rifle barrel into the Egyptian's mouth. "Shut the fuck up."

After using zip ties to immobilize the prisoners Lopez left them lying on the bed. Kydd heard firing and knew the other marines were holding the bandits back. He turned his radio on. "One-Six to Mambo-Four. Over."

The response was immediate. "This is Mambo-Four. Over."

"We have the target, but we're under attack, and could use some help. Over."

"Roger that," Lieutenant Sommers replied. "On the way. Over."

"First right, second left, next right. And be careful … More bandits are arriving. Over."

That was when Cole broke into the conversation. "Sailor boy, is that *you*? Over."

"None other," Kydd replied. "Where are you? Over."

"Directly across from your location. I have two-zero friends with me. Don't fire into the plaza. Over."

"Roger that, over."

The steady bang, bang, bang, of an AK-47 could be heard from the 2nd floor landing. "We have hajis coming from above *and* below," Stiles said calmly. "Over."

Kydd turned to Lopez. "Get on their radio … Chances are that some of Urabi's men speak English. Tell them to back off, or we'll cut his throat."

Givens followed Kydd out onto the central landing. Stiles was firing *down* the stairs, and Givens was over at the other stairwell firing *up*. And, as Kydd went over to join him, a grenade bounced down, to land at Kydd's feet. Time seemed slow as he bent to grab the bomblet and throw it. The grenade was sailing though the air when it went off. There was a loud bang and shrapnel flew every which-way. Kydd was untouched.

Givens was climbing the stairs by then, firing short bursts, and yelling obscenities. Kydd hurried to support the marine—and together they were able to clear the third floor. "Stiles … Give me a sitrep. Over."

"I took a round, but I'm functional, and I can hear firing out front. Over."

"Be careful who you shoot … We have two sets of friendlies inbound. Over."

Kydd turned to Givens. "I've got this. Check on Stiles."

Cole's voice came over the radio. "The plaza is clear. A perimeter has been set. Over."

Then it was Sommers' turn. "Mambo-Four … Incoming from the southeast. Over."

Friendlies flooded the mansion two-minutes later. And Cole was among them. She surfaced on the 2nd floor accompanied by two heavily armed civilians. Both wore skull masks. "So," Cole said, "where is he?"

"In there," Kydd said, as he pointed to the double doors.

"Is he alive?"

"Sadly, yes," Kydd replied. "I appreciate the help, but why are you here?"

Cole frowned. "This is what I do sailor ... *What?* You thought no one else would go after Urabi? Goolsby sent me."

"And your friends?"

"They're contractors," Cole replied enigmatically. "All right, let's collect our prize, and get out of here."

In actuality it took nearly an hour to scour the house for Intel, free the prisoners being held in the mansion's cavernous basement, and retreat to the river. At some point during the journey Cole's "contractors" vanished into the night.

Dawn was an hour away... And it looked as if every light the *Nile* had was lit. An order was waiting: "Report to Colonel Goolsby immediately."

Kydd ignored the directive long enough to make sure that Stiles was receiving medical attention. "After taking a bullet in the left shoulder, and holding the stairs by herself, Lance Corporal Stiles continued to fight until relieved." That's how Kydd planned to write it up.

"All three of your marines deserve medals," Kydd told Sommers. "Let's push some recs through."

Then, like a criminal on the way to the electric chair, Kydd made his way up to deck three, where Cole was waiting. "You lucked out," Cole said. "We're on hold while Goolsby chats with General someone-or-other."

"His boss probably."

"Probably," Cole agreed. "Shed the hardware, or the sentries won't let us in."

After surrendering his weapons, Kydd was about to sit down, when the door swung open. "You can enter now," a sergeant told them.

"Oh, goody," Kydd said sotto voice, as he followed the CIA agent through the door. Goolsby was seated behind his desk. And, for the first time in Kydd's experience, the marine had a smile on his face. "Congratulations on a well-fought naval engagement Commander Kydd... Even if you did exceed the scope of your orders.

"As for you, Agent Cole, an excellent performance as always. I, for one, appreciate the manner in which you saved Commander Kydd's ass."

Kydd couldn't help but admire the way in which Goolsby had been able to dole out a lump of praise, *and* dress him down, all in two succinct paragraphs. Never mind Goolsby's failure to share information related to Cole's activities. But Kydd felt lucky to get off so easily.

Goolsby's face turned somber at that point. "Please accept my condolences regarding the loss of Ensign Miller, her crew, and one of my marines. I will write a letter to each family for inclusion with yours."

Kydd nodded. "Thank you, sir."

"All right," Goolsby said, "the locks belong to us. But, from what the captain of the *Nile* tells me, it will take an entire day to push the convoy through. Get some sleep. The dam is still 100-miles away."

***

After a hand-over to Lieutenant Altman, and an hour spent reviewing all of the documents Evans had prepared for him, Kydd hit the rack. It was midmorning by then ... And time for the convoy to move upriver. Despite the noise associated with that process Kydd slept like a log. His alarm went off at 1500 which, according to the way he felt, was far too soon. But, considering all the things that demanded his attention, he didn't dare sleep longer.

Kydd felt better after a shower and a shave. After donning a fresh set of cammies, courtesy of the *Nile's* civilian laundry service, Kydd was ready for breakfast.

Upon finishing the meal Kydd made use of his radio to request a pickup. SURC-2 was idling at the bottom of the stairs when Kydd arrived. Murphy stood waiting to greet Kydd as he crossed the gap. "Good morning, sir ... And welcome to crazy town."

"Uh, oh ... What's wrong?"

"Everything," Murphy replied. "The lockmaster took off during the fighting last night, nobody's been able to find him, and there's the language barrier to deal with.

"A combat engineer is working the problem, but the lock controls are thirty years old, and hard to figure out."

"How's the colonel taking it?"

"Not well, skipper ... Not well at all."

"Alright, Murph ... Let's head upstream and see the craziness firsthand."

The sun was approaching its zenith and, if it hadn't been for the SURC's speed, the heat would have been oppressive. Spray flew as the open boat came on step—and the twin diesels pushed the SURC up to 30mph. It wasn't long before the burned-out cruise boat appeared off to starboard, followed by a tug and two barges, all of which had been forced to anchor until the lock opened.

The helmsman brought the SURC in alongside the dock and, as Kydd made his way up the stairs, he paused to inspect the western gun emplacement. All that remained of the artillery piece was some twisted metal and a blackened crater.

The road across the top of the dam was crowded with people. Altman and a combat engineer were at the center of a mob of mostly civilians who were bombarding a marine with rapid-fire Arabic. Except the marine was barely out of language school and badly outmatched. "Good morning," Kydd said, as he approached Altman. "I hear the lockmaster is AWOL."

The sun was beating down on them. Altman wiped the sweat off his forehead with a sleeve. "That's right, sir ... These people say they know where he is, and they'll tell us, for a fee. And I'd pay if I knew who to believe."

"In that case," a man in a grubby *thawb* (robe) said, "pay *me*. I know where the lockmaster is."

"How much?"

"Fifty-dollars American."

"Here's twenty-five," Altman said, as he removed the money from his wallet. "Where is he? In town?"

"No," the Egyptian replied, "he's right *there*."

The man in question saw the pointing finger and tried to run. Kydd chased him down, grabbed a skinny arm, and towed the Egyptian back to where the translator stood. "Is this the lockmaster? Ask him."

The marine posed the question and received a nod. "He's the lockmaster alright," the corporal said. "He was scared to identify himself."

"Alright," Kydd said. "Let's get to work."

The lockmaster's assistant showed up minutes later. And with both men on the job the locks were open for business 30-minutes later. However the cycle rate for the locks had been notoriously slow before the takeover and still was. That, combined with the number of vessels that needed to pass through, meant the process was going to take at least a day.

The sun was hanging low in the western sky when *Nile* arrived, entered a lock, and slowly rose. Kydd was there when the brightly lit cruise ship emerged. He expected her to proceed upriver, to the point where other vessels were anchored, but she didn't.

The starboard paddlewheel stopped, while the port wheel continued to thrash the water, pushing the *Nile's* bow in next to the riverside promenade. Orders were shouted and lines went ashore. Then a gangplank was extended and secured.

Though unexpected Kydd welcomed the opportunity to walk aboard, go to his cabin, and take a shower. But all such thoughts vanished from his mind as Colonel Goolsby and Hussain Urabi appeared. Then, much to Kydd's shock, they shook hands! Urabi waved as he strolled ashore and crossed the promenade to the street where a white Land Rover was waiting for him.

Kydd felt the anger boil up inside him. Miller, and six more, all dead because of Urabi... And Goolsby let the bastard go! The gangplank bounced as Kydd hurried across, shoved a marine sentry aside, and yelled "Colonel! What did you do? That bastard killed seven sailors and a marine! What the hell is wrong with you?"

Goolsby was walking away. He stopped. He turned. His eyes were narrowed, his lips were drawn, and his body was stiff with barely contained rage. "Corporal... Confine that officer to his quarters." Then Goolsby turned and walked away.

The corporal was the same marine that Kydd had pushed. His right hand was resting on his pistol. His voice was tight. "You heard the colonel."

"Yeah," Kydd said. "I heard him." And with that he made his way up to his cabin, went in, and closed the door. Evans was gone for the day. Would the marines station a guard outside his door? Probably.

The shower felt good, even if *he* didn't, and Kydd emerged feeling refreshed. He was dressed in nothing more than a towel when there was a knock on the door. He went over to open it. A marine was standing outside. "Yes?"

"You are to report to Colonel Goolsby's quarters at 1830." After delivering his message the private turned and marched away. Kydd looked left and right. If a guard had been stationed there earlier, he or she was gone. What, if anything, did that portend? He was about to find out.

Kydd got dressed and spent the next twenty minutes writing a letter to Miller's parents. "I regret to inform you that at such and such time, on such and such day, your daughter Ensign Karen Miller was killed in action.

"I'm not at liberty to say where her death took place, or under what circumstances, except to assure you that she died in the service of our country..." And so on, just like thousands of others being written that day, all over the world.

What Miller's parents wouldn't know, *couldn't* know, was that the man responsible for their daughter's death had been set free. Kydd glanced at his watch, and put the pen aside. He was at peace. He'd said what he'd said... And meant every word of it.

Kydd left his cabin, made the long trip to Goolsby's cabin, and showed his ID. The marine nodded. "Thank you, sir... The colonel is expecting you."

Kydd opened the door and went in. Goolsby was at a side table with his back turned to the room. "Have a seat Commander... I hope you like gin because that's all I have. In the absence of tonic water, I'm mixing it with orange juice. That constitutes an Orange Blossom which can be served 'up,' like a martini, or on the rocks. The latter being my preference."

When Goolsby turned he was holding a drink in each hand. He brought them over, handed one to Kydd, and sat in a guest chair. Then he raised his glass. "Forged by the Sea."

Kydd nodded. "Semper Fi." Their glasses clinked.

Each took a sip. Goolsby looked Kydd in the eye. "Please allow me to apologize. I lost my temper. If I were you, and if I saw what you saw, I'd like to believe that I would react the way you did."

Kydd opened his mouth to speak, but stopped as Goolsby raised a hand. "Hear me out... The U.S. State Department is a big organization. The Under Secretary for Political Affairs has responsibility for the Bureau of Near Eastern Affairs, which employs a dickhead named Victor Danby—he's the Bureau's Country Desk Manager for Egypt.

"More than that, from what Agent Cole tells me, he's a fixture around here. So much so that he refused a promotion to stay in-country. *Why* you ask? Because the bastard is on the take. How else can you explain the mansion in Cairo, the S-Class Mercedes, and all the rest of it?

"So, when Danby got wind of the fact that we had Urabi, he sent a 6,000 word screed to the Under Secretary suggesting that although Colonel Urabi had been a bad boy in the past, we could rehabilitate the bastard and use his paramilitary forces to help capture the dam. Thereby lessening the need for conventional forces.

"And never having been to Egypt, much less Africa, the Under Secretary bought it." Goolsby drained his glass and slammed it down. "The bitch."

"So don't tell me, let me guess," Kydd said. "Danby and Urabi are friends."

Goolsby nodded. "You're pretty smart for a navy officer. The upshot is that I received orders to turn him loose."

"To do whatever he wants."

"Pretty much ... Although Cole will try to keep track of him."

"I was wrong to do what I did," Kydd said. "I should have told you off privately."

Goolsby laughed. "Please do so next time. So much for item one on the agenda. Now it's time for item two."

Kydd swallowed what remained of his drink. "Which *is?*"

"We've been summoned," Goolsby said. "As you know Operation Pharaoh falls under Admiral Charles Larson. And, now that we're within striking distance of the dam, he wants to have a chat."

"About *what?*"

"About how to keep Kantar from blowing the dam."

"There's no plan?"

"Nope."

"Cole told me there was back in Port Ashdod."

Goolsby smiled. "She lied to you."

"Shit."

"Would you like another drink?"

Kydd held his glass out. "Yes, please."

***

The sun was up, but just barely. The air was filled with the hysterical shrieking of the Senegal Thick-knee wading bird. The incessant pvi, pvi, pvi sound originated from the edge of the river, where the Thick-knee was searching for its breakfast.

The screeching combined with the call to morning prayer produced a strange chorus. What had been a farmer's field, and would be again, was the site of a makeshift landing zone. Red smoke boiled up into the sky. And, as the call to prayer came to an end, the drone of aircraft engines took its place.

Kydd was wearing sunglasses but still felt the need to shade his eyes as he looked up. He'd been expecting a helicopter rather than a V-22 Osprey. He'd ridden in them on prior occasions and knew the tiltrotor aircraft were capable of vertical takeoff and landings (VTOL), as well as short takeoff and landings. They could carry 30 passengers, and had a range of 1,000 miles, which would be more than enough to reach the carrier *Hornet*. The ninth ship to bear that name.

As the V-22 circled, Goolsby appeared with Cole in tow. She was wearing her trademark shades, a heavily loaded tac vest, and toting an MP7. The combat loadout was SOP. If the Osprey went down, and the passengers survived, they would find themselves in what amounted to enemy territory.

Both engines began to tilt upwards as the Osprey made its final approach and, by the time the VTOL was in position over the LZ, the rotors were pointed at the sky.

Everyone knew that V-22s were allergic to dust. But the field consisted of black loam. And there was very little blowback as the aircraft touched down.

Goolsby went to speak with a lieutenant leaving Cole to fend for herself. "Good morning," Kydd said, as the agent approached. "This is a pleasant surprise. I like the way your submachine gun matches your boots. "

Cole removed her glasses. "You never quit, do you?"

"Don't be a quitter," Kydd replied. "That's what mom told me."

A smile tugged at the corners of Cole's mouth and disappeared. "The fact that we had to let Urabi go sucks. I understand you went cray-cray on the colonel."

"We had a spat," Kydd allowed. "But we're besties now."

Cole laughed. "You are entirely full of shit."

"I choose to interpret that as a compliment," Kydd replied.

"Excuse me," a marine said. "Names please."

After checking their names off his list, the crew chief told them to clear their weapons and place them on safety. "And keep your PFDs handy," he added. "The last leg of the trip will be over water. You can board."

The Osprey's rear loading ramp was down and in contact with the ground. Cole entered followed by Kydd. Inward facing fold-down seats lined both bulkheads, cable bundles ran every which-way, and recessed tie-downs were set into the deck. A crewman was there to greet them. "Sit wherever you like…We have twelve passengers, so there's plenty of choices."

Goolsby got on, produced a laptop, and went to work. The rest of the passengers were marines who required more medical treatment than the battalion's surgeon could offer them. One was strapped to a stretcher, with a hospital corpsman at his side. "Ramp's coming up," the crew chief announced. "Fasten your seat belts."

The engine noise increased, the VTOL began to taxi, and suddenly it was up in the air. That's how it felt anyway, although there weren't any windows in the cabin, so Kydd couldn't see.

It would have been nice to chat with Cole during the trip, but she had chosen to sit across the aisle, and was busy reading her Kindle. A clear message if there ever was one. That left Kydd to do what Evans wanted him to do, which was catch up on his paperwork. He opened his pack, removed the laptop, and turned it on. *Maintenance logs… Oh, goody.*

Kydd worked. Then he napped, or pretended to nap, while watching Cole through slitted eyes. What was it about her anyway? The way she looked? Her smarts? All of the above? Not that it mattered, because she wasn't interested.

Eventually, after nearly 3 hours in the air, the pilot made an announcement. "We crossed the coast, we're over the Med, and 20-minutes out. More when I have it."

The landing was somewhat anticlimactic since Kydd couldn't see anything. He felt the shift from forward to vertical flight however, knew the Osprey was going to land on a moving target, and hoped the pilot was competent. She was. There was a pronounced thump as the wheels made contact with the flight deck.

Another wait followed as the V-22 was towed to an elevator and moved to the deck below. The ramp was lowered at that point, and a team of corpsmen came aboard to carry the stretcher off. Then, and only then, were the rest of the passengers allowed to disembark.

A first class petty officer was waiting for them at the reception desk where the visitors had to check-in. They were then handed off to an ensign who welcomed them aboard, and led them into what felt like an endless maze.

That was one of the reasons why Kydd disliked the "big" navy. He liked smaller boats, smaller crews, and smaller objectives. He couldn't imagine being in charge of a carrier strike group like Admiral Larson's.

In addition to the *Hornet*, Larson's command included approximately 7,500 sailors, a cruiser, a destroyer squadron, an air wing, ancillary vessels, and at least one submarine. That was way too much responsibility in Kydd's opinion, and boring to boot, since most of the admiral's time was spent on politics.

After climbing ladders, and making their way down corridors, the party arrived in officer country—where they were assigned to tiny cabins. The ensign eyed his watch. "You have thirty minutes to freshen up … Then it's off to lunch in the wardroom, followed by a meeting in the briefing room next door. That's where Admiral Larson will join you."

True to his promise the ensign returned half an hour later, to escort them to the wardroom, and sign in with the mess treasurer, who would collect payment for their food before they left the ship. Lunch was a relaxed affair that included officers from various departments: operations, administration, maintenance, safety, and more.

Kydd found himself sitting next to a helicopter pilot who knew someone that he knew. That happened a lot in the navy. They traded sea stories until the ensign came to collect the visitors.

The briefing room was only steps down the corridor on the right. It was a large brightly- lit space with theatre-style seating and a low-rise stage. The *Hornet's* emblem was located between two flat screens that were mounted on the bulkhead.

About 15 people were present. Some were seated while the rest were milling around a table where refreshments awaited. Goolsby, Cole and Kydd sat in the second row amongst a mix of civilian and military personnel. Suddenly a voice in the back said, "Attention on deck!" and Admiral Larson entered. Everyone stood.

Larson said, "As you were," as he made his way to the podium. Larson had "the look." Meaning the look of a senior officer, most of whom were tall and fit. Blue eyes roamed the audience. "Good morning. We're here to figure out what the hell to do."

That got a chorus of laughs just as it was supposed to. Larson smiled. "Before we get into our discussions I would like to extend a special welcome to Colonel Martin Goolsby, commanding officer of Operation Pharaoh, Commander Harley Kydd, commanding officer of RIVGRU 6, and adviser Cassandra Cole—on loan from somewhere." Everyone in the room knew Cole was a CIA agent and they laughed.

Larson turned serious. "They, along with their marines and sailors, have done a hell of a job in the face of stiff resistance from warlords and insurgents. The battalion is located just south of Esna now—about 100 miles from the dam. But at a price.

"Now," Larson continued, "we have to face the prospect of two possible outcomes. One is success, and the other is failure. Strangely enough both possibilities could be good or bad where the Allied war effort is concerned. *If* we ignore what's good for the Egyptian people.

"Here's an example," Larson said, as a word chart appeared on the screen to his left. "If the terrorists blow the dam, the best estimate is that 10-million people will die. That would be horrible for the Egyptians. But, if we don't care, it would be good for us. We could jump in and seize control of Egypt. And by doing so, deny the country to the Axis.

"But we *do* care what happens to the Egyptians … And allowing 10-million people to die would be unconscionable.

"By the same token," Larson continued, "we can win *and* lose. Let's say we manage to take the dam, we neutralize the bomb, and we leave. What is likely to happen *then*?"

Larson pointed to Cole, and she was ready. "A warlord, or an alliance of warlords will take control of the dam, and the whole thing will start over."

"Exactly," Larson agreed. "And that brings us to the purpose of this meeting. We need to generate a plan that enables us to win, helps us deal with success, and will minimize the effects of failure if it comes to that. You will work in three groups … The first group will tackle the Operation Pharaoh's most pressing problem, and that is how to prevent the terrorists from detonating the nuclear device when the task force nears the dam.

"The second group will work on a plan to hold the dam, and keep it safe after neutralizing the bomb, without committing a substantial number of Allied troops to Egypt.

"The third group will identify the appropriate actions to take if the dam is blown, 10-million people plus our own personnel are killed, and the Axis attempts to occupy Egypt.

"You will have until this time tomorrow to create and codify you plans. You have already been divided into groups—and Lieutenant Powell will sort you out. I'll return at 1500 tomorrow for the read-outs. Do your best work." And with that Larson left.

Kydd had been assigned to group 1, Cole to group 2, and Goolsby to group 3. Group 1 consisted of six people, and was sent to a smaller space, which was equipped with all the supplies they might need—including a coffee urn.

The first order of business was for each person to introduce themselves. That's when Kydd learned he would be working with a navy pilot, an air force officer on loan from the Pentagon, a Sunni cleric, a retired army general and a reformed member of Hezbollah.

Each member of the group had a different point of view. And that was no accident. After electing the general to chair the process they went to work.

First they watched the video posted by Hezbollah immediately after their fighters took control of the dam. Then came a very interesting Intel briefing from an Israeli officer. "Here's the situation," he said. "After the Hezbollah fighters killed their Russian counterparts their leader Kantar took possession of the nuclear key. He carries it with him 24 hours a day."

"How do we know that?" the pilot wanted to know.

"We know that because some of his men wanted to blow the dam, and kill millions of Sunnis without regard to Hezbollah's master plan," the Israeli replied. "They attempted to assassinate Kantar and failed. After he turned the tables on them two of the fanatics ran. They were captured by Coptic Christians, subsequently sold to Egyptian gun smugglers, and purchased by us. Then they spilled their guts."

Kydd's already high opinion of Israeli Intelligence went up a notch. "So we know Kantar was in no hurry to blow the dam, and we know he has the switch," Kydd mused.

"Correct," the briefer said. "We believe Kantar has orders to pull a collaborationist government together. The most likely arrangement would be a deal where well-known Sunnis agree to front for the Shias in return for money or power. The Axis wants to control Egypt. But they'd like to achieve that goal without killing 10-million Muslims."

The meeting ran all afternoon and continued after dinner. The problem was tactical, rather than strategic, and eventually the discussion boiled down to a simple syllogism: (1) To prevent a disastrous flood the Allies had to capture or destroy the nuclear key. (2) Kantar had the key. (3) Destroy Kantar.

The use of the word "destroy" was intentional. Killing Kantar wouldn't be sufficient. But if Kantar were "destroyed" the key would be destroyed as well. And that was critical lest the object be recovered by a terrorist or some other bad actor.

So a variety of scenarios were considered. If the Allies threw waves of missiles at the dam's SAM system they could overwhelm it. But Kantar would destroy the dam long before Goolsby's marines could reach him.

A Sunni suicide bomber could blow him or herself up while standing next to Kantar. Assuming Kantar was that careless.

And so it went with each scenario becoming more and more unlikely. Finally, when time ran out, only one realistic possibility remained. And that was the idea the air force officer had put forward in the beginning: Kill Kantar with a drone. Or, as he put it, "We'll blow his ass up. And the trigger too."

Each group had the opportunity to present their conclusions to Admiral Larson the following day. And after group 3 presented their findings, he went to the podium. "I'm impressed," Larson told them. "Your plans will be forwarded to the Pentagon and the State Department for final approval."

That produced a chorus of groans. Larson smiled. "I know what you're thinking... But, they understand the stakes, and we expect a two-day turnaround. Once I receive their feedback, my staff will make adjustments if any are required, and tasking orders will follow. Thank you."

A group dinner was held that evening, and once it was over, the participants were invited to rotate through the bridge to watch planes come and go. It was an amazing sight, and one that left Kydd wondering how anyone could master all the skills required to fly a plane off a carrier, or why they would want to.

Kydd fell asleep only seconds after hitting his rack, only to be awoken at what seemed like ten-minutes later. After packing up, eating a quick breakfast, and paying their mess bills—Goolsby and his subordinates were escorted to the main deck where a V-22 Osprey stood waiting. Once lifted up onto the flight deck, the Osprey had to wait its turn before taxiing into the wind, tilting its rotors up, and lifting off. And that beat the heck out of being shot from a catapult.

The Osprey was carrying six passengers besides Goolsby, Cole and Kydd. All were replacements for marines who'd been killed or wounded.

Goolsby was staring at his laptop, and Cole was listening to music, so Kydd took a nap. And that's what he was doing when the Osprey began to shake and the noise level changed. Kydd opened his eyes as the pilot's voice came over the intercom. "Please check your seatbelts. We just lost an engine. The good news is that we're over land, and can fly on one engine."

Kydd tightened his belt, and saw Cole do likewise. Then came a bang, followed by relative silence, as the second engine quit. The pilot's voice was tight but calm. "Cairo is directly ahead. Hang on. We're going in."

CHAPTER TEN

Cairo, Egypt

The V-22 Osprey had the glide characteristics of a rock. It couldn't autorotate the way a helicopter could. So, without power, all the pilots could do was look for a place to crash. Kydd looked at Cole. Their eyes met. Something jumped the gap. She shrugged.

Kydd was thinking about that, thinking about what might have been, when the VTOL crashed. Kydd couldn't see anything. But there was no mistaking the violent impact, followed by a brief moment of weightlessness, and a second hard landing.

Then the passengers were thrown sideways as the Osprey's forward motion caused it to skip like a stone. Metal screeched, groaned, and rattled as an engine came off, and the front end of the plane slammed into something. Kydd's body was jerked sideways as the journey came to a sudden end.

Kydd was alive. It took a moment to process that. He could move his arms. And his legs. He fumbled for the release on his seat belt and felt it give. Goolsby began to bark orders. "Get up! Check the people around you ... Give aid if necessary.

"Grab your pack and load your weapons. We're in enemy territory, marines ... And people *will* try to kill us."

"I think that sums it up," Cole said, as she shouldered her pack.

"Yeah," Kydd replied. "Are you okay?"

"Never better."

Kydd laughed.

"Quit fucking around," Goolsby ordered. "Get your asses in gear. Sergeant! Check the pilots."

The crew chief was donning his tac gear. "I did, sir. Both are KIA. The cockpit hit the backend of a semi-truck."

"Get their tags," Goolsby said grimly.

A semi? We landed on a street, Kydd concluded. *Or in a parking lot.*

The six marines had survived. They were young, just out of advanced infantry training, and understandably frightened. But not *too* frightened—judging from the way they were strapping their gear on.

The rear hatch was partially open thanks to the crew chief. Goolsby made his way to the opening, paused, and disappeared. The marines followed one-by-one.

Cole followed with Kydd behind her. There was a four-foot drop to the ground. The navy officer paused to insert a magazine into the HK416 assault rifle. A car horn blared nearby. A woman was screaming. A distant boom was heard.

Kydd scanned his surroundings. The Osprey was resting on two flattened cars. A quick look confirmed what Kydd already knew. The people in them were dead.

Buildings rose like cliffs around them; the sky was a ribbon above. Goolsby shouted. "Follow me!"

Did Goolsby know where he was going? That seemed unlikely. But the colonel had been a lieutenant once. And he knew they should clear the crash site quickly. Fire was a possibility, as was an explosion. There were other threats too. The VTOL would attract bandits, thieves and terrorists, all bent on capturing survivors—and looting the wreckage.

Traffic was lighter than it had been before the war. But there were still plenty of cars on the streets. And when the VTOL fell out of the sky the crash triggered dozens of collisions. Some minor, some serious. Drivers were slumped over their wheels. Others were out of their vehicles shouting at each other.

As Goolsby led the party through the maze of stalled cars, Kydd saw something shiny coming their way. The off-the-shelf drone made a mosquito-like whining sound as it slowed and circled above them. Had the device been sent by the authorities? No, that seemed unlikely.

Kydd paused, raised the HK416, and pulled the trigger. The drone ran into the stream of bullets and exploded. Bits of metal fell like confetti.

The team was up ahead, twisting and turning through cars, but Cole was waiting with her MP7 at the ready. "Come on, sailor ... That's enough target practice."

Kydd followed the agent through the traffic jam. They had just crossed *Youssef Wahbi* street when a group of armed men emerged from hiding. One of them fired two shots into the air, and instructed Goolsby to stop. The marine had no choice but to comply.

"Place your weapons on the ground," the Egyptian ordered.

"Fuck you," Goolsby said, as he kept the M4 carbine leveled.

The Egyptian's eyebrows rose. "You're American?"

"Yes. How did you know?"

"I went to medical school in Boston. And Americans say 'fuck' all the time."

The Egyptian raised his weapon, and issued an order in Arabic. His men tilted their rifle barrels up toward the sky. "I am Dr. Dacey Boutros ... Commanding officer of the Coptic Guard. Welcome to the hood."

The "hood" as it turned out was part of the Daher district of downtown Cairo. The Guard's territory consisted of four-square blocks. They were bordered by the Ramsis freeway on the north, El-Zaher on the south, and side streets to the east and west. The

Guard's mission was to protect the Arch Angels Greek Orthodox Church from the Sunni groups that wanted to purge the city of Christians.

After passing through a sparsely defended perimeter, Kydd found himself looking up at the church. It consisted of two towers, each topped by a rounded cupola, and separated by a peaked arch. The windows were shaped like gun slits. As if the architect *knew* that his edifice would come under attack.

The church's facade was pockmarked with bullet holes. A large chunk of the left-hand tower was missing. And at least two-dozen shell craters marked spots where incoming mortar bombs had exploded. "The Sunnis attack us every few weeks," Boutros explained. "They want to kill us and demolish the church."

"You're a Coptic," Goolsby said. "And this is a Greek Orthodox Church. Why risk your life to defend it?"

"I'm a Christian," Boutros explained. "And that comes first."

Their conversation was interrupted by a man dressed in combat gear. He spoke rapid-fire Arabic and Boutros frowned. "I'm sorry," the Coptic said in English. "A Sudanese gang called the Outlaws captured one of your pilots. They know you're here ... And they want 50-thousand dollars for him."

"Our pilots are dead," Goolsby replied.

Boutros spoke to the fighter who replied. Cole translated. "The gang says the pilot's name is Riley, and in order to prove that he's alive, they'll put him on the radio. He's injured though ... And a bit confused."

Goolsby nodded. "Go ahead. Put him on the radio."

It took a full minute to complete the necessary arrangements. Goolsby accepted a radio from Boutros. "What's your name?" Then, after a pause, "What's the Marine Corps motto?"

The answer must have been correct, because Goolsby nodded. "I'm sorry, Lieutenant Riley ... Hang in there. The State Department will try to get you out."

Goolsby thumbed the radio off and gave it back. "Where are these bastards?"

"Most of the Sudanese live on the outskirts of the city," Boutros replied. "But, because of the chaos, the Outlaws were able to infiltrate the central area. They control an abandoned Hilton hotel. It's five-miles west of here. Why?"

"Because we're going to pull Riley's ass out of there," Goolsby replied. "That's why."

"I can't spare any men," Boutros said. "We're barely holding the church as it is."

"All we need is *one* man. A guide," Goolsby said.

Boutros nodded. "I have the right person for you. She's an Iraqi Christian. We call her Sneakers."

"Good," Goolsby said. "Please ask Sneakers if she's willing to help us."

As Boutros departed to find Sneakers the VTOL's crew chief snapped to attention. "Sergeant George Martin, sir, requesting permission to join the extraction team."

Goolsby stared at him. "You told me that *both* pilots were dead."

The expression on Martin's face was one of pure misery. "I checked, sir. After the crash *and* when you sent me to get their tags. I couldn't find a pulse either time."

Goolsby relented. "Don't worry about it son... That's the most anyone could do. Your request is approved."

"I'll go too," Cole said. "I speak Arabic."

"I'm in," Kydd added. "Because I belong to the Hilton rewards program."

"And that's all the people we can afford to send," Goolsby said. "The bad guys know we're here. So it's my guess that they'll attack the church."

Goolsby was about to say something more when Boutros appeared. "This is Sneakers."

Kydd figured the girl was 15 or 16 years old. She had a buzz cut, and was dressed in boy's clothing, including a pair of red Nikes. Brown eyes scanned the marines. "Too many," she said. "Small group better. Night have eyes."

Goolsby gave in. "Okay, four people."

"You'll need this, sir," Martin said, as he offered a hand-held radio to Goolsby. "An automatic distress call went out the moment we crashed. The SAR (Search and Rescue) people will contact you soon." Goolsby accepted the unit.

"Get rest," Sneakers said. "We go when dark come. Have to walk. Many checkpoints."

"Are you hungry?" Boutros asked them. "We have a kitchen…And there's always something to eat. Church members make sure of that."

Sneakers led them into the church through the front door. The interior was beautiful. Perfectly-lit religious paintings and tapestries decorated the walls. Rows of benches lined the main aisle which led straight to the altar. Two of the slit-shaped windows were located so as to direct sunlight onto an oil painting and the effect was stunning.

A side door led to a flight of stone stairs and the basement below. The kitchen, which was normally used for religious celebrations, had been transformed into a mess hall. Kydd, Cole and Martin took advantage of the opportunity to eat lunch.

The *ful* sandwiches consisted of stewed fava beans that had been mashed and mixed with olive oil, chopped parsley, onion, and garlic all stuffed in hot pitas. The texture was similar to that of hummus, but filling in the way that meaty sandwiches are filling, and therefore satisfying.

It would have been nice to have a serious chat with Cole. But that was impossible with Martin present. Assuming the agent *wanted* to talk, which was by no means certain.

After lunch the three Americans were shown into an adjoining room. Padded sleeping mats had been laid on the stone floor. Each was topped with a neatly placed pillow and blanket.

Kydd lay down expecting to lie there—waiting for the necessary hours to pass. But he fell asleep at some point. And when he woke it was to discover that someone had laid a blanket over him. Cole was kneeling at his side. "Rise and shine sailor ... We have work to do."

Kydd wondered if Cole was the one who had placed the blanket over him. He hoped so.

After a visit to a restroom, and a cup of strong coffee, Kydd was ready to leave. Or thought he was ready until Sneakers appeared holding a bundle of black cloth. "These *niqab*," she said. "You wear. Hide you. Hide weapons."

After Sneakers shook one of the garments out Kydd discovered that he was going to be wearing a female garment that was supposed to cover a woman from head to toe.

Except most women weren't six-two. So his *niqab* ended ankle high, thereby revealing his combat boots. "Very sorry," Sneakers said. "Biggest I could get. Nighttime. No one see."

Kydd wasn't so sure about that. Nor was Sergeant Martin. But it couldn't be helped. Some sort of disguise was better than none. The plan called for Sneakers, dressed as a boy, to accompany the three "women" to the Hilton. "There be checkpoints," Sneakers warned them. "I talk. I pay access fees."

"Access fees?" Kydd inquired.

"Batteries," Sneakers said. "New ones. Or toothpaste. Or cigarettes. But bullets best."

It was dark outside and the air was cooler. Kydd's assault rifle was on a makeshift sling, hanging inside the *niqab*, where it would be impossible to access in an emergency.

So he was holding his nine-mil in his right hand. And, as long as he kept the pistol pointing down, only an inch of barrel showed below his sleeve. That wasn't perfect by any means, but beat the heck out of the alternative.

Sneakers led the way… She was wearing a boy's *thawb* (ankle-length robe), and a white skull cap. The hope being that observers would assume that "he," as a male was serving as an escort for three adult women. A common sight in neighboring Saudi Arabia.

Sneakers and Cole led the way. The men followed. They were paired to make them seem smaller. And because they didn't speak Arabic.

Kydd hadn't been to Cairo before, but was pretty sure that the prewar sidewalks had been a good deal more crowded in the evening, especially downtown. Some streetlights were on. But many had been shot out. Businesses that would normally remain open after dark were closing. And most were equipped with roll-down doors or makeshift fences to protect them from thieves.

The rattle of distant gunfire could be heard as gangs battled over turf, warring militias clashed, and citizens defended their homes. A flare soared in the distance and floated down. The sound of a pop song emanated from an alley.

Meanwhile the Americans were subjected to the unrelenting attentions of street vendors. They were teens mostly, peddling trinkets, street food, and tee shirts.

Sneakers did an excellent job of driving them away with machine gun-like bursts of Arabic invective. But more swarmed in to replace them. Sneakers had just dispatched a woeful one-armed beggar when Kydd spotted the checkpoint ahead.

It wasn't much to look at. Just a folding card table with a pot-bellied man sitting behind it, a couple of thuggish youngsters, and a mangy dog. Cars were forced to stop at a boom barrier operated by two men. The motorists paid up without being ordered to.

The same was true of the checkpoint on the sidewalk. The dog lapped water out of a bowl as the rescue party approached. Sneakers was clutching four 7.62x39mm rounds. The cartridges produced a rattling sound as she dropped them into a red plastic bowl.

The fat man said "*Shukraan jazilaan,*" (thank you) and Sneakers continued on her way. The Americans followed. Kydd wanted to look back, but knew a woman in a *niqab* wouldn't do that.

And so it went. Each checkpoint was slightly different, but the price was constant, and no one challenged them. After an hour of walking, Sneakers pulled them aside. "The Hilton ahead. We go in. I ask directions. You kill everyone."

The plan was so direct, and so brutal, Kydd could hardly believe his ears. But Sneakers had been through some shit... That much was obvious. And she was smart. A more nuanced strategy wouldn't work. *Use the nine first,* Kydd thought.

Thanks to the ambient light Kydd could see the building's facade. Most of the windows were shot out. And everything above the fourth floor had been damaged by fire.

Sneakers led the way to the front door where three armed men were talking and smoking cigarettes. A sandbagged gun emplacement was positioned off to one side—complete with an unmanned heavy machine gun.

When Sneakers spoke one of the men turned her way. He had just opened his mouth to speak when Sneakers shot him in the face a Helwan 920 pistol.

That was Kydd's cue to shoot a second man as Cole fired the stubby MP7 submachine gun *through* her *niqab*. The garment flared, and smoke dribbled out of the holes, as the third man jerked spastically. He went down in a heap.

Martin had thrown his *niqab* off by then. The combat shotgun was up and ready as he entered the lobby. Two gang members were coming his way. Martin blew both away with single shots. Blood sprayed across the huge "H" set into the terrazzo floor.

Sneakers entered the hotel like an angel of death. And, even though Martin's targets were down, the teenager shot each as she passed. "The basement," Sneakers said, as she hurried over to a circular staircase. Cole and Martin were right behind her.

Kydd threw his *niqab* off in time to holster the nine and chase Martin down the stairs. Sneakers shot a gang member as he hurried up the stairs. Then she vaulted over the railing to land six-feet below.

What had been a combination bar and restaurant was directly in front of them. Kydd fired the HK416 as outlaws poured out of it. Men were snatched off their feet as a series of three-round bursts cut them down.

Then, as suddenly as the fight began, it was over. Or nearly over… Because the Americans had to stand and wait while Sneakers shot each Outlaw in the face.

"Jeez," Martin said. "What's up with that?"

"Sneakers was raped by three Isis fighters when she was ten," Cole replied. "Her goal is to kill as many Sunnis as she can. And she likes to make sure."

Kydd looked at her. "How do you know that?"

"Girl talk," Cole replied.

"Come!" Sneakers said, as she reloaded. "We must hurry."

Lieutenant Riley was in the bar tied to a chair. His head was hanging low—and one side of his face was caked with dried blood. "Lieutenant!" Martin said. "It's me, Sergeant Martin."

Riley struggled to raise his head. He'd been beaten. One eye was swollen shut. "Martin?" he said groggily. "What are you doing here? Did they capture you?"

"No sir," Martin replied as he hurried to cut the pilot free. "We came to get you. Can you walk?"

"I don't know," Riley answered. "Help me up."

With Martin's assistance Riley was able to stand and shuffle forward. But he was in bad shape. And it didn't take a medical degree to see that he wouldn't be able to walk a mile, never mind the four required to reach the church. Sneakers had been on her radio. She put it away. "More come... We go."

"Paul," Riley croaked. "I can't leave without Paul."

"Lieutenant Omada didn't make it," Martin said. "Now help us get out of here."

By supporting Riley between them Martin and Kydd were able to walk the pilot over to the stairs and help him up. Sneakers and Cole had preceded them.

Kydd could hear bursts of submachine gun fire—interspersed with the harsh bang, bang, bang of a 9mm pistol. And when they arrived at the top of the stairs Kydd saw that more bodies lay sprawled in the lobby. Sneakers waved. "Come!"

Riley's legs had gone limp by then. The toes of his boots cut trails through the pools of blood as the two men dragged him across the lobby and out into the humid air. "Hurry!" Sneakers said, as she led them to the left, and away from the street they'd arrived on.

"One-block!" Sneakers said. "Then safe."

It seemed hard to believe, but Kydd figured that some chance was better than none. Together with Martin, he carried Riley down the shadowy street to a structure with graffiti scrawled all over it, and a sign that said "Metro" above an entrance. "Subway," Sneakers said, before ducking inside.

Was the church a short train ride away? Kydd wondered. The possibility seemed too good to be true, and it was. A frozen escalator with stairs on both sides led down. The stairs were covered with trash, piles of human excrement, and stray pieces of clothing. The smell was nauseating and became increasingly worse as they carried Riley down. It was hard work, and Kydd wondered how far they'd be able to go.

A light appeared at the bottom of the stairs, and Sneakers hurried toward it. Four armed men were waiting on a trash-strewn platform. They wore headlamps and scarves which hid their faces. A stretcher sat next to them. Kydd and Martin lowered Riley into place and strapped him in.

Cole spoke to one of the men in Arabic before turning to Kydd. "Boutros sent them. They will carry the stretcher. After the trains stopped running people began to bring their dead down here. Now it's a business. The crypt keepers charge the equivalent of one-hundred U.S. dollars to wash each corpse, cover the body with a shroud, and make sure that its head points toward Mecca when they push it into a slot."

Kydd wrinkled his nose. "It smells down here."

"And it's going to get worse," Cole warned him. "The Guardsmen brought scarves for us to use. Wrap this around your face." Kydd accepted the *rezza,* and soon discovered that the piece of cloth was large enough to circle his head twice, before securing it in place.

Once everyone was ready the journey began. First they had to jump down onto the track. Then it was time to manhandle the stretcher down. With that accomplished the party left. The combined illumination from four headlamps was enough to light the way.

There wasn't much to see at first. Just trash, graffiti, and tracks. Then men with guns emerged from the darkness. They were wearing respirators. A stretcher bearer spoke to them and a security guard waved the party through. Some sort of deal had been done. A fee perhaps? Probably.

The light level increased as they entered a section of the tunnel that was being excavated. A machine had been brought in to dig graves. It consisted of an articulated drill, an enclosed cab, and a large engine compartment.

Safety barriers kept the stretcher party away from it. Kydd caught a glimpse of a partially drilled wall. Vertically aligned holes could be seen. Some were occupied, while others waited to be filled. And, despite the industrial strength fans and ducting, the stench was terrible.

Once past the active work area the group entered a section of finished crypts. There were rows of graves. Each with a plastic lid and a code number. It was very impressive in a way... But, in a city where up to 4-million people a day used the subway before the war, there would be transportation problems later on. *Unless Kantar blows the dam*, Kydd thought. *Then it won't matter.*

Riley passed in and out of consciousness. He shouted things, tossed his head from side-to-side, and moaned occasionally. There was nothing the others could do except get the pilot to the church as quickly as possible. But another forty-five minutes passed before they arrived at what Sneakers said was the correct stop.

It took the better part of ten minutes to get people into position and hoist the stretcher up onto the platform. Then it was time for the rest of the party to climb the access ladder.

That was followed by the long up-the-escalator trip to the street above. "We two blocks from church," Sneakers announced. And that was good.

But, as they left the metro for the street, the sounds of a firefight could be heard. Bursts of automatic gunfire were punctuated by the occasional boom of a grenade. That was followed by the steady bang, bang, bang of a Kalashnikov firing one round at a time.

"They attack," Sneakers said. "You wait."

"Bullshit," Kydd said. "Lead the way. We'll attack the bastards from behind."

He turned to Cole. "Tell the stretcher bearers to stay close, but not *too* close."

Cole passed the word. Kydd turned to Sneakers. "Lead the way. But go slow."

The streets were nearly deserted by then. And Sneakers made good use of the available cover as she led them across the street and into the narrow passageway between two buildings. Sneakers paused to use her radio at that point. It was important to warn the defenders lest Boutros and his Guards open fire on the stretcher party.

There was no way to know who the attackers were. But one thing was for sure. They weren't soldiers. The attackers were so focused on firing at the church that Sneakers was able to sneak up and shoot a man in the back. And the sound was lost in the clatter generated by at least a dozen AK-47s.

Then the defensive fire stopped. And, had the attackers been better led, a noncom or officer might have wondered why. But certain of victory, the attackers emerged from cover, and started to advance. More than that, they bunched up in order to pass through a gate.

That was when Kydd, Cole, and Martin opened up on them. What ensued was more of a slaughter than a fight. The attackers near the gate died. The rest fled. Sneakers went to work shooting the wounded and dead.

Kydd waved the stretcher bearers forward. Then he, Cole, and Martin stood guard until everyone else was safely beyond the six-foot-high stone wall. Goolsby was waiting for them. "Good job! Come 0500 the navy will pull us out of here."

Boutros was kneeling by the stretcher. He took Riley's pulse, checked the pilot's pupils with a pen light, and stood. "Take him to the infirmary... Tell them I'll be there in a minute."

He turned to the Americans. "Don't worry, he'll make it. I'll make sure of that." Then he was gone.

Kydd and Cole took the opportunity to get something to eat. And it was then, as Kydd went over to pour himself a cup of coffee, that he realized his hands were shaking.

Would Cole understand? Would she think less of him? Fortunately his back was to her. By holding the mug with both hands Kydd could keep his hands from trembling.

They sat across from each other but neither chose to reference the rescue mission. "You lied to me," Kydd said. 'When I asked how we were going to stop Kantar from triggering the bomb, you said the plan had an additional element that you couldn't reveal."

Cole smiled. "You can't share something you don't have."

Kydd laughed. "You're a devious woman."

Cole eyed him over the edge of her cup. Her eyes were very blue. "That's right, sailor … And don't forget it."

***

"The show," as Goolsby referred to it, began at exactly 0500. Two F/A-18 Hornets appeared. One from the north, and one from the south. They broke the sound barrier within seconds of each other. "Good morning, Cairo!" Goolsby said gleefully, as the Americans watched from the churchyard. "Things are about to get real."

The response came moments later when three heat-seeking MANPADS (man-portable air-defense systems) flashed up out of different parts of the city. The fighters fired chaff, entered tight turns, and went looking for people to kill.

However the Soviet-made second-generation SA-14s weren't fooled by the chaff. So they zeroed in. Or attempted to.

But the Hornets were equipped with ECs (electronic countermeasures) which prevented the enemy missiles from achieving lock-on. Meanwhile the jets were preparing to make gun runs with their M61 Vulcan cannons.

The six-barrel, electrically-fired Gatling-style weapons could fire 6,000 rounds per minute. They were being employed to avoid the collateral damage often associated with missiles and bombs.

But as the cannons roared, and 20mm shells ploughed through streets and buildings, the difference was more theoretical than real.

The attacks were over in seconds and so was the resistance. The missile attacks stopped as the F/A-18 Hornets circled the city. "That was act one," Goolsby announced. "Act two is on the way."

Two specks appeared from the north, and quickly resolved into HH-60H "Rescue Hawk" helicopters, and both were armed. They came in high to avoid ground fire to the extent that such a thing was possible, and as RPGs lashed up at them, helos were ready to reply with GAU-17A door guns.

A pillar of red smoke was rising from the church, and the Hawks followed it in. Fortunately the garden behind the church was large enough for two helicopters to land at once.

Riley had been brought up from the church's basement. Navy hospital corpsmen took over from the Egyptian nurses. But, before they could load the pilot, a significant quantity of guns and ammo had to be unloaded. The rotors continued to turn, and the engines were loud. Kydd had to yell in order for Cole to hear him. "What's the hardware for?"

"We owe the Coptic Guards," Cole shouted. "Plus they might come in handy later on."

Kydd was surprised, but shouldn't have been. Even as the shit went down Cole was busy cutting a deal between Boutros and the CIA. It was a different kind of mindset. Rescue Riley and get him out. That's what Kydd had been focused on. *Cole's something else,* Kydd thought. *Something special.* Once the last crates had been unloaded the corpsmen lifted Riley into a Rescue Hawk. Martin followed.

The jets made low passes over the city as the first helo took off. The message was clear: "Shoot at the helicopter and we will we kill you." No one did.

The HH-60H was a quickly dwindling speck when the crew chief yelled at Goolsby. "You're good to go, sir! Let's load 'em up!"

Goolsby turned to shake hands with Boutros before making his way over to stand by the chopper. Kydd had to give him credit. Rather than get on, Goolsby planned to count heads and be the last jarhead out.

The second helicopter departed without incident, the flight from Cairo to Esna took two-and-a-half hours, and the Rescue Hawks landed on the same field from which they had departed. It soon became apparent that while the convoy had transited the locks it hadn't gone any further. And there was a reason for that.

"We're stalling," Goolsby told Kydd. "While the people in D.C. do their thing. So if your people need to catch up on maintenance now's the time."

Kydd passed the word. There was always maintenance to do, and his sailors went to work. More than that there was the question of the poorly armed British boats.

The wrench turners agreed that they couldn't add heavy weapons to the boats without making the kind of structural changes that could only be carried out in a navy yard. But they could add a layer of ballistic fabric to the interiors of both wheelhouses and up-gun the boats by adding shield-protected grenade launchers in the front.

Thanks to the fact that the launchers could fire 40 rounds a minute, and reach targets that were 2,000 yards away, the additional firepower would make a very significant difference in any sort of bow-on action. Lieutenant Fox-Smith professed himself to be "Very happy indeed."

While those things were happening Kydd tackled all the administrative tasks Evans had waiting for him. After working on it for an entire day Kydd was finally caught up.

That meant he could join the command boat for a trip to Outpost Oscar, which was located about 25 miles up-river just north of Al Kilh Sharq, at a point where the Nile narrowed.

The detachment consisted of a platoon strength unit located in the ruins of an old fortress. The leathernecks were charged with watching the river—and preventing players like Urabi from setting up shore batteries, laying minefields, or otherwise making preparations to attack the convoy. Kydd's flotilla was responsible for keeping the advance party supplied, and for providing fire support if needed.

But, when Kydd made his way down the riverboat's stairs to board the RCB, he was in for a surprise. Cole was on the boat and chatting with Chief Petty Officer Jones. She was wearing a headscarf and a blue *gallabya*. Cole turned to greet him. "Hi! I'd like to hitch a ride with Jonesy. I hope that's okay."

Jonesy? No one dared call the chief Jonesy. Yet the man in question hadn't blinked an eye. "Sure," Kydd replied. "That's fine. Where are you headed?"

"I'm scheduled to meet with someone at the Pyramid of Al Kola. Dump me off. I'll be waiting when you return."

Kydd frowned. "Shouldn't you take a fireteam with you?"

Cole shook her head. "That would spook the guy I'm meeting with. Don't worry, I know what I'm doing."

Yes, you do, Kydd thought. *But you push it.* "Roger that. Okay, Chief…Let's shove off."

It was a beautiful morning. The local feluccas were out on the river as usual. And, as the patrol boat motored south, well-watered farms were visible on both sides. An island appeared ahead. "We took the left channel last time," Jones said. So we'll take the right channel today."

Kydd nodded. Rivers don't provide a lot of choices. They flow where they flow. But it made sense to vary routes to the extent possible. Cole was standing by the port rail. The slip stream tugged at her gown. He went to stand beside her. "So, what have you heard? Did a decision come down?"

"Yes," Cole replied. "Our request was approved."

"So it's up to the drone jockeys."

"Yes. But, even if they succeed, we'll have to fight Hezbollah."

"Yeah," Kydd agreed. "What about the Chinese? Will we have to fight them too?"

"They're still moving north," Cole replied.

"So the answer is 'yes.'"

"That's how it looks."

Kydd took advantage of the momentary silence. "So, what's your favorite book?"

Cole broke into laughter. "You're incorrigible."

"*What?*" Kydd asked innocently. "We can't discuss literature?"

Cole smiled. "*Pride and Prejudice.* And yours?"

"*Into The Heart of Darkness.*"

"How appropriate."

"I guess it is … That hadn't occurred to me."

"This is it," Jones announced, as the boat slowed. "The dock looks rickety … Watch your step."

Kydd looked into Cole's eyes. "You have a radio? And a weapon?"

"Yes, daddy."

"Call and we'll come running."

Cole nodded. "I'll be waiting when you come downriver."

***

Cole stepped off the boat and onto the dock. The sunbaked wood was in need of repair, birds had been pooping on it for years, and a beat-up felucca was tugging at its rope. There were no people to be seen.

A worn path led west from the river and through a well-watered banana plantation. The muted thump, thump, thump of an irrigation pump could be heard but nothing more. No birds. No anything.

It felt spooky. Cole slid her right hand into the *gallabya*, felt for the pistol, and drew it. With the weapon pointing down along her leg she continued to walk. Her head was on a swivel, the way it was supposed to be, and her gut felt empty.

The purpose of the trip was to meet with a man named Burhan Al-Bishi. He was, among other things, one of Hussain Urabi's underlings. And Cole was supposed to keep track of Urabi's activities. Was the warlord keeping his part of the bargain with the United States Government? Or was he preparing to attack the convoy? Inquiring minds wanted to know.

Thanks to one of Cole's Egyptian contractors she'd been able to make contact with Al-Bishi and set a meeting. But only if she came alone.

Cole arrived at a T-shaped intersection where her path met with another. A pond blocked the way which meant the agent had to go left or right. Based on the drone footage Cole had seen she turned right. The trail led to a bridge. And the bridge crossed the pond to a spot just east of the Al Kola Pyramid.

Cole had done her research. The Al Kola had been constructed to honor an unknown personage and dated back to Egypt's third dynasty. It had been 40-feet tall originally. But now, after more than 2,000 years of weather, it had been reduced to a 32-foot-high mound of rubble. And looked like a pile of stone blocks. So it wasn't, nor would it ever be, a major tourist attraction.

The pyramid was a roadside stop for the nearby highway though … And prior to the war the site had been home to half a dozen food vendors. They were gone now leaving little more than a clutch of picnic tables. And except for a lone figure who was slumped over a table the area was deserted.

Cole stopped to check her surroundings. A truck rattled past on the highway. The sun beat down on her shoulders and flies buzzed. Cole didn't like the feel of it, but she couldn't skip the meeting without a reason.

The person was taking a nap. Or so it appeared from a distance. But as Cole drew closer she saw the knife that protruded from the man's back and his blood-soaked *thawb*.

Cole's heart beat faster. She raised the pistol and performed a complete 360. Nothing. The killer, or killers, were gone. She wanted to leave. And she *would* leave. Right after she checked the body. Was she looking at Al-Bishi? Or someone else?

Cole made her way over to the corpse. The dagger wasn't just any old blade. The pommel consisted of a red gemstone, or what *looked* like a gemstone, and glowed in the sun. The handle was wrapped with silver wire. Why so fancy? Unless...

Cole heard the scrape of a boot, turned, and fired. The bullet hit the man in the shoulder. He staggered, and regained his balance, only to take one in the head.

Cole whirled in time to shoot *another* assailant. The first shot took half of his left ear. The next slug killed him. Then she ran. A male voice yelled, "Catch her!" The river was a long ways off.

CHAPTER ELEVEN

Aswan Dam, Egypt

B lood flew as Kantar brought the sword down on Sergeant Boustani's unprotected neck. The noncom turned his head and laughed. "You call that a cut? My five-year-old could do better."

Kantar awoke with a jerk. The nightmares had been plaguing him for days. There were a number of permutations, but all of them had common elements: The sword, Boustani, and a feeling of failure.

Not only had Kantar failed to kill the mutineer with a single blow, his efforts to create a Shia friendly government had thus far come to naught, and Secretary General Hassan Haddad was going to arrive in a few hours. But *why*? Was Haddad planning to deliver a pep talk? Or chew him out? Kantar turned a light on, put his feet on the tiny carpet, and grabbed his radio. "Marwan."

"Sir!" Newly promoted *Lieutenant* Babak Marwan was an even better officer than Allawi had been. The Iranian was equally industrious, better educated, and a trained missile technician.

"Is everything ready?"

"Yes, sir. The control tower is manned. The airport has been searched and secured. All the missile batteries have been notified—and will allow the secretary general's plane to land."

"Excellent. And the refreshments? The secretary general might be hungry."

"Mr. El Saa promised a feast," Marwan assured him.

El Saa was the battalion's Nubian chef who, along with the other members of his enormous family, kept the battalion fed. Even the men stationed in the outlying missile batteries ate well and that was good for morale.

"Thank you, Marwan," Kantar said. "And remember…It will be your job to keep everything running smoothly while I'm at the airport."

"Yes, sir."

Kantar broke the connection and began the laborious process of getting ready. The "bomb" room had never been intended for sleeping. It lacked running water, never mind a shower. Kantar had to take his toiletries, his radio, the bomb's remote, *and* a pistol to a distant utility room in order to take a sponge bath and shave.

Once that ritual was complete Kantar returned to the bomb room, put his toiletries away, and got dressed. Then it was time to button the remote into a cargo pocket and lock the door behind him. From there Kantar made his way to the control room and his office. Most of the engineers didn't bother to turn and look.

Once Kantar sat down he found the usual stack of reports waiting on his desk. Marwan was a member of the Iranian Army which, unlike Hezbollah, had a penchant for all things bureaucratic.

That was an improvement in many ways. But it forced Kantar to spend at least an hour of every day plowing through paperwork. Kantar was reading a technician's fitness report when his lead driver appeared in the doorway. "We're ready, sir."

Kantar put the report aside and stood. "Good."

After following the driver out into the cool night air, Kantar looked up at the blanket of stars. Marwan said there was nothing to worry about. But what if the Iranian was mistaken?

An Al Qaeda leader named Musa Abu Dawud had been killed by a drone near the city of Ubari in Libya. *But he didn't have radars and a missile system to protect him*, Kantar thought.

Still, it was best to leave nothing to chance. That's why *three* cars stood waiting at the curb. No one knew which vehicle Kantar would choose to ride in. Not even the man himself. Kantar paused for a moment, chose car two, and got inside. The driver had a radio. "Car one can depart." Car one left on a drive to nowhere. "Car three can go." Car three pulled away.

Then, and only then, did car two leave for the airport. It was a short drive. As the car pulled up in front of the terminal building Kantar saw that all of the lights were blazing.

A sergeant offered a salute. Kantar returned it. They entered together and made their way to the west side of the terminal. A civilian employee was waiting to greet them. He bowed. "Good evening, Wahda Kantar. My name is Abbad Omar. All is in readiness. The plane is on time."

Kantar nodded. "Thank you." He knew that the plane Omar referred to was a Kenya Airways jet. Did Allied intelligence agents know that Secretary General Hassan Haddad was on board? Probably. But, they couldn't shoot a neutral plane down, so Haddad was safe.

Kantar was thirty-minutes early. Time seemed to drag. But finally, after what seemed like an eternity, Omar reappeared. "The plane is on final approach, sir."

"Take me down to the tarmac. I want to be there when the secretary general deplanes."

It took a full fifteen-minutes for the jet to land and taxi in. An honor guard consisting of twelve fighters marched onto the field and came to attention. One of them carried a green-on-yellow Hezbollah flag.

Once the stairs were rolled into place Kantar stood at the foot of them. But rather than the secretary general, the first man off the plane was a heavily laden Hezbollah noncom. He tossed a salute, received one in return, and began to bawl orders. "Move it, move it, move it!" The stairs rattled as fighters hurried to deplane. "Form up!" the sergeant ordered. "That means you Abdullah."

That was when Secretary General Haddad appeared at the top of the stairs. He looked even more corpulent than before. And, as Haddad made his way down the stairs, his bodyguards followed. "*Mar Haban*," Haddad said. (Hello, greetings.)

"*Ahlan wa sahlan*," Kantar replied. (Welcome.)

Kantar was ready for the air kisses this time. "It's good to see you, sir…Mr. Omar will lead the way. Refreshments are waiting."

"Ah, you know me too well," Haddad said. "I am a bit peckish."

Stairs led up to the main floor where the elevator was waiting. There was barely enough room for Omar, Kantar, Haddad and his bodyguards.

After arriving on the second floor it was a short walk to the executive dining room where a table loaded with food awaited. There was hummus, manakish, falafel and more.

El Saa and two of his sons stood on the opposite side of the table ready to serve. "This is a remarkable feast," Haddad said, as he made his selections. "I assume you will join me."

Kantar wasn't in the least bit hungry, but forced himself to eat anyway. He listened as Haddad rambled on about the war, his granddaughter who was learning to walk, and diabetes.

The diatribe seemed to last forever. But eventually the meal came to an end, and Haddad turned his attention to business. "I brought you a present."

Kantar knew Haddad was referring to the newly arrived fighters. "Thank you. What a wonderful surprise."

"You will need them," Haddad said. "The Allies are closing in from the north."

"True," Kantar agreed. "Although they haven't left Esna. They're afraid to."

"Possibly," Haddad allowed. "But what if they're waiting for the Chinese?"

Kantar frowned. "I don't understand. The Chinese will make my position stronger."

"No," Haddad said. "They won't. The Chinese oppose using the bomb ... And, should they manage to get this far, they will try to dissuade you. And failing that, who knows? It's possible that the Allies know these things and are waiting for the Chinese to arrive."

"But *why?*" Kantar demanded.

"Because there's something like 20-million Sunnis in China," Haddad answered. "The Chinese fear that they will revolt if you blow the dam."

Kantar thought about Allawi. Now he knew the truth. The helicopter hadn't crashed. Allawi had been murdered. To prevent him from reporting back.

Should he mention that to Haddad? No. There was no benefit to doing so. "So what should I do?"

"Do what you were sent here to do," Haddad said. "And that is to cajole, nudge, or bully the Egyptians into forming a government we can deal with."

"My attempts have failed thus far," Kantar confessed. "But I have a plan."

"Tell me about your plan," Haddad said, as he popped a stuffed date into his mouth.

"There is a man," Kantar began. "His name is Umar al-Hudaybi. He's one of three men who claim to be President. When I meet with him I will offer our assistance in return for military access to Egypt."

"I like it," Haddad said. "And our friends in Iran and Pakistan will like it too. As for the Russians, they are angry at you, but won't object. Not if they can base planes here. But understand this, Mustafa … You're running out of time."

"Yes, sir," Kantar replied soberly. "I know."

***

Al Farafra, Egypt

Cirrus clouds marbled the blue sky as the gray S-class Mercedes entered town. Al Farafra was unexpectedly green. Everywhere Victor Danby looked he saw palm, apricot, and citrus trees. And there was a reason for that.

Al Farafra was home to the Roman spring of Ain Bishay which, along with one-hundred natural wells, made the oasis a tourist attraction before the war. But now, with political uncertainty and gas rationing, the town had few visitors.

But Danby wasn't there to see the sights. No, he was in Farafra to take care of State Department business, and make some side-money. One-hundred-thousand smackers to be exact. That was the price the Russians had on Mustafa Kantar's head.

A week earlier Danby had been ordered to make contact with an ex-government official named Umar al-Hudaybi, and convince the Egyptian to take a meeting with terrorist Mustafa Kantar, for which he would be paid fifty-thousand dollars. Al-Hudaybi had agreed, and today was the day.

Then, as Kantar left town, the CIA would kill him. That's when Danby would go to the spot where Kantar had been killed and take *two* tissue samples. One for the U.S. government and, unbeknownst to them, one for Russia's military foreign-intelligence service.

The side-hustle would put a sweet one-hundred-thou in Danby's Caribbean account. And the Caymans were a much better place for his stash than Switzerland which was very close to the action in Europe.

So Danby was in a good mood as Farook, his driver-bodyguard, turned onto a well-paved driveway. It curved through a grove of trees to end in front of a magnificent residence.

Having toured the home a week earlier, Danby knew the sprawling mansion was made of limestone blocks, just like the pyramids of Giza. The Arab-style house included a formal reception area, a family hall, a circular staircase beyond, separate dining rooms for men and women, two salons, and a spa one level below. All paid for with the money that al-Hudaybi siphoned out of Egypt's coffers during his tenure as a cabinet minister.

Uniformed guards, all dressed like soldiers from the late 19th century, came forward to check identities and search the car. Then it was time for a bearded major domo wearing a red fez to escort Danby into the house. Danby had to pass through a full-body scanner, and allow his briefcase to be X-rayed, before being free to proceed.

Al-Hudaybi was waiting for him, as were refreshments, and a comfortable chair. *This*, Danby thought, *is the way life is meant to be.*

* * *

Cavallero Airbase, Libya

Cavallero Airbase had been built by the Italians during World War II, and used to launch raids on Allied shipping in the Mediterranean. However, by the spring of 1943 Axis airpower had nearly been eliminated in North Africa, which caused Cavallero to be abandoned.

But shortly after the beginning of World War III Cavallero had been reconstituted as a CIA drone base. It consisted of the original runways, which had been repaired, and three "clam-shell" style hangars, each large enough to house Predator drones.

There were trailer-like habs as well, one of which was commonly referred to as "The Crypt." The windowless box was divided into two "control pods." Each operation center was manned by a three-person team 24/7. The Pod 2 duty team consisted of Pilot Karen Ho, CIA Case Officer Tim Buxton, and Mission Coordinator Larry Elwood.

Together they were running a Pred B mission over Al Farafra, Egypt. According to the data on the screens in front of Ho, the drone was at 25,000 feet, traveling at a minimal speed of 100mph, and all of its systems were green. "I have the handoff," Ho said. "The target is ten out from Farafra."

Elwood took a swig from his can of Liquid X energy drink. The target, a bad boy named Mustafa Kantar, was currently flying from Ar Rashidah, where his Russian-made plane had been forced to refuel, to Al Farafra.

During the flight Kantar's ride had been under surveillance by a RQ-4B surveillance drone cruising at 50,000 feet. And because that was well above the biplane's operational ceiling of 15,000 feet the Global Hawk had gone undetected. Now, having completed its mission, the surveillance aircraft was headed home. "Roger that," Elwood said, as Ho's Predator looked down on the ancient plane. "What *is* that thing?"

"It's a combination crop-duster and passenger plane," Buxton said, without looking up from his laptop. "The first ones were manufactured in 1947. About 18,000 were produced and sold all over the world."

"How do you know this shit?" Elwood inquired, as the Antonov An-2 prepared to land.

"I'm linked to the Cho'ja hive mind," Buxton replied. "Which means I am all-knowing."

Both Elwood and Ho were familiar with Buxton's science fiction references. "In that case you know the plane is on the ground," Ho said, as she put the Pred into a turn. "And the target is walking to a car."

The drone was lower now, and Elwood was able to watch, as the tiny figure entered a vehicle. It seemed that Kantar had enough green stuff to hire a plane plus ground transpo.

He took another swig of Liquid X. "Okay, people ... This shit is about to get real. Pee while you can."

***

Al Farafra, Egypt

Kantar felt a heady combination of anticipation and fear as he entered the taxi. The AC wasn't working, so the windows were down, and hot air blew against his face as the road-weary car made its way through streets lined with mudbrick buildings.

The overhead power lines suggested the presence of modern conveniences. But the unpaved streets, a caravan of Bedouin-led camels, and an open air bazaar were like scenes from the distant past.

Most of Kantar's attention was focused on his personal safety and the meeting with al- Hudaybi. After a great deal of delib-eration Kantar made the decision to travel alone. Bodyguards could protect him from thieves. But their presence could draw unwanted attention, and prompt a drone strike.

As for the meeting, it would have been nice to bring an entourage, in an effort to impress al-Hudaybi. But that had a flip side too .... By making the journey alone Kantar was signaling strength and confidence. He hoped so anyway, as the cab turned into a driveway, and stopped in front of a large house.

After paying the driver Kantar got out and was met by half-a-dozen uniformed guards. Kantar wasn't carrying official ID. But he was expected and, after surrendering his pistol, was shown into the front lobby where a body scanner awaited.

Kantar couldn't trust anyone with the bomb's remote, and he couldn't bring the device with him. So it had been left behind, hidden deep within the dam.

After passing through the security checkpoint Kantar entered the family hall where al- Hudaybi and another man stood waiting. Al-Hudaybi was wearing a bespoke suit and a pair of shiny shoes. *"Mar Haban."* (Hello, greetings.)

"Iinah lamin diwaeiin saruri 'an 'altaqi bikum," (It is a pleasure to meet you), Kantar replied respectfully.

"And you," al-Hudaybi replied. "I would like to introduce Mr. Tanner, my secretary. He'll be joining us to take notes."

Danby offered his hand. He spoke flawless Arabic. "This is an honor Wahda Kantar. The entire world knows of your accomplishments."

The compliment triggered a momentary surge of pleasure, which Kantar hurried to suppress lest he be manipulated. "It's a pleasure to meet you Mr. Tanner."

"Come," al-Hudaybi said expansively. "You came a long way, and are no doubt hungry. We will have something to eat and talk."

The large table that normally graced the male dining room had been replaced by a smaller version set for three. Tea was served, followed by appetizers, and a steady flow of beautifully prepared dishes. Kantar barely noticed them as he made his presentation.

Kantar began by praising al-Hudaybi's many accomplishments, and assuring the ex-government official that *he*, above all others, was the person best suited to lead Egypt through troubled times. And more than that—all the Axis countries stood ready to pour resources both military and commercial into Egypt, thereby ensuring al-Hudaybi's success and safety were he to convene a Shia-friendly government.

"I know the concept will be met with resistance at first," Kantar said. "But the Shias' history with Egypt is a long one. The Shia Fatimids came to power 969 years before Christ, and they founded Fustat, the city that became Cairo.

"Fatimids ruled Egypt for 200 years, and helped shape its culture, Kantar added. "They founded the famous Al-Azhar University which, as you know, exists today.

"All of which means that in spite of subsequent changes Sunnis share a common heritage with their Shia brothers and sisters. And," Kantar said, "once you assume the presidency we will work with you to remind the population of this common history.

"In the meantime our troops will help keep the peace, and prevent the Allied countries from infringing on your sovereignty." That was a disingenuous statement to say the least, but at the core of the argument al-Hudaybi could make to the Egyptian people.

During the presentation Mr. Tanner scribbled on a yellow legal pad, and al-Hudaybi nodded occasionally. Finally, when Kantar was finished, his host weighed in. And al-Hudaybi's response was clear. He was impressed, he was enthusiastic, and he was in.

Kantar felt as if an enormous weight had been lifted from his shoulders. He thanked al- Hudaybi, asked for directions to a restroom, and excused himself. To relieve himself, yes, but to celebrate as well.

***

Cavallero Airbase, Libya

The Pred was circling high above al-Hudaybi's mansion as Buxton paced back and forth. He was speaking over a scrambled sat phone. "So he's in there. Yeah, I get that. Have you seen any non-combatants?"

That was followed by a pause and another question. "But they're wearing uniforms, right? Okay, that's a wrap. Get out of there."

Buxton broke the connection. "Okay, let's do this thing. Get ready to hit the house."

Elwood stared. "*What?* The plan calls for greasing Kantar on his way to the airport."

"That was draft one," Buxton replied calmly. "This is draft three. Kantar is in the house. So is al-Hudaybi, who played a role in destabilizing Egypt's government, and a shithead named Victor Danby. See the Mercedes? The one that's leaving? That's his... Bought and paid for with Russian money. The man at the wheel is one of my guys."

Buxton met Elwood's gaze. "Once Danby received orders to work with al-Hudaybi, and try to sucker Kantar in, he sold the hit to the GRU. They want revenge for the way Kantar double-crossed them. So, if you look at today's disposition matrix, you'll see that all three names are on the to-do list. This is what I call a three-fer."

Keys rattled as Elwood typed. "Holy shit... You're right."

"Of course I'm right," Buxton said confidently. "So here goes... I want two Hellfires on the house—followed by two 500-pound Paveways."

"Coming up," Ho acknowledged. "Ask, and the bad guys shall receive."

All eyes went to the main screen. The house was directly ahead, and locked in the video crosshairs. Ho fired.

***

Al Farafra, Egypt

After washing his hands Kantar splashed water on his face. It was refreshing. Then he examined himself in the mirror. *You did it*, Kantar thought. *You did it.*

Kantar was one level below the men's dining room in the spa-like area that opened onto the pool deck. And he was about to go back upstairs when the entire world seemed to explode.

There was a loud BOOM. The building shook, a crystal chandelier crashed to the floor, and Kantar began to run.

A *second* explosion followed the first as Kantar sprinted out through the open door. The pressure wave from the *third* explosion propelled him over the water.

As Kantar sank into the cool water, he heard the muffled thud associated with a fourth weapon, and pieces of debris splashed into the water. Some fell past him to land at the bottom of the pool. *Who are they trying to kill?* Kantar wondered. *Me? Or al-Hudaybi?* Not that it mattered in the moment. What mattered was oxygen… And getting enough of it.

***

Cavallero Airbase, Libya

"Right on the money," Buxton said, as the weapons exploded in sequence. "No bug splat (collateral damage) so far as I can see."

"Roger that," Elwood agreed.

"Bring the bird home," Buxton said. "My guy will perform the BDA (battle damage assessment)."

"It's Miller time," Elwood said. "And I'm buying."

***

Al Farafra, Egypt

Once the airstrike was over Farook returned to the mansion, parked on the street, and hurried up the drive. Chunks of debris lay scattered about. His digital camera was ready, as was the tissue collection kit in his pocket.

But as Farook rounded a curve he saw that the previously beautiful mansion was mostly rubble now. Fires were burning here and there, smoke poured up into the sky, and whatever passed for a fire department in Farafra would respond soon. That meant the chances of finding the correct bodies were negligible. But that was the task—and Farook was determined to try.

The front of the building had collapsed. That forced Farook to circle north in hopes of gaining access from the east. The swimming pool was to his right. Shards of wood floated here and there—along with what might have been a hand.

But Farook needed more than a hand. What he needed… Farook's thoughts were interrupted as a man erupted out of the pool beside him.

Then, before Farook could draw the pistol at his waist, the man pulled him off-balance and into the water. Farook didn't know how to swim—but found that his feet could touch bottom. So he fought. But Farook's opponent was bigger and stronger.

Farook struggled to dislodge the arm that was wrapped around his neck, failed, and found it was impossible to breath. *Nayla,* he thought. *Nayla.* Then he was gone.

***

Kantar let go. *Hurry,* he thought. *Hurry. People will come soon.* Hands fumbled with wet clothing. Kantar found a wallet, a set of keys, and the holstered pistol. He kept those items but threw the case containing a scalpel and vials away.

A siren could be heard by then, and when the firemen appeared, Kantar was dragging the body out of the pool. "The explosion threw him into the water," he told them. "I tried to revive him, but he's dead."

The fireman opened his mouth to ask a question but never got the chance. Somewhere, deep inside the remains of the mansion, flames found al-Hudaybi's armory. The resulting blast tossed chunks of debris high into the air. Some splashed into the pool, as Kantar ran for the street.

The keys were in his hand...All on a Mercedes Benz ring. Was that the kind of car the little man *wanted* to own? Or was that the kind of car he actually had?

The answer to the question was parked on the street. And, when Kantar pressed the key fob, lights flashed. *Thanks be to Allah*, Kantar thought, as he opened the door. The driver's seat was too far forward, but slid back at the touch of a button.

Kantar looked for the ignition switch and realized there wasn't any. There was a button though...And the engine started right away.

An alarm sounded as Kantar drove away. That forced him to stop and buckle up. Then he took off. But for *where*? To the airport, where the chartered plane was waiting? Or to Aswan?

Kantar looked for a place to pull over and did. There was a map in the glove box. And the situation was clear. There was no direct route from Al Farafra to Aswan. And the indirect routes would take forever. So the plane was the way to go.

Maybe the attackers were after him, and maybe they weren't. Maybe they knew about the plane, and maybe they didn't. All Kantar could do was take the chance.

After asking an old man for directions Kantar drove to the little airport, rousted his pilot out of a nearby restaurant, and ordered him back to the plane. Kantar's clothes were soaking wet. But, if the aviator was curious, he kept the questions to himself.

They were in the air twenty minutes later. "Contact the tower at the Aswan Dam," Kantar said. "Tell them we're enroute, and give them an ETA. The authorization code is seven-zero-seven. Got it?"

"Seven-zero-seven," the pilot said dutifully.

Kantar felt tired and depressed. He made his way back into the cargo compartment where the pilot had a thin mattress and a couple of blankets. *Maybe they're tracking me*, Kantar thought. *Maybe I'll die in my sleep.* And that, Kantar decided, would be just fine.

But Kantar *didn't* die in his sleep. He was awake for the refueling stop in Ar Rashdah, and the subsequent flight to the dam, where Lieutenant Marwan was waiting on the tarmac. The sun was setting by then—and the airport's lights were on. "Welcome back, sir ... How did it go?"

"It went badly," Kantar told him. "*Very* badly."

Marwan's eyes grew wider as Kantar described the meeting with al-Hudaybi, the drone attack, and his escape. "Allah was with you," the Iranian said. "Nothing else could explain how you survived."

Kantar assumed that was true. But to what end? Al-Hudaybi was dead. And so was the possibility of a deal. Time was running through his fingers like grains of desert sand. But, much to Kantar's surprise, the answer to his dilemma was there waiting for him.

"I have a message for you," Marwan said, "from a man named Hussain Urabi."

Kantar frowned. Urabi ... He'd heard the name before. But in connection with *what?* Then it came to him. Urabi was the warlord who had done battle with the Chinese who, according to Secretary General Haddad, planned to attack him. "What does Urabi want?"

"He wants to meet with you," Marwan said. "To discuss the creation of a new government."

Kantar felt his heart leap. Urabi was hostile to the Chinese. And the Chinese were hostile to *him.* So Urabi was a potential ally. "You're sure?"

"Yes. He would like to meet with you tomorrow. In Aswan."

"Get back to him," Kantar said. "And set it up. Pay attention to security though ... The meeting could be a ruse."

The promise of a new initiative was just the tonic that Kantar needed. He slept well that night, exercised the following morning, and was ready by ten. Marwan had chosen six bodyguards to protect Kantar, all of whom were combat veterans, and large in stature. Urabi was entitled to bring an equal number of retainers. But Kantar's troops controlled the city of Aswan. So, if the warlord were to try something, he and his men would have no way to escape. And Kantar took comfort from that.

Even though Kantar was back inside the protective umbrella that the SAM launchers provided, he was even more paranoid about drones after the attack in Al Farafra, and determined to deceive the Allies should they be spying on him. So the bodyguards were sent off in a truck. And, in a departure from his past practices, Kantar rode a motorcycle from the dam to the city. Kantar's fighters knew their commander was coming and waved him through the checkpoint.

Despite Hezbollah's efforts to prevent Aswan from being reoccupied, people had been leaking in for some time. And Kantar saw evidence of that as he rode through the streets. Laundry could be seen hanging from lines, plants were being watered, and a healthy looking camel stood tethered to a lamppost.

But what could Kantar do? He lacked the number of fighters required to go house-to-house and clear the city. And, even if he were able to force a complete evacuation, doing so would foster even more hatred. It was a conundrum.

The restaurant Urabi had chosen for the meeting was a well-known spot that fronted the Nile. Kantar parked the bike next to Hezbollah's truck. His bodyguards formed up around him. One man in front, followed by two more, followed by Kantar himself. Two fighters had been assigned to protect his back, while a third spent half his time looking backwards, in case of an attack.

The upscale eatery was plush but empty. White linen covered the tables, silver gleamed, and the floor to ceiling windows were crystal clear. Fishing boats weren't supposed to operate off Aswan city anymore, but there they were, tacking back and forth. It was a pretty sight.

Urabi was seated at a table in front of the window and rose as Kantar appeared. The warlord's bodyguards stood in pairs, their backs to Urabi. The warlord had a receding hairline, a moon-shaped face, and heavy eyebrows. He spoke with a British accent. "Greetings! I'm happy to see that you survived."

Kantar's alarm bells went off. *Be careful*, the inner voice said. *He's good at this sort of thing, and more experienced than you are.* "News travels quickly," Kantar replied, in what he hoped was a nonchalant manner.

"Please," Urabi said, "have a seat. Yes, I have contacts in Al Farafra, and they keep me advised. I assume that Minister al-Hudaybi was killed."

"Yes," Kantar replied. "That seems likely. But I didn't search the ruins."

"No," Urabi said, as tall glasses of iced tea arrived. "I wouldn't think so.

"We're men of action, you and I. So, let's get down to business. I, like everyone else in Egypt, would like to prevent a catastrophe. But I'm a businessman as well … And, like all businessmen, I'm interested in making a profit.

"You on the other hand are a soldier, and a diplomat, who wants Egypt on your side. I believe we can work together to achieve all of those goals. Would you like to hear more?"

Appetizers arrived and sat untouched as the men eyed each other. "Yes, I would," Kantar replied. "Coming together is a beginning; keeping together is progress; working together is success."

The proverb caused Urabi to smile. "Good. My proposal is this: Others, men like myself, will listen to me. I will invite them to a meeting which you will attend. We will put forward a proposal to create an Egyptian government led by me, in which each of them will occupy an important post, thereby ensuring their ability to have a say.

"Immediately after the creation of this government, I will announce that Egypt has aligned itself with the Axis. Subsequent to that the Axis countries will be allowed to establish a limited number of airbases in Egypt, all in locations well away from population centers, and all subject to limits on aircraft and personnel.

"But, my friend," Urabi continued, "that's only part of it! Saudi Arabia will fall once Axis aircraft can operate from Egypt, and The House of Saud will topple with it. And that will liberate a great deal of wealth. In recognition of the role that my associates and I will play, it only seems fair that a small portion of that bounty be paid to us. I think something on the order of a hundred-million each would be right."

Kantar was amazed by the other man's audacity. What Urabi proposed was nothing less than a full-scale kleptocracy in which he and his fellow warlords would milk Egypt like a cow. And, once the Saudi Arabian kingdom was dissolved, Urabi and his friends would receive cash bonuses. But so what? *I'm not Egyptian*, Kantar thought. *And the means justifies the end.*

"I think your proposal is quite interesting," Kantar said. "But the decision isn't up to me. I will relay the plan to my superiors, along with a recommendation that they approve it."

"Excellent," Urabi replied. "But tell them to hurry. The Allies are only a hundred miles away."

Yes, Kantar mused, *and who knows how close the Chinese are.*

"I will tell them that," Kantar promised. "I most certainly will."

CHAPTER TWELVE

The Pyramid of Al Kola, Egypt

It was hot, so Kydd went looking for some shade, and found a cool spot under some palm trees. A white plastic chair was waiting for him. Where was the person who liked to sit on it? Where were the women who normally came down for water? Where were the farmers? The area was quiet. *Too* quiet.

Kydd sat down and placed the HK416 across his knees. A fly buzzed around his head. He tried to swat it and missed. Kydd should have been on the command boat motoring upstream. He *wanted* to be on the command boat motoring upstream.

But Cole was somewhere to the west of him, intent on meeting with a mysterious contact, and unwilling to take marines with her. What was that anyway? A necessary risk? Or some stubborn bullshit?

The silence was shattered by four shots. They came one after another. Kydd jumped to his feet and began to run. He was wearing a headset—and had a radio clipped to his vest. "One-Six to One-Seven. Shots fired west of the river. I'm headed that way. Over."

"Roger that, One-Six," Chief Jones replied. "We're on the way. Over."

Kydd's pulse was pounding as he followed the trail along the edge of a field. He heard a shout followed by another shot. "I'm coming your way ... Don't shoot me."

Cole was breathing hard. "Three on my six."

Kydd saw the agent ahead. He stopped, brought the rifle up, and squinted. The men were roughly thirty feet behind Cole and gaining on her. "You're in my line of fire."

Cole veered off the trail, hit the dirt, and rolled. Kydd fired a series of three-shot bursts. The men were bunched up. That made it easy. Bodies jerked and fell.

All of the attackers were down, but Kydd kept the 416 up and ready, as he advanced to a point just short of the bodies. With no other pursuers in sight, Kydd lowered his weapon. He turned to find that Cole was searching each corpse. Once she had their wallets and other effects she stood. Her eyes were sky blue. "Thanks."

"You're welcome. And?"

"And *what?*"

"You know what."

Cole sighed. "You were right. Do you feel better now?"

Kydd grinned. "Yes, I do. What happened?"

Cole told him. "It was a set up," she finished.

"Yeah," Kydd agreed. "You shot at them, but they didn't shoot at *you?* That's strange."

"Exactly," Cole agreed. "I think it's safe to assume they had orders to capture me."

The conversation was interrupted as Jones and two heavily armed sailors arrived on the scene. Kydd turned to greet them. "Thanks for the fast response...Three tangos are down—and we're ready to pull out."

"Not so fast," Cole said. "I need to go back, and search the guy at the table."

Kydd made a face. "Okay, let's get this over with. I'll take the point and the chief will walk drag. Let's go."

Kydd half expected an attack, but there was none. And, when they arrived at the pyramid, the bodies were still there. "The girl's a badass," Jones observed, as he looked around. "Don't piss her off."

A man sat slumped over a picnic table. Cole went over to search him. Kydd followed. "A dagger?" he inquired. "That's kind of old-school."

"It is," Cole agreed, as she found a wallet and flipped it open. "Burhan Al-Bishi. This is the man I was supposed to meet."

"The guy who worked for Urabi."

"Exactly," Cole replied. "And the guy who was going to give me information about what Urabi is up to. It's my guess that Urabi was onto Al-Bishi, learned about the meeting, and had him killed. The dagger was supposed to hold my attention while Urabi's men grabbed me. And it very nearly worked."

"So he could ransom you?"

"Possibly," Cole allowed. "Urabi has done that kind of thing before as you have reason to know. But I think he planned to drain me dry."

Kydd winced. "We need to kill that bastard."

"Sounds good to me," Cole agreed. "It was a big mistake to let him go."

Jones had been monitoring the emergency frequency. "We've got a problem," he announced. "Outpost Oscar is under attack."

"Come on!" Kydd said. "Let's get to the boat. Tell the ops center that we're headed upriver to provide support."

They ran east along the trail and out onto the rickety dock. The RCB was waiting with her bow out, and took off the moment the last sailor jumped aboard.

Waves rolled away from the bow as the helmsman opened both throttles and sent the boat racing upriver. The crew were already at battle stations so there was no need for an order. "What's our ETA?" Kydd inquired.

"About forty minutes," Jones replied.

Kydd made a face. Forty minutes was an eternity in combat. Jones turned a radio up so all of them could listen. The platoon leader, who was likely to be a second lieutenant, and in the shit for the first time—was doing his best. But there was no denying the desperation in the kid's voice. The bang, bang, bang of semi-automatic weapon fire could be heard in the background. "This is Oscar-Six actual…Fifty-percent casualties…Final protective fire. Requesting an airstrike on this position."

"Shit," Jones said. "They're about to be overrun! And if Goolsby had attack helicopters, which he doesn't, the missiles at the dam would shoot them down."

Kydd grabbed the mike. "Oscar-Six…This is Riverine One-Six actual…Hang in there, son. We're fifteen out. Over."

There was a moment of silence followed by a new voice. It was grim. "This is Oscar-Seven. Six is down. We…" Then the transmission ended.

There was nothing to say. Cole looked away. Kydd knew that tears were rolling down her cheeks. Was she thinking about John? Probably.

There was a lot of radio traffic as Goolsby sent marines north in every boat he had— including the two-boat, the British boats, and both of the SURCs. Kydd saw the column of black smoke rising from Outpost Oscar well before the RCB arrived. But not a sound could be heard.

Then, as they got closer, he saw the empty feluccas on the beach that fronted the old fort. "Look!" Cole said. "They're tied together. End-to-end."

The agent was correct, and Kydd thought he knew why. *That's how the bad guys arrived*, Kydd thought, *in stolen boats. All roped together so they couldn't go astray.*

The fact that the boats were still there meant one of two things: Either the hajis were waiting to attack the relief force, or they'd gone east into the desert.

So why not attack from the east? Kydd wondered.

Because, Kydd decided, *the platoon leader was more concerned about the desert than the river. So when the feluccas came downriver, his heavy weapons were facing east.*

"Keep your heads on a swivel!" Kydd yelled, as the boat came within gunshot of the fort. "They could be waiting for us!"

Ellis had the minigun trained on the fort as the RCB's bow slid up onto soft sand and most of the crew bailed out. Jones had removed an LMG from its mount and was ready to fire it from the hip as he waded ashore. Kydd, Cole, and a gunners' mate followed.

Doc Niles was carrying *two* Unit One medical kits, and armed with a pistol. "Take it slow," Kydd cautioned. "Watch for IEDs."

The steps were made of limestone. A depression was centered in the middle of each tread. There was no telling how many thousands of feet had climbed and descended the stairway over hundreds of years. Not thousands of years, because gun ports in the west wall suggested that the crumbling fortification might have been new when Napoleon arrived in 1798. Or been built by his army. The stairs led to a pool of blood and some dead Arabs. All shot from above as they tried to advance.

But when they came to a landing two marines lay there, stripped of their gear, faces slack. Niles paused to check each body, and shook his head.

More stairs led up to ground level. The east side of the fortress was open to the desert. Bodies lay everywhere. A private moaned. Doc rushed to help. Other marines, all stripped of their weapons and gear, were sprawled in heaps.

A mortar pit marked the center of the area, fronted by a wall of badly shot-up sandbags, with a gun emplacement at each corner. Except the mortar tube and the machine guns were missing. *And that,* Kydd thought, *may have been the purpose of the raid.*

Then something else occurred to him. He turned to Jones. "Call ops... Find out how many marines were stationed here."

A sailor named Martinez was standing nearby, weapon at the ready. Kydd waved him over. "Count the dead and wounded. Marines only. And don't forget the bodies on the lower landing."

Martinez said, "Aye, aye, sir," and disappeared.

"I see where this is going," Cole said. "Some of the marines are prisoners."

"That's how it appears," Kydd agreed. "A typical platoon consists of something like 40 men. And, since I don't see that many bodies, some of the marines survived.

"I think the raid had two objectives. The first was to acquire heavy weapons. The second was to kidnap marines and sell them back."

"Well, at least we know who the raiders are," Cole said.

Kydd's eyebrows rose. "We do?"

"In the general sense, yes," Cole replied. She pointed at a body. "That man *looks* like a Bedouin the same way a cowboy looks like a cowboy. The type of headdress, the robe, and the knife are similar to what Bedouin men usually wear. Now look around. You'll see what I mean."

Kydd scanned the area. Cole was right... The other civilian casualties were wearing nearly identical attire. Jones appeared at his side. "The platoon had been reinforced with heavy weapons teams, Skipper. It consisted of 46 marines."

Martinez returned. "I found 25 marines, sir. Dead *and* wounded."

"So the Bedouins have 21 prisoners," Cole put in.

"Damn it," Kydd said. "We've got to find them, and fast, before they fade into the desert."

"Which Bedouins excel at," Cole added. "The Bedouins who practice traditional ways are nomads. They tend to live in areas that get under 2 inches of rain each year. And they see themselves as the *true* Arabs, and the rest as pretenders."

Kydd turned to Jones. "Call the ops center. Tell them that 21 marines are MIA, and presumed to be prisoners. Ask them to launch a drone if they have one that can travel this far. Something the SAMs won't target. And tell them that we're sending a party out to get eyes-on if that's possible."

Kydd turned to Cole as Jones worked the radio. "It would be nice to have a translator. Not to mention another gun. Are you in?"

Cole nodded. "You know I am."

"Good. Hey, Martinez! Would you like to volunteer for a walk in the desert?"

Martinez grinned. "Sounds good, sir."

"Great. Tell Harris that he volunteered too ... And make up four packs. Lots of water, extra ammo, and night vision stuff. You have fifteen minutes." Martinez left for the boat.

"I'm going too," Jones said.

"Sorry," Kydd replied. "But you are in command of the RCB. Not to mention the fact that the XO will need your help when he arrives. How's the Doc doing?"

It turned out that Niles was doing as well as he could. Three marines were wounded, one critically, and all were being loaded onto the RCB. "I want to take them downriver as quickly as I can," the corpsman said.

"Of course," Kydd answered. "And the attackers?"

"One survivor," Niles said. "A boy. He took a bullet, but he'll make it."

"He's on the boat?"

"Yes, sir."

"Okay, get moving. And be sure to let the surgeon know you're coming."

Martinez and Harris appeared at that point, wearing floppy hats, and toting two packs each. "The chief sent this," Harris said, as he gave a rangefinder binocular to Kydd.

"He's a genius," Kydd said.

"Yup," Harris replied expressionlessly. "That's what he tells me."

Outpost Oscar was located in that spot for a reason. The Nile was narrower at that point, which made it easier to monitor river traffic, and the nearest habitation from there was miles away. That meant the marines could open fire without worrying about civilians.

But the locals didn't live adjacent to the fort for a reason. Due to the topography, and the force of prevailing winds, sand dunes were pushed west—and into the Nile. Making it narrower.

So as the foursome followed the tracks east, they had to walk on loose sand, which required more effort. "At least it's easy to follow them," Kydd observed, as they topped a rise. "Look! The trail is at least six-feet wide."

"True," Cole agreed, as she knelt beside him. "But look at this... See the way the wind is blowing sand into each depression? The tracks will disappear in a matter of hours."

"Then we'd better get going," Kydd replied.

Thus began a long and arduous hike. Kydd figured the temperature was something like 95 degrees. Scraps of shade were visible near outcroppings of rock. But the team couldn't take advantage of the cool spots without departing from the trail.

The sand shifted under Kydd's boots and raw spots had begun to develop around his ankles. And, precious though they were, the bottles of water in his pack were heavy. *But that's okay,* Kydd told himself, as he paused to take a sip. *You're lucky to have it.*

The march dragged on. *What would I do if I was a Bedouin?* Kydd wondered dully. *And I knew the U S of A might come looking for me? I'd leave at least one guy behind that's what … A guy with a radio. And I'd give him orders to watch for kafirs on my back trail.*

Kydd came to a sudden stop, brought the binoculars up, and glassed the horizon. There were two ridges in the distance with a gap between them. *There*, he thought. *That's where the lookout would be. Hidden among the rocks.*

The others had gone a bit further when Kydd stopped, figuring that he would sip some water, and catch up. Now they returned. Cole eyed him. "Are you okay?"

"Never better," Kydd lied. "But I have a concern."

Kydd told the others what he'd been thinking about. Martinez nodded. "That makes sense, sir … But what can we do about it?"

"We can pass the buck," Kydd replied. "Let's see what the ops center says."

The hot sun continued to beat down on the team, as Kydd radioed in, and wound up delivering a sitrep to Goolsby. "So," Kydd concluded. "If we pass through the gap, I'm afraid they'll make us. Over."

There was a burst of static followed by the sound of Goolsby's voice. "Find some shade One-Six. And keep your eyes peeled. One-five backups are on the way, and will arrive before nightfall. They will deal with the lookout if there is one. Sorry about the drone … But the SAMs would blow a Pred out of the sky. And our UAVs (unmanned aerial vehicles) don't have enough range. Good job by the way … Maybe you should transfer to the corps. Over." That was followed by a click.

The team was waiting. "The colonel wants us to find some shade, and wait for reinforcements," Kydd told them. "Fifteen marines are on the way."

It took the team twenty-minutes to reach a patch of shade on the east side of a rocky spire. "Drink water," Kydd told them. "And nap if you can. I'll take the first watch."

Kydd spent the next hour watching Egyptian vultures ride thermals above the desert, as contrails clawed the sky high above them, and cloud-shadows crossed the land. Then it was time to wake Martinez and grab some shut-eye.

It seemed like only a few seconds had passed when the sailor woke him. "Sorry, sir ... But a marine, call-sign 'Four-Three,' is on the horn. He wants our twenty."

Kydd rolled over, did a pushup, and stood. If the leathernecks were off to the west he couldn't see them. Martinez gave him the radio. "One-Six to Four-Three. Can you see reddish spire? We're at the base of it. Over."

"Roger that," Four-Three replied. "We'll be there shortly. Over."

The binoculars were resting on top of Kydd's pack. He held them to his eyes. Dry desert slipped past as he panned from right to left. Nothing, nothing, bingo! There they were, barely visible in their camos, running cross-country! Carrying packs and weapons. *Force Recon*, Kydd thought. *Celer, Silens, Mortalis.* (Swift, Silent, Deadly.) *One, two, three, four, who loves the Marine Corps? They do.*

The first marine arrived fifteen-minutes later. He was sweating, but otherwise fresh as a daisy, and in good spirits. "Good afternoon, sir ... I'm Corporal Lansing. The rest of the team will arrive shortly."

A first lieutenant named Givens was the fifth man in. He had dark skin, a lanky frame, and a southern drawl. "No offense sir, but the water's that-a-way."

Kydd laughed. "Thanks, Lieutenant ... I'd love to jump in the Nile right now. Are you up for a sitrep?"

"Yes, sir," Givens replied. "Lay it on me."

Kydd pointed to the gap, and told Givens about his theory. He finished by saying, "So, given the fact the Bedouins are on foot, I figure they'll make camp no more than five miles beyond the gap."

Givens nodded. "That makes sense, sir. The light is starting to fade. I'll send a team forward to eliminate the sentry—assuming he's there. Then we'll push through. Do you plan to go with us? Or return to the river?"

"Where would the corps be without the navy? We're in. But you're in command."

Givens smiled. "Roger that, sir. I'll keep you in the loop."

Kydd was eating a candy bar, and washing it down with sips of warm water, as the two-man sniper team departed. One marine was carrying a Barrett XM500 sniper rifle with a bipod. His spotter was armed with an M4 carbine and a powerful spotting scope. Kydd tried to follow their progress. But it wasn't long before the leathernecks seemed to merge with the desert landscape.

The sun was slipping down below the western horizon when Givens made the rounds. "On your feet marines ... Take a whiz if you need to. The enemy lookout is down. We leave in five."

And that was that. No fuss, no muss, and no sound. "One shot, one kill." The sniper's motto.

The marines took off at a steady jog. Kydd, Cole, and the sailors managed to keep up at first, but soon fell behind. So the best the smaller team could do was don night vision gear, and follow the newly made tracks.

The *other* footprints, the ones left by the Bedouins and their prisoners, were partially obscured by that time and hard to discern. Kydd was glad that Givens had the responsibility for tracking the bad guys instead of him.

Minutes stretched into an hour, followed by another hour, before Givens whispered in his ear. "Four-Three to One-Six ... Eyes-on. Close slowly. No noise. Over."

Kydd clicked his mike twice by way of an acknowledgement. He turned to the others. "The marines have eyes-on. Move slowly. Keep it quiet."

Like any competent platoon leader Givens had a man stationed on his six. And when the naval contingent appeared he waved the newcomers forward. "Keep down," he whispered. "There's some strange shit going on."

And the marine was correct. A glow appeared as Kydd worked his way up a slope to the top of a ridge. The kind of glow produced by electric lights! Givens was staring at the depression below as Kydd plopped down beside him. "Here," Givens said, as he handed a pair of night vision binoculars over to Kydd. "Check it out."

Kydd had to remove his night vision gear to use the binoculars. The encampment looked green. He saw tents, two of which were military rather than nomadic, along with some parked vehicles. Bedouins were present, but so were uniformed soldiers. "What the hell?"

"They're Russians," Givens whispered. "Or that's my guess."

And it seemed like a good guess. After being suckered by Hezbollah off the top, the Ruskies were back, and determined to reassert themselves. In order to help Kantar? Or with plans to displace him? Either one was a possibility.

The marines, or the figures Kydd assumed to be marines, were seated with hands behind their heads. "I see trucks," Kydd said. "I wonder if they intend to move the prisoners."

"That ain't gonna happen," Givens replied. "I have orders to free our guys—not let a bunch of A-holes drive them away."

"I like the way you think, Lieutenant," Kydd replied. "What can we do to help?"

"How about a diversion?" Givens suggested. "You take your team over to the west side of the depression—and lob some grenades at the tangos. Then, as they surge your way, we'll advance from the north. As we do, my snipers will thin out their command and control. It's my opinion that we should attack sooner rather than later."

"I agree," Kydd said. "We'll move out. I'll let you know once we're in position."

Kydd held a whispered conference with his team. "I'll take the point," Cole said, as she screwed a suppressor onto her pistol.

That made sense, so Kydd nodded. "I'll walk drag. Let's keep it tight."

Cole had been an infantry officer, and it showed in the way that she advanced, weapon ready, looking for trip wires. The Bedouin weren't likely to lay any but the Russians were. And sure enough, once they reached the bottom of the slope, Cole raised her hand palm out. It was the signal for "stop." The team froze.

Then, using exaggerated movements, the agent stepped over something the rest of them couldn't see. Not until they reached the same spot. Then the piece of tightly-stretched, monofilament line became visible. Kydd figured it was connected to a mine or a flare. Not that it mattered.

One-by-one the team members crossed the obstacle, and followed Cole through a scattering of rocks, to the point where open desert began. The glow was directly ahead. And there, silhouetted against the light, was a Bedouin armed with an M16A4. Taken from a dead marine? Or a prisoner? Of course.

A lighter flared as the sentry lit a cigarette. He took a deep drag. That was when Cole shot him in the head. Smoke dribbled out the man's nostrils as he fell. Cole patted the body in hopes of finding a radio but came up empty.

From there the agent led the team forward toward some sand-drifted rocks where they could take cover. And they were halfway to that objective when an engine roared into life. That was followed by a second one. "They're loading the prisoners!" Givens said over the radio. "Throw the grenades!"

Kydd removed a grenade from his vest, held it with the pin up, and pressed his thumb against the safety lever. After pulling the pin Kydd threw the grenade overhand. Like a baseball player.

Harris did likewise and both men hit the dirt. The explosives went off in quick succession. The response was immediate. Auto, and semiauto weapons opened fire, and all the diversionary team could do was hug the ground as bullets whined, snapped, and buzzed over their heads.

The Force Recon marines were halfway down the slope by that time, and firing at targets of opportunity. The defenders shifted fire accordingly. And that was when Kydd stood, and shouted, "Follow me!"

Blood pounded in Kydd's head, his breath came in short gasps, and someone screamed. Each muzzle flash was a target and he paused to fire at one of them. Then Kydd was off and running again. The camp was closer by that time as were the tents. Kydd was still picking up speed when he tripped on a guyline. The crash landing occurred just as Givens yelled, "Cease fire from the west!"

And that made sense, because the marines were in the enemy encampment by then, and could be hit. Kydd had to roll over in order to relay the order. "Cease fire!"

"Hello, sailor," Cole said, as she paused to offer him a hand. "What a slacker."

Kydd got to his feet. "Just taking a short break, that's all ... Come on, let's lend a hand."

But the marines had the situation under control by then. The Bedouins and the Russians had been sorted into two groups— and their wrists were being secured with zip ties.

In the meantime the marine prisoners were being released and armed with their own weapons. "Find 'em all!" a noncom hollered. "And that includes the heavy stuff."

"I don't speak Russian," Cole said. "But I'll chat with the Bedouins. Maybe they can tell me what's going on here."

With Harris and Martinez in tow, Kydd went looking for Givens, and found him near the encampment's generator. It rattled softly. Givens was on his radio. "Roger that, we have all of them. Over. Yes, sir ... I'll tell them, over." Then he broke the connection.

Givens spotted Kydd and frowned. "Where's Cole? Is everybody okay?"

"She's chatting with the Bedouins," Kydd answered. "How about your guys?"

"One KIA, and three WIA," Givens answered glumly. "We can't call for an air evac so we'll use a Russian truck to take them out."

Kydd nodded. "I'm sorry. That makes sense. So they *are* Russians?"

"Absolutely," Givens replied. "None of them are willing to talk at the moment. But I figure the S2 will unzip at least some of these bastards. Then we'll learn more."

"I can give you some preliminary scoop," Cole said, as she joined them. "According to the Bedouins, who see themselves as employees rather than Axis loyalists, the Russians came ashore at the port of Al-Ghardaqah on the Red Sea. This group is the advance party for a larger force."

Kydd frowned. "Why would the Russians order an advance party attack the fort?"

"They didn't," Cole replied. "A Bedouin chieftain came up with that idea. And, according to my guy, the Russians were mightily pissed."

Kydd could imagine it. The chieftain, who had no interest in geopolitics, had seen an opportunity to raid the fort—and acquire heavy weapons.

End of story. Except that Goolsby would have to be on the lookout for *more* Russians, and send a larger force should they decide to double down.

Kydd and his party were on the first truck out, along with a body bag, and two wounded marines. A trip that had required hours of hard slogging on foot took about forty-five minutes. The two-boat was waiting to take the casualties downriver.

As for the fort, the bodies had been removed, and another platoon had been brought in. But not for long, if what Chief Jones said was accurate. "We're headed upriver," the NCO said. "That's the scuttlebutt anyway."

The sun was starting to rise as Kydd boarded the *Nile* and went to his cabin. Evans was waiting there along with a list of administrative tasks. "We're falling behind," the petty officer warned, as if Kydd was at fault.

That was annoying, but Kydd understood. More than that, Kydd knew Evans was trying to protect him from Goolsby's wrath, which he would certainly feel if his reports were late. "We'll dig in," Kydd promised. "Right after I take a nap. I'm wasted."

"The Colonel is holding a staff meeting at 1500," Evans said, as he prepared to leave.

Kydd eyed his watch. "Come back at 1200. We'll work until 1430."

Evans looked pleased, and said, "Yes, sir." The door closed behind him.

After five hours of sleep Kydd arose feeling much better. Then, following a shower and a hurried brunch, he returned to the cabin where Evans was waiting.

There were supply requisitions to sign, missing equipment to justify, fitness reports to review, watch schedules to approve, patrol rotations to eyeball, and endless Goolsby-grams to read. Most of them were of the "don't forget to write home" sort. The kind his sailors referred to as "ass wipes."

But there were exceptions. Like the bulletin that began, "The USS Destroyer *Susan Kelly* lost with all hands." Kydd couldn't bear to read it. A friend of his had been on the *Kelly*. The BIG war, the one outside of Egypt, continued to grind on.

By 1430 ninety percent of the to-do list had been accomplished and Evans was in a good mood. "We kicked some ass, sir ... I'll finish up."

Kydd arrived at the meeting on time, spotted Cole, and went over to sit beside her. "You look tired."

Cole made a face. "The agency doesn't know about our stroll in the desert. Nor would they care if they did."

Kydd was about to sympathize when Goolsby called the meeting to order. "Good afternoon. I would like to begin the meeting by acknowledging the loss of twenty-two marines at Outpost Oscar, and still another marine lost inland, for a total of twenty-three men and women lost. But the wounded are doing well. Once the after-action reports have been reviewed and analyzed a report will go up the chain of command."

Unsaid, but obvious to all of the officers in the room, was the fact that mistakes had been made by the platoon's inexperienced leader. Mistakes he paid for with his life.

Was the company commander going to take some heat? Probably. He, or she, should have taken notice of the way the heavy weapons were placed—and ordered some changes.

But the buck didn't stop there. The colonel's superiors might or might not feel that some of the responsibility was Goolsby's. Such was the price of command.

"Thanks to Lieutenant Givens, Lieutenant Commander Kydd, force recon marines, and our intrepid sailors, our POWs were freed and will return to duty soon.

"Unfortunately," Goolsby continued, "I have some bad news to share. As all of you know, a Hezbollah officer named Mustafa Kantar has control of the dam, *and* the bomb that could destroy it. And so long as he remains inside the ring of SAM installations around the dam he's safe from drone attacks. But Kantar needs to create a Shia friendly government if he can. And, to that end, he traveled to the town of Al Farafrah—for a meeting with an ex-minister named al-Hudaybi."

Goolsby's eyes made contact with Kydd's. "Another man was present as well. An American who was passing information to the Russians.

"Long story short—someone fired two Hellfires, and dropped some 500 pound bombs on the house where the meeting was taking place."

That produced applause, but Goolsby raised his hand. "Sorry, but there's no happy ending. A contractor was dispatched to perform a BDA. He was murdered. So *another* asset was sent to do the job. He was able to confirm that both al-Hudaybi and the American were killed in the attack. But Kantar's body was nowhere to be found. And, based on signals intelligence, we know he's back in Aswan."

Goolsby paused for a moment. Kydd and Cole traded glances. It didn't take a genius to figure out that the CIA was responsible for the attack. Maybe they figured that two out of three was a fairly good score. But they weren't sitting in the Nile valley waiting for a religious fanatic to send a tsunami downriver.

"So our mission continues," Goolsby said. "At 0800 tomorrow morning we'll cast off, and head upriver to the town of Nagaa Al Jami. That will put us only thirty-miles away from the city of Aswan.

"Will Kantar view that as a provocation? Most likely. But so long as we remain in place our analysts believe that Kantar will continue his efforts to form a government. And, when the time comes, we'll be within striking distance of the dam."

Kydd tried to imagine taking his flotilla upstream in a doomed attempt to reach the dam and prevent 10-million people from dying. Talk about a bad day.

There was more, but nothing so consequential for Kydd's flotilla, as the need to prepare for the 77-mile advance. So once the meeting was over Kydd brought his officers and senior noncoms together for a planning session.

The open air get-together was held ashore in a park once frequented by tour boat passengers. "The way I see it we have the following priorities," Kydd told them. "Reconnaissance will commence at 1800 hours this evening. Both SURCs will head upriver for 10 miles, paying close attention to both riverbanks. They will keep a sharp lookout for navigational hazards, potential ambush sites, and floating IEDs.

"Force protection activities will begin at 0600 in the morning. That's when the British one-boat will head north and clear feluccas off the river. SURC-1 will follow and act as enforcer.

"At 0800 the American one- and two-boats will lead the *Nile* upriver and stand ready to repel waterborne or shore based attacks.

"The British two-boat will fall back," Kydd added, "and prevent hostiles from attacking the convoy's six. That boat will also have a search and rescue responsibility, should someone fall overboard, and drift downstream.

"Meanwhile SURC-2 will serve as a VIP taxi, an ambulance should there be some sort of accident, and a felucca chaser if needed. Are there any questions?"

There were questions—ranging from how to deal with engine failures, the need for more translators, and the ongoing friction with recalcitrant tug captains. But eventually all the issues that *could* be resolved were resolved. And it was time for the group to repair onto the *Nile* where Evans had a buffet waiting for them. It wasn't fancy, but it made a nice change from MREs, and Goolsby stopped by for a chat.

Then it was time for Kydd to gear-up and board Murphy's SURC. He wanted to see the next stretch of river for himself—and get back to what he enjoyed the most. A clear night, a fast boat, and a river to run on. The brown water navy. *His* navy.

CHAPTER THIRTEEN

RAF Deversoir Air Base, Egypt

Cole was tired and for good reason. In order to tackle her next assignment, the agent had been forced to ride a boat downriver to a location where a navy CH-53E helicopter could pick her up without being shot down by the dam's air defense capability. And not just her. As the helo carried them east Egyptian air force officer Hasan Farook sat chained to the seat across from Cole.

Farook had been captured by Kydd and his sailors when he and a second pilot attacked the Riverines with Russian-made Black Shark helicopters. They'd been acting on orders from an Egyptian general named Ahmar.

Now Cole was taking Farook to Ahmar by way of a gift. But only after a long and tiring ride. "Their SAMs have a lock on us," the pilot announced via the intercom. "And we have company. Two SA-342 Gazelles are escorting us in."

Cole had no idea what a SA-342 was, and there weren't any windows to look out of. But it didn't matter. They were expected but an ambush wasn't beyond the realm of possibility. And if that occurred then Cole and her bodyguards wouldn't last long.

Cole would die, or she wouldn't. There were reasons to live though ... And maybe Kydd was one of them. Cole pushed the thought away. *Not now. Focus on what you're doing.*

Cole felt a thump as the helicopter's the landing gear made contact with the tarmac. She released her seatbelt. It fell away. "Welcome to Deversoir Air Base. You're home."

"*Not* home," Farook said. "I shamed. Kill me."

Cole sighed. "You never stop, do you?"

She turned to the sailors. There were five of them, all heavily armed, and on loan from the navy. "Free Farook and keep him ready. In the meantime I need a couple of guys to make me look important."

A first class petty officer named Wilson was in charge. He grinned. "No prob ma'am ... Foss and I have your back."

Cole drew a semiauto pistol from her shoulder holster and worked a round into the chamber. Then she scanned the faces around her. "If this turns out to be an ambush, kill as many of them as you can. Oh, and don't forget to pop Farook. He *wants* to die ... So he'll be grateful. "

Wilson nodded. He was carrying an MP7 muzzle-up. "Roger that, ma'am."

"Good. Let's go."

***

General Abdu Ahmar was in the control tower at Deversoir Air Base. His binoculars were focused on the scene below. The field was located 72-miles northeast of Cairo. Prior to WWII it had been known as RAF Deversoir. Now it was home to a half-dozen Russian-made Black Sharks, a few French-built Gazelles, and the 2,000 or so men that he was struggling to hold, equip and feed.

Yes, the once glorious Republican Guard had fallen on hard times. The division consisted of 10,000 men prior to the war, and was supposed to defend Egypt's President, a variety of strategic institutions, and key airports. One of which was Deversoir.

But, in spite of its best efforts, the Guard failed. *You failed*, Ahmar told himself for the thousandth time. *And, when the day comes, you must pay.*

But not today, Ahmar thought, as he watched the American walk off the helicopter. She had blond hair, and was wearing sunglasses, a white pantsuit and yes—red high heels. Oh, and she was holding a pistol down along her right leg! Two soldiers, both armed, followed.

Those were the days, Ahmar thought. *When I was young, when such women wanted me, and when I wanted them.*

***

Once on the ground Cole paused. A battalion of Republican Guard troops stood waiting. They were dressed in camouflage uniforms and blue berets. And, when an officer yelled a command, they crashed to attention. Then, with a single voice, they shouted, "*Alfawz 'aw almawt!*" (Win or die.)

A *ra'id* (major) took three paces forward and saluted. "Major Din, at your service ma'am." Din's English was excellent.

"It's a pleasure to meet you, Major," Cole replied. "My name is Linda Faraday. I'm a foreign affairs officer with the U.S. State Department."

Din dropped the salute. "General Ahmar sends his compliments, and will see you at dinner. Suitable quarters will be provided for you and your crew."

Cole had been hoping to meet with Ahmar right away, get the job done, and haul butt. Was Ahmar busy? Away from the base? Or just jerking her around? "Please thank the general for me. I look forward to meeting him. In the meantime, as a gesture of goodwill, the United States government has authorized me to repatriate Republican Guard Lieutenant Hasan Farook."

Din frowned. "He's *alive?*"

"Very much so," Cole assured him. She turned to Wilson. "Tell the guys to send Farook out."

Wilson spoke into his boom mike. Then, looking very lonely, the pilot made his way down the ramp. Din was visibly shocked. "Farook?"

Farook came to attention. "Sir!"

"Did you win?"

"No, sir."

"Then die." Din shot Farook in the chest. The pilot collapsed.

Cole had seen some really bad things, but knew that would go down as one of the worst. She wanted to throw up and cry at the same time. But that would show weakness.

Cole cleared her throat. "Thank you for your offer of accommodations. But our regulations require that all the helicopter crew remain with their aircraft while away from their ship."

Cole had no idea what the actual regulation was and didn't care. She wanted Wilson and the rest of the crew ready to go in case of an emergency. And she wanted to prevent the Egyptians from boarding the ship.

"Of course," Din replied. "Please inform your personnel that our regulations require that security personnel guard your aircraft until the moment of departure." Tit for tat.

"Naturally," Cole said. "My men will need to use a restroom."

"Escorts will be provided," Din assured her. "And one more thing... You can continue to carry your pistol in your hand if you wish to. But rest assured that there's no need for you to do so."

Cole returned the pistol to its holster. "Thank you."

Din turned to wave two soldiers forward. Both were noncoms. If they were shocked by the summary execution their faces revealed no sign of it. "Sergeant Faheem will show you to your quarters. Sergeant Naceri will assist your men. Both speak English."

Cole turned to Wilson. "Please ask the pilots to file a verbal report. And set watches. Do you have sleeping bags? What about food and water?"

Wilson nodded. "Always."

"Good. The local stuff might not agree with you."

Wilson knew what she meant, and smiled. "I read you five-by-five ma'am." He offered a radio. "Please stay in touch."

Cole turned back. Farook's blood had dried by then. Flies buzzed around the body. "It's a pleasure to meet you Sergeant Faheem. Please lead the way."

The heat was fierce, and the low-lying operations center seemed to shimmer, as Cole followed Faheem across the tarmac. A private was waiting to open the door—and the building's interior was refreshingly cool. Cole got the feeling that WWII RAF pilots would recognize the pea-green paint on the walls, and the well-worn linoleum floor.

Deversoir Air Base had been built during the 1930s to help defend the Suez Canal. Then, during WWII, the Allies used it to battle Axis forces in North Africa. Now, 80-years later, the Allies were fighting Axis countries again. The alliances were different—but the essence of the conflict was the same. If that was progress, Cole couldn't see how.

Cole's high heels produced a clicking sound as she followed the noncom down a long hall. Offices lined both sides of the corridor. Most of the doors were open, and soldiers turned to stare, as a blond woman strode past. A pair of wooden doors parted to provide access to what Americans would refer to as "officer country."

The lounge was empty. The air smelled of stale cigarette smoke, and furniture consisted of badly worn 1950's era chrome chairs with red vinyl upholstery. Windows looked out onto the tarmac—and a board labeled "Flight Schedules" covered most of the opposite wall.

A second set of doors opened onto a hallway with evenly spaced rooms to either side. Each bore a name. Faheem paused to let her catch up. "The officers will stay elsewhere tonight. You have no worries."

Was that arrangement a recognition of how aggressive Egyptian men could be? Or a way to observe a social norm? Maybe both. "Thank you," Cole said.

"You down here," Faheem said. "Guest quarters."

Faheem opened a door and gestured for Cole to enter. He followed. "You need, you call," the noncom said, as he pointed to a phone. "Dinner at six. I come to take you."

Cole thanked the noncom, closed the door, and locked it. Was the room bugged? Maybe, but maybe not. How many Egyptian generals would want to be taped? Still, better safe than sorry.

After checking in with Wilson, Cole glanced at her watch. It was a little past four, and she was tired. After removing the fluffy white bathrobe from the closet, Cole entered the bathroom, where she spent five-minutes searching for cameras before disrobing.

The white pantsuit had been an impulse buy while waiting around in Esna. As were the red shoes. But the outfit made an excellent disguise, and Cole didn't want to wrinkle it. Not until the meeting with General Ahmar was over.

The room was quiet, the bed was comfortable, and the pistol felt good in Cole's hand. She went to sleep. Her Garmin watch had an alarm. And the gentle beep, beep, beep woke her up. It took a moment to remember where she was. And another moment to remember why.

Cole rolled off the bed and took the pistol into the bathroom with her. That's where she made a miraculous discovery. Hot water! *Really* hot water … After weeks of tepid showers and sponge baths.

Cole took the gun into the shower stall with her, turned the water on, and spent ten wonderful minutes luxuriating beneath the stiff spray. When Cole emerged she felt reinvigorated, and ready to cope with rogue generals.

Once she was dressed Cole spoke to Wilson by radio. "No problems here, ma'am," the petty officer assured her. "Except for the usual whining."

Cole laughed. "Good. I'm about to have din-din with the general. I'll check in when it's over."

"Have a good time," Wilson replied. "And remember what you told me. 'The local stuff might not agree with you.'"

"Roger that," Cole said. "Over and out."

A knock came at the door. Cole put the radio in her handbag and took the pistol off the bed. "Who's there?"

"Faheem."

Cole aimed at the door. "Come in."

When Faheem opened the door Cole saw his eyes widen. No one appeared behind him.

Cole smiled as she returned the gun to its holster. "Nothing personal, Sergeant. I always answer the door that way."

Faheem nodded as if one should expect such things from a *kafir* woman. He led the way back through the empty lounge, and out into the operations center. Two soldiers, both armed with brooms, stared.

From there Cole followed Faheem outside. It was dark by then. But the heat lingered. And an engine roared as an Egyptian helicopter took off. The Sea Stallion was right where she'd left it—and surrounded by guards.

From there Faheem took Cole along a sun-faded yellow line to a WWII era hangar. "It a museum," Faheem explained. "You like."

The plane-sized hangar door was closed. So they made use of a side entrance. The museum's interior was well lit, and there was a lot to see.

Cole wasn't a WWII aviation buff, but even she could recognize the British Spitfire in one corner, and the German

Messerschmitt parked across from it. Both were dusty and in need of restoration.

And there, in a pool of light, was a beautifully set table. An officer rose from his chair to greet her. He had a British accent. "Miss Faraday... This is a pleasure. I'm General Ahmar."

The general was about five-ten or so, with thinning hair, and a prominent nose. His uniform was just so, and decorated with all manner of tabs, badges and medals. Cole offered her hand. "It's an honor to meet you, General... I love the museum by the way. What a great place to have dinner."

"Yes," Ahmar agreed. "Especially since we're here to discuss war. I was surprised to receive a sat call from Ambassador Darwish. Or *is* he Egypt's ambassador? It's so hard to tell when your country has no official government. But enough of that for now... We will discuss such things later. First a drink... Would champagne be acceptable?"

Cole assumed that Ahmar was Muslim, which meant he *shouldn't* drink, but was one of the many who did. And like any woman Cole was sensitive to what she thought of as "the vibe." And the vibe was mixed.

Ahmar was clearly ready to talk business. But champagne, the candles on the table, and the regimental silver suggested something else. It would pay to be careful. "Of course," Cole answered. "I would love a glass of champagne."

After allowing Ahmar to seat her Cole watched the officer open the champagne and pour. The *same* liquid, from the *same* bottle, filled both glasses. A good start. And when Ahmar raised his to make a toast, she was careful to follow his movements. "Confusion to the enemy!"

Cole echoed the words, but waited for Ahmar to take a sip, before tasting the champagne herself. "It's very nice," she said truthfully.

"Thank you," Ahmar replied. "Back before the war Egypt produced half-a-million gallons of wine a year. That in spite of the fact that 75 percent of the population is Muslim. Our wine is however, almost uniformly bad, so who knows where the swill goes? *This* however, is from France. I hope their vineyards survive the war."

Thus began a lengthy, and interesting conversation about Egyptian history, and the country's politics. "That's where I failed," Ahmar confessed. "It was my job, *our* job, to protect the president above all else—yet he was assassinated. Yes, others share responsibility. But that fact in no way shields the Republican Guard from blame."

Cole took the plunge as a military orderly removed the latest set of dishes. "I understand how you feel General . . . Yet the possibility of redemption remains."

Ahmar pushed his chair back. "Really? I hope you are correct. Please tell me more."

"You know about the dam, the bomb, and Hezbollah's threat."

Ahmar nodded. "Everyone does. They have a knife at our throats."

"Yes," Cole agreed. "They do. But the Allies sent a force up the Nile."

"And I sent helicopters to attack it," Ahmar said. "A mistake for which I must apologize."

"Your perspective was clouded by the fog of war," Cole said, even though it was only partially true. In the wake of his failure Ahmar had seen the flotilla as another violation of Egypt's sovereignty and struck out at it. Never mind the big picture.

Ahmar shrugged. "You are too kind."

Yes, Cole thought. *I am. Get him back on track.*

"So," Cole said. "There is reason to hope. Our forces are 30 miles from the dam. And, if we can find a way to capture it without triggering nuclear explosion, 10-million Egyptian lives will be saved."

"May Allah make it so," Ahmar responded. "You came here to tell me this?"

"No," Cole replied. "I came here to talk about the problem we will face *after* the dam has been recaptured and secured. Hezbollah has shown the way. He who controls the dam, controls Egypt.

"Yes," Cole continued, "the Allies could send troops to protect the dam. But we don't want to. That would mean diverting resources away from the war effort. Plus, your countrymen might see the move as an invasion, leading to more bloodshed.

"There's an alternative however. And that would be to place the dam under the protection of the Republican Guard which, led by *you*, would protect the facility until such time as Egypt can reconstitute its government."

Ahmar stared at her. Cole watched the comprehension dawn in his eyes. Then a spark appeared, followed by what might have been a flame. "You're serious?"

"Yes, I'm serious," Cole assured him. "Of course such a role would be very demanding. And some of the warlords might resent your power. So rather than leave your family vulnerable to kidnapping attempts we will take them to the United States. Your wife and children will live in a very nice home, and your daughters can attend college."

Ahmar stared at her. "Hostages! You plan to use my wife and daughters as hostages."

Cole took a sip of champagne. "That seems prudent, don't you think?"

Ahmar was silent for a full ten seconds. Then he nodded. "Yes, it does."

"Good," Cole said. "So, there's only one thing left to do."

"Which is?"

"To take control of the dam."

***

Aswan City, Egypt

The sun was rising as Kantar departed for the Sudan. He began the journey by descending down through the interior of the dam and exiting onto the peninsula of land that pointed north. The *same* peninsula Kantar and his loyalists used the night they went after Boustani and his mutineers.

From there Kantar stepped into an open fishing boat. The *felucca* carried him to Aswan City where a squad of his men were waiting. They took him to a Christian carpenter's house where a coffin was waiting. The kind Coptics used.

Then, with Kantar inside, the oblong box was loaded onto a truck, and driven up to the cruise terminal located a half mile from the dam.

That was where six black clad pallbearers, all of whom were Hezbollah fighters, carried the coffin onto a steamer. The sun was up by then. If the eyes in the sky were watching, they had every reason to believe that a dead Christian was on his, or her, way to Sudan for burial.

Other passengers, all of whom were Hezbollah dressed as civilians, milled about as the coffin was lowered into a hold. That was where Kantar left the box.

"I'm back from the dead," Kantar announced, and his men laughed. A nice cabin was ready for Kantar up on the main deck. And that's where he spent his time during the two-day trip to the town of Wadi Halfa in northern Sudan.

Kantar felt it was safe to venture out by then. And, as he stood in the stern, looking back across Lake Nasser, Kantar knew he was looking at thirty-one cubic miles of water. All backed up behind the dam. And, if he triggered the bomb, the lake would empty into the Nile valley all at once.

Kantar's thoughts were interrupted as the ship's whistle blew. He made his way forward as the steamer neared the dock. The pier wasn't much to look at. Nor was Wadi Halfa itself. There was no business area to speak of. Just a scattering of flat-roofed warehouses and mudbrick homes.

The town of 15,000 people had been the terminus of the rail line from Khartoum, and the point where goods were transferred to ferries, for the trip into Egypt. But that was before the SLM (Sudan Liberation Movement) destroyed three key bridges. Now, without the railroad, Wadi Halfa was a ghost town. Three grubby children were waiting on the pier. They waved, and Kantar waved back.

Orders were shouted, lines were passed, and the boat bumped into the dock. A gangplank was lowered shortly thereafter and the captain went ashore with a leather folder tucked under his arm. To pay some sort of fee? Probably.

Kantar needed to hire some trucks in order to find the Chinese and kill them. He was about to follow the captain ashore when a man with dark skin and prominent teeth walked up the gangplank. "Good afternoon!" he said, cheerfully. "My name is John Jal … Is this steamer available for hire?"

Kantar was carrying a pistol, but it was hidden under a blue *gallabiya*. So there was nothing to suggest that he was anything other than a member of the ship's crew.

It was tempting to dismiss Jal, or refer him to the captain, but why did the man want to hire a steamer? Unless he was planning to move a lot of something to Aswan. And, for the moment at least, the city of Aswan belonged to Kantar. "It could be available," Kantar allowed cautiously. "What do you need to move?"

"People," Jal replied. "Tourists."

Jal was lying. There weren't any tourists. Not any more. So who was he working for? Could it be the Chinese? They would need to cross the lake at some point. Maybe they were that close. Kantar smiled. "Come my friend... Be truthful. I heard that a group of Cambodian soldiers are headed this way."

Jal made a face. "Yes, they're soldiers, but *Chinese* soldiers, not Cambodians. And they pay well."

"Then a deal can be struck," Kantar said. "Come, we'll drink tea, and go over the details."

Kantar herded Jal across the deck to a narrow set of stairs. They led down into a lounge filled with Hezbollah soldiers. They were preparing to disembark. Jal had just started to take that in when Kantar barked a name. "Sergeant Safar! Take this man into custody!"

Jal turned to flee but Safar blocked the stairs. Two soldiers hurried to help. "Who are *you*?" Jal demanded.

"Wahda Kantar."

Jal flinched. "Yes," Kantar said. "I'm the man your Chinese friends want to kill."

* * *

Kerma, Sudan

After eating and drinking in the city of Dongola, and traveling north to Kerma, 75% of Bo's command had been infected by what his surgeon said was cholera. Then after three days of continuous vomiting and shitting the man died.

The cure for cholera, if administrated in time, was to rehydrate patients with clean water.

To protect themselves Bo's troops had to draw water from the Nile and boil it. So those who weren't infected had to work long days providing assistance to those who were.

Now, after six fatalities and nearly two weeks of delay, the unit had arrived in the ancient city of Kerma, and was ready to proceed. Or would have been ready, had it not been for the latest weather forecast from Khartoum. It called for a major *haboob* (dust storm) of the sort that often resulted when a surge of moisture arrived from the Gulf of Guinea. And that, Bo knew, could be extremely dangerous.

Prior to leaving Khartoum Bo had gone to great lengths to download every scrap of information he could regarding the battalion's route and the dangers it might face. And that included the way dust storms were created.

Haboobs were caused by strong winds that flowed down, and out of thunderstorms, picking up dirt and sand as they did so. A process that could result in a wall of dust that was 60-miles wide and a mile high.

So instead of running the risk that he and his men would be caught in the open, Bo decided remain in Kerma until the threat had passed.

Kerma was a sprawling scimitar-shaped city that bordered the Nile. And rather than try to take shelter in the town's one-story buildings Bo chose to place his troops in among the sprawl of ancient temples, buildings and burial markers located immediately to the east.

Bo didn't have respirators for his men. But there were enough dust masks to go around, plus goggles, and plenty of water. There were three groups. Bo placed each in the lee of a major structure with an officer in charge. Then all they could do was wait. Bo stood out in the open. The air was moist. Lightning crackled in the distance. The storm was coming.

***

Mustafa Kantar heard the roll of thunder. He and his men were hiding around the base of a rocky outcropping just north of Kerma, and had been since 4:00am. After hiring trucks in Wadi Halfa, and driving for hours, the Hezbollah troops were within half-a-mile of the enemy. The Chinese were camped in the ruins east of Kerma, and clearly preparing for the coming dust storm.

It was difficult to get an accurate headcount. But, as Kantar panned his binoculars across the area, he estimated that his force was outnumbered two to one. Fear began to seep into the pit of his stomach. Had he come so far, only to die in an obscure firefight?

Another bolt of lightning flashed across the sky—and Kantar felt raindrops hit his face. They were warm, *blood* warm. And suddenly, by the grace of Allah, Kantar knew how to win. *Alawi*, Kantar thought. *We will kill them for Alawi.*

***

The battalion was ready, or as ready as Bo could make it, as the sky grew even darker. Rain began to fall. "It's on the way," Bo said over the radio. "Take cover."

After a final 360 Bo followed his own advice. The group he had chosen to weather the storm with were camped in the ruins of an ancient temple. The intersection of two intact walls and a partial ceiling formed a cave. Tarps had been used to screen a large opening. One of them began to flap as the wind picked up. The temperature was starting to drop.

***

The Chinese soldiers had taken cover. It was time to move. The more distance the snake-like formation could cover before the storm struck the better.

Kantar held his compass in the palm of his hand. His men were roped into a line that was stretched out behind him. "Now!" Kantar yelled, knowing that the company's radios, like their weapons, were wrapped to protect them from the dust storm. A well-established trail led from the rocky outcropping onto the desert floor and toward the ruins.

The going was easy at first. That was to be expected. But as the sky continued to darken, and as the air became colder, Kantar could see the towering wave of dust coming from the west. It was *huge!* And it looked like a tan tsunami.

Then, with a degree of speed that caught Kantar by surprise, the *haboob* consumed them. Suddenly Kantar found himself inside a pitch-black maelstrom of airborne grit. *The compass*, he thought. *Keep your eyes on the compass. The ruins are due south.*

The rope seemed to assume a life of its own as men struggled to keep up. The line was slack one moment—and taut the next.

At one point Kantar was jerked off his feet when someone fell. He swore, struggled to stand, and eyed the compass. *South. Go south.* A slight turn to the right put Kantar back on the correct course. He had to shake dust off the glowing compass in order to read it.

In spite of Kantar's efforts to button up, the dust found its way into his clothing and filtered into his shorts, where it started to chafe. His thoughts turned to the company's weapons. Would the makeshift dust covers and the barrel plugs work? Or would he and his men arrive only to discover that they were helpless? The Chinese would slaughter them. *I made a mistake*, Kantar decided. *Now I'm going to pay for it.*

It was pitch black by then. And Kantar found the temple by running into it. The unexpected contact frightened Kantar, and men began to pile up behind him, as he ran a hand over smooth sandstone. They had arrived!

Kantar turned to reel the rope in as dust sleeted in around him and threatened to clog his mask. Could the men see him? *No better than you can see them*, Kantar thought. *But we're still roped together.*

After watching the Chinese Kantar knew that the entrance to the temple was to his left. He felt along the wall, found the edge of a doorway, and located the tarp. Kantar turned to tug on the rope. Men gathered, freed themselves, and readied their weapons. They were little more than half-seen shadows as the dust sleeted in around them.

Kantar drew his knife, raised it high, and stabbed. The blade went through. Then, with one long stroke, he sliced downward.

It was pitch black inside the refuge. Kantar brought the men in by feel. Then, hoping for the best, he lit a flare and threw it. Dozens of faces were revealed by the reddish glare. They looked confused. "Fire!" Kantar shouted. "Kill them all!"

It was nothing less than a slaughter. Chinese solders jerked spastically as the withering automatic fire swept across them. Then, in less than a minute, it was over.

"Stop!" Kantar told them. "You're wasting ammo. There are more. We will follow the Chinese ropes."

Kantar led his men back to the entrance, felt for the rope, and found it. Then it was time to step out into the raging storm again. There were *more kafirs* to kill. Then, and only then could he return to the dam, and the work that awaited him.

***

Bo floated up out of the darkness. His head hurt. Memories stuttered through his mind. A flare ... Sudden gunfire. Soldiers dying. A blow. Darkness.

Then came the knowledge that he'd failed. Followed by a deep soul-etching grief from which he would never be able to recover. His men ... So many dead ... So many ...

"Look!" a voice said. "His eyes blinked!"

Bo tried to force them open. All he could see was a fog. "Here," the voice said. "This will help."

Bo felt someone place a wet compress over his eyes. The warmth felt good. After the washcloth was removed a face swam into focus. Medical specialist Huang! "Can you see me?" the medic inquired.

"Yes," Bo croaked. "How many, Huang? How many are left?"

Huang's normally cheerful face darkened. "Twelve, sir. Counting you."

"No, it can't be."

Another face appeared. Sergeant Chen was wearing a patch over his right eye. "It wasn't your fault, sir. They captured Jal … And he told the bastards where to find us."

Bo tried to sit, failed, and fell back against the pillow. He was in a tent. "How do you know?"

"They put Jal's head on a stake," Huang replied. "Then they left."

Bo could imagine it. After being sent to Wadi Haifa to hire a boat Jal had been compromised somehow. Tears began to flow. And Bo couldn't make them stop.

"Don't worry," Huang said, as if speaking to a child. "Things will get better." Bo felt the needle prick. He tried to object, but darkness pulled him down.

Days passed. They were bad at first. *Very* bad. But gradually, bit-by-bit, Bo began to recover. He couldn't forgive himself. But, by concentrating on the objective he'd been sent to accomplish, Bo could ease the pain. *If* he could reach the dam, *if* his remaining expert could neutralize the bomb, the deaths would have meaning. The thought gave Bo strength.

Bo's head wound was healing nicely, and by day three he could walk without assistance. Decisions had to be made. Bo could request reinforcements from Khartoum. But that would weaken the battalion's capacity to respond to an emergency.

So Bo wrote a report by hand, and filed it by radio, being careful to enumerate his failings as he did so. Then he hired locals to make markers and bury the dead. Bo apologized to each man as sand was shoveled onto his face.

When the burials were complete Bo hired two trucks. After loading the unit's excess equipment onto them, the vehicles were sent to Khartoum, with four soldiers to guard them.

Bo watched as the trucks departed, dwindled to specks, and disappeared. Then, with the seven men who remained, Bo turned to look north. The dam was waiting for him. And so was Mustafa Kantar.

CHAPTER FOURTEEN

Nagaa Al Jami, Egypt

The *Nile* was exactly where it had been more than a week earlier, which was moored to the cruise ship dock at Nagaa Al Jami, waiting for orders that never came. Orders that *couldn't* come until Kantar and his remote were destroyed.

But even though the battalion was stationary it had a voracious appetite for food, supplies, and fuel—all of which had to be brought upriver from the Med. That alone was sufficient to keep the Riverine flotilla busy, because every time a tugboat pushed barges upriver, hostiles were sure to fire on it.

The patrol boats took turns on escort duty, and even though Kydd could have remained at Nagaa Al Jami, he felt obliged to take part. To share the risks, yes. But for other reasons too. His presence was good for morale, and it offered an opportunity to evaluate his officers.

So Kydd was on board the British one-boat, as a tired looking tug completed the long haul upriver, and nudged its barges in against the dock. Marines were waiting to help secure the barges in place and no wonder. Each time a convoy arrived there were cases of beer aboard. Two cans per person which, according to standing orders, had to be consumed within the Allied compound.

An enterprising leatherneck could acquire more beer if he or she was willing to pay for it, or win a can while playing poker.

Even so it was difficult to get drunk on three cans of beer. So disciplinary problems were rare—and well worth the positive impact on morale.

The patrol boat had to go alongside the fuel barge before returning to its berth. Once the vessel was secured Kydd thanked each crew member and said goodbye to Lieutenant Fox-Smith. Then with his HK416 and pack in hand, Kydd transferred to the barge, and from it to shore. A five-minute walk took him to the *Nile*.

Stairs had been lowered, but before Kydd could board, he had to show ID. Evans was waiting on the main deck. "Welcome back, sir ... Did you run into any trouble?"

"People took pot shots at us," Kydd replied. "And some kids dropped a rock off a bridge. It landed on barge two."

Evans looked alarmed. "But the beer is okay?"

Kydd laughed. "The beer is safe. And cold too ... It was in a reefer hooked to a Honda generator."

"Thank God," Evans said. "The usual pile of administrative crap awaits you. And you're scheduled to participate in a recon briefing at 1400."

"A reconnaissance of *what?*"

"That's above my pay grade," Evans replied. "But why would anyone run a recon downriver?"

Kydd laughed. "Your powers of deduction are unparalleled. Let's tackle the pile of administrative crap."

Kydd stopped by the dining room to grab a sandwich before heading to his cabin. Evans had "the crap" stacked in priority order. And Kydd was through most of it when 1330 rolled around. "I need to shower and change," Kydd announced. "Take the rest of the day off. I will finish up as soon as I can." Evans was gone thirty-seconds later.

The meeting was slated for the ship's library. It was a small room located midship on deck two. Shelves loaded with ancient paperbacks lined the inner wall.

Kydd arrived to find that the battalion's S2 Major Waller was present, as was Cassandra Cole, and the Egyptian engineer named Asem El-Baz. El-Baz had thinning hair, and a sizeable nose, upon which a pair of wire rimmed spectacles were perched. Kydd nodded. "We meet again, sir ... I was there when you left Ezbet Sherif."

Cole spoke some rapid-fire Arabic, to which the engineer responded. "Mr. El-Baz remembers you," Cole said. "But not fondly."

Kydd frowned. "Why not?"

"You kidnapped him."

"Bullshit ... *You* kidnapped him."

"Don't be childish."

Major Waller was watching with a look of amusement on his face. "You two should take your act on the road. Have a seat commander ... We're here to discuss the recon scheduled for 2100 tonight. My mission is go up river as quietly as possible, determine the best route through the Cataract Islands, and take a look at some potential landing spots."

"And mine is to take Mr. El-Baz to a meeting in Aswan City," Cole added.

Kydd frowned. "A meeting? Why?"

Cole paused to translate before framing her answer. "As you know, we plan to use Mr. El-Baz as a guide after the dam comes under our control, and Kantar is holding about a dozen engineers hostage."

Kydd frowned. "*And?*"

"And there's the possibility that by the time we enter the dam all of those engineers will be dead," Cole explained. "But others have the necessary skills. People who, like Mr. El-Baz, are retired. And many of them live in the area around Aswan City. We're building a B-team."

The need for a B-team hadn't occurred to Kydd. "Okay," he allowed. "A meeting in Aswan City. What could possibly go wrong?"

Waller laughed. "'What' indeed? I'm going to bring a squad of Force Recon marines. They'll deal with whatever trouble may arise."

Kydd looked at Cole. "What kind of trouble?"

Cole shrugged. "Your guess is as good as mine. But, given the fact that Mr. El-Baz had to use word of mouth to organize the meeting, a lot of people know we're coming. Too many. But that's the chance we have to take. Taking the dam is one thing. Running it is another. And electricity is crucial to hospitals and emergency responders. People will die if the dam goes offline."

"Okay," Kydd said. "I get it. We'll take the one-boat. Meet me there at 2030."

"So you're going?" Waller inquired.

"Of course," Kydd said. "Cole is helpless without me."

That was when the Egyptian surprised all of them. "On the contrary," El-Baz said in perfect English. "Agent Cole is quite self-sufficient."

Cole laughed along with the others. Such was Egypt. Nothing was the way it appeared.

* * *

After warning Chief Jones about the coming mission, Kydd took a much needed nap, and got up at 1900. That provided enough time for a shower and a hot meal before gearing up.

Kydd arrived at the boat early, only to discover that Major Waller and his marines were already aboard, and crammed into the stern. Cole brought El-Baz aboard at 2100 straight up. "Cast off," Kydd ordered, "and take her out. Keep it down to 20 knots."

Twenty-knots would have been fast on a lake. But 20-knots upstream, on a river flowing at roughly 6-knots per hour, was a conservative 14-knots.

It was dark. But the helmsman had night vision gear on, as did the gunners, who did double duty as lookouts.

Kydd felt the tension he always experienced when departing on a mission. But there was a certain eagerness too, because the Cataract islands served as natural barriers to any invasion, and the more he knew about them the better. The islets were located immediately north of the dam. Many of them were not only farmed but settled. Something to keep in mind when the invasion came.

Also, downstream from the so-called "high" dam, where the bomb had been planted, was the "low dam," built in 1902. That was as far as boats could go. Which meant Major Waller, and ultimately Colonel Goolsby, would have to decide what to do at that point.

The marines could land on the east bank in a town called Nagaa Al Kaur. It was located just south of Aswan City and virtually uninhabited thanks to Kantar's draconian efforts to clear people out. But based on the satellite images Kydd had seen, he knew that dozens of small islands fronted Nagaa Al Kaur, and would increase the chances of a grounding.

That's why Kydd favored a landing on the *west* bank, which could be accessed via a clear channel, once the invading force got past the Cataract islands.

In either case Waller had to figure out how to move his marines roughly 5-miles upstream from the low dam and do so quickly. The leathernecks were in great shape of course... And could follow the river road south. But the march was still likely to take a couple of hours.

On the other hand, if the bomb threat had been eliminated, it wouldn't matter how long the marines took to get there—so long as they won the ensuing battle. And Kydd figured they would.

The patrol boat was about ten-miles upriver by that time. And, as the RCB rounded a curve in the river, an amazing sight came into view. Thousands of campfires were burning on both sides of the Nile. So many that the light level increased. "What's going on?" Kydd wondered aloud.

Cole was at his side. And the jarheads were crammed into the stern. "They're refugees," she told him. "Tens of thousands of men, women and children, driven out of Nagaa Al Kaur and Aswan City by Hezbollah."

"But why stay *here?*" Kydd inquired. "What if Kantar blows the dam?"

"They have nowhere to go," Cole replied. "And, thanks to how fertile the land is, there's been enough to eat. But that will change soon. The farmers can't keep up."

Kydd looked at her. "You've been there, haven't you?"

"Yes," Cole said. "And it isn't pretty."

The number of fires dwindled after that and eventually disappeared as the boat approached Aswan. Kydd was surprised to see that something like 25 percent of the lights were still on.

"Don't let the lights deceive you," Waller said. "Most of the ex-residents are sitting around the fires you saw. Hezbollah left the remaining street lights on for *their* convenience. So they can find their way around the city at night. They don't have any night vision equipment."

The Cataract islands were just ahead, and Kydd ordered the helmsman to reduce speed. Other than the burbling noise the exhaust pipes produced the engines made very little noise as they pushed the RCB upstream. A scattering of lights marked the islands that were populated.

"Damn," Chief Jones said. "It's tight through here. It's hard to imagine how a tug captain is going to push barges loaded with marines through the maze at night."

"Yeah," Waller agreed. "It could turn into a real shit show. That's for sure."

Once the boat drew abreast of Seheil Island Kydd ordered a turn to port. Then they motored north along the east bank toward Aswan City. "Watch for a blinking red light," Cole told him. "Pull in when you see it."

There was no need to send the crew to battle stations. They were already there. But Kydd couldn't resist saying "Stay sharp," as the red light appeared, and the helmsman put the wheel over.

"A guide is going to meet us," Cole said. "A person Mr. El-Baz trusts. He will lead us to a location two blocks off the waterfront, where the meeting will take place. Once it's over, we'll return to the boat. Do you have any questions?"

No one did. But Kydd had doubts. *But doubts are natural*, he told himself. *So is fear. Don't pee yourself.*

As the boat bumped the dock a sergeant led the marines over the side and onto the dock. They surged past the man with the light to take up positions beyond him. Kydd waited for the storm of incoming fire. There was none.

Cole stepped ashore followed by El-Baz. The man with the red light hurried to embrace the engineer. They were gabbling in Arabic, but Cole was there to monitor the conversation, and that made Kydd feel more secure.

El-Baz turned to Cole. "We're ready. Mr. Bensaid will lead the way."

The sergeant gave orders and a marine took the point position. Two jarheads were right behind him, followed by the sergeant, Waller, Kydd, the Egyptians, Cole, and more marines. Everyone other than El-Baz and Bensaid was wearing night vision gear.

Most of the streetlights had burned out, or been shot out, but the rest were on. They threw pools of light surrounded by heavy shadows. There was no movement other than that of the mangy dog which was following the unit. Kydd could feel eyes though ... Or believed he could. And that was to be expected in a city where the few remaining residents couldn't show themselves without being shot by Hezbollah.

But what if the night had *other* eyes? Watching and waiting to take the group down. That was Kydd's fear—but he hoped it was baseless.

A woman was waiting next to a drab one-story building. She opened the front door and motioned for the group to enter. "Hold on," the sergeant whispered. "Mack, Daniels, Ortiz ... Check it out."

The marines went in weapons at the ready, and returned minutes later. "Five civvies, no weapons," Ortiz reported.

"Good," the sergeant said. "Boost Daniels up onto the roof. The rest of the team will take defensive positions." He turned to Waller. We're ready, sir."

Waller nodded. "Take 'em in, Cole. Commander Kydd and I will follow."

Cole, El-Baz and Bensaid followed the Egyptian woman into the building's darkened interior. Then, after passing through heavy curtains, they entered what looked like a conference room. Four people were seated at a long table. They rose to greet El-Baz. All of them were older and deferential toward El-Baz.

Once the greetings were over the participants sat at the table while Kydd and Waller remained near the door. The conversation took place in Arabic, but was well peppered with English tech terms, and western slang. It seemed to last forever but stopped when Kydd's radio burped static. "One-Seven to One-Six. Over."

"This is One-Six. Go. Over."

"Hez vehicles approaching from the north. It looks like they made us. Over."

Kydd looked to Waller who nodded. "Engage them," Kydd said. "Warn the gunners ... The shore party will be returning from the east. Over."

Kydd turned to Cole. "This meeting is adjourned. It's time to amscray." The last sentence was punctuated by the roar of the RCB's minigun.

Cole said something in Arabic, and everyone other than El-Baz made for the back door. Waller was talking to his marines. "Standby to exfil. Bring Daniels down. Four people coming out. Over." He received two clicks by way of an acknowledgement.

"Alright," Waller said. "Women and swabbies first."

Both Cole and Kydd flipped the army officer off as they made for the door. Waller grinned happily. The marines were waiting for them and a firefight was underway. The sound of the minigun was overlaid by a loud boom as an RPG exploded.

Waller had been a platoon leader in his younger days. "Larson will take the point, I have the two slot, and Sergeant Foley has drag. Let's hit those assholes from the east."

Larson took off at a jog with the rest of them following behind. Kydd was in the six slot, behind Cole, and worried about the boat. Under normal circumstances the crew would cast off and haul butt. But that was impossible until the shore party was back on board. That left the tangos free to move left, right and center, as they poured fire into the stationary RCB.

Larson slowed as he neared the riverfront and spoke over his radio. "Charlie-One-Four … Two vehicles, one on fire, one engaged. Over."

"Eyes open," Kydd said. "We're coming in. Over."

"Charlie Six," Waller said. "Move left to avoid firing on the boat."

Larson rounded a corner and ran forward. The rest followed. A gun truck was positioned in the middle of the street. And, because it was mostly sheltered by a burning pickup, Ellis hadn't been able to target it. "All at once now, fire!" Waller ordered.

The marines plus Cole and Kydd opened fire. What happened next was reminiscent of the Bonnie and Clyde movie when a gazillion police fired all at once. The gun truck shook like a thing possessed, the gunner jerked spastically, and the loader collapsed.

Larson led the team forward. The driver was slumped over the steering wheel and Waller shot him again. "All right people, let's board the boat."

Kydd held the stern line until the rest of them were aboard. Then he threw the rope to a sailor. The bow was swinging free by then. And, one the RCB found the current, the Nile gave it a push. That's when the throttles went forward and the patrol boat angled away.

Jones was sitting on the deck, just aft of the cabin, holding Doc Niles in his arms. "He died on me," Jones said, as tears rolled down his cheeks. "The bastard died on me."

Cole knelt next to him. "I'm sorry, Chief... I'm very sorry."

Kydd checked each member of the crew. There were wounds, three of them, but none of them were too serious. And while the boat had suffered some damage, all of it was above the waterline. Then he could grieve.

***

Aswan Dam, Egypt

Kantar was dreaming about his brother's wife when someone banged on the door. He sat up in bed. Damn it. He kept a pistol next to his cot. His fingers closed around the butt as his feet hit the floor. The banging continued. "Stop that! I'm coming."

Kantar never felt safe. So he stood next to the steel door with the weapon ready. "Who is it?"

"Abdi," came the answer.

"Back away from the door," Kantar replied.

Kantar gave the fighter a moment to move and opened the door. Corporal Abdi was alone. Kantar lowered the pistol. "What's the problem? Why did you wake me up?"

"Lieutenant Marwan is on the radio, sir … There was a fire-fight in Aswan City. He wants to speak with you."

Kantar didn't like the sound of that. He put a robe on, slipped his feet into a pair of leather sandals, and followed Abdi through the control area to the tiny com center located adjacent to his office. A tech was waiting. Kantar accepted the mike. "What's going on?"

"A truck patrol spotted a *kafir* boat and fired on it," Marwan replied. "The boat returned fire with a machine gun and killed the men on the truck. Then *another* truck arrived. It took cover behind the first vehicle and opened fire. That's when Allied soldiers attacked from the east. All of our men were killed. The boat escaped."

Kantar felt a stab of fear. Were the Allies about to push up river and attack? "What about our lookouts north of Aswan City? What are they reporting?"

"The outpost on the west bank heard the sound of engines as a boat passed them," Marwan reported. "But smugglers go by nearly every night. So they assumed that was the case. And they heard a boat go downstream after the firefight. But that's all."

Kantar felt a sense of relief. It had been a scouting mission then … The sort of thing he should expect. "All right," Kantar said. "Give orders to fire on *any* boat that comes up river during the hours of darkness. Smugglers included. That will make it even harder for the holdouts to remain in Aswan City."

"Yes, sir," Marwan said.

"And make sure that our men receive proper burials," Kantar added. "I would attend, but I'm supposed to be elsewhere, as you know."

"Yes, sir. I'll take care of it."

Good. Keep a sharp lookout Babak … And stay in touch with our spies. If the Allies begin to move notify me immediately."

"I will," Marwan assured him. "Allah be with you."

Kantar handed the mike to the tech. *Would* Allah be with him? Kantar hoped so. He was scheduled to leave for an important meeting in two hours. If it went well Egypt would have a Shia friendly government. If the talks failed he would have no choice but to blow the dam.

The gathering had been arranged by warlord Hussain Urabi for the purpose of enriching himself and others like him. That was distasteful. But Kantar was willing to pay the price so long as the right result was forthcoming.

The next couple of hours were spent getting ready. Then, along with five handpicked to accompany him, Kantar left for the meeting. The possibility of a drone attack was on his mind. Marwan swore that the SAMs would protect Kantar while on the dam. But what if the *kafirs* tracked him to a point *beyond* the missiles' effective range? What then?

But everything hinged on the meeting. So Kantar had to leave the relative safety of the dam. No one could be trusted, *especially* Urabi, so it would be stupid to take the remote with him. That's why Kantar slipped away to hide the device. Once the task was complete Kantar made his way back to the control area.

A pair of identical Land Rovers were waiting outside. The streetlights that ran east and west across the top of the dam imbued the scene a greenish glow. A man in a white thobe came forward and bowed. "Greetings Wahda Kantar," the man said. "My name is Abdul Fadel. Please choose a vehicle and make yourselves comfortable. The journey will last approximately four hours."

Both SUVs were equipped with puddle lights that threw the Land Rover logo onto the pavement when a door opened. Kantar chose to ride in the front passenger seat next to the first SUV's driver. The seats were covered with butter-soft leather. A bottle of water and a bag of snacks were waiting on the floor. *This*, Kantar thought to himself, *is decadent. But I like it. Is that wrong?*

No one answered as the Rovers left the curb, and proceeded west across the top of the dam. The road led past the airport on the left and out into the vast desert beyond. They were on Highway 75, otherwise known as Aswan-Abu Simbel Road, which soon left civilization for the wasteland beyond.

The driver wasn't the talky type, or was afraid to speak, lest he make some sort of mistake. And the bodyguards were no less withdrawn. Prior to departure a noncom had taken the fighters aside and lectured them on decorum. "Do not spit, do not fart, and do not say one damned word unless spoken to. Do you understand?" They understood.

So the four men sat in silence as the sun rose behind them, and threw its harsh glare over the desert land, as if determined to kill anything larger than a lizard. Time passed and Kantar napped.

But, when the Rover lurched from side-to-side, Kantar awoke to find that they were turning off the pavement and onto a dirt road. That caused Kantar to sit up and look around.

They were off-road, but other vehicles had passed that way, and recently too—judging from the tire tracks. Finally. They were getting close to their destination. Or so Kantar assumed.

He was wrong. The trip continued for another 15- miles before the Land Rovers stopped at a checkpoint. A large awning was held aloft by metal poles. Folding chairs plus a cooler sat in the shade.

The Bedouins got up and ambled out to meet the incoming vehicles. They were armed. But anyone who wished to circumvent the guards could have done so. And that led Kantar to believe that their purpose was to let Urabi know who was on the way rather than try to stop them.

Kantar's driver offered an ID card and a guard waved him through. The makeshift road continued for half-a-mile, before entering a dry wash, and climbing over the embankment beyond. That's when the sprawling encampment appeared.

The SUVs passed a herd of camels. The noisy creatures were under the supervision of young boys, and due to the smell, were well separated from the crisp white tents visible in the distance. Next came a parking lot for the vehicles and trailers, all baking in the sun.

As the Rovers drew closer Kantar saw the white tents had vertical stripes. They were aligned with military precision, and connected by a network of red carpet runners, to ensure that guests wouldn't have to walk on hot sand.

A second parking lot was visible to the right where three upscale SUVs were parked under a large awning. And there, beyond the encampment, a radio antenna and a satellite dish were visible. A sure sign that even though they were in the desert, Urabi and his friends could communicate with the outside world.

Something else could be discerned as well. The encampment was well protected. Guards with automatic weapons were patrolling the camp's perimeter.

And, as Kantar's Land Rover passed a sandbagged gun emplacement, he spotted a man with Russian-made shoulder-launched Verba missile. He'd been trained to fire Verbas and knew they were effective against aircraft, drones *and* cruise missiles. That made Kantar feel more secure.

The SUV came to a stop. A servant wearing a thobe and a white skull cap hurried to open the door. A tall dignified looking man stepped forward. He was wearing a red and white *keffiyeh* head scarf, a thobe, and sandals. "My name is Bashar Nohas, Wahda Kantar, and I bring you greetings from his excellency General Hussain Urabi."

Kantar tried to remember. Hadn't Urabi been a *colonel?* Not that it mattered. "Thank you. Please inform the general that I am most impressed by the quality and extent of his hospitality."

Nohas was clearly pleased. "Of course, that would be my pleasure. Your tent is waiting, and in accordance with your wishes, a second tent for your staff."

Kantar and his men followed Nohas along a sand-drifted red runner to a pair of side-by-side tents. "This," Nohas said, as he paused in front of a shelter large enough for six people, "is yours."

The other equally spacious tent was for Kantar's bodyguards who took their gear inside. "Dinner will be served early," Nohas said, "so that you and the other guests can watch the camel race before it gets dark. Entertainment will follow. Breakfast will be available at 8:00am in the dining tent, and the meeting is scheduled for 9:30. Do you have any questions?"

Kantar didn't want to watch a camel race or the entertainment. All *he* wanted to do was make his pitch, convince the principals to participate in a new government, and return to the dam.

But Urabi was in charge. And the warlord clearly believed that a show of ostentatious wealth was necessary in order to make the sale. Kantar forced a smile. "No, I don't have any questions. Thank you."

That left Kantar free to enter his tent. It was fully carpeted and furnished with a king sized bed, two side tables, a dangling chandelier, a wardrobe and a spacious cubicle that boasted a tank-fed shower, sink and chemical toilet. It was all very posh compared to the cold-damp "bomb room" that Kantar normally slept in.

After conferring with the noncom in charge of his security team Kantar took a nap. The air inside the tent was too warm. But Kantar managed to sleep in spite of that. He awoke to the clatter of a helicopter passing overhead. A servant arrived shortly thereafter with a pitcher of iced tea and a bowl of chilled fruit.

After slaking his thirst, and eating a snack, Kantar emerged from his tent to find that two of his bodyguards and a teenage guide were waiting for him. The boy led Kantar along freshly swept carpeting and out to the point where a three-sided tent faced onto open desert.

Urabi was present, along with three other men, all wearing thobes. "Here he is!" Urabi said enthusiastically. "Gentlemen, it is my pleasure to introduce Wahda Kantar. You are, needless to say, acquainted with his exploits.

"Mustafa, please meet my friend Sattar Amari, a business-man of considerable renown, Baki Shamon, Egypt's ex-finance minister, and Fathi Wasem, a spiritual leader with whom you are likely to be familiar."

Kantar *was* familiar with Wasem. Most Muslims were. That was due to the fact that because of his moderate teachings, Wasem was a fixture on television, and a wide variety of social media platforms, largely. He'd been quick to condemn Osama bin Laden *and* Hezbollah, which was why Wasem was critical to the plan.

Everyone knew that Shias had taken control of the dam. But if Wasem was to announce an interim government comprised of Shias *and* Sunnis, which would not only neutralize the threat to the Nile river valley's population, but restore the country to its former prominence—then most Egyptians would go along. Even if that meant hostilities with Saudi Arabia.

The relationship between the two countries had once been cordial. But after the Saudis backed the Egyptian military coup in 2013, followed by friction over Saudi Arabia's stance toward Syria, the relationship had cooled.

So Kantar knew it was in his best interest to make a good impression on the cleric. And, based on Wasem's greeting, that would be hard to do. "I can't pretend to approve of what you and your men are doing," the Imam said. "It's wrong. But General Urabi believes that some good could come from it. So I'm willing to listen."

Kantar knew Wasem was likely to be a hard sell. But dur-ing the meal that followed there were opportunities to discuss the ways in which a Shia-Sunni government could implement Wasem's dream of improving society via what he called "Faith Based Development."

Beyond that Wasem wanted to bring *all* Muslims closer to Allah. "Honesty, humbleness, and good manners," Wasem said. "Those are the values upon which a new Egypt should be built."

Though normally served as a family style repast, dinner was served buffet style on the long tables located at the back of the three-sided tent, and there were lots of choices. Once the men were finished eating Urabi announced the camel race. "Come," he said. "Camel races are as old as the pyramids. And my animals are among the finest."

Kantar had never been to a camel race, but he'd seen video clips, and knew the contests were especially popular in Dubai. But unlike the races there, what was shaping up before him harkened back to the days when children rather than robots rode the camels, and enormous amounts of money were wagered on the outcomes.

The tent was situated on a rise looking out over a natural depression. As the other men settled into their seats Kantar could see that four animals were already in position with jockeys on their backs. And he knew that even though camels *look* awkward, they can reach speeds of up to 40mph in short sprints, and maintain a speed of 25mph for an hour or so.

"There's a camel for each one of you," Urabi announced. "The Wahda's animal is wearing yellow livery, Mr. Amari's steed is dressed in red, Mr. Shamon's camel has green accessories, and the Imam's beast is the one with a white saddle blanket. The winner will receive a prize. So be sure to cheer your rider on!"

Binoculars had been issued to each guest. Kantar brought his to bear on the camel "dressed" in yellow. A boy who might have been six or seven years old sat perched behind the beast's hump.

He was wearing a yellow helmet, had the reins with one hand, and a whip in the other. "Get set!" Urabi yelled. "Go!" Nohas fired an ancient flintlock pistol into the air.

The whips came down, the camels took off, and the race was on. Sand flew as Mr. Amari came to his feet. "Go, go, go!" the billionaire shouted as he pumped a fist in the air.

Shamon was standing as well... "Whip it!" he yelled, as his camel fell behind Amari's.

Kantar felt obliged to get up and Wasem did the same. "I hope none of those boys get hurt," the Imam said to Kantar. "Camel races are very dangerous."

Rather than imitate Amari, the way he'd been planning to, Kantar switched to a more sober approach. "That's my concern as well, Imam Wasem. I'm glad they're wearing helmets."

Amari's animal was in the lead by that time, and the normally staid businessman was literally jumping up and down with excitement. As Kantar looked that way his eyes made contact with Urabi's. The warlord winked. That was when Kantar realized what he should have realized all along. The race was fixed.

And sure enough, as the racers finished the third and last circuit of the track, the "red" camel was slightly in the lead. And air horn sounded as the competitors crossed the finish line and Amari was ecstatic. "Did you see that?" he demanded. "*My* camel was the best!"

Shamon smiled indulgently. "It was Sattar, it certainly was. Congratulations."

Urabi was ready with a filigree covered silver pitcher. "I said there was a prize, and here it is," the warlord said. "You'll notice that it's engraved: '*To the Victor Go the Spoils.*'"

"I love it!" Amari said. "Thank you."

Was it that simple? Kantar wondered. Would Amari agree to a Shia-Sunni government? He would know soon.

The light was starting to fade by then, the camels were being led away, and the time had come for the "entertainment" Nohas had mentioned earlier. The major domo led the way.

The air was starting to cool, and in spite of Kantar's focus on his mission, he was enjoying himself. It was hard not to given the lavish surroundings, and the feeling of bonhomie that followed the men into the dining tent. Except the dining tables had been replaced by five well upholstered chairs, a low stage, and dramatic lighting. "You're in for a treat," Urabi promised them. "Nyla Badri has agreed to dance for us."

Kantar hadn't heard of Nyla Badri before, but the other men had, and Amari was quick to sing the performer's praises. "She's beautiful!" he said. "And very evocative."

Kantar took that to mean that Badri was sexy, and that would be welcome, because he'd been living with men for too long. Refreshments were served once the group was seated.

The lights went down after that, and the rhythmic rise and fall of *shaabi*, or Egyptian folk music began. And that was when Badri danced her way out from behind a backlit screen and onto the stage. *Raqs sharqi*, or belly dance, had been around for a long time. And though entertaining the form was very predictable.

Not Badri though. The first thing Kantar noticed was the scimitar. It was balanced cutting-edge up on the top of her head. A cloth winding covered her eyes. She was wearing a simple top, which like the mask, was black.

Badri had a narrow waist and flared hips. A black skirt fell all the way to her feet. It swayed as Badri moved. But the *way* she moved was remarkable. Badri had transformed *Raqs sharqi* into a *new* dance form that combined belly dancing with modern dance, and martial arts. The sword came off her head to cut the air into geometric shapes familiar to anyone acquainted with Japanese Samurai movies. It was both entrancing and arousing.

Badri was, Kantar thought, like an Arabic goddess of war, somehow brought to life.

But all good things must end, and when Badri came forward to present the scimitar, it was to Baki Shamon. Kantar was reminded of his own sword, the *Sayif al-Dawla,* and realized that Urabi was using the weapon in the same way that Secretary General Haddad had. As a way to motivate someone.

Urabi's clever, Kantar thought, *too clever. And once the government is established, and the Axis has its way with Egypt, I will arrange to kill him.*

But for his part Shamon was clearly taken in. And as Badri backed away there was a look of desperate yearning on his face. The lights dipped to black. And, when they came back on, Badri was gone. Everyone clapped. "I'm glad you enjoyed the performance," Urabi said. "Breakfast will be served at 8:00. I'll see you there."

Kantar slept well that night. There were dreams, wonderful dreams, in which Badri danced—and delivered the sword to *him.* Then it was time to get up, take a tepid shower, and shave. Urabi had done an admirable job of setting things up. Now it was Kantar's turn—and he was determined to succeed.

Breakfast consisted of warm beans flavored with cumin, onion, tomato, garlic and parsley, plus a variety of side dishes— including flat breads, hard boiled eggs, and salads made of chopped tomato and cucumber. Kantar barely noticed. His mind was on the presentation ahead.

The meeting took place in a smaller tent set up for the purpose. The chairs used during the camel race had been brought in, along with a circular table, and a blank whiteboard.

Urabi wasted no time getting down to business. "All of you know why we're here. And that's to not only secure the lives of those who live in the Nile valley, but to rescue Egypt from chaos, and restore the country to its rightful place among nations.

"Doing so will involve a geopolitical realignment in which Egypt will, while providing certain forms of assistance to the Axis, still retain its sovereignty. And with Imam Wasem's guidance become a bright light illuminating the path that other Arabic nations can follow. And here, to elaborate on that plan, is our friend Mustafa Kantar."

Kantar had done his research. And he spoke eloquently about how the Shia Fatimids came to power in 969 AD, how they established a capital called Cairo, and ruled Egypt for the next 200 years. "Even today," Kantar said, "there are ties. Many Egyptian Sunnis, especially those who follow Sufi denominations, visit Shia shrines and Mosques. And we are Muslims, just as you are Muslims, and natural enemies of the crusader countries.

"Plus," Kantar added, "change is coming. Soon after the Axis starts to base aircraft and troops in Egypt, Saudi Arabia will fall, causing thousands of Saudi royals to be captured or killed. At that point a great deal of wealth will be liberated and, I have been authorized to offer each of you 50-million dollars of it, to do with as you please."

That was a lie of course, because the secretary general hadn't agreed to any such thing, but Kantar felt sure that he would if given the chance. "Think of it as compensation for the hard work that lies ahead," Kantar told them. "Yes, you will receive government salaries, but those will be relatively modest."

"I will use the money to help the poor," Wasem volunteered, and Kantar believed him. As for the others they planned to use the money on new homes, yachts, and other absurdities. But Kantar didn't care what they did so long as they agreed.

"So," Urabi said. "You heard what the Wahda had to say … Let's go around the table. Mr. Amari, are you in?"

"Yes."

"Mr. Shamon … How about you?"

"Yes."

"Imam Wasem … Can we count on your support?"

"Yes."

"And I vote yes as well," Urabi told them. "May Allah bless us and all that we do."

Kantar felt as if an enormous weight had been lifted from his shoulders. He had, against all odds, accomplished his mission. But the opportunity for celebration was brief.

An office manager and his assistants appeared seemingly from nowhere. And it wasn't long before the communications gear Kantar had noticed earlier was put to work sending and receiving encrypted messages. Each of the men with the exception of Kantar had a network of contacts, allies and, in Amar's case, employees who had to be alerted and supplied with talking points.

And, as messages went out, a TV crew appeared. A script was ready; all the men had to do was review the content, and change it into their own words.

"Our announcement will be released to Al Jazeera first," Urabi informed them. "And to major news outlets worldwide immediately thereafter. The video will appear on all the major social network sites too."

It was all very professional, and Kantar gave thanks for it, because he and his men would have been incapable of putting the whole thing together without the warlord's help.

Then came the second order tasks. So many of them that Kantar had trouble keeping track of it all. Finally, by 10:00 pm the basics were in place for an announcement at 6:00 am the following morning.

Kantar returned to his tent so tired he fell on the bed, and went to sleep without getting undressed. But, after what felt like fifteen minutes, a bodyguard came to rouse him. "It's Corporal Kattan, sir … Lieutenant Marwan's on the radio. It's an emergency."

Kantar groaned, rolled off the bed, and followed Kattan into the next tent. A bodyguard gave him the mike. "This is Kantar... What's wrong?"

"I was making the rounds," Marwan said, as a loud boom was heard in the background. The *kafirs* are attacking our launch sites with missiles. "

"And we're shooting them down," Kantar replied. "Correct?"

"We shot some of them down," Marwan agreed cautiously. "But they're sending flight-after-flight of cruise missiles. So many we won't be able to counter them."

Kantar head another explosion and winced. "Okay, rally the men. The Allies will attack Aswan city first. Stop them there. I will come as quickly as I can."

"Where is the remote?" Marwan demanded. "I need it. We must blow the dam!"

'No," Kantar said. "Success is within our grasp... Fight, and fight hard. I will be there soon. Over."

Kantar turned to the corporal. "Find Mr. Nohas. Tell him I need General Urabi's helicopter—and I need it *now*."

CHAPTER FIFTEEN

South of Nagaa Al Jami, Egypt

Man-made lightning flashed, and thunder rolled, as the submarine launched missiles fell. The Allies knew exactly where the Hezbollah-controlled SAM sites were. And, after intercepting six land-attack missiles, the Russian system was rendered toothless. The end came quickly.

The capability had been there all along. But the Allies couldn't attack the SAM system until Kantar had been killed, or failing that, well away from the bomb. Because at that point the terrorist would either: A. Have the remote with him, but be unable to trigger the bomb, being out of range, or B. Kantar would have left the device hidden inside the dam.

In the second case Kantar could reveal the remote's location to a subordinate, and order that individual to blow the dam, but the experts didn't think he would.

A fanatic like Sergeant Boustani would obey Kantar—but what about the rest of them? What would a nuclear device be worth on the black market? Five-million? Fifty-million? A payday like that would be very tempting to some of Kantar's men.

So the experts were willing to bet 10-million lives on the proposition that Kantar wouldn't entrust the remote to anyone else. And based on information supplied by a high-flying reconnaissance drone, the command team knew Kantar was at a desert encampment hundreds of miles to the west, wouldn't be able to return in anything less than two hours.

Orders went out and missiles were launched. None of that surprised Kydd as the RCB carried him and a squad of Force Recon marines upriver to the so-called "low" dam.

What *did* surprise him was the fact that he and his team were the only people who had been assigned to attack the dam head-on. But, according to the briefing Kydd had attended eight hours earlier, a river-based assault had been ruled out from the beginning.

"Because boats and barges couldn't get past the low dam," Goolsby told the officers, "we knew it would be impossible to deliver our marines to the high dam fast enough to secure it in time. But by sending the convoy up river we kept the enemy focused on that.

"Meanwhile contractor-driven trucks arrived in Esna a week ago, and stand ready to take our marines to the dam via the Luxor-Aswan highway, located just west of here."

That announcement produced chuckles *and* moans. Goolsby nodded. "I know…It took lots of effort to bring the battalion upriver. But the fake worked. The highway is virtually undefended.

"Meanwhile, once Hezbollah's SAM system goes down, a battalion of British Paras will drop into Aswan City and lock the area down."

The announcement drew lots of applause because all of them knew that the Paras were among the most elite special forces units in the world. Goolsby nodded. "Yes, I think it's safe to say that Hezbollah forces in the city will wish they were somewhere else.

"But that isn't all. While it's true that the main attacks will envelope the dam from the west and east, Commander Kydd is going to lead a team upriver. They will do everything in their power to convince Hezbollah that a large force of marines is attacking the dam head-on."

"Go navy," someone said. "Squids rule," another voice added. "Easy day," a third marine said. But Kydd never thought the assignment would be "easy." And now, as the RCB slowed, a difficult task was about to begin. "Standby," Jones said. "Man the starboard side. Put the fenders over."

The helmsman applied a touch of reverse at precisely the right moment. The patrol boat came to a dead stop. Two men made the jump to a concrete breakwater and used lines to pull the RCB in.

Thirteen-marines were standing in the cockpit. All were armed and carrying heavy packs. Three sailors stood ready as well. Each had a 2.5hp outboard in one hand and a backup fuel container in the other. The team members were equipped with night vision gear, tac vests, and personal radios. "What the hell are you waiting for?" Sergeant Meeks inquired. "A fucking invitation? Deass the boat."

The marines grinned. Meeks was a lifer, their squad leader, and a guy who thought he was playing the part of a noncom. Once the marines were ashore he sorted them into patrol order. The sailors fell in forward of the drag slot occupied by Kydd.

And that made sense. The staff sergeant was more qualified to lead from the front. And, with Kydd in the tail-end-Charlie slot, both halves of the column would have leadership should it be cut in two.

It was dark but a scattering of streetlights remained on. Meeks followed the top of the breakwater to a path that led past a cluster of trees, across a street, and over a pedestrian causeway. Stairs connected it to the ground.

Meeks guided the team south to the elevated road that crossed the dam. After passing below it they continued on to the west bank where the lake-sized reservoir was backed up behind the low dam. That's where the feluccas were. Some were moored close to shore, while others were tied to buoys, and only accessible by rowboat. "Make a perimeter," Meeks growled. "And keep the noise down."

Confident that Meeks had the defensive situation in hand, Kydd was free to eyeball the feluccas, and to choose ones that met his criteria. He preferred those that were large enough to accommodate six people, made of aluminum rather than wood, and equipped with easy-to-remove pintle-style rudders.

Second class petty officer Tucker was in charge of the sailors. Kydd motioned him over. "I want *that* one," Kydd said, as he pointed to a boat. "Plus that one and that one. Pull the rudders and mount the engines."

The sailors went to work and were finished 10-minutes later. The second task was to install homemade sound systems on each boat. "Good work," Kydd told them. "Let's have a final radio check. Then we'll push off."

As soon as the radio checks were complete, and the subteams were aboard their boats, the engines were started. The outboards had been tuned prior to the mission. But Kydd held his breath until all of them were actually running.

Each felucca boat was assigned a slightly different route. Kydd's boat was slated to pass between the mainland and Agilkia Island before heading south past the town of Nagaa Jabal Shishah. Kydd took a quick look around prior to eyeing his watch. They were right on time. The diversion was to start at 2200 hours, followed by the all-out attack at 2300. He opened his mike. "This is One-Six. Execute. Over."

Shortly after the one-boat got underway a marine flipped a switch. The sounds of marine engines, overlaid by the rattle of automatic rifle fire, and a series of incomprehensible orders blared from the bow-mounted loudspeaker.

Then the leatherneck and his buddies began to fire their flare guns. It looked like the 4th of July as the boats launched red, green, and white flares into the night sky. "Dial it down a bit," Kydd ordered. "Space 'em out. And drop a floater every once in awhile."

The so-called "floaters" were empty water bottles attached to waterproof lights. By setting them adrift Kydd hoped to further confuse the Hezbollah fighters.

And, as his felucca drew abreast of Agilkia Island, Kydd saw a flash of light to port. That was followed by a loud boom and a gout of water up ahead! A cannon? A mortar? It didn't matter. What *did* matter was the fact that a Hezbollah weapon was pre-registered on the center of the passageway. Kydd had just opened his mouth to give an order, when a *second* round struck the surface of the water, and exploded not 10-feet away.

The force of the blast tipped the boat over—and dumped all of them into the water. Kydd started to sink.

***

The Aswan Dam, Egypt

The 50-foot long fishing boat was named the "*Perch*," and it smelled like one. The *Perch* was anchored on the south side of an uninhabited island, not more than half-a-mile from the high dam. And that, unfortunately, was as close as a boatload of Chinese soldiers could get without being identified.

The original plan was for Bo and his men to land, force their way into the dam, locate the bomb, disarm it and call for an extraction. But with only eleven-men, all Bo could do was wait for something to break his way. And now it had.

Or so it seemed as a series of explosions to the west and east signaled what Bo assumed was a missile attack. Not on the dam itself—but the SAM system that protected it.

Time had passed since then. And, as Bo scanned the top of the dam with a pair of binoculars, flares appeared in the distance.

Allied forces were motoring up the Nile. No other explanation made sense.

So what to do? There were two choices. The first was to wait for the Allied forces to arrive, take control of the dam, and disarm the bomb.

But what if the Allied force was poorly led? Or what if their experts made a mistake? The bomb would go off—and 10-million people would lose their lives.

The second possibility was to take his men, row ashore, and attempt an entry. Bo knew that course of action was likely to fail. And get the rest of his men killed.

But maybe, just maybe, the impending attack would cause so much confusion that Bo and his men would be able to complete their mission.

Which path would General Leong want him to pursue? The answer was obvious. Bo lowered the binoculars. "Sergeant Chen!"

The noncom materialized out of the darkness. "Sir!"

"The men are ready?"

"Yes, sir."

"Load them into the boat. Leave nothing behind. We won't be back."

A flare went off. It lit Chen's face. Bo could see the look of understanding reflected in the noncom's remaining eye. This was it. All or nothing. Chen nodded. "Yes, sir. I'll tell them." And with that the sergeant disappeared.

***

North of the Aswan Dam, Egypt

Kydd was drowning. He kicked, and kicked hard, as the tac vest, pistol, and boots tried to drag him down. A shell exploded nearby… The concussion threatened to force the remaining air out of his lungs. The Type V PFD had inflated by then.

Kydd gasped for air as his head broke the surface. One arm was reflexively reaching, trying to grab something, before the water swallowed him.

A hand found Kydd's wrist. "Got him," a voice said. "Get a grip on his vest."

Suddenly Kydd was being pulled up and over the side of a felucca to collapse at the bottom of it. He coughed and struggled to speak. "The others ... Find them."

"We have Ford, and Smitty," a sailor named Clemmons responded. "But Owens and Abbot are missing."

Kydd realized that he was in the two-boat. A shell exploded and that caused the boat to rock back and forth. Kydd had a choice ... He could order Clemmons to search, and thereby risk the lives of seven men, or tell the sailor to break it off and continue the mission. It was one of the most difficult decisions he had ever been forced to make. "Head south," Kydd ordered. "Toward the dam. We have a job to do."

***

West of the Aswan Dam, Egypt

Kantar was seated in the back of Urabi's ancient Russian-made Mil Mi-4 transport helicopter. His bodyguards were aboard, as were Urabi's security men, all armed to the teeth. The warlord was seated upfront next to the pilot. Could Urabi fly the machine? Or did he like to look out through the window? The answer wasn't clear.

But one thing *was* clear ... Kantar needed to reach the dam, and reach it quickly. According to the most recent report from Lieutenant Marwan, *all* of the SAM launchers had been destroyed. And contrary to expectations, the Allies had been able to move boats up onto the reservoir behind the low dam. Now they were motoring south.

It's over, Kantar thought. *The agreement came too late. Urabi doesn't realize that yet ... So he and his men will fight the kafirs in Aswan City. But not for long. When I detonate the bomb he'll be swept away! And paradise will be mine.*

The certainty of that made Kantar feel better. *Much* better. "We're 10-minutes from the dam," Urabi announced over the intercom. "We'll put you right on top of it. Then we'll proceed to Aswan City, where my men are waiting for me."

Kantar laughed. His bodyguards stared at him. Their leader was crazy, and be it for better or for worse, they were along for the ride.

* * *

The Aswan Dam, Egypt

After firing more flares Kydd and his men had been on the receiving end of small arms fire from Philae Island, but the identity of the shooters was unknown, and the boats escaped unscathed.

Then came the open channel that led to the dam. That was when Kydd heard aircraft engines, and the rattle of distant gunfire, as British Paras hit the ground. Explosions followed. And Kydd hoped the bad guys were on the receiving end of whatever was going down.

There was no further need to fire flares, and every reason not to, as the boats approached the high dam. How many men were waiting for the imaginary invasion force? Kydd knew that "Blue-Bird" was the call sign for a drone operator at Cavallero Air Base in Libya. "One-Six to Blue-Bird. Over."

"I read you Six. Over."

"What, if anything, is waiting for us? Over."

"Three-zero tangos are deployed on the peninsula that extends north from the dam. Over."

Kydd wasn't surprised. After motoring straight at the dam, while shooting off fireworks, it would have been strange if no enemy troops had been laying in wait. "Roger that … What kind of support can you give me? Over."

"I have a Pred B, with two Hellfires, and two 500lb Paveways still on the racks. Over."

Kydd knew that a Pred B was capable of carrying more ordinance than that. A clear indication that his team was second or third on Blue-Bird's list of things to do. "Let's save the Hellfires for someone more deserving," Kydd suggested. "Put both Paveways on the bastards. Over."

"I like the way you think," Bird replied. "Standby. Over."

There was a 10-second pause followed by two almost simultaneous flashes of light. The sounds generated by the explosions overlapped. Five-seconds passed. "This is the Bird. At least twenty tangos are down. Over."

"Roger that," Kydd replied. "We'll tidy up. Thank you. Over."

"Okay," Kydd said over the team freq. "We're going to land under fire. Take cover and let Corporal Givens earn his pay."

"That'll be the day," a voice said.

"Belay the bullshit," Meeks responded. "Over."

A Hezbollah flare went off, lit the peninsula with a whitish glare, and floated gently down. After sustaining heavy casualties the Hez fighters were understandably trigger happy. They opened fire right away.

That was a mistake. Each muzzle flash was a target for Givens. The sniper was belly- down in the two-boat. He fired as the coxswain ran the felucca up onto the beach. "Tango down," a voice said, as the second boat arrived.

Kydd's assault rifle had been lost but he still had his pistol. Cold water overtopped his boots as he left the felucca and ran a few yards before flopping down beside a dead body. An AK-47 lay next to it. Kydd took the weapon and checked to ensure that it was loaded.

Automatic fire lashed back and forth between the Hezbollah fighters and the marines. There was no contest however. The leathernecks had night vision gear and the tangos didn't. That, plus the winnowing fire from Givens, brought the fight to a speedy conclusion. "We own this place," Meeks announced.

"Did we take any casualties?" Kydd inquired.

"Wells caught one, and the Doc's on it," a marine replied.

Kydd had a decision to make. His mission had been completed. So he could wrap things up and retreat downstream if he chose. But what if he and his team could enter the dam? And catch Kantar by surprise? The choice was, in the final analysis, a no brainer.

***

"We're five minutes out," Urabi announced over the intercom. "We won't be on the ground for long, so be ready to jump. Flares and explosions are visible to the north."

Kantar could hardly wait. He wanted to retrieve the remote as quickly as possible. He wished he could look out a window but there was none.

The helicopter hit hard. "The immediate area appears to be clear," Urabi informed them. "Secure the dam. I'll be in touch."

Cool night air rushed in as Urabi's crew chief opened the door. With duffle bag in hand Kantar jumped to the ground and paused to look around.

Two sentries were on duty behind the sandbagged gun emplacement that fronted the door. They came to attention as Kantar paused to watch the ancient helicopter lurch into the air.

Once aloft the aircraft turned onto a northwest heading. A course that would take the helo *away* from the fighting in Aswan City. *The bastard is running for his life*, Kantar thought. *I hope the kafir kill him.* He turned to the door, returned a salute, and went inside. The remote. He had to retrieve the remote.

* * *

After rowing ashore Bo and his soldiers made their way up the steep slope and onto the road that crossed the dam. That's where they were when a helicopter appeared out of the west, lost altitude, and landed in front of them. Six men left the helo before it took off. They entered the building leaving two sentries outside. Bo turned to Sergeant Chen. "Send Khoo forward."

Khoo arrived moments later. He was armed with a QBZ-95 bullpup-style assault rifle, and a PLA issue crossbow, which was slung across his back. Bo gave him the glasses. "Look across the street... Can your crossbow reach the sentries from here?"

Khoo gave the binoculars back. "Yes, sir."

"Kill one of them. When your target falls the rest of us will charge."

It would have been nice to kill *both* men. But reloading a crossbow takes time. Khoo nodded, freed the weapon, and brought it around. Then he settled in. A minute passed.

Bo had fired almost every weapon the PLA had, including crossbows. So he understood the challenge. Especially for a shot that far away. Elevation was the key. It would be necessary to aim high, so as to allow for the effect gravity would have on the bolt, but not *too* high lest Khoo overshoot.

There was a dull thud. The quarrel flew across the street and hit one of the sentries in the forehead. That was no accident, and Bo understood Khoo's reasoning. Military targets are likely to wear body armor. He jumped to his feet. "Follow me!"

The second sentry was bent over his buddy, trying to understand what had occurred, when Bo shot him with a suppressed Norinco Type 92 pistol. It produced a popping sound.

"Hide the bodies behind the sandbags," Bo ordered. "Assign two men to take their places. Try the door." Sergeant Chen obeyed. It opened smoothly. They were in.

***

Goolsby's marines were due to arrive soon. So Kydd put in a call to the battalion surgeon who promised to send help within fifteen-minutes.

It didn't take long to find the access door which, not surprisingly, was unlocked. What remained of the team totaled thirteen men counting Kydd. A PFC named Jayson was armed with a shotgun—so Sergeant Meeks sent him up the switch-backing ramps first.

Kydd expected to encounter heavy resistance but there was none. Because Kantar was elsewhere? Or because a lot of the Hez fighters were in Aswan City?

Whatever the reason Kydd welcomed it. He was in the two slot with Meeks on drag. Jayson rounded the first turn and hurried up a ramp. Kydd could hear the thrum of generators, smell the ozone in the air, and feel the emptiness in his gut.

The ceiling appeared to be a hundred feet high, color-coded pipes twisted and turned down along concrete pillars, and warning signs decorated the walls.

Jayson made another turn and continued upwards. His head was on a swivel and for good reason. If Hez fighters were waiting to ambush the team Jayson would be the first man to die.

***

The bodyguards followed single-file as Kantar ran the length of the vast turbine room. The ramps were located at the other end of the cavernous space. Kantar felt a sense of relief as he passed the last turbine and spotted the first ramp.

Kantar was on it, and hurrying down, when he saw a man with a shotgun below. Kantar fired his pistol, heard the bullet spang off metal, and withdrew just in time. The shotgun blast passed through the space where Kantar had been standing.

Hezbollah fighters rushed forward to pour automatic fire down on the invaders. Kantar was frantic. The Americans had passed the point where the remote was hidden! The only way to retrieve the device was to push them back down. "Grenades!" Kantar shouted. "Throw *all* of them!"

Half a dozen Russian "*limoka*" (lemon) hand grenades arced through the air. They clanged, bounced and rattled as they rolled downhill. Then they exploded. The Americans had to withdraw. "Hold your fire!" Kantar ordered, as he made his way down the first ramp.

The aluminum panel was located at the first turn. Kantar fumbled with the multipurpose pocketknife, managed to deploy the screwdriver blade, and went to work. He had to remove four stainless steel screws and his hands were shaking.

A weapon began to fire from below and the bullets produced a clang each time they struck the metal ramp. Something buzzed past Kantar's right ear. *Ricochets!* The kafir were trying to bounce a bullet into his body. He couldn't stop. A screw fell to the floor, followed by another, and a third.

Then a grenade landed ten feet away. But, thanks to the downward sloping ramp, it rolled back toward the Americans! The resulting explosion produced a loud scream.

Once the final screw was loosened the panel rotated down and out of the way. The remote was waiting. Kantar grabbed the device, turned, and ran. The Americans surged up the ramp, firing as they came.

Kantar felt a sense of relief as he arrived on the main floor, only to have it snatched away, as soldiers fired on his men from the opposite direction!

Kantar caught a glimpse of an Asian face as a man backed into cover. The Chinese! It appeared that some of them had survived the slaughter at Kerma. And here they were blocking his line of retreat. "Kill them!" Kantar ordered, and half of his men obeyed. The rest were busy trying to hold the Americans at bay.

***

Jayson was dead, Alvarez was wounded, and Kydd was pissed. He had taken the point position. He fired the AK-47 until it ran dry. After tossing it aside he drew the pistol.

As Kydd neared the top of the ramp it was necessary to drop to the floor and elbow his way forward. A bullet spanged off the rail to his right. But that didn't explain the firefight that was under way. It seemed as if the Hez fighters were caught between his team and another group. Goolsby's marines were the best bet.

Meeks led the rest of the team up onto the floor. "One grenade would get you all," he told them, "so spread out!" They joined the fight and it soon became obvious that the Hezbollah fighters were about to lose. A voice shouted, "Surrender! Or I'll blow the dam!"

"Hold your fire," Kydd ordered, as a man stood. There was something in his right hand … The remote! Kydd got to his feet. "Captain Kantar?"

"*Wahda* Kantar," the man said defiantly, his eyes aglow. "Place your weapons on the floor."

He wants hostages, Kydd thought. *Well, fuck him*. It was a reckless thing to do, and Kydd knew that, as he brought the pistol up. What if he missed?

But there was no going back. *Don't get fancy,* Kydd thought. *Hit him in the torso.* The gun bucked. The sound of the shot rang in his ears. The bullet was high. *So* high it blew the top of Kantar's skull off.

Kantar jerked, the remote went flying, and a Hezbollah fighter pounced on it. The man shouted, *"Allahu Akbar!"* (Allah is great) and thumbed a button.

Kydd waited to die. Nothing happened. The fighter thumbed it again. And that's when a man in an unfamiliar uniform stepped out of hiding and aimed a weapon. Kydd heard what sounded like a cough. The Hez went limp.

The man with the pistol placed it on the floor, and took three paces forward. "Colonel Shin Bo, the People's Liberation Army. And you are?"

"Lieutenant Commander Harley Kydd, United States Navy."

"It's a pleasure to meet you Commander... My men located the bomb with help from an Egyptian engineer."

"And you disarmed it?"

"No," Bo replied. "That will take more time. We removed a metal floor plate, cut the wires connecting the radio receiver to the bomb, and replaced the lid. Your experts will be able to carry out the work required to neutralize the device."

Kydd stared at him. "You and your men came all this way... *Why?*"

"I'm a soldier," Bo replied simply. "Such were my orders."

***

Esna, Egypt

Urabi was in a hurry, and for good reason. After speaking to his field commanders the situation was clear. British Paras had engaged the Hezbollah irregulars stationed in Aswan city and the *kafir* were winning. So Urabi ordered his people to pull back and let the Shias to fend for themselves. Allah would be pleased. And now, as his helicopter passed over Esna, the warlord was trying to salvage what he could.

The helicopter hovered over the mansion prior to settling on its flat roof. Guards were waiting to greet him as he left the helo. Their faces were hidden behind scarves and their weapons ready as they accompanied Urabi to the stairs.

Then, as the warlord disappeared below, the guards turned to fire on Urabi's bodyguards. The suppressed submachine guns produced little more than a series of clacking sounds. The helo pilot saw what was taking place and tried to take off. Bullets riddled the windscreen. The aviator slumped in his harness.

Urabi took the stairs two-at-a-time in his rush to reach the bedroom, remove the box of Canadian gold wafers, and depart. But Urabi entered the room only to find a blond woman seated in his favorite chair. She smiled. "Well, well … Look at what we have here. Welcome home."

Urabi frowned. "How did you know I would come here?"

"I figured you would have a stash," Cole replied. "Plus I have eyes in the sky."

Urabi sighed and offered his wrists. "Nope," Cole said. "It isn't going to be that easy this time. If you want to live, which I assume you do, you're going to accompany me on a trip to Lebanon."

Urabi stared. "Lebanon. *Why?*"

"*That,*" Cole replied, "is for me to know, and for you to find out."

***

Beirut, Lebanon

Lebanon was theoretically neutral. But, since Hezbollah was in control of the nation's coalition government, it called the shots.

Had it been left to the Hez hotheads, the country might belong to the Axis.

But Hezbollah did what the Supreme Leader in Tehran told it to do. And the Ayatollah knew that if Lebanon were to join the Axis, Israel would invade, and take control within two days.

Besides, Lebanon gave Iran access to the Mediterranean via the client state of Iraq. All of which meant that while Beirut was an "open" city, it was lousy with spies, more of whom had just arrived.

The sleek, 68-foot long super yacht *Alexis* was registered to a Lebanese business tycoon named Giorgio Asmar, who was living in the Virgin Islands while leasing the vessel to the CIA. Thanks to that provenance the *Alexis* had been allowed to enter the well-defended harbor, and tie up to the customs dock, shortly after 9 a.m.

Though unfailingly polite, the Lebanese customs officers were very conscientious, and spent the better part of an hour searching the yacht from bow-to-stern. All while stealing surreptitious looks at the scantily clad blond woman. She was sitting in a lounger next to an older man who they assumed to be her husband.

The crew consisted of young males dressed in white Polos, blue shorts, and deck shoes. Some spoke Arabic, and some didn't, but that was typical where large yachts were concerned.

Eventually both the *Alexis* and her passengers were cleared for the marina, where a long, and very expensive slip was waiting. Once the mooring lines were secured, and the shore power was on, the operation began. In and out. That was the plan.

Urabi was supposed to be himself... A task he was well suited for.

As for Cole, she was to play the part of Urabi's bodyguard, and planned to look the part. Her hair was pulled back into a tight ponytail. Her red lips matched her nails and high heels. The shoes would be a liability in a fight. But they served a purpose, and that was to get men to perceive Cole as a sex object, rather than a threat.

Once everything was ready Urabi, Cole, and a crewman left the boat, made their way down a long dock, and passed through a gate. A parking lot lay beyond. That's where the black Mercedes was waiting. The driver stood next to the rear door which was open.

Urabi paused, as if looking for a way out, but the driver and the crewman were only a few feet away. The warlord slid inside.

Cole paused to speak with the driver. He looked like a local, but hailed from Hoboken, New Jersey. There was no chitchat. Cole spoke first. "What's in the sky?"

"The Israelis have an IAI Heron over the city, and the Iranians have a Fotros II in the area."

"How 'bout the US of A?"

"An RQ-4 Global Hawk is watching the watchers."

"And if we run into trouble?"

"We'll dump the car, make our way to a MOSSAD (Israeli Intelligence Agency) safe house, and travel from there to Israel."

Cole nodded. "Good. You have the address?"

"Yes."

"Let's go."

As the Mercedes threaded its way through narrow streets Cole saw stunning buildings clad with golden stone, drab apartment blocks decorated with graffiti, and mirror-bright banks which reflected their surroundings.

Christian churches sat side-by-side with mosques, political posters drooped from balconies, and fashionable men and women, many of whom wore western clothes, shared the streets with people in traditional dress. It was a beautiful, yet ominous city, where politics seethed just below the surface.

There was a lot of traffic, but that was to be expected, and had been built into the schedule. They were stopped at a light when Urabi made his move or tried to. But the attempt to open the door failed. "The driver controls the locks," Cole told him. "Behave yourself."

"I have money," Urabi pleaded. "You could be rich."

"Not any more you don't," Cole responded. "We have the gold from your mansion, and we know where your loot is. Your ex-girlfriend has been most helpful."

Urabi stared at her. "So, I have nothing."

"You have your life," Cole replied.

"You won't kill me?"

"Not if you're a good boy."

Urabi turned away. It took the better part of an additional half-hour to reach south Beirut. Some of the buildings still showed signs of the damage suffered as a result of past bombings.

Others, strangely modern in among the drab structures of the past, occupied sites where damaged apartment buildings had been demolished.

When the sedan came to a stop, it was in front of a bank, so solid it looked as if it could withstand a direct hit from a 1,000 pound bomb. That made sense because the bank was the local branch of *Bayt al-Mal Lil Muslimeen*, which meant the "House of Money," and served as Hezbollah's financial arm.

"This is it," Cole announced, as the car pulled over. "Let's review your story again. Once the Allies took control of the dam the plan to form a Shia-Sunni government collapsed. But the pieces remain, just waiting to be assembled, and you're the man who's equipped to get the job done. Got it?"

"That's it? That's all?" Urabi inquired.

"Yes," Cole said. "It is. We can't script it further than that. He might tell you to fuck off. Or, he might buy in hook, line and sinker. If he does, then play him."

Urabi brightened slightly. "You can count on me."

"Unlock my door," Cole said.

There was a click. Cole got out and paused to look around the way any good bodyguard would. Then she went around to the other side of the car. The passenger door was unlocked. Urabi got out. That was his chance, or would have been, except that the driver was there to stop him. "Don't," the agent said. His right hand hovered near his belt buckle. A pistol was only inches away.

Urabi straightened his tie, turned, and made his way toward the bank. Cole followed.

Other people were entering and leaving the bank. Cole was carrying what felt like a lead weight in her stomach. Could they make it through security? That was by no means certain.

And, if the guards took Cole away for a strip search, Urabi would run. But there was a tracker in his left shoe … And the CIA would find him. Even if Cole was dead.

Urabi opened the door, Cole followed him in, and the security checkpoint was directly ahead. Muslim women couldn't submit to full body scanners so there weren't any. Cole was counting on that.

Personal possessions *could* be scanned however. So both Urabi and Cole were required to place their cell phones and wallets in baskets and put them on a conveyer belt.

Armed guards motioned for them to step forward and hold their arms over their heads. Cole could feel the weight of male eyes and knew the guards were staring at her tits.

Handheld scanners were used to determine whether either one of them was carrying something metallic. And, with the exception of zippers, they weren't.

Cole felt a tremendous sense of relief as a guard waved them through, and into the lobby beyond. Some of the granite wall was obscured by a row of green and yellow flags, each bearing the silhouette of the first letter in *"Allah,"* which was reaching up to grasp a stylized assault rifle.

Banks of elevators were located to the left and right. And, according to the signage, the high-rise lifts were on the left.

Cole escorted Urabi over to that side. Other people were waiting. There was a loud "ding" as an elevator arrived. Cole waited for Urabi to board and stepped aboard. The button for the 20th floor was already lit.

The car made three stops before arriving on 20, where Cole and Urabi followed a man off. He took a right and disappeared as they approached the counter. "Mr. Urabi is here to meet with Secretary General Haddad," Cole announced.

The receptionist was male. His eyes shifted to Urabi and back to Cole. "Yes," he said. "You are right on time. But the Secretary-General is running ten-minutes late. Please have a seat. I will let him know that you're here."

The waiting area was furnished with comfortable chairs, a glass-topped coffee table, and lots of Hezbollah literature. Urabi fidgeted, and Cole did her best not to, as fifteen long minutes dragged by. They came to an end when the receptionist stood and came out from behind the counter. "The Secretary-General is free now ... Please follow me."

The receptionist led them along a red carpet, past an open conference room, to the point where two bearded men waited. *Bodyguards*, Cole thought. *Will they search us?*

The answer was yes. Both visitors were required to empty their pockets onto a table before being wanded. Then, after passing muster, they were allowed to collect their belongings and enter what turned out to be a large, comfortably furnished room.

Two additional bodyguards were present, both standing against the left wall, but well separated from each other.

Secretary General Haddad was seated behind a desk so cluttered that hardly any of the wood surface was visible.

Haddad was momentarily backlit as he heaved his considerable bulk up out of a swivel chair, and waddled over to greet Urabi. *"Marhaban bik!"* (Welcome.)

"Yashrifuni," (I am honored) Urabi replied, as they shook hands.

Cole turned to watch, as the receptionist backed out of the room, and closed the double doors behind him. That was good. But the additional guards were a surprise. *It's all about process*, Cole thought. *You can do this.*

"Please have a seat," Haddad said, as he returned to his chair. "Mustafa and I were in frequent contact. He told me about you, and the plan to form a government."

Haddad was doing Urabi's work for him … But Cole's attention was elsewhere.

Her arms were crossed as she reached under the jacket. The guns were about the size and shape of a Glock 26, but made almost entirely of plastic, and designed to fire custom-made caseless ammo. The bullets were small. *Too* small in Cole's opinion. But the fact that each weapon held 18-rounds helped compensate for the lack of punch.

The bodyguard on the left had been staring at Cole, saw the motion, and was reaching for his weapon when the agent drew. The semiauto pistols were *so* light that it was easy to come up over a target forcing the shooter to pull back down. And the wasted millisecond could mean the difference between life and death.

The left-hand gun produced a gentle cough as Cole shot the left-hand target. The pistol in her right hand went off a second later. A headshot for each guard. Both collapsed.

It was a feat of marksmanship that only a truly ambidextrous person could execute. Cole put an extra bullet into each man before swinging to the right. Secretary General Haddad was staring, his mouth agape, as Cole pointed a pistol at him. "So," Cole said. "*You're* the person who came up with the idea to weaponize the dam. Would you like to know who told us that?"

Haddad nodded.

"The Russians did," Cole said. She waited for a second, just long enough for Haddad to process the information, and smiled. "Yeah—payback is a bitch."

Then Cole shot him. Three times. Haddad slumped sideways and fell to the floor. The body landed with a thump.

The left-hand pistol had been on Urabi all along. Cole turned to face him. The warlord was terrified. "You said you wouldn't kill me."

"I lied," Cole replied, and shot him twice.

Urabi's head jerked and fell back. *Four for four*, Cole thought. *Two to go.*

She went to the doors, opened one of them, and spoke to a guard. Her voice was urgent. "The Secretary General needs you! Hurry!"

Both men rushed through the door, and were still moving forward, when Cole shot them. Two between the shoulder blades, followed by two in the head, in case they were wearing armor. They crashed face down on the floor. Cole closed the door. Her cellphone was ready. "The meeting is over. I'm coming out."

The reply was equally succinct. "Black helmet, red scooter."

Cole closed the doors behind her, followed the red carpet to the receptionist's desk, where she paused. "The Secretary General asked me to tell you that he can't take any calls." She shrugged. "They told me to take a break. I'll be back soon."

The receptionist nodded and Cole got the feeling that private meetings weren't unusual. "I'll see you soon," he said. Never dreaming what he would find within the hour.

The elevator took Cole down to the main floor where she followed two men out onto the street. A red Vespa was waiting at the curb. The driver was wearing a black helmet and had one to her.

Cole climbed on the back, wrapped her arms around the driver's torso, and placed her high heels on the foot pegs. The scooter sped away. Cole relished the way that Beirut looked and smelled. It felt good to be alive.

CHAPTER SIXTEEN

Navagio Beach, Zakynthos Island, Greece

Navagio Beach was located in a picturesque cove, on the Greek island of Zakynthos, and accessible only by boat. Tourists flocked to it before the war. But, as Kydd gazed at the azure-blue water, he was one of only six people enjoying the spot. A couple was snorkeling as a family ate a picnic lunch two-hundred feet away.

A little more than a month had passed since the confrontation with Kantar, the near annihilation of the terrorist's battalion, and the subsequent liberation of Aswan City.

General Abdu Ahmar's Republican Guard unit was brought in soon thereafter, with orders to "… protect the dam against all enemies foreign and domestic, until relieved by the elected representatives of an Egyptian government."

Even so a twelve-person team of UN observers was dispatched to ensure that Ahmar behaved himself. Plus, if the rumors were true, the general's wife and children were "guests" of the United States government. All in an effort to prevent the dam from being weaponized again.

Colonel Shin Bo and his men were sent to a POW camp where they would likely spend the balance of the war. Then came the work required to take the Allied troops out. After an evening spent drinking beer with their "Yank" comrades, the Brits piled onto their boats, and pulled out.

The *Nile* departed the next day. And with the Riverines to protect her, the cruise ship steamed north until arriving in Port Said, where Goolsby and his marines went ashore for the last time. That was followed by a truly raucous Hail and Farewell party in a waterfront hotel.

And, when it came time to part company, Goolsby shook Kydd's hand. "I have some good news for you Harley... You made commander. The paperwork will catch up with you soon. And you sure as hell deserve it." High praise indeed, coming from the marine.

All of RIVGRU 6's boats were loaded on a freighter two days later for transshipment to parts unknown. The chief and his sailors had orders to join other units, return to the states for training courses, or to take leave. Kydd was there to thank each one, and see him or her off. He couldn't help but think of those who *weren't* shipping out. Like the kid named Bower... Like so many others his face was little more than a blur.

Kydd had leave on the books himself. Lots of it. But he didn't want to go home and face his parents. They meant well, but dad would go on-and-on about the war, and mom would cry. So before returning to duty Kydd decided to treat himself to a vacation on the island of Zakynthos. A decision the officer was quite content with, as he lay on the lounger, and tried to summon the energy required to read a book.

Movement caught his eye. Gentle waves fled from the bow of a Bermuda-rigged sloop as it motored into the bay. A tour boat perhaps, like the one that would return for him that evening, or some rich person's plaything.

The sailboat was towing a skiff which drifted forward as the owner cut power. Kydd watched the anchor splash and closed his eyes. *A nap*, he thought. *Followed by a swim, lunch, and a cold beer. Life doesn't get any better than that.*

Kydd was floating somewhere between sleep and wakefulness when he heard a familiar voice. "Hey, sailor … Wake up. We have things to do."

Kydd's eyes flew open. There, standing in front of him, was Cassandra Cole! She was wearing shades, a white crop-top and matching shorts. A smile tugged at the corners of her mouth. He stood. "You disappeared."

"I had things to do," Cole explained. "They sent me to the states for my annual sexual harassment training."

"I don't believe it."

Cole shrugged. "Does it matter? I'm here."

"How did you find me?"

"The CIA knows everything."

"Do they know I want to kiss you?"

"Yes," Cole replied. "They do. And I hope you will."

Kydd took Cole into his arms. They kissed. Her lips were soft and she smelled like soap. The kiss lasted a long time, and felt like a promise of things to come.

"Grab your stuff," Cole said as the moment ended. "The boat is ours for five days. You know how to sail, right?"

"I do," Kydd replied. "But I need to drop by the hotel."

"No," Cole said, "you don't. Your duffle bag is on board."

Kydd chuckled. "You think of everything."

"I do," Cole agreed, as she looked up at him. "But it takes me a while sometimes." He kissed her again.

They loaded the boat. Then, with Kydd at the oars, they got underway. He pulled and Cole smiled. "Put your back into it, sailor … We have a long way to go."

ABOUT THE WINDS OF WAR SERIES

In RED DRAGON, volume three of the Winds of War series, WWIII rages on as a Chinese hit team targets the Dalai Lama for assassination in an effort to choose his successor, and retain their steely grip on Tibet, which constitutes nearly a quarter of China's land mass.

In the meantime Green Beret Captain Jon Lee and his team are behind enemy lines in Nepal, and living with a tribe of nomadic hunter-gatherers, who could become valuable assets.

But it isn't long before Lee, a Chinese American army doctor, and a company of Nepalese Gurkha soldiers, are given orders to find the reincarnated Dalai Lama—and bring him out of enemy held territory.

Meanwhile as the assassins who killed the Dalai Lama continue to search for the baby, the Chinese and the Pakistanis are planning a major push aimed at conquering India.

But moving 10,000 Chinese soldiers through rugged mountains on a narrow highway won't be easy. Not with Lee, his Green Berets, and a team of Gurkhas doing all that they can to slow the enemy advance—in hopes of giving Allied forces time to prepare.

Never before have the hopes of so many depended on the efforts of so few.

ABOUT WILLIAM C. DIETZ

For more about William C. Dietz and his fiction, please visit williamcdietz.com. You can find Bill on Facebook at: www.facebook.com/williamcdietz and you can follow him on Twitter: William C. Dietz @wcdietz

Made in the USA
Middletown, DE
23 June 2019